in a Melting Fire
of Sensation. . . .

The clean masculine smell of him clouded rational thought, as did his demanding hands and lips. She tried to hold onto her scattering wits, but she was rapidly sinking beneath his seduction, resistance to his burning touch melting away. She arched against him, pressing her naked breasts to his chest as her arms rose by their own volition around his neck. . . .

Dear Reader:

We trust you will enjoy this Richard Gallen romance. We plan to bring you more of the best in both contemporary and historical romantic fiction with four exciting new titles each month.

We'd like your help.

We value your suggestions and opinions. They will help us to publish the kind of romances you want to read. Please send us your comments, or just let us know which Richard Gallen romances you have especially enjoyed. Write to the address below. We're looking forward to hearing from you!

Happy reading!

The Editors of
Richard Gallen Books
8-10 West 36th St.
New York, N.Y. 10018

Conquer The Memories

JANET JOYCE

PUBLISHED BY RICHARD GALLEN BOOKS
Distributed by POCKET BOOKS

This novel is a work of historical fiction. Names, characters, places and incidents relating to non-historical figures are either the product of the author's imagination or are used fictitiously. Any resemblance of such non-historical incidents, places or figures to actual events or locales or persons, living or dead, is entirely coincidental.

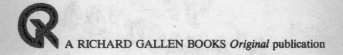

A RICHARD GALLEN BOOKS *Original* publication

Distributed by
POCKET BOOKS, a Simon & Schuster division of
GULF & WESTERN CORPORATION
1230 Avenue of the Americas, New York, N.Y. 10020

ISBN: 0-671-45144-8

First Pocket Books printing June, 1982

10 9 8 7 6 5 4 3 2 1

RICHARD GALLEN and colophon are trademarks of Simon & Schuster and Richard Gallen & Co., Inc.

Printed in the U.S.A.

Dedicated to Sue,
who brought us together
and made this possible

Our life is like some vast lake that is slowly filling with the stream of our years. As the waters creep surely upward, the landmarks of the past are one by one submerged. But there shall always be memory to lift its head above the tide until the lake is overflowing.

—Alexandre Charles Auguste Bisson

AUTHOR'S NOTE

The characters and action in this story are fictional, with the exception of the well-known historical persons and the location and dates of actual battles during the Mexican-American War. The Colt-Walker revolver was not developed until 1847. American troops received the first shipment in midsummer of 1847. There is no documentation to support the premise that the guns might have been spirited into Texas as they are in this story, although they were indeed distributed to the Texas Rangers and the Army Sharpshooters first. The weapon was designed by Samuel Colt, owner of the Colt Munitions Company, and Samuel H. Walker, Captain, Texas Rangers. It was an improvement over the Colt-Paterson, or Texas Paterson, which had received its greatest success in the hands of the Texas Rangers. It was the development of the "Walker" and the subsequent large order by the Federal Ordnance Department that saved the floundering Colt Company.

Conquer The Memories

Chapter 1

London, England, 1846

With a flick of his wrist, Garrett Browning dropped his cards on the green baize surface of the gaming table, showing his opponent, Lord William Maxfield, earl of Brockmere, that he had been defeated once again by Browning's ability to bluff. He watched the older man struggle to contain his disbelief. Out of the corner of his eye, Garrett glimpsed his English cousin, Sir Allen Winslow, release his pent-up breath and shake his head.

"Who would have believed you could pull off a stunt like that two hands in a row? I was positive that you held at least a straight," Winslow said to Garrett as he smiled sympathetically at Maxfield, who had just lost a fortune.

"I'd be interested to learn where you acquired your skill, Browning. I could almost believe that I had been bested by a professional." Two mottled red spots stood out on Lord Maxfield's cheeks as he eyed the brash young Texan with suspicion. Maxfield thought that Browning was slightly too adept in the skills of draw poker. Winslow had introduced Browning as his cousin and a Texas landowner. New to London and to the club rules under which they played, Browning should have been easily culled of his purse. Instead, Lord Maxfield, who was familiarly known as Brockmere after the name of his earldom, found himself losing heavily to a commoner, duped by a steely-eyed foreigner who was young enough to be his son. Like many of his peers, Brockmere considered the English a superior race. After all, wasn't England the most progressive, the most powerful and the richest nation on earth?

Browning ignored the earl's distrustful tone. "My father taught me the game when I was a boy, and I've played with some excellent teachers. Texas isn't all prairie grass and cactus, Brockmere."

The earl made no reply.

"It's getting late, gentlemen. Perhaps we should call it a night," Garrett continued quietly, placing Brockmere in the position of having to decide whether the game should continue. The American showed no emotion when the earl immediately demanded another chance to recoup his losses.

"Deal," Garrett ordered. It was nothing to him if Brockmere preferred to leave his club several thousand pounds lighter. Although Lord Maxfield was a skillful player, he had one glaring weakness. When he was bluffing, a tiny vessel in his temple would throb, and when he had a good hand, his gray eyes would refuse to meet his opponent's until the round was over.

The cards were dealt, and Garrett watched for the signs. After two rounds, the pulsing vein in Brockmere's forehead signaled yet another victory. Apparently the man was desperate to win, because instead of folding under the pressure of Garrett's increasing raises, he stayed in the game. Garrett made his final raise, betting more than Brockmere had showing on the table.

"It's to you, Brockmere." Garrett relaxed in the velvet high-back chair and reached for his brandy snifter.

"Not this time, Browning." Lord Maxfield smiled malevolently. "The deed to my estate is my share of the pot."

Garrett leaned forward and reached for the folded parchment the earl had thrown nonchalantly onto the center of the table. Was Brockmere insane to risk everything he possessed on the odd chance that Garrett was bluffing again?

Allen squirmed in his seat. "Lord Maxfield, I don't think that is necessary. My cousin will trust you for the money. Why don't you sign a note for the amount required?"

"I won't sign for what I don't have, Winslow," Lord Maxfield said sharply, surprising Allen and Garrett with his vehemence.

"Am I correct in assuming that you have been playing with the last of your funds?" Garrett frowned at the brittle parchment he held in his hands. An amusing game of cards between two wealthy men had suddenly changed into a battle for survival for one of them. He wasn't sure he liked the idea of winning the earl's home as easily as plucking a ripe plum from the branch.

"What's the matter, Browning? You've been bluffing all night and making me look like a blithering fool. Don't let my financial condition stop you from trying again. I'm quite willing to stake my home in order to prove that we English are not as gullible as you ill-bred Americans believe."

"Ill-bred?" Garrett cocked an eyebrow.

"You're not the first upstart American who has tried to show up his betters, Browning. Every man in this club has had to deal with your kind occasionally." Lord Maxfield looked disdainfully down his thin nose at Garrett, his taunting words a brazen attempt to prove how confident he was of his cards.

Garrett raked a hand through his black hair, trying to decide if he cared to show Brockmere how easily an "ill-bred American" could best a member of the English nobility. He had no use for an ancient ancestral mansion. It was imperative that he leave for America in two weeks' time. He was going to be much too busy trying to fulfill the requirements of his father's will to devote any time to the sale of an estate.

Allen realized what Garrett was thinking and said worriedly, "Garrett doesn't want to play for anything that would mean a longer stay in England. He's left his holdings in the hands of his younger brothers, and he has some rather pressing affairs to complete before he journeys back to Texas."

"Indeed?" Lord Maxfield was beginning to sense his opponent's unwillingness to proceed. Most men would have jumped at the chance of winning the huge estate, but Browning was hesitating. Browning's indecision increased the earl's self-confidence.

"You realize, Browning, that if you don't accept the deed, I have every right to declare myself the winner by forfeit. Of course, we both know that I will win in any case. Next time you attempt to toy with your superiors, you would be wise to familiarize yourself with the rules under which we play."

Allen slumped back in his chair. Brockmere had just sealed his own fate. Garrett grimly threw the deed back onto the table and stared at the earl. He slowly placed his cards face up and watched the color drain from the earl's face.

"The first lesson I learned was that a man never bluffs during the last hand of the game." Garrett's full house, kings over jacks, beat the earl's three queens easily. An unnatural silence permeated the game room as the two men stared at one another.

Lord Maxfield closed his eyes, bitter defeat in every line of his face. His shaking hand went to an inside pocket of his gray cutaway coat. He pulled out a gilded miniature of a young woman. The two younger men watched Brockmere finger the picture as if trying to attain strength from the artificial likeness.

"Is that your daughter?" Allen asked gently.

"I had thought to win enough tonight to establish a suitable dowry for her." Brockmere spoke shakily, hoping to arouse sympathy. "When word of my bankruptcy reaches the ears of her suitors, none shall offer for her."

"May I see that?" Garrett asked. He took the small portrait and studied it for a long time. If the painter had accurately depicted her features, the girl was a beauty. An array of silver-gold curls surrounded a perfectly oval face. Two large violet eyes sparkled back at him from beneath long, gold-tipped lashes, and a teasing smile pulled at the corners of a pleasingly shaped mouth. Garrett was almost tempted to smile back at the painted image in his hand. If the rest of her was as exquisite as her face, she would suit his purposes very well.

"I'm a wealthy man, Brockmere. I don't need or want your home. However, I do require a wife. If I find that your daughter is the type I'm looking for, would you consider exchanging the deed to your estate for her hand in marriage?" He kept his tone businesslike. To him, the acquisition of a wife was just that: business.

"You're joking, of course." Lord Maxfield attempted to match Garrett's tone.

"I assure you, I'm serious. My cousin will verify it for you, if you like. My time in London is running out, and it might be fortunate for us both if we come to some kind of an arrangement."

The earl's eyes widened as he received Allen's affirmative nod. It was possible that he would not lose Bannerfield after all. His glance became speculative.

Guessing the reason for the look of curiosity on the

earl's face, Garrett grinned—a lopsided, boyish grin that immediately made his face less hard. "My father didn't approve of my reputation with the ladies. He felt it was high time I settled down and produced an heir. So he added a codicil to his will on the day he died. He gave me little choice in the matter, stipulating that the girl be English. Pa believed that just as we choose horses to improve the strain, wives should be chosen for their bloodlines. With that purpose in mind, I came to my mother's family in London." Garrett paused. "What Pa didn't take into account is that Texas is about to get into a war with Mexico. I shouldn't be here at all."

Lord Maxfield perceived correctly that Garrett was deeply committed to his land. He anticipated Catherine's reaction to this outrageous proposal, and the thought of her indignation brought him considerable pleasure. The earl had slight affection for his daughter, who had never lived up to his expectations. Though she was intelligent, Catherine refused to behave properly and was far too strong-minded. Her refusal to marry the suitors Brockmere proposed was a constant thorn in his side. He eyed his opponent shrewdly. Catherine might find Browning attractive at first, but she'd balk when she discovered how different he was from the men she was used to. Perhaps Browning was a perfect match for her unladylike high spirits.

"I can see you are considering my proposal." Garrett quirked his mouth at the earl's thorough appraisal. His eyes narrowed when Brockmere looked almost amused. Maybe the young woman in the picture had become a fat shrew with pockmarks.

"I will have the papers of our agreement drawn up this very night," Lord Maxfield said quickly, as Garrett frowned and looked at Allen. Garrett got the uncanny feeling that he was walking into a trap.

"Is there some reason for that dazed look on your face, Cousin?" he asked, nonchalantly finishing the contents of his glass.

"Brockmere, you can't mean to go through with this!" Allen said, stunned. "I must protest on Lady Catherine's behalf. She is one of the most beautiful women in London, and I would gladly offer for her myself if I thought there were any chance she would accept me, dowry or no."

"Well, that's a relief." If Allen was eager to marry the girl, she couldn't be so bad, Garrett decided. The portrait must be accurate after all.

"You can't do this, Garrett. She's not a slave, to be sold like chattel. Please, give Brockmere back his deed." Allen moved his hazel gaze from one man to the other. Neither seemed willing to change his stand.

"Shall we adjourn to the bar to await the conclusion of these arrangements?" Brockmere reached for his deed, but Garrett's hand closed over the parchment and relegated it to the inside pocket of his coat.

"I believe I'd like to meet the lady before I make up my mind," he said, observing the earl's struggle to control his irritation and wondering at his reasons for wanting to close the deal before Garrett got a chance to meet Lady Catherine.

Brockmere grudgingly agreed to arrange a meeting, suggesting that it be done without informing Catherine of what was afoot. They agreed to meet the next night at a private party being given by the duke and duchess of Strathmore.

In a bedroom of the Winslows' town house, Garrett stood gazing at his reflection, not appreciating the classic lines of the dark evening clothes he saw in the mirror or the efforts of the fawning tailor, Mannering. The man was boring him with details about the latest men's fashions. Garrett shrugged his broad shoulders and twisted his neck inside the high cravat tied beneath the snug-fitting cutaway jacket. He ignored the kneeling tailor as he held out his arms, noting the ruffled cuffs of his fine linen shirt. His lips twisted wryly.

The invitation to the Strathmore ball had arrived early, and Allen had suggested that Garrett be fitted with new evening clothes to help ensure his success with Catherine.

The tailor's soft fingers patted the American's backside and hips. Garrett glared with exasperation at Allen, who was overseeing the fitting. Allen returned the look, his lean face benign, indicating that the tailor's actions were not unusual. The little man, still on his knees, fitted a tape to the inside of Garrett's muscular thigh and let it drop to the floor.

Astounded, Garrett stepped away from the cringing tailor. "Listen, friend," he snarled, "you keep your hands to yourself or you'll go out of here minus a few fingers."

The startled clothier drew back his hands. "Sir Allen, if this . . . this . . . gentleman expects me to complete my work by tonight, he must allow me to continue." He pleaded with his fellow countryman, totally intimidated by the tall, muscular specimen who was threatening him. He wanted to leave the room with all his appendages intact, and from the smoldering look in the dangerous blue eyes of the big Texan, his well-being was highly in doubt.

Allen stifled a laugh. He felt Garrett's presence as strongly as the drooping tailor, but he knew his cousin's irritation was directed more at himself than at the wizened man who was trying his best to be quick. "Garrett, you have to stop scaring this poor fellow. Believe me, he is only doing what is necessary to ensure a proper fit. Mannering is the finest tailor in London." Allen searched Garrett's face, seeing a disbelieving frown furrow the tanned brow and an exasperated glitter in his deep blue eyes.

It was remarkable that Garrett was his cousin. They were entirely different. While Allen was pale and thin, Garrett looked as if he had been born and raised in the outdoors. His lean, powerful body exuded strength and vitality.

"Do you go through this kind of ordeal every time you need a new suit?" Garrett asked, glaring at the tailor with dislike.

"Every time, and well worth the trouble it is," Allen assured him, and gestured to Mannering to continue his work.

"Do you dress to the right or the left, Mr. Browning?" The little man waited impatiently for his answer before he brought the tape to Garrett's long legs.

"What the hell is he talking about now?" Garrett demanded, highly suspicious of the little tailor's hesitation.

Allen's hazel eyes rolled up to the ceiling. He had no choice but to explain the fine points of expensive tailoring, though he feared that Garrett would throw Mannering out before answering a question he would consider much too personal.

"Ah . . . he wants to know if you are going to need more material to the right or to the left of your inseam. I think you know why, and for heaven's sake, don't take offense."

He winced when he saw the explosive light in Garrett's eyes. Garrett twisted his lips and barked, "The left, then, but you damned well better be quick about it!"

The tailor was finished minutes later and gathered his

equipment in nervous haste. He left, stating that he would return the suit in a few hours. Garrett immediately looked for his comfortable clothes.

Waiting for Garrett to get dressed, Allen recalled their first meeting and how impressed he had been with his first glimpse of Garrett's powerful figure striding down the gangway of the ship. He was glad that Garrett had come and was fascinated by his tales of Texas. But when word got out that Garrett had up and married Lady Catherine Maxfield and carted her back with him to the wilds, Allen would be left to answer all the curious questions.

"Mother will be upset if we don't join her for brunch." Allen decided not to approach the subject of Catherine. It was futile. Her fate was sealed. "She's a stickler for etiquette and schedules."

"As was my mother," Garrett said distractedly, buttoning his shirt.

"Oh?" Allen asked. It was the first time Garrett had referred to his mother. All Allen knew about Celeste Browning was that she had married an American and there had been some kind of scandal.

Garrett had no idea how much Allen knew about his mother, but he had no intention of discussing her. Every time he thought about the promiscuous Celeste, Garrett wanted to strike out in rage. He forced himself to look blank, stifling further comments about her. Keeping his voice even, he said, "Let's not keep Aunt Estelle waiting."

It was almost eleven o'clock that evening before Allen and Garrett entered the Palladian mansion of the duke of Strathmore. Their cloaks were taken by a liveried footman, and they were shown to a crowded ballroom. Garrett conveyed a polite greeting to their hostess and began searching for Brockmere. He found him talking to a group of elderly gentlemen. As if feeling Garrett's gaze, Brockmere excused himself from his conference.

"Browning." The earl saluted him with a glass of red wine. His gray eyes were slightly glazed, and his face was very red, as if he had drunk a great deal of alcohol. "I must have your decision tonight. I can't take any more of this waiting. Bannerfield means everything to me."

"More than your daughter?" Garrett couldn't help asking.

"Women are useless encumbrances," the earl said. "Do you want a formal introduction or do you want to meet her on your own?"

"Point her out to me, Brockmere." Garrett followed the earl's eyes. He was beginning to dislike Maxfield intensely. The man was a pompous sot. His annoyance increased when he discovered that the subject of his interest was surrounded by a herd of finely dressed young men. All he could see of her was a glimpse of green silk. Then he heard her feminine laugh, and his eyes flashed angrily. Catherine Maxfield obviously enjoyed the attentions of her countless admirers. He knew all too well where such flirtations led. How many times had he seen his beautiful mother flirting with fawning men? His brow furrowed in a scowl. "Is she always surrounded like that?"

"Afraid of the competition?" Brockmere chided snidely.

"Not at all," Garrett replied smoothly as he took a glass of champagne from a passing servant. He walked diffidently toward the circle of young men, sipping from the crystal goblet as he shouldered himself into their midst. He'd be damned if he'd stand in line with her English admirers.

Catherine had danced until her feet hurt. She wished

she could escape from the good-natured men who prattled around her. At nineteen, Catherine was older than many unmarried young women in Victorian England, but she would rather stay single than marry one of the foolish young bachelors who courted her. She'd had what many considered an unseemly education, and her knowledge of history and politics made her different from the simpering debutantes who were paraded like gaily wrapped packages to the eligible young men of the nobility. Her grandmother, the dowager duchess of Brockmere, had demanded that Catherine be well tutored, and William Maxfield had acquiesced to his domineering mother's command. However, upon the elderly lady's death four years ago, he had promptly dismissed Catherine's tutors. Catherine had continued her education in secret, poring over the newspapers and books she found in her father's library.

Strangely enough, her suitors were not put off by her ability to talk on what were generally considered masculine subjects. They were intrigued by her soft violet eyes and her intelligence and wit. Her father had been adamant that she attend the Strathmore ball, but she was tired of the meaningless society of London and would rather have been home at Bannerfield, riding with her brother Colin over an open meadow, than enduring another party. She pursed her soft lips with resignation when Lord David Longley reached for her gloved hand and claimed his dance.

"Oh, David," she pleaded wearily, "I had hoped to sit through this set."

"Be fair, Catherine," Longley declared. "I was promised the first dance and you gave it to that prig Stanton. My heart is probably in shambles inside my chest."

"You don't look any the worse for it." Catherine laughed up into his ruddy, round face as she allowed him to draw her onto the floor. Because of his slight stature, she could look over his shoulder to her vacated seat. It was at that moment that she became aware of a peculiar awareness. She sensed someone's eyes upon her, could almost feel an invisible thread drift sensuously down her face and neck to linger on the gentle curves of her breast. Startled, she searched the faces of the men who had stood near her chair. She couldn't shake the sensation of being watched.

Finally, she saw him. Dark blue eyes magnetized and held hers, searched their violet depths and then slowly dropped to the shadowed cleft between her breasts. The delicate hairs at her nape prickled in reaction to the startlingly handsome man's insolent perusal of her body. Longley swung her toward the center of the dance floor, but Catherine sensed that her movements were being closely followed by the tall, lean stranger. Trying not to let his rude scrutiny unnerve her, she forced herself to concentrate on the steps to the dance, but each time she was turned to the outside wall he was there, watching, and coming closer. He disappeared during a short turn, and she found herself searching for him. Twirled around again, she spotted him leaning casually against a white pillar, his arms folded across his chest. Then the bold creature winked at her! Actually winked at her! She missed a step, almost losing her balance. Before she could stop herself, she glanced to see if he had noticed. He had.

An amused smile lifted the corners of his mouth, making her stumble yet again. This brought a wide, flashing grin across his devilishly attractive face. He was much too sure of his looks and his effect on her. She glared at him furiously, leaning toward Longley as if he were the only man in the world.

During the next few dances, she pretended not to see the stranger but was more aware of him than ever. He had taken a new approach, which was even more devastating than being ogled from a distance. Choosing a partner from among the women, he danced as close to her as possible. When she said something flattering to her dance partner, he would issue a similar comment to her feminine counterpart. Sometimes he used her exact words! The women he claimed fairly glowed beneath his charm, but Catherine knew that she was the subject of his interest. He was playing with her, challenging her; and it was working. She began to resent the young women he held too closely in his arms. Curiosity was eating her up. He was an obvious rake, but impatience flared in her eyes, as she waited, knowing that she was the woman he wanted to partner. At length, unable to dance another step, she asked her escort to take her outside. As soon as they reached the hedged garden, she sank down upon a white wrought-iron bench. She requested a glass of lemonade and sat back to wait.

She spread her green silk skirt around her on the seat and brushed a hand across her flushed brow, pushing a stray tendril of hair away from her face. Her head rested against the cooling stones of the garden wall, and she closed her eyes to erase the mental picture of a pair of mocking blue eyes and a flashing grin. When the acrid smell of cigar smoke assailed her nostrils, her eyes flew open.

"Waiting for me?" The image became reality. He stood before her with his legs spread, his brazen presumption that she had anticipated his arrival bringing her swiftly to her feet.

"I beg your pardon?" she flared up at him, feeling small all of a sudden, for he was inordinately tall. She didn't know what game he was playing, but she wanted no part of it. He was too experienced, and she didn't know how to deal with him. She tried to sound haughty, needing to erect some kind of barrier. "Who has given you leave to speak to me?" She took a worried step backward when he moved closer.

"I don't need permission, little one," he announced, and pulled her quickly into his arms. Then he covered her mouth with his lips.

Catherine was stunned, unable to break out of his enveloping embrace. He plundered her mouth, his tongue invading the soft interior, exploring and tasting until she thought she would faint. His hand slipped beneath the flimsy material of her gown at the shoulder and slid it from her, exposing one creamy breast. Catherine was horrified. His warm hand cupped the soft flesh, and his thumb circled the rosy nipple. There was nothing she could do, and she was mortified when the nipple grew taut and tingled in response to his tender stroking. When she thought she would die of the exquisite torment he was inflicting, he abruptly released her.

"You'll do." He grinned and disappeared into the dark shadows.

Catherine stood shaking with shock and fury. She pulled up her bodice with trembling fingers, still feeling the warm imprint of his hand upon her breast and the seductive pressure of his mouth. She pressed her hand to her branded lips and dropped to the bench.

"Your lemonade, milady." The young officer held out the sparkling liquid and sat down beside her.

Catherine's thoughts were so chaotic she barely heard him, and she ignored the drink. How could that man, a stranger, have dared touch her so intimately?

"Is something the matter? You're pale as a ghost," Captain Parker said. His question brought a flaming blush to her cheeks as her eyes dropped guiltily to her bosom.

"I'm afraid I have a headache, Captain. The air is

heavy this evening." As the man took her inside, she glanced warily back, her cheeks warm with the thought that a tall, mocking stranger might emerge from the darkness.

Chapter 2

Catherine turned her mare toward the upcoming row of hedges, and she and her horse sailed effortlessly over the tall shrubs. She turned breathlessly in the saddle to call to her younger brother, who was riding behind her on a chestnut gelding. "C'mon, Colin. Give Sampson his head."

Seconds later, the twelve-year-old boy joined her on the other side and grinned. "I've missed you, Kay. When you go up to London with Father, there is nothing fun to do around here."

"I'm glad to be home." Catherine pulled her slouched cap down over her eyes and tightened her grip on the reins of her horse. "What do you want to do next?"

Their mother had died shortly after Colin's birth, and seven-year-old Catherine's life had been shattered. Catherine gave her infant brother all the love she could possibly give him in place of the beautiful, loving mother he would never know. Their father had never shown great affection for either of them, spending most of his time in London. Bannerfield was Catherine's haven. Here she could drop the pretenses society demanded and become the free spirit she really was. Colin and she were always together until he had been sent off to Eton. Since then, only holidays were spent together, and these were the times they both enjoyed most.

"According to Leeds, Father and some man from London are talking business in the garden. Do you want to scare the devil out of some unsuspecting old codger from town? I'll never forget that time we jumped over the vicar and he spilled his tea all over Father's lap." At this distance, they couldn't tell who the visitor was, but Lord Maxfield's friends were always stuffy in the extreme.

Catherine was reluctant to agree to the childish prank, but the hoyden in her won out. She was dressed in her brother's clothes, so their startled victim wouldn't guess her identity. Besides, after the confining weeks in London, she was enjoying her freedom and Colin's company too much to deny herself or Colin a bit of harmless fun. "Let's go!"

Looking like two stable boys, they raced neck and neck toward the garden wall. "Tallyho!" Colin yelled as both horses rose up and sailed within inches of the heads of the two unsuspecting men sitting in the garden. The riders disappeared out of sight as they raced across the lawn.

"What the hell was that?" Garrett Browning jumped up and shouted at Lord Maxfield. "Do you often have horses leaping over your guests?" He grimaced at the brandy staining his tan breeches. He had felt a moment's fear when two sets of hooves passed so closely above his head. Even so, he admired the daring feat of horsemanship he had just witnessed. It was one hell of a good stunt!

Lord Maxfield picked up the signed marriage contract and quickly deposited it inside his coat. "That was my son, Colin, and his . . . ah . . . usual cohort."

"I'll say this much for them—those boys can ride."

Garrett began wiping his trousers with a linen napkin. "I'd like to join your son and his friend for a ride sometime."

The two men were unaware that Catherine and Colin were sneaking up behind them. Colin formed a stirrup with his hands, and Catherine took a leg up in order to peek over the wall that hid their victims from view.

As soon as she caught sight of Garrett, Catherine gasped and lost her grip on the stones, falling backward to land with a thump in the middle of a large puddle.

"What did you let go for?" Colin whispered, surprised that his usually agile sister had lost her balance and landed unceremoniously on her backside in a mud hole. The boy turned swiftly at the chuckle he heard behind him and found himself staring at a man with sparkling blue eyes and a wide grin.

Before Colin could reach his sprawling sister, the man had jumped nimbly over the wall and was hauling her up by the collar of her jacket. Colin supposed by the stranger's actions that they were about to be delivered a scathing lecture, and he backed away from the powerful figure. "I don't suppose you would accept an apology," Colin said cheekily. Then he shouted, "Hey! Don't choke Kay!"

"Is that your name?" Garrett demanded of the dripping youth still in his grip. The head went down, and the boy nodded.

"C'mon, Kay, let's get our horses and clear out of here." Colin was prepared to make a run for it. This man was nothing like the village vicar. But before he took a step, he was collected and collared, and they were both dragged inside the gate to the garden.

"Gentlemen, let's see what my host has to say about the way you greet his guests." Garrett made his voice sound stern to hide his amusement. At least one of the boys was afraid, for he could feel him quivering beneath his hand. The other one was too high-spirited to give in without saying something.

"Do something, Kay!" Colin begged.

Garrett would have thought Colin was the leader of this terrible twosome. His cohort hadn't uttered a word since he had been dragged from the puddle. Personally, he preferred Colin's spunk to the other boy's downcast face and refusal to meet Garrett's stern expression.

"Be quiet, Colin," Lord Maxfield said exasperatedly as the two cowed figures stood before him. He cleared his throat and patted the pocket that held the marriage contract. "Garrett Browning, may I present my children. The young man who is looking to your other prisoner for aid is my son, Colin, and his silent partner in crime is my daughter, Lady Catherine Elizabeth Maxfield."

Garrett released both his prisoners and whisked the cap from Catherine's head. A mass of curls tumbled down her back as she turned a flushed and furious face to the man she had hoped never to lay eyes on again. Garrett bowed from the waist and drawled silkily, "How charming! What delightful children you have, Lord Maxfield." He reached for Catherine's hand and brushed the grubby palm with his lips.

Colin grinned when he saw the brazen wink the man gave his sister. He was relieved that the stranger had a sense of humor and was not another stuffed shirt from London. His accent was foreign, and Colin wondered where he was from.

Catherine finally found her voice. "What are you doing here?"

"I was invited, bright eyes," Garrett returned, his mouth twitching.

"Catherine, you are being rude to our guest," Lord Maxfield snapped. "I suggest you excuse yourself and go change those disgraceful wet clothes. Perhaps Mr.

Browning will forget this unfortunate incident when you appear later, dressed like a proper young woman."

Colin burst out laughing, and Catherine glared at him. Trying to act as dignified as possible under the humiliating circumstances, she turned on her heel and walked briskly toward the hall.

"Lady Catherine." The deep voice stopped her, and she turned around. "You forgot this." Garrett grinned and threw her the soiled cap she had been wearing. She reached out automatically and caught it. Then, furious, she stuffed the hat inside a pocket of her short jacket and raced into the mansion. The man was a mocking, arrogant beast!

Catherine reached her bedroom and slammed the heavy door behind her. She pulled the bellcord hanging at the side of her canopied bed, then paced back and forth until her maid answered the call. She ordered a tub of hot water, and as she stripped out of her muddied clothes, her temper began to soar. Of all the people on earth to find in the garden, Garrett Browning was the last person she would have expected. At least now she knew his name and could curse him in more personal terms. Ever since that night when he had swept her into his arms and kissed her as if she were a harlot, she had thought of little else.

Who did he think he was to intimately explore her body, then coolly present himself at Bannerfield as if he had every right to be there? She was going to find out how that had happened, that was for certain. This time she was prepared for him, and she wouldn't make it easy for him to subdue her, kiss her, maul her. "You'll do? I'll just show you what I'll do!" Catherine declared out loud. He would regret ever laying a hand on her.

Catherine stepped into her tub of warm, scented water and scrubbed away the mud. She knew that men found her attractive, but never had one of her suitors taken such liberties. She had accepted a few kisses from the gentlemen who pursued her, but none had branded her lips with flame.

She had to admit that Garrett Browning was a magnificent specimen of masculinity. The night of the ball he had looked like a roguish prince of darkness, his black evening clothes hugging his lean body, his white teeth flashing in his tanned face. Her pulses had begun to race when he first looked at her with those eyes, so liquid and dark blue as the sea. Some women might fall into his arms at a snap of his fingers, but she had no intention of becoming one of them.

She spent the remainder of the afternoon in her room, discarding gown after gown until she located the exact one she wanted—a lavender sprigged muslin that sported a hundred tiny pearled buttons from its hem to the top of its high neck. She didn't wear it often, as it was too time consuming to put on. It took her maid, Jenny, almost ten minutes to fasten each tiny button within the loops. Satisfied that she was well armored, Catherine smiled into the vanity mirror before her and waited for the little maid to brush her hair up into a regal mass of curls atop her head. When dinner was announced, she descended the stairs and walked gracefully into the formal sitting room.

"Ah, Catherine, you look charming." Lord Maxfield bestowed the first genuine smile he had given her in a long time. He escorted her to a green brocade chair, and she sank down upon the soft seat. She carefully surveyed the room and was relieved to discover that they were alone.

"Where is Mr. Browning?" she asked casually, trying to sound disinterested.

"Leeds took him upstairs to his room in order for him to change out of the clothes you ruined," Lord Maxfield said in irritation.

"What is he doing here, Father?" She stared pointedly at Lord Maxfield, anxious for details about Garrett Browning's relationship with him.

"When I feel the need to discuss my affairs with one of my children, I shall let you know. In the meantime, I think you would find it judicious to treat Mr. Browning politely. It's possible that his opinion of you could threaten our business arrangements."

"Rubbish!" Catherine burst out. "That man couldn't care less what a woman thinks."

A strange smile turned up the corners of the earl's thin lips as he turned at the sound of footsteps.

Colin burst into the room attired in a flamboyant cutaway coat and ill-matched trousers. "Kay! You should see what Mr. Browning had under his shirt. A knife! I bet he knows how to use it, too. Just think, he's probably had to kill Indians and fight off dangerous cutthroats!"

"That will be enough, Colin." Lord Maxfield glared at his son. "How did you discover what our guest wears beneath his clothing?"

"I went through the passage and peeked through the panel next to the fireplace," Colin admitted sheepishly. The earl would have delivered an angry tirade, but at the moment the subject of Colin's obsessive interest walked into the room. Lord Maxfield composed his outraged features and suggested that it was time they proceeded to the dining room.

As the footmen brought in the first course of the evening meal, Colin hurled one question after another at their guest.

"Texas is a vast wilderness, Colin. My home is far away from the closest settlement, so I rarely see anyone who doesn't live on Tierra Nueva," Garrett was saying as a steaming bowl of saffron-colored liquid was placed in front of him. He waited a long moment before dipping into the substance, unused to tasting anything that looked so unappetizing.

Catherine was having difficulty keeping her eyes off him. She was grateful for her younger brother's demanding curiosity about their guest. He was asking all the questions she wanted the answers to and yet enabling her to appear coolly unconcerned as she hung on every word. Garrett swallowed a spoonful of soup, and his brows rose at the taste. He replaced the spoon on his plate and hoped the oddly flavored fish soup would be taken away before he had to eat any more.

"You don't have to eat this stuff, Mr. Browning. It's made from slimy eels and ground-up crocuses." Colin pushed his serving away untouched. "Kay used to water the centerpiece with it when Father wasn't looking."

"Colin!" Catherine croaked, wishing she could kick her brother under the table and throw her soup in Garrett Browning's face. He saluted her with his spoon, his amused chuckle increasing her embarrassment.

"Forgive him, Lady Catherine. Whenever my adopted sister, Elena, is entertaining a gentleman, I tend to point out what she was like as a child." His words were meant to soothe her ire, but Catherine almost choked on her Elys en Brewet. Entertaining a gentleman? Garrett Browning was no gentleman, and she certainly had no intention of entertaining him.

Her violet eyes darkened to onyx black orbs as she retorted, "Your adopted sister has my sympathies." She made sure he could tell from the inflection of her voice that she was sympathetic for more reasons than the teasing Elena suffered.

Lord Maxfield cleared his throat and quickly changed the subject, sending Catherine a warning with a quick, sharp glance. Garrett was studying her features, his warm gaze probing her thoughts. She forced herself to look at him, denying him the right to lay claim to her form with his arrogant survey. She found his interest in her increasing as the meal progressed, and questions about what this meant filled her mind. She forced herself to enter the conversation. "Colin, you were telling me that you wanted to ride over to the village tomorrow and purchase a new pair of riding boots. I'm sure Mr. Browning and Father will be otherwise occupied, so why don't we meet after breakfast?"

"On the contrary, Catherine," Lord Maxfield said smoothly, "Mr. Browning has told me that he wishes to put his horse to the test. Since I no longer ride, I offered your company to our guest. Colin will have to attend to his lessons with his tutor. If he is to continue at Eton next semester, he must improve his Latin."

Catherine would have said something to reject that suggestion, but Mr. Browning obviously didn't like the idea any better himself. His frown was a vast relief. "I doubt very much if Lady Catherine would be able to complete the course I intend to put to Trojan. I would like it if you asked one of your stable men to accompany me. I intend no insult, Lady Catherine, but I doubt your ability extends to the steeplechase. I saw the difficult course you have built for such riding on my way in. Do you breed horses of that caliber, Brockmere?" He ignored Catherine, but the implications of his speech made her furious.

Before her father could comment, Catherine interrupted. "Perhaps you didn't realize it this morning, Mr. Browning, but the jump through the garden could only have been made by a rider of considerable skill. Both my brother and I have ridden the steeplechase course many times."

Garrett dismissed her declaration with a wave of his

hand. "Childish pranks usually succeed out of sheer luck. One jump over a low garden wall is no evidence of skill."

Catherine was fuming. Before stopping to think, she declared, "Very well. I challenge you to the course. I hope the plug you have purchased can keep up with my mare." She glared across the table, and then her mouth dropped open. Garrett's face reflected a satisfaction he made no attempt to hide. His eyes were sparkling, and his lips were twitching with amusement. She had walked right into the trap he had set for her!

"I accept the challenge, Lady Catherine," he said softly, and she had the distinct feeling that he was challenging her to far more than a race. His knowing gaze traveled slowly over her face until the pink color in her cheeks told him that she was conscious of what he had just accomplished. She turned to her father and saw the same smug look. She was sure these two were conspirators in something that would affect her. If that was the case, she would do her best to foil them.

Her thoughts went back to the night in the garden when Garrett had fondled her breast, making her writhe beneath his sensual fingers. Her eyes dropped to his hand, and a pulse began beating in her cheeks. Her thoughts lingered on that night when Garrett Browning had taken unheard-of liberties. She didn't want to think about it any longer and lifted her eyes, only to discover that Garrett was watching her. A sensual darkness invaded his eyes, and his grin became mocking as he looked at his hand and then at her breast.

With her heart fluttering like a captured bird's, Catherine forced her attention to the next course of the meal, knowing that he had read her mind. She was immensely grateful that neither Colin nor her father was aware of the exchange that had just taken place.

"Do you have real savages in Texas?" Colin asked

between bites. "I saw some pictures of the red devils in school, and they looked ferocious. One even had a hank of human hair hanging from his belt."

"Colin, will you please refrain from such discussions at the table," the earl ordered.

"Don't concern yourself on my account, Brockmere." Garrett smiled. "The boy is naturally interested. At his age, I loved hearing bloodthirsty tales. I agree, however, that such subjects should be discussed at another time. I will tell you, Colin, that I have met several Indians. Some are as dignified and civilized as your father, and others were like the ones you see in books. In Texas, we have an equal number of both."

"I must say, Browning, that I do not particularly like being compared to a savage." Lord Maxfield looked appalled.

"I apologize, Brockmere. Perhaps it would be better if I kept my comments about Texas until tomorrow."

Colin looked disappointed. It was apparent to Catherine that her young brother was completely enthralled by Garrett Browning. His gray eyes looked worshipful as he listened to every word the Texan spoke with rapt attention. He would not be so enamored if he knew how the man had treated his sister, she thought darkly.

"My compliments to Cook," the earl said to the head footman as they completed dinner. "Catherine, show Mr. Browning our gardens. I have some papers to look over in my study. Colin, I believe you have a few things to attend to in your room." The stern look the earl turned on Colin indicated that the boy had better acquiesce to his father's suggestion.

About to refuse her father's orders, Catherine changed her mind and decided to confront their unwelcome guest with a few well-chosen words. She did not like the possessive way he looked at her, his arrogance or the feeling that she was dealing with an unknown quantity. She rose from her chair and patiently waited for Colin to bid them good night.

"This way, Mr. Browning." She walked toward the French doors with a swish of her skirt and many petticoats and led him outside. She was struck by his height when he joined her at the open doors. She barely came to his shoulder, and she frowned at her natural disadvantage, hoping that intelligence would more than make up for her lack of stature. She was determined to find out exactly what he had been implying when he had stated, "You'll do."

Her thoughts must have been mirrored on her face, for she heard his low chuckle and the words, "I deserve better." Catherine was disconcerted. What did he mean by that?

She remained silent as they walked out into the warm spring air. The smell of roses became stronger as they wandered toward the small gazebo in the middle of the hedged garden. Catherine had no intention of straying far. His nearness was making her more nervous with each passing moment. The white latticework structure would serve her purposes very well and would also offer a direct route back inside, if necessary. As soon as she had taken the last step up to the wooden floor of the gazebo, she turned to face him.

"Why have you come here, Mr. Browning? I can't believe someone like my father would have anything to do with a man like you." She tried to see his expression, but his face was in shadow, and her only impression was of how large he seemed as his lean form loomed before her in the darkness.

"I can't believe someone like your father sired anyone like you. I would say we are equally astonished." He leaned back against the frame of the enclosure, a shaft of moonlight lighting his features as he slowly folded his arms across his chest and surveyed her from head to foot.

"Will you stop looking at me like that?" Catherine demanded. She wanted to ask him what he meant by saying she had come as a surprise to him, but she was suddenly afraid of his answer. Somehow she would have to show him that he couldn't unsettle her with his challenging words and dangerously expressive blue eyes.

Garrett took a step toward her. "I like looking at you. I liked the feel of you in my arms, all soft and melting. You have a delectable mouth, and I was never one to deny myself the pleasure of laying claim to a particularly enticing pair of lips." He took another step toward her, smiling as she backed away. She frantically thought about how to halt his advance. His capacity to reduce her to gulping frustration with his entirely too personal remarks overwhelmed her. She straightened her shoulders and looked firmly up at his face.

"If you lay your disgusting hands on me one more time, I will have you thrown out on your ear," she threatened, hoping he would not notice the betraying quiver of her lower lip.

"Ah . . . I was wondering how long it would take you to bring up our first meeting. Although brief, it was memorable, was it not?" He cocked his head, obviously considering himself entirely safe from her rather hysterical threat.

"Memorable!" Catherine's voice rose. "All I remember is being pawed by an animal and then insulted by your disgusting estimation of me. I'll do? Let me tell you, I will do nothing that involves you. I want you to pack up and leave here before I tell my father what liberties you have taken with me!"

Garrett's deep laugh set her back considerably. "I was hoping you would remember what I said. I must have made quite an impression on you. I wanted to see if the passion sleeping beneath your luscious exterior could be aroused by my touch. You responded tolerably. And I see that I made a lasting impression."

"Why, you conceited, arrogant swine! All I remember is my revulsion!" she almost shouted, wishing to wipe the tolerant grin from his face.

"How disappointing." He continued to grin down at her. "Here I thought you had invited me out here to begin where we left off the first time we met. At dinner, I recall that your thoughts were not so chaste."

Catherine's mouth dropped open in astonishment. He was uncannily adept in his ability to read her thoughts. He had known that she was thinking about his hands on her body and had interpreted it to mean she wanted him to touch her again. The realization hit her that she *had* responded to his touch. In her tormented dreams, she had relived the moment again and again.

"You should go back to the wilderness where you belong," she said defensively. "I will not spend another second in your company." She turned to leave the gazebo, but his hand snaked out and grabbed her wrist.

"Let go of me!" Catherine raged.

He loosened his grip but still retained firm control of her wrist. "I have no intention of letting you go, little spitfire. If you stop shouting at me long enough, I'll tell you what you need to know."

She looked furiously up at him. "I don't want to know anything. I don't want to be forced to spend any time in your company." She tried to wrench free of his grasp, but he pulled her closer to him until she could feel every muscle of his hard body through her gown.

Desperate, she brought up her free hand and issued a sharp slap to his cheek, inadvertently scratching his neck with her nails. His reaction was instantaneous.

He grabbed her wrist and pinned her arms to her sides, holding her helpless in his embrace. "You are one hell of a lot more than I bargained for, lady." He looked down at her angry face, her eyes glinting mutiny in the moonlight. "I think you should have been called Kate. I hope I have as easy a time taming you as Petruchio did taming Shakespeare's termagant."

"I am not yours to tame," she announced courageously, feeling as if he had already tamed her considerably. "If women in Texas allow men to treat them like this, I'm surprised you haven't all been murdered in your sleep. Let go of me before I scream."

"You don't really want to scream, Catherine. You want me to kiss you. But before I do, I want you to know that my intentions are honorable. I plan to marry you before I leave for Texas next week. We don't have much time to get to know one another."

Catherine's eyes widened with shock. "You are joking!" she exclaimed.

"I assure you, I am not. You were mine the night I first met you, and you are mine now." He brought up his hand and caught her chin. "Mine," he whispered, bending his head to give her a gentle kiss on the lips, lips that quivered beneath his.

She pulled away after the first tentative contact with his warm lips. Slightly dazed, she stammered, "I . . . I don't understand."

"Understand this." His voice was soft and husky against her lips as he swept her up into his arms, and his mouth took possession of hers while he carried her down the gazebo steps and lowered her gently upon the soft grass of the lawn. Her breasts were crushed to his chest as he plundered her petal-soft lips. He began a slow, expert exploration of her body, trailing his hand along the delicate column of her throat and down the closed fastenings of her gown. Tiny buttons meant to ensure her safety were slipped from their loops until he had opened the gown to her waist and exposed the satiny mounds. He placed a hand over each breast and felt them swell in his palm as he sensually molded them to taut peaks of awareness.

She felt that she was about to drown in a melting fire of sensation. The clean, masculine smell of him clouded rational thought, as did his demanding hands and lips. She tried to hold onto her scattering wits, but she was rapidly sinking beneath his seduction, resistance to his burning touch melting away. She arched against him, pressing her naked breasts to his chest as her arms rose by their own volition around his neck. Her fingers gloried in the feel of his crisp black hair. She wanted to get closer yet, drawing his face to her own and twisting beneath him, her body on fire with a delicious need.

He raised himself up on one elbow, intending to bring the interlude to a close before he lost control and took her. He was astounded when she pulled him back down to her. Her soft lips were a sweet invitation he could not refuse, and the feel of her dainty hand as it slipped between the buttons of his shirt to the skin beneath made his breath catch in his throat. He gave a low growl, captivated by her touch.

Catherine exulted with each quickened beat of his heart. She was sure he must love her. She had never felt such overwhelming desire and was filled with joy at the thought of being married to a man who could inspire such wondrous feelings within her. It seemed like a miracle that this man could feel for her what she felt for him. Now she truly did understand. He was in love with her and was not going to leave for America without her.

His lips moved across her cheek and down her throat, and she murmured, "I am glad you love me."

There was an immediate stiffening of the muscles in his body as he abruptly pulled away. She didn't understand the shuttered expression that came down over his face. She only knew that something was wrong. She sat up, shaking, humiliated by his sudden withdrawal, and began refastening her gown with trembling fingers.

Garrett wouldn't look at her. He stood up and turned his back, waiting for her to finish covering herself. There had been triumph in her voice. She had not responded to him like an innocent but like an experienced woman, sure of her seductive power. He wondered how many others had fallen into the silken trap she had woven around him so easily. She might have the face of an angel, but her body had responded like that of a temptress. All women were alike! "In order to gain my inheritance, I have to marry an Englishwoman within the year. As I told you once before, you'll do," he announced cruelly.

Catherine stood up in shocked silence. There was no tenderness or warmth in his voice or in the forbidding, stiff line of his spine. He had turned his back on her as if she meant nothing to him. "Why have you chosen me?" Confusion and hurt were present in her every word.

She heard his soft curse as he slowly turned around to face her, his eyes riveting on her pale face. "I won you in a poker game."

"No," she breathed, horrified. The gentle seduction of his mouth and hands had been a sham, a deceitful trick to gain himself a willing wife. "That's impossible."

"I suggest you take that up with your father," he stated, not willing to meet her shattered gaze with his cold eyes.

She hurled herself at him like an angry lioness. "I

hate you, Garrett Browning. I hate you and I won't ever let you touch me again!"

Ignoring her threat and her tiny, pummeling fists, he picked her up and carried her through the garden and directly into the hall. "You can cool off in your room." He took the grand staircase two steps at a time, paying no attention to her outrage as he carried her to her bedroom. When they were inside, he sat her down on her bed and stood towering over her, his hands on his hips. "After we're married, I'll teach you to control that temper. I hope you respond as well to that lesson as you have to our sessions of lovemaking."

"Oh!" She shook her head until her hair fell completely free of its pins, making her look like a wild kitten spitting with temper. "I'll never marry you! You are a madman and should be locked away from decent people." She scrambled to her knees and reached across the bed for a vase to throw at his head. "Get out of here! Get out of my room!"

"You must learn to accept your fate." He smiled dangerously, easily ducking the flying missile. "You are as much mine as my horse. I signed the bill of sale this morning."

"I'm not for sale." She hurled another vase, which he quickly sidestepped. It crashed to the floor and shattered.

He flashed her a teasing grin as he got out of the way of a flying piece of pottery. "I can wait." He turned on his heel and left.

Catherine continued pitching everything she could reach at the closed door before sitting back on her heels in exasperation. Her breath came in short, harsh pants as she glared at the closed mahogany door. Seconds later, Colin entered, opening his mouth with amazement when he saw the heap of shattered china on the floor and the look of fury on his disheveled sister's face.

Carefully stepping over the shards near the threshold, he came to the side of the bed. "Whew! What happened? I saw Garrett going downstairs. What did he say that made you start throwing things? Father would have a fit if he found out you brought a man to your room. You could have tried to be a little more quiet."

"I did not bring that despicable excuse for a man to my room. I'd love to know how he knew which one was mine." She started pulling dried leaves and grass from her hair, glaring at Colin.

"I showed him this afternoon when he came up to change his clothes." Colin frowned at Catherine's glare. "Well, he did ask me. Why don't you like him, Kay?" He walked to the door and began picking up the broken pieces of glass. "I think you should give in and marry him before he decides you aren't worth the trouble. He said he would give you a fair chance to impress him, even after I told him you don't do a good job of acting like a grand lady."

"What?" Catherine squeaked. Did everyone but her know about and approve of Garrett's outrageous plans? Give her a fair chance to impress him! He'd be impressed when she stuck a knife in his ribs and laughed while he bled to death!

"He told me he is going to marry you and take you home with him. Wouldn't that be wonderful? I could come and visit you and maybe see a real Indian." Colin dug Garrett's grave deeper and deeper as he blithely continued. "He says he'll buy me a horse to ride on the ranch when I come."

"He had the effrontery to tell you he plans to marry me?" She jumped off the bed and faced him, her arms akimbo.

"Sure. Why do you think I stayed in the house when you two went courting in the garden? Father said you needed some time alone." Colin grinned at her sheepishly. "I know grown-ups like to get all mushy and kiss. It looks like he kissed you quite a lot, Kay."

"I'll kill him!" she said vehemently, shocked to the core that Garrett would apprise everyone, especially her little brother, that he planned to marry her. But if her father knew what he had done to her, he would throw him out rather than agree to such a match. The earl might not be a loving parent, but Catherine was sure he would protect her honor.

Colin looked upset. "Why? You're almost an old maid. I think you had better marry him while you have the chance. Your life will be an adventure. You will be able to ride all day long and do anything you want."

"Colin, will you please stop spouting about Texas as if it were a piece of heaven? Would you have me marry a man I despise so you can have a new horse?"

Colin looked wounded; his lower lip drooped. "Well, I think you're being a bad sport about this. You should be flattered that he wants to marry you."

"Just what did he tell you?"

"He said it was man talk," Colin said proudly.

"Listen here, Colin Edward Maxfield, Garrett Browning is a total stranger. If you owe anyone allegiance, it's me. Now, you tell me what nonsense he has put into your head, this very minute!"

"Well . . . he said you were his woman but you just didn't know it yet. And . . . he said women are like horses, and you were like a spirited filly refusing the bit. And I think you are!" Colin tossed this phrase over his shoulder as he edged toward the door. His parting remark left Catherine fuming. "I bet you like the way he kissed you and that's why you're so mad."

Was that true? She had had no idea who Garrett Browning was when he walked into her life and branded her with his lips. She still knew little about him, other than that he had the power to make her respond to him until she was clinging to him and welcoming his caresses. It was appalling that this complete stranger could so overpower her and then announce that she was to be his wife! She would have to talk to her father and find out just how far this arrangement had progressed.

She straightened her gown and brushed her hair until all the dried leaves were gone, no evidence remaining to show that she had recently lain on the moist grasses of the lawn and reveled in the touch of a demanding seducer.

She walked to the study, where she expected to find her father drinking his usual brandy before retiring. She hoped he would be up to discussing Garrett Browning with her and not completely inebriated.

When she entered the dark-paneled room and walked directly to the wide mahogany desk in the center, she did not see the tall figure reclining in a leather-upholstered chair before the fireplace.

The earl looked up from his desk, and his lips tightened. He had hoped to delay the inevitable a bit longer, but Browning had told him that Catherine was already aware of her impending marriage. He disliked unpleasantness and hoped she wouldn't embarrass him with her actions once he had informed her how much was at stake. "Shut the door, Catherine. I don't want Colin to hear this conversation, and you know his penchant for eavesdropping." The earl watched her retrace her steps and close the study door, saw her falter slightly when she discovered Garrett and then stubbornly refuse to acknowledge his presence.

"Father, I demand to know what is going on." She took a chair before the desk and stiffly sat on its edge.

The earl glanced at Garrett. Receiving a nod to proceed, he turned back to his daughter. "As you know, Catherine, you have reached an age when proper young ladies are usually married, or at least betrothed. Since you have not accepted even the most influential suitor, I have taken the matter into my own hands and arranged a match with Mr. Browning."

"You must be as mad as he!" She stood up, rigid with anger, and gripped the edge of the desk, glaring. "You will just unarrange any contract made between the two of you."

"Excuse me, Brockmere," Garrett interrupted, and he came to stand beside his intended. He leaned indolently back against the hardwood desk and caught Catherine's eyes with his brilliant blue gaze.

"Lady Catherine, your father has neglected to explain that you have little choice in the matter." Pulling out a document from his coat and opening the folded parchment, he continued. "Unfortunately, your father lost Bannerfield to me some days ago. Thinking I would be doing myself no favor by saddling myself with a rather expensive liability, I told your father of my need to find a bride before leaving the country. It was most fortunate that your father had you to offer, or at this very moment, you would be without a roof over your pretty head.

"Now, you can choose to refuse my offer, and then Bannerfield will pass out of Maxfield hands and into mine, but I doubt you would like explaining to your young brother that it was you who allowed his birthright to pass to a stranger." He watched the warring emotions on her face: disbelief, rage, shock and finally horrified understanding. He remained silent, following her train of thought as she reached the only possible conclusion. She lifted her eyes to her father's face.

"It's rather late to question your father's judgment. I admit that he was most unwise to sit down to cards with me, but as it turned out, nothing disastrous need

happen. It is high time you married, and I need a wife."
He coolly inspected her as she vainly tried to control
her emotions.

She was caught in his trap and could think of no way
out. "Is this true?" Catherine spit out, her face tight.

"It is," Lord Maxfield admitted. "And you need not
look so betrayed. You have been a constant bane to
me, Catherine, and a bad influence on Colin. If the
truth be known, I am glad that Browning will take you
off my hands."

Catherine had known all her life that her father did
not love her, but never had she suspected the degree of
hatred she saw mirrored in the cold depths of his gray
eyes. Her face paled to deathly white when he continued. "I thought I was free of strong-minded women
when your mother and finally your grandmother died,
but I have been forced to endure you. I will have your
answer now! We both know you won't refuse, don't
we? You love Colin and will do anything to bring him
happiness." The earl leaned back in his chair, his face
revealing his pleasure in his daughter's distress.

Catherine looked straight into his eyes. condemning
his actions and words with her silence until he began to
squirm under her withering gaze. When her answer
came, her voice was so low that both men had to strain
to hear her.

"I will marry Mr. Browning. You have chained me to
a man I despise, and I will hate you forever for it." She
looked at Garrett, loathing in her glance. He almost
winced at the accusing look on her face, cursing both
himself and the stupid man who was her father for
being so brutal with her. Perhaps he should have taken
her when she had wanted him as strongly as he wanted
her. Now all that was left for him to do was to marry
her and worry about the situation that had been
created.

She walked out of the room with a dignity that impressed him greatly. Her father might consider her a bane to his existence, but Garrett felt a rising admiration. Something deep within him felt as wounded as her eyes had looked when she had acknowledged her defeat. She belonged to him now, if nothing else, he could protect her from any further pain from this man.

"We are both fools, Brockmere," he ground out from between his teeth before stalking out of the room and going upstairs.

Chapter 3

"Saddle my mare!" Catherine ordered the groom. While the young boy went to do her bidding, she began impatiently slapping her crop against her gloved palm, striding back and forth outside the stable door.

A grizzled, gray-haired figure came out of the tack room. "Riding alone, Miss Kay?" Thomas Binning asked, his leathery face creased by a smile. "Where is young Colin this morning?"

Catherine turned to the old man who had been her friend since birth and attempted to smile. She had little success, and Binning's brow rose as she said tightly, "Colin is busy, so I will be riding alone."

Observant brown eyes accurately judged her mood, wondering who had caused her high temper. "I would have thought that young scallywag would be out here first thing. I heard that American guest of yours tell the boy he could take a ride on his big roan stallion. Come see that magnificent animal; that will put the smile back on your pretty face." The old man put his arm around her and drew her into the stable.

Catherine hung back. "I don't want to see anything that belongs to him!"

A glint appeared in Binning's eyes as he read her resentful expression. "Him being that young, good-looking Texan?"

"His looks don't impress me. He's an arrogant beast. He actually believes I shall marry him, but he is very wrong."

The groom brought Glory out, and Catherine quickly mounted. She whipped her horse into a gallop and raced out of the stable yard.

Binning scratched his head, surprised by her announcement but not by her reaction. It would take a very unusual man to capture Catherine's heart. As he turned to go back to his chores, he spied Garrett Browning walking toward the stables.

"Good morning—Binning, isn't it?" Garrett held out his hand and clasped the old man's in a firm grasp. "Where is the lady off to so fast?"

"Away from you, I gather," Binning returned gruffly.

Garrett grinned and turned his gaze after the rapidly disappearing horse and rider. "I don't think she approves of me as a husband. I guess she told you that."

"That's putting it mildly, sir." Binning chuckled. "She says she doesn't approve of the looks of you."

"But she's exactly what I am looking for," Garrett responded.

Binning laughed out loud at the man's confidence. "It's going to take some time to bring her around—if you ever do at all."

"I'd best get at it, then." Garrett shrugged and called to the groom for his horse. "Where would she go?"

"I'd say she'd take her mare to the steeplechase. Whenever she's angry, she goes out there to work it off."

"Thanks, Binning." Garrett mounted and turned in the direction his reluctant fiancée had gone.

Catherine was riding at a gallop, taking the first series of fences at a dangerous speed. Her horse responded to her slightest touch, sailing effortlessly over the increasingly taller jumps. Concentrating on the movements of her mount, she almost forgot her troubles until she heard the sound of hooves pounding behind her. Turning in the saddle, she saw the great roan gaining ground. Instantly she brought her crop to Glory's flanks and increased her pace. The sight of Garrett flying toward her at incredible speed filled her with a reckless excitement. On horseback she was any man's equal, and this was the perfect opportunity to prove it.

She took the next fence, landing unsteadily on the other side. Glory stumbled and almost fell, but Catherine's expert handling brought the mare back under control. They rode furiously through the field toward the upcoming obstacle. Pressing her thighs to the saddle, Catherine urged Glory on, ignoring her mare's lathered coat and foaming mouth.

As she prepared to take the water obstacle, she felt the stallion come close; too close. Before she could prevent it, Garrett reached across the space between them and grabbed Glory's reins, pulling her to a stop. Swiftly dismounting, he yanked Catherine from the saddle and shook her. "You little idiot! What are you trying to do? Kill yourself, or your horse?"

Unable to speak, she glared up at him, knowing he had good reason to be angry but not wanting to admit it. She had endangered her horse and herself as well, because she had been hell-bent on proving her capability. She lifted her chin defiantly, intending to brazen it out. "How dare you question my skill? I was in no danger. I have ridden this course a hundred times."

"Then you are lucky that you haven't put down several fine animals. You showed no thought for your mare's safety."

"That is not your concern."

"I won't stand by and watch a beautiful animal ruined by a spoiled little vixen. Besides, I have a great deal invested in you, and I don't want *you* destroyed, either." He was furious with her. When he had watched her wildly jumping her horse at breakneck speed, his heart had nearly stopped beating. Fearing that she would fall and break her neck, he had raced to cut her off. The thought of her crumpled body lying broken on the turf had frightened him more than he would have thought possible. But now that she was safely within his grasp, he felt an urge to choke her.

Catherine threw her whip down in disgust, pulling out of his grasp and walking toward her exhausted mare.

"Where do you think you are going?" he growled.

"As far away from you as possible," she threw at him.

"That's what you think!" Garrett grabbed her wrist and pulled. "You deserve to be beaten, but perhaps you'll understand this." His mouth captured hers in a bruising kiss. He made sure she felt every muscle of his long form. He forced her head back, grasping her hair in a painful grip. Her gasp gave him the chance to thrust his tongue inside her mouth, ruthlessly taking what she refused to give willingly. When he was finished, he thrust her away from him, and she fell to the ground. Anger apparent in every taut line of his body, he mounted his horse and took Glory's reins. "The walk back will give you the chance to think about your mistreatment of this horse. You can think about this as well: Any more stunts like this and you will get a whole lot worse."

"You can't leave me stranded here!" She ran to her horse, but Garrett was already leading the mare away. "It's over four miles to the hall, you beast," she cried. "Come back here!"

He turned in the saddle, gave her a mocking salute and continued riding.

"I hate him!" she declared out loud, and began walking.

It was a warm, humid day, and Catherine's riding boots were not designed for walking. By the time she had climbed to the top of one rolling hill, her feet were beginning to blister and rivulets of perspiration ran between her breasts. She hated Garrett more with each painful step. There had to be a way out of it. If only she could get her hands on the deed. A plan began taking shape in her mind. Tonight, after he had fallen asleep, she could sneak into his room and steal back the parchment. He didn't know that she could enter the room via a secret passageway. She began to smile as the pleasurable picture of a thoroughly thwarted Garrett emerged in her head.

Colin was waiting when Garrett arrived back at the stable with the mare in tow. With large, curious eyes, Colin asked the whereabouts of his sister.

"I decided she needed a long walk. She'll probably arrive in a little while, so it would be wise for us to be elsewhere. I doubt she'll return in good spirits. It might be a good time for you to give me that tour of Bannerfield Hall I've been promised."

Colin's eyes lit up with anticipation. At last, he would be alone with his new friend.

Garrett draped an affectionate arm around Colin's shoulder. "Lead on." The twosome proceeded amiably to the hall.

Perspiring, miserable and furious, Catherine arrived

an hour later. Slowly and painfully, she limped up the stairs to her room. She heard a deep chuckle coming from the guest room down the hallway. Evidently Colin and Garrett had been having a good time while she suffered. "We'll just see who's laughing tomorrow, Mr. Browning!" She pulled savagely on the bell rope.

A short time later, she sank gratefully into the warm, scented water of her bath. Her hot skin cooled, and it helped her gain control of her emotions. She had to face her tormentor coolly. It would be a trying afternoon, but soon she would have the deed back in Maxfield possession.

Dressed in a pale blue day dress of Indian cotton that exposed her neck and shoulders, Catherine was ready to descend the stairs. Her freshly bathed skin glowed, and her shining blond hair was pulled back at the temples, then cascaded down her back in riotous curls. Minutes later, she entered the dining room. She walked regally to her seat across the table from Garrett. She surprised a look of desire on his face, which swiftly changed and became considering. She gave him a blazing smile as he politely stood up while she took her seat.

"I'm sorry if I'm late." Her voice was soft and sensuous, and his liquid gaze stayed on her. It was as if he couldn't get enough of the sight of her. "Colin, what have you been up to this morning?"

"Mostly waiting for you to show up, so we could eat," Colin teased. She barely managed to hide the flash of temper she felt and politely gestured for the meal to begin. She would not be provoked; she would play the genteel lady to the hilt.

"Enjoy your walk?" Colin said slyly, unable to suppress a wide grin.

"As a matter of fact, I did," she agreed sweetly.

Garrett's eyes narrowed speculatively. What was she up to? So far, she had totally ignored her father. He was not forgiven, but something had changed. The smile she had bestowed on him was almost triumphant. Garrett didn't trust her. She was a devious little minx, and from the sparkle in her eyes, she was pleased about something. He sensed it concerned him and knew he had better prepare himself.

Colin was annoyed that Catherine hadn't risen to his taunts. "You're lucky you don't have a sister like her," he complained to Garrett. "Even when she's got something to be howling mad about, she doesn't give me the satisfaction of teasing her about it. Are you sure you want to marry her?"

"Your sister knows what I want. Don't you, my sweet?" He tilted an inquiring head in Catherine's direction, meeting her eyes with sensual suggestion. Lord Maxfield shifted uneasily in his seat.

"It's unfortunate we can't always get what we want." She forced down the fluttering of her heart as he looked at her. "Some of us aspire to the impossible and are sorely disappointed when we fail."

"I couldn't agree more, milady. At last, a philosophy we hold in common."

Lord Maxfield interrupted their byplay. "If you approve, I will go to the vicar to formalize the arrangements. Catherine, I suggest you wear your mother's gown. You are much the same size. There is no time for fittings for a new dress. I expect you to see to it this afternoon."

Colin clapped his hands. "I knew you'd come around, Kay. This is jolly good. When is the wedding?"

"Thursday morning." Garrett spoke quickly, his eyes dancing.

Catherine offered a wide, insincere smile. "I must plan an appropriate ensemble for the occasion. If you'll excuse me . . ." If she married Garrett, she'd wear sackcloth and ashes. She rose majestically and followed Lord Maxfield from the room.

Colin picked up his plate and moved closer to Garrett, waving the hovering footmen away. "Just think, in two days, we'll be brothers. I was beginning to think old Kay would end up a spinster. She's getting pretty old."

Garrett laughed uproariously. "Your sister has a few good years left. When you reach my age, Colin, believe me, you'll appreciate a woman like her."

"You like her, don't you?"

Garrett surprised himself by admitting, "Yes, I do."

"She can be sweet sometimes. You can have a lot of fun with her when she's not mad."

Garrett choked on his wine. If only Colin knew how much fun! He said aloud, "You may be right, Colin."

Catherine didn't know or care how Garrett and her traitorous family spent their day. She suffered through the fitting of her mother's gown, not wanting to arouse suspicion. Positive she would explode if she had to sit through another meal with Garrett, she pleaded a headache and had a tray sent up to her room for dinner.

She grew increasingly nervous as it grew late. The hours seemed to drag by as she detailed her plan until she was sure of success. She heard Garrett come up the stairs and walk down the hall to his room. She waited another hour to make sure he was asleep. It was close to midnight, the house silent, when she donned a thin silk wrapper over her white lace nightgown and approached the panel beside the fireplace. Her fingers slid along the polished wood until she felt the small hidden lever. She pressed it and waited for the heavy panel to move. Then she picked up a candle and ducked into the dark passageway.

She crept along the dusty hall as silently as a cat, her slippered feet making no sound on the stone floor. She had gone several yards by the time she reached the access to Garrett's room. She blew out her candle and pressed her ear to the wall. All was quiet. She peeped through the peekhole and saw nothing. She pressed another lever, and the wall slid open. Gathering her courage, she waited for her eyes to adjust to the darkness before she entered the room.

Garrett's even breathing allayed her fears. He was asleep. Silently she edged toward his waistcoat, which hung over the back of a chair. The pockets were empty. This was going to be difficult. She stole a glance at the figure on the bed. A bare thigh told her that he slept nude, and her heart leaped to her throat. His tanned, muscular chest stood out against the white linen, and she stood staring, mesmerized by the sight of him. There was something happening inside her. She couldn't keep her eyes from hungrily drinking in every inch of the smooth, lithe muscles of his chest. Her eyes followed the line of dark, curling hair that stopped where the sheet was drawn across his flat belly. Her reverie was broken, a startled gasp coming from her lips, when he turned in his sleep and the sheet fell away. Her breath came unnaturally fast. His body was beautiful to look at. She shook herself. What am I doing, she rebuked herself. Now was not the time to admire the man's physique!

Then she spied what she was looking for. She almost groaned when she saw the white parchment peeking out from beneath his pillow. Slowly she approached the bed, her heart beating louder and louder. Her fingers shook as she reached for the paper. The second she touched the stiff parchment, Garrett muttered something unintelligible in his sleep and brought up his hand beside his head, inches from the deed. Catherine held her breath and waited, praying he wouldn't wake up. When his body relaxed again, she reached for the pillow. Her hand slipped beneath the linen case. Instantly it was trapped and held.

"Looking for something?"

Speechless with shock, Catherine pulled back, but with a slight twist on her wrist, he jerked her off balance and she fell headfirst across his chest.

"Let me go!" she screamed.

"Oh, no, my beloved." He laughed. "You can't enter a man's bedroom dressed like that and not expect him to give you what you are inviting."

"I'm not inviting anything." She struggled against him. Her wrapper fell open, leaving only the flimsy lace of her nightgown between her and his smoothly muscled flesh. "You know what I came for," she cried, but melting desire was hot in his eyes, and she was afraid her words were no deterrent to what he planned for her.

"You will have something to remember when you go," he promised softly and chuckled as she fought him, her arms flailing uselessly as she desperately twisted her body from side to side.

"The movements are much the same in passion, my love," he chided gently, pinning her arms to her sides and bringing her body under his. "But first things first."

Keeping her securely trapped, he quickly slipped off her wrapper. Her nightgown followed. She was now as naked as he.

"Lovely," he whispered huskily. Then he silenced her protests with his lips. His hands began a slow exploration of her nakedness, caressing her flesh with a fevered touch as arousing as his tantalizing lips. Her struggles grew weaker as a delicious languor spread throughout her body until she couldn't struggle at all.

Her flesh alternately burned and tingled wherever he touched. He sensed her capitulation and rained light butterfly kisses across her throat until his mouth captured one breast on its downward journey. She was lost. His tongue caressed one nipple to a throbbing peak and traveled to the other while small, kittenish moans escaped her quivering lips.

"Oh, please," she whispered as the pleasure built, but he had no intention of allowing her to regain control. He kept her exquisite torment at a fever pitch, her inexperienced body overwhelmed with new, wonderful sensations. He brought his hands to the undersides of her breasts, his tongue tantalizing the swollen, taut flesh while his hands molded the creamy mounds. She wanted to scream with pleasure. The clean, masculine smell of him was like an aphrodisiac. Her body reveled in the feel of his bare skin along hers. Her hands moved to his shoulders and down the corded muscles. Nothing could have prepared her for this. No one could have explained how tumultuous lovemaking could be, how the feel of his nakedness would fill her with need.

She gasped when his hand slid slowly down her side and across her thigh, seeking the place no man had ever touched. She flinched instinctively when his fingers pressed between her legs, but a flood of feeling welled up like a tidal wave as he stroked the delicate skin. A shuddering began deep inside her belly and rose up until her whole body trembled in his arms. He claimed her mouth in a deep, searching kiss as he eased himself between her thighs. His tongue thrust into the recesses of her soft mouth, exploring the honeyed interior and seeking a fervent answer, which she gave without restraint. Her back arched as his hands slid beneath her hips and he brought her to himself. His first burning thrust shook her, but the tight pain immediately spread into a fiery warmth as he began moving inside her. Her hips began to move in rhythm with his, and they became one.

Garrett groaned. The frenzied movements of the temptress beneath him were driving him further and further into the warm, moist center of her being. It was like sinking inside warm velvet. He had never had the sensation before, never felt that a woman was staking an irrevocable claim upon his manhood. They climaxed together, and he didn't know if he was the seducer or the seduced. He wanted to keep her with him forever, be caught in her tender possession eternally.

It was a vast relief to discover that she had been a virgin. He hoped that she understood that she belonged solely to him, for he could never let her go. At last, he understood how his father must have felt about his mother. If Catherine ever gave herself to another man, it would destroy him. This vulnerability to a woman was frightening to Garrett.

Catherine lay panting, immersed in conflicting emotions. She had just been masterfully possessed by a man she professed to despise, yet she felt nothing but incredible joy. His hard chest was crushed to her breast, and his demanding lips were still against her throat. Her fingers were entwined in the crisp, dark curls upon his head. She wanted to stay like this forever, his dark head cradled upon her soft bosom, his strong legs entwined with hers. She felt him shudder and wondered if his emotions were the same as hers. Her breathing slowly returned to normal. She felt the soft down mattress beneath her, the warm night air caressing her naked skin. She opened her eyes.

"You were just as I hoped you would be," Garrett said softly, not letting her move. His blue eyes were warm and soft as he stared down at her flushed face and tousled hair. "I think you got a bit more than you bargained for, didn't you, my love? Your eyes look like dew-drenched pansies."

Catherine's mouth dropped open, horrified that he could tease her after what had just happened. Nothing would ever be the same for her again. She had truly gotten much more than she bargained for. Nothing in her experience could have prepared her for this, for the power this man had over her body. A few well-placed caresses and she had gone wild with desire. The only thing that had kept her from loving him with all her being was her knowledge of why he was marrying her. She had disregarded her good breeding, the rules of society, in order to partake of the pleasure he offered. Shame darkened her eyes to violet pools. She remembered how she had moved with him, arched to meet every thrust of his manhood. She couldn't bear to look at him.

Garrett rolled gently to one side, placing an arm possessively across her waist while he nuzzled her neck. "Next time it will be even better. I'm going to thoroughly enjoy teaching you how to make love."

He stroked the golden tendrils of hair away from her temples. "I knew you were a passionate woman," he said. "Since I have to marry, at least I haven't saddled myself with a cold stick."

Catherine rolled away from him. "Let go of me." Her mission to steal back the deed was a failure, her pride was in shreds and she couldn't bear to listen to another word. She scrambled out of bed and quickly put on the nightgown he had discarded on the floor.

"What's wrong?" Garrett looked flummoxed as he raised up on one elbow.

"Everything is wrong," she snapped, scurrying about

to find her wrapper, panicking, needing to run away from him. He was a devil and he had everything under control, including her.

Garrett got up, dragging the sheets with him as he reached for her to drag her back to the warmth of the four-poster. "You can't be sorry for what happened. We will be married in two days. You belong to me, Catherine, now more than ever."

"No!" she shouted, pulling away and running to the passageway. "I don't belong to anyone. You . . . planned this. You . . . you seduced me and made me respond. I hate you!"

His voice, like a glacier, stopped her at the open passageway. "You wanted me. If you plan to run away, do it now. When you are my wife, you won't get the chance."

"I don't want to be your wife. I . . . I don't want to be your anything." She didn't cringe from the biting fury in his eyes. "I meant to marry someone . . . someone . . ."

"Who?" His question came like a bullet. His features had suddenly turned granite-hard.

Catherine stepped back, desperately frightened by the coldness in his face. All she had meant to say was that she had planned to marry someone who was gentle and kind, who wouldn't take what he wanted without asking or caring about her feelings, but she realized that he thought she was in love with another man. Perhaps it would be better if he did think that. Maybe then he wouldn't want her.

"Does it matter?" she asked. "You have ruined me for anyone else. Who would have me now? You have taken me, just as you took Bannerfield from my father, but you cannot take my heart."

"Very true," Garrett said, a muscle twitching in his jaw and a strange gleam in his eyes. "It's not your heart that holds my interest. You came here to steal the deed and you failed. You're a poor loser, Catherine, a spoiled child. I thought I held a woman in my arms, but I was wrong. I suggest you accept the inevitable and realize that you can't get out of your commitment to me without destroying your brother's future."

He dragged the sheets tighter around his slim hips. "I should tell this man you profess to love how easy it was to have you moaning with desire." He turned away from her and reached for the candle she had left on the nightstand. He threw it at her. "Better take this. I don't want you hurting yourself on the way back. I haven't gotten my money's worth out of you yet."

She fled through the dark passage and didn't see his clenched fists or the pained furrow of his brow.

Chapter 4

Catherine remained in her room the entire next day. Shame and humiliation vacillated with hot rage as she remembered over and over again the preceding night. How could I have let that happen? How could I have responded as I did? What kind of woman am I? She paced endless miles back and forth across the Persian carpet in her room.

She could think of no way to avoid her arranged marriage, but she vowed never to respond so warmly to Garrett again. Somehow she would find a way to make him curse the day he had first laid eyes on her. She would be so cold and unresponsive that he would not want her. The nagging thought that she had enjoyed his caresses was pushed aside as she planned her future.

When Colin rapped on her door asking to talk to her,

she sent him away. She would not leave her room until the wedding, would not look at Garrett and see his intimate knowledge of her in his cerulean eyes.

In the midst of an awful nightmare, Garrett twisted and turned on his bed. He had kicked the bedclothes into a tangled mess that twined around his perspiring body.

Garrett's knees were shaking as he backed away from his mother, edging toward the door of the cabin. He had to stay out of the reach of the knotted whip, had to get away before she . . . before she . . . "I didn't touch your perfume, Ma! Honest!" It was useless to deny her accusation; he could see that. She didn't believe him. Her blue eyes were glittering like frosted crystal. Her beautiful face was twisted into an ugly scowl of rage. She stood between him and the door, brandishing the whip, and he was too panic-stricken to move.

"So! You dare lie to me yet again. Stand still or it will go worse for you," Celeste warned, eyeing him as a pouncing cat eyes a harmless mouse. "I will deliver the punishment you deserve. Why can't you be like your brother? He never lies to me or displeases me like you do. You deliberately poured out my favorite scent, didn't you?" Her voice rose in a shrill cry as she brought the lash down inches from his right leg, the snap of leather dulled on the dirt floor of the cabin. "You thought the Mexican families would hide you from me, didn't you? Ana won't stop me from beating the wildness out of you. It is I who am *la patrona*, and these stupid people answer to me! She can care for you when I am finished with you."

Garrett tried to step out of the way of the lash as it came down again, but he stumbled over a low cot and fell to the floor. There would be no escape. He rolled frantically from side to side, evading the blows until a sharp pain cut into his hip and a cry of anguish was forced from between his gritted teeth.

"Stop, *Patrona!* It is enough!" Ana Morales begged from the doorway, her large brown eyes wet with tears. Garrett tried to crawl to her, but the leather strap stopped him, and he curled himself into a tight ball of misery. At last, the whipping was over. "Take care of the sniveling little liar, Ana. One word of this to his father and you and your family will have no place on Tierra. Do you understand?"

"*Sí, Patrona, sí,*" Ana murmured, looking down at the floor to avoid Garrett's eyes. Celeste marched to the door but looked back before leaving. "You know that your father's happiness depends on me, don't you, boy?"

Garrett nodded dully, trying to get up from the cot. "I won't touch your things anymore." He, like Ana, had learned how to answer Celeste.

"I'm sure you won't." Celeste laughed cruelly. He met her eyes, unaware that his clear-eyed stare sent shivers up his mother's spine. "You are too much like him," Celeste said softly, and it sounded like some sort of strange apology. Her figure seemed to fade before his eyes, wavering like disturbed water in a clear pool. Eventually she disappeared altogether, and all that was left was the pain. He groaned and sat up on the cot, sweat dripping from every pore in his body.

A shaft of sunlight from a mullioned window fell across the whitened scar on his hip and highlighted the blue satin counterpane that fell away from his thigh. He was no longer ten years old but a grown man, and Celeste Browning was dead. It had only been a dream. His mouth twisted at the sight of the small scar on his hip, a visual reminder that his nightmare had once been a reality. He shook his head to clear away the last vestiges of the painful memory and swung his legs off the bed. He was still at Bannerfield Hall in England and about to marry a girl who spoke in the same accented tones as his mother.

Would Catherine turn out to be as bitter toward him as Celeste had been toward his father? He admitted to himself that he had never been as drawn to a woman as he was to Catherine, but would she use her power against him? Would she turn on him, wield her lovely body like a weapon to destroy him? "If I'm not careful, she'll have me . . . No! Not like Pa! Never like Pa!" He stood up fast, pulling on his clothes swiftly.

His father's will had taken the decision out of his hands. He would marry her, but she would never discover how strong his feelings for her had become. He couldn't allow himself to trust her and must never show her how vulnerable he was where she was concerned. He was afraid to contemplate the possibilities if Catherine sensed his weakness. What a powerful weapon she would have at her disposal!

It was a relief when his dark thoughts were interrupted by a knock on the door and Colin's voice calling his name.

"Garrett? Are you going to sulk in your room all day like Kay? Is this the way a bride and groom act before their wedding? Doesn't seem too happy to me. I'm glad I'm not getting married."

Garrett answered Colin's disgruntled summons, breaking into a wide smile when he opened the door and looked down on the shining head, the face so much like Catherine's. He tousled the blond curls and said, "Sorry, Colin. I have a few things on my mind. You say your sister is still in her room?"

"Kay says she's not coming out all day. She is sure mad about something, because she hates to waste time in her room. Is she angry with you, Garrett?"

"I'm afraid so. You might say we've had a minor disagreement." He wished that were all it was. "That's enough about that. I have some business to handle. Can a wire be sent to London from here?"

"Sure. You can send a footman to the village."

"Good." He gave Colin an affectionate cuff as they went to the morning room.

Shortly after breakfast, a footman was dispatched to the village, and Garrett was waiting in the library for the arrival of the estate overseer, John Willcott. Garrett convinced him with some difficulty to present the estate books, telling Willcott that he was engaged to Catherine and that he wanted to help out before he and his bride left for America.

It was apparent that the earl had spent little time handling his affairs, and Willcott was relieved to have someone take an interest in the estate. Garrett was inwardly thankful that Willcott was an honest, upstanding man, for if it had not been for him, the estate would be in an even sorrier condition than it was. The two men spent the better part of the morning going over the books and discussing the planting, the rents and possible improvements. After satisfying himself that everything was in order and that Bannerfield was safe in Willcott's capable hands, Garrett excused the overseer and asked Colin to give him a tour of the estate.

The remainder of the day was spent visiting the tenant farms and talking with the farmers. Garrett offered a few suggestions as he talked with the men. He listened with growing interest when Henry Dalton showed him a herd of fat English shorthorns. Dalton was the tenant of the largest of Bannerfield's farms. His father and grandfather both had worked on the estate. Garrett plied the man with questions about the shorthorns' stamina, disease resistance and breeding. The short-legged, boxlike creatures represented a greater and higher quality yield of beef than did his Texas longhorns, but the possibility of their thriving in the harsh Texas climate was doubtful. Garrett pondered the possibilities of cross-breeding, storing the idea away for the future.

Upon their return to the hall, a footman handed Garrett the return wire from Allen Winslow. Garrett folded the thin paper in his hand and placed it in his pocket. He walked up the stairs lost in thought.

The next morning Garrett impatiently awaited the arrival of his cousin. He wanted a private confrontation with the earl and had convinced Colin to persuade Catherine away from the hall. He watched them leave, hoping they would enjoy the short time they had left together.

It was late morning when Allen finally arrived with a solicitor in tow. Garrett met privately with them. After some persuasion, Allen agreed to accept the continuing income Garrett offered in exchange for his services. "You know, Cousin, I would do this for you without any remuneration. I—"

"I know that; that's why I chose you." Garrett cut off any arguments. "I will feel better about the arrangement if you receive some compensation for your efforts. You will be accepting the money as a favor to me." He knew Allen was in financial straits but would not insult him by revealing his knowledge.

After the solicitor left the room to draw up the necessary papers, Allen asked, "How has Lady Catherine dealt with your marriage proposal? She is actually willing to marry you tomorrow?" He caught the slight frown on Garrett's face. "I had hoped you would have come to your senses by now. You are marrying for all the wrong reasons." Garrett held up his hand, not liking the turn in the conversation. Allen continued, regardless. "What will people say when they hear how quickly this marriage took place? Lady Catherine needs time, and it would not harm you, either."

"I will agree that the ceremony is taking place abruptly and that the lady probably deserves more time. Unfortunately, I don't have more time. However, the more I get to know her, the better my reasons become for marrying her." He walked to the table and picked up a bottle of brandy to pour himself a drink. "It's academic now, anyway," he said under his breath.

Allen heard the low words. Standing up and striding to Garrett, he pulled him around. "You don't mean what I think you mean? Surely you have not taken advantage of her?"

Garrett looked at the hand on his shoulder, and Allen quickly removed it. "I needed every advantage I could get," he said quietly, smiling. "Believe me, I have not done anything the lady did not want. We can continue discussing my bride another time. Here comes Haversham."

He ignored Allen's astonishment and ushered the solicitor inside the room. "Gentlemen, I believe it is time to confront Brockmere. Hopefully the man will be sober enough to understand." Acknowledging their nods of assent, Garrett led the two men out of the library. They located the earl in his study, downing a large snifter of brandy. Hiding his repugnance, Garrett politely introduced his cousin and the solicitor, expecting and getting bleary-eyed suspicion.

"You are not asking for more from our deal now, are you?" the earl inquired sharply, ignoring the other two men.

"The lady is not all I was led to expect, Brockmere. Beauty is one thing, but I can't say I am pleased with much else. You cannot deny that her manner leaves much to be desired." Garrett frowned for Allen's silence as he began his attack. He did not see the slight figure lurking outside the study window and listening to every word. He received Allen's silent look of comprehension and continued. "I have purchased a woman who behaves like a child and does all she can to infuriate me. I'm demanding more, Brockmere, and if you want to rid yourself of your hellion of a daughter, you will go along with me on this. No one else would have her, not when she is so violent. Not a lady at all." Garrett pulled down his collar to reveal a reddened scratch on his neck.

The earl was horrified. "What do you have in mind, Browning?" he asked, seeing his plans for a future without Catherine and her hoydenish behavior fading fast. The small figure at the window turned and ran away, too humiliated to listen any longer.

"Simple," Garrett said easily, accurately judging the earl's willingness to do almost anything to rid himself of Catherine. "I want to ensure the prosperity of Bannerfield. If the vixen isn't barren as well as everything else, I could very well be the father of one of the estate's heirs. In the meantime, I would like to see Colin prepared for his future role here. You have been remiss with both your children, Brockmere. I want your signature on a document Haversham has prepared. You sign it, and I'll take your daughter off your hands."

"What kind of document?"

"Entailment, Brockmere." Garrett kept his voice steady. "It will prevent you from losing Bannerfield to the next gambler who can outwit you in cards."

"Now see here—" the earl began.

"I'm taking all possibilities into account. If Colin never marries, my children will be next in line for this place. I don't want to take the risk that Colin will fritter his wealth away and leave nothing to a son of mine. He could end up like you, Brockmere. Look at yourself, man; you almost lost everything you own to me." Garrett attacked ruthlessly, playing on the earl's adherence to convention, pressing his advantage in any direction he thought might succeed.

"And if I do not agree to this extortion?" Lord Maxfield asked belligerently.

"Then I'm taking Bannerfield. In fact, I might be better off. Think about it, Brockmere. I could have both Catherine and Bannerfield if I had more time. If not for Colin, I'd do just that. I like your son, Brockmere. I plan to make sure he gets what he deserves."

They locked eyes, steely resolve in Garrett's, frustration and anger in the earl's. "Damn you, Browning! Give me the document and let me read it." The earl reached for the parchment with hands that shook. "Winslow," he turned an accusing eye at Allen, "why would you want to saddle yourself with a twelve-year-old boy and an estate up to its ears in debt? Or does Browning have something to hold over your head, like he is holding Catherine over mine?"

Allen explained the arrangement. He would be Colin's financial counselor and guide, make sure Bannerfield was run efficiently through Willcott and make the best investments possible, to be held in trust for Colin until he reached his majority. The earl would retain a healthy income, more than enough for his needs if he did not gamble it away, and Colin would receive the best education Allen could arrange.

"You realize you are assisting Browning in blackmailing me, Winslow?" the earl accused before signing the document. For generations, the Maxfields had existed without outside intervention. It galled him to think that a commoner, an American upstart, was determining Bannerfield's future. "I wish to God I had never met you, Browning. I hope my daughter is a burden on you for all the years to come." He stood up. "I need a drink," he muttered harshly as he left.

"I believe you have just been cursed, Garrett." Allen shook his head and gathered up the papers, handing them to Haversham.

Garrett laughed dryly. "Worse things have been wished on me." A picture of Catherine dressed in her lacy white nightgown floated before him.

"I'm sure," Allen said. "But Catherine Maxfield may surprise you. I realize women fall all over themselves to get your attention, but Catherine is different. You cannot treat her callously; she will not let you get away with it."

"What do you know about it?" Garrett shrugged, but a flame of jealousy ignited inside him at the thought that Allen knew his future bride better than he did. If his dealings with Brockmere had not occurred and he had met her on his own, he would probably have pursued her differently. Thoughts of her sweet body beneath his were occurring with increasing frequency. She already occupied more of his thoughts than he cared to admit.

After dispatching Haversham, Allen returned to the study to find Garrett still seated, his long legs stretched out before him and a half-empty brandy glass beside him on the table. Allen took a seat in the opposite chair. "When will I see Lady Catherine?" he asked. "It has been months since I last had the pleasure. I don't recall the occasion, but I remember that she was having trouble fending off the advances of David Longley. He has been after her for two years."

Instantly Allen had Garrett's complete attention. Allen barely hid the smile before Garrett began questioning him about Longley. He was beginning to believe that his cousin had finally met his match. He returned Garrett's questions with vague answers, for he really had no idea how far Lady Catherine's association with Longley had progressed. Garrett had a distinctly dissatisfied look on his face.

"You have certainly become deeply involved with the Maxfields in a very short time. Are you happy with the results?" asked Allen.

"I'm beginning to wonder." Garrett smiled in self-derision. He leaned back in the comfortable leather chair. "I'm glad my session with the earl is over. To tell you the truth, Allen, I had no idea I would get this involved. My plan was to ride out here, marry the girl and be done with it. Then I met Colin. He's so much like my youngest brother, Rob, that I discovered I couldn't leave him to deal with Brockmere. It's the damndest thing—I feel like I've taken on the whole family.

"You'll like Colin. He's both intelligent and spirited. He'll miss Catherine like the devil, but he's more concerned with her happiness than his own. He was afraid she would end up an old maid. That's a laugh, isn't it? The first night I saw her, she had half the men in London hovering around her."

"True," Allen agreed, remembering how Garrett had reacted to his first sight of the gentlemen clustered around Catherine at the Strathmore ball. "Her intelligence scares a lot of men, however. If she were a man, you would not have gotten one step inside this door."

"If Catherine were a man, I wouldn't be here," Garrett quipped. "I've already discovered she's more of a woman than I bargained for." He straightened when he heard footsteps approaching, recognizing the light step.

"Sir Allen Winslow, isn't it?" Catherine swept into the room in a cloud of frothy gold silk. Allen's eyes widened with appreciation as the vision approached him on satin-slippered feet and offered her tiny hand for his kiss. He thought he had accurately remembered how striking she was, but he was not prepared for this. He had forgotten the incredible violet color of her eyes and the provocative tilt to her smile.

"Lady Catherine, you are more beautiful each time I see you," Allen complimented, ignoring his cousin's raised eyebrows and slight frown. Catherine was ignoring Garrett altogether.

"I had no idea you were related to that . . . to Mr. Browning." She made Garrett's name sound unwelcome to her lips. "What brings you to Bannerfield, Sir Allen? Surely news of my . . . wedding has not reached London yet? I was hoping to leave before any of my friends knew my fate." She made it sound as if she were the victim of some heinous crime.

"Ah . . ." Allen hesitated. "I wish you every happiness, Lady Catherine."

"Happiness is hardly considered when the bride is no more than chattel sold to the groom, Sir Allen." She made her statement sweetly, though her eyes flashed and her words were a direct jibe at Garrett. No matter what Garrett thought, she did not look ready to walk meekly down the aisle. Allen felt extremely uncomfortable as he eyed the man and the woman challenging each other.

"That will be enough, Kate," Garrett said softly. Catherine returned her attention to Allen, who was not at all sure he wanted it.

"Of course," she said coldly. "I believe the call to dinner has been sounded. Would you escort me, Sir Allen?"

Cheerfully Allen took Catherine's arm and braved the daggers in his back as he walked with her to the dining room. Garrett followed closely behind, a deep furrow creasing his brow as Catherine deliberately began flirting with Allen. That he was going to be completely ignored was obvious, but he hoped she had the good sense not to push it too far. He had had enough experience with coquettish females to last him a lifetime, and he wouldn't allow his wife to put him through that kind of torment.

Colin came into the room from the hall entrance, walking tipsily as he imitated his father's gait. "Father won't be joining us," he lisped drunkenly.

"That will be enough, Colin," Catherine snapped. "We have a guest." She excused her brother to Allen. "I'd like you to meet the last of the Maxfields, Sir Allen."

As soon as Colin discovered Allen's relationship to Garrett, he accepted him. Catherine was extremely annoyed that this was enough to make Colin befriend a total stranger, and she glared at her fiancé. He smiled back at her and raised his eyebrows as if he had no idea what she was thinking.

Garrett was very glad to see that Allen and Colin were getting along well. His cousin made no attempt to talk down to the boy, and Garrett was satisfied he had made the right choice. He listened with interest to their conversation and then, reassured, he concentrated on his meal and on his woman.

"Did you enjoy your day with Colin?"

"My brother is quite smitten with you, Mr. Browning. You might have been along, for we discussed little else." She hoped her sarcasm could get through the barrier of confidence that surrounded him.

"How bad for you, Kate," he said, amused. "Odd that you still refer to me as Mr. Browning after all we mean to one another."

"I believe I've made it clear what you mean to me," Catherine returned, looking furtively at Allen to make sure their conversation wasn't being overheard. Allen and Colin were talking horses and were completely engrossed, so she continued. "You cannot command my speech as you try to command everything else."

"Try, Kate? I did much more than try. It is you who are trying to deny what is between us, and you're having little luck. Your feelings are apparent to everyone. I warn you, little one, don't bring my wrath down on your head if you can avoid it." He resumed eating, satisfied that she would not dare press him any further. He was wrong—underestimating her defiance yet again.

She lifted her chin and spoke to Allen, her features composed. "You must stay for the wedding, Sir Allen. What fun you will have telling the people in London of my father's folly. I'm sure they will think twice before playing cards with an American. The story should provide fuel for the gossips for months."

Allen was startled, almost spilling his wine as he watched the sparks emitting from two sets of eyes, a battle of wills that raised the hairs on the back of his neck. He didn't know what to say.

Colin, however, seemed used to the atmosphere of tension. He smiled happily at his sister and future brother-in-law and shook his blond head. "She's angry at Garrett 'cause he never lets her have her way."

"Don't tease your sister, Colin," Garrett said, surprising everyone. "You have to forgive us, Allen. Our family squabbles shouldn't concern you. As I told you earlier, Catherine isn't going to do anything she doesn't want to do. She doesn't like to admit it, but I have proof that she thinks I'm the right man for her. Haven't I, darling?"

Catherine's face paled, his challenge more than she could meet without bringing about her total humiliation. Garrett meant to tell Allen that he had bedded her and she had enjoyed it, if she disagreed with him. She knew it, could see the smoldering fire in his blue eyes, a fire that would burn her if she didn't put it out. She said softly, "If you say so."

"Oh, I do." He laughed.

Allen watched them. Colin looked happy with the whole world; Catherine was seething; and Garrett looked satisfied. Allen could feel the attraction between Catherine and Garrett as if it were tangible. Although the circumstances were highly unusual, he found himself thinking that these two might be right for each other. He shuddered at the thought of the battles that would rage between them and looked heavenward, offering a silent prayer of thanks that he wouldn't be around during the fiery interludes he foresaw in their future.

After dinner and for the remainder of the evening, Catherine did everything in her power to avoid conversation with Garrett. He was expert at fielding her sarcasm and dishing it back in ways that were damaging. She played the piano for Allen and sang a few songs in a low voice that sent shivers down his spine. She hoped Garrett noticed that she was showing Allen the accomplishments of refinement expected of a lady.

Colin and Garrett were enjoying a boisterous game of chess. The harder Catherine tried to ignore them, the louder their laughter became. Allen was grateful when the hour grew late enough for him to gracefully retire. "I will see you both in the morning." He made his good nights, and Catherine would have followed but for Garrett's clasping of her arm.

"I suppose you two want to kiss or something?" Colin shook his head in disgust. "I'll see you tomorrow." He shuffled out quickly, hoping he would never lower himself to like some girl.

"Good night, Colin," Garrett called and waited until he heard the boy's footsteps on the stairs. Then he turned Catherine into his arms, ignoring her attempts to free herself. He kissed her thoroughly, invading her mouth until he felt her response. "Sweet dreams, my lovely," he whispered at her ear as he released her. Without speaking, she ran up the stairs to her room.

Safely in her bedchamber, Catherine donned a mauve silk nightgown and matching satin wrapper. She couldn't sleep. Tomorrow she would be married to a man who by his own admission considered her an unladylike hellion. He was a devilishly handsome man, totally without scruples and as much a mystery to her as he had been the night she first met him. If he disliked her so much, why did he want to marry her? She wondered what else he had bargained for with her father. If she hadn't been so upset by his scathing estimation of her, she would have listened longer and discovered how great his compensation was for marrying her.

"There you are, Catherine." Lord Maxfield came in unannounced, his red-rimmed eyes barely focusing as he sank down in a brocade chair. "Glad to see you appear no more happy than I. Damned, cursed American, giving orders, arranging things that are none of his business. Had the gall to bring in a solicitor from London. Hope you are satisfied. If you had offered yourself willingly, none of this would have happened. Why couldn't you act like a mature woman for once?"

Catherine tried not to react as he ranted. He was drunk, and as usual when he was the worse for liquor, he blamed others for his own faults. His belief that she should have offered herself to Garrett, when it was his own foolishness and weakness that had gotten them into this affair, rankled. She hid her contempt and asked him what the solicitor had wanted.

"Entailment! That's what the scoundrel arranged! Bannerfield is hardly mine now. That devil's cousin will be keeping his hand on the purse strings until Colin reaches his majority. If you ask me, Browning will dupe the boy out of his inheritance just as he cheated me out of my home and daughter. If I could have married you off to a wealthy title, all my problems would have been solved. But what gentleman would have you? Even that animal had doubts. This is all on your head, you wayward chit!" He collapsed back in his chair, muttering curses under his fetid breath.

Catherine was amazed. So he hadn't tried to finagle more from her father at all. Colin would be safe! Tears gathered in her eyes as she acknowledged Garrett's wisdom. He might not care for her any more than for one of his horses, but he had had the decency to provide for Colin. Why had he done it? She didn't understand him. Garrett held her interest like no other man, but he was the last man she wanted to marry. Thinking about him, she almost forgot her besotted father until she heard him snort.

"I think it would be best if you left, Father." She called for his valet. If nothing good came out of this marriage, at least she would no longer have to worry about her little brother. It was strange, but where Colin was concerned, she trusted Garrett completely.

She continued her restless pacing after her father left her room, aided by his valet. What was America like? What was waiting for her there? How could she bear to leave England and never see Bannerfield again? Great tears began rolling down her cheeks when she thought about having to leave Colin. She walked to the open mullioned windows of her room and looked out. She surveyed the smooth green lawns of Bannerfield through a mist of tears. The stars were shining and the moon was a gigantic gold crescent overlooking the rose garden. This sight would be denied her after tomorrow. Turning away, she flung herself down on her bed, fear and homesickness gnawing at her insides.

She did not hear the panel of her wall slide open or see Garrett approach the bed and look down at her for several seconds. Not until he sat down on the bed and drew her unresistingly into his arms did she realize anyone else was in the room. She could do nothing but continue to sob.

"Who would have thought my little lioness could cry like an infant?" he whispered in a husky voice, gently holding her head against his shoulder.

She valiantly tried to stop crying, gulping the tears down her throat until it ached. "Go away," came out in a muffled plea against his shirt.

"Not yet. I understand the pain you feel. If I had a choice, it would not be like this for you. Believe me, I didn't intend to hurt you." The soft words were most odd coming from one who was usually hatefully mocking. It took several minutes, but finally Catherine was able to pull away and look at him. She gazed into his face, searching his deep blue eyes for an answer, pleading in mute misery for him to let her go.

"I want to thank you," Catherine murmured, unable to look away, holding his gaze with eyes as wet and soft as lilacs after a spring rain. His brow lifted and he tilted his head, unsure of what she was thanking him for.

"I know what you did for my brother. I . . . I still don't want to marry you, but I . . . I'm grateful for Colin's safety." Seeing the soft, almost tender look on his face, she forgot her intentions to stay cool and pleaded, "Can't you leave me alone? Won't you marry someone who really wants you, who loves you? Can't you let me do the same?"

"No, I can't." He fought against the soft entreaty, feeling an overwhelming remorse that this proud creature would beg him for her release, hating the fact that her fiery nature was no help to her now. Her tears were genuine and her words were from the heart, but he couldn't let her go. He could handle her wild tantrums and flaming passion, her mischief and icy taunts, but her tears were beyond him. He almost found himself telling her he would wait to marry her until she fell in love with him, but he stopped himself just in time. That was impossible. He was responsible for fifty people on Tierra.

"Catherine, I have as little choice in this as you. I have to get back to Texas, and I must bring back an English wife. My father willed it, and I have no say in the matter."

"I see," she murmured softly, and he felt an overwhelming relief. He brought her chin up, touching her lips lightly. Then, covering her face with feather-light kisses, he whispered, "Let me love you again . . . tonight could result in my heir."

Catherine stiffened in his arms. "Your heir?"

His mouth continued a tantalizing trail of light kisses down her throat as he said, "Could be. After all, you are a healthy young woman." He buried his face between her breasts. "I told you we Americans appreciate good bloodlines, and yours are magnificent." He was puzzled when she pushed him away.

"Good bloodlines! You make me sound like some kind of brood mare you've purchased!"

"I just told you that I had to marry an English aristocrat. You give me a great deal of pleasure, and I plan to enjoy my part in improving the Browning strain."

He thought her nothing but a fancy breeder, an object of pleasure. She wanted to be more, wanted to mean everything to him, but now she knew all he wanted was to ensure the continuation of the Browning name. "Get away from me!" she shrieked. "You won't improve your bloodlines with me. You will have to take your pleasures elsewhere. I won't be your brood mare!"

"Very well," he said coldly. "But you will marry me, tomorrow. After that, you'll be anything I want you to be. I won't allow you to deny me or yourself ever again. Sleep while you can, my dear." The endearment was carved out of ice. With a piercing look of his hard blue eyes, he left the room.

Chapter 5

Catherine stood in the chapel alcove, preparing to take the short walk down the aisle. Lord Maxfield's perspiring hand under her elbow was not reassuring and did not stop the quaking in her limbs. She was stunning in the simple gown her mother had worn. The ivory satin, trimmed with orange blossoms, fell from the bodice in soft folds. The enveloping veil of Honiton lace had been worn by Maxfield brides for generations.

The earl escorted her down the aisle to the altar, where Garrett stood waiting. She didn't look at him, didn't see how the charcoal-gray striped cutaway coat emphasized his broad shoulders or how the straight black trousers hugged his powerful thighs. A starched white collar stood up against his bronzed skin, and his eyes sparkled as he watched her approach.

The instant he claimed her hand with his strong fingers, she knew there would be no escape. The beautiful words of the ceremony were barely heard as she murmured the required responses. Garrett's vows were made in a clear, deep voice.

* * *

At the wedding breakfast, Lord Maxfield opened a chilled bottle of champagne and offered a brief toast. "Happiness," he said dutifully.

Catherine knew her goblet was full, but her hand was shaking so badly she could not raise it to her lips. Her husband's hand covered hers, and he raised the glass first to her lips, then to his. "Mrs. Browning." He placed a kiss on her cold hand.

Colin and Allen applauded, bestowing their best wishes on them. "You are a lucky man, Cousin." Allen smiled widely, hoping Catherine's pale face was more from nerves than unhappiness.

"Kay is the lucky one," Colin declared, sipping his first glass of champagne and grimacing at the taste. "I thought she would marry that dandy Longley. What a stuffy brother-in-law he would make."

Garrett had looked amused, but Catherine saw the slight stiffening of his shoulders when her brother mentioned her past suitor. At least her strong-willed, arrogant husband might still think that she was involved with another man.

"I hate to hurry this along, but Catherine and I will have to get started. Allen, we plan to be at your mother's house by midday tomorrow. Please tell Grandmother that she will see us then."

Garrett seemed reluctant to discuss his relatives further. He stood up and took Catherine's hand. "Are you finished packing?" he asked, showing his impatience to depart.

"I am." Catherine glared at him, finally released from the shock that had held her in its grip all morning. A little imp of mischief danced behind her eyes. He would not find traveling with her easy. She had packed almost every article of clothing she owned.

Lord Maxfield cleared his throat and told Garrett that the servants had loaded Catherine's luggage into the carriage. He looked at her disapprovingly, but she lifted her chin and stared back at him, unashamed. She brushed past her father to go up to her room and change into her traveling clothes.

Her movements were slow as she pulled her mother's wedding gown from her body and let it drop to the floor. Jenny picked up the gown and laid it away while Catherine put on a traveling suit of dark gray, the color matching her mood. She faced herself in the cheval glass, slowly drawing her gloves over her hands. Mrs. Garrett Browning; that was her name. The delicate emerald ring she wore on her left hand declared it to the world. She blinked back her tears and straightened her shoulders. It was time to make her farewells to Colin, and it was going to be the most difficult thing she had ever done. She found him waiting outside her room. Wordlessly she pulled him against her, hugging him tightly.

"Don't get all mushy, Kay," he said, his voice quivering.

"Of course not. When were we ever mushy?" She smiled brightly, her throat aching. "I shall miss you, little brother. You must trust Allen Winslow. Learn everything he can teach you. Will you promise?"

"Sure. I like Allen. Garrett says I can come see you next year, if my grades improve. I can hardly wait. Don't worry about me. I'll be stuck in the books while you are having all the fun."

Catherine smiled. "Some of us are born lucky." They walked arm in arm down the stairs, where Allen, Garrett and their father were waiting. They all walked outside, where the staff were assembled. Catherine went to each and bid them good-bye.

"Let's go," Garrett said quietly, watching her efforts

to remain in control, her pain ricocheting back to him. Minutes later, they were traveling out of the gates, the cold metal closing behind them. He grasped her gloved hand as she sat stiffly beside him, fighting her tears.

"Don't touch me!" she snapped, jerking her hand away and moving as far from him as possible.

"Are you going to jump away from me forever?" he asked, leaning back against the velvet seat and taking inventory of her.

"Just because we are married does not mean I will let you touch me."

"You have a strange idea about marriage. It gives me the right to touch you whenever I wish." The smoldering blue of his eyes was replaced by a frigid glare.

Fury snapped in her eyes. "I'll kill you first!"

He laughed, folding his hands over his chest and bringing his long legs up to the opposite seat. "I'll consider the danger while I take a nap. We will be at the inn by dusk. You won't have to kill me until then." He brought his arms behind his head to make a pillow.

Minutes later, his even breathing told her he was asleep, and for the first time all day, Catherine relaxed. She felt totally exhausted. She looked at Garrett. His luxuriously long eyelashes swept down upon his cheeks, making him look years younger. The lines of his mouth had softened. His chin bobbed on his chest while he unconsciously searched for a more comfortable position.

She could look at him without having to answer the challenge that was constantly in his blue eyes. She noticed the way his crisp black hair curled slightly over his ears, one unruly wave falling over his forehead. His immaculate clothing fit his tall body like a glove. She watched the steady rise and fall of his chest, then allowed her gaze to slip lower, down the flat belly to the bulge his tight trousers could not hide. Completely startled, her eyes flew quickly to his face, but he was still asleep. A slight smile played over his face, and a hot blush rose to her cheeks. She stifled the urge to shriek at him, though, and resigned herself to silence, resting her head against the carriage frame, letting the swaying motion lull her to sleep.

She awakened when she felt the carriage slowing and heard the sound of the hostlers shouting orders as they entered the cobblestone courtyard of the inn. As soon as they came to a halt, Garrett opened the carriage and jumped down. He had evidently been awake for some time, for there was no hint of drowsiness in his movements. Catherine's stiffened limbs, however, seemed cemented to the seat. She blinked and turned her head away from the sudden glare of a lantern.

"Do you intend to stay curled up in your corner all night, or do you wish to eat some dinner and then sleep in a soft bed?" He watched her slow movements as she disentangled her lethargic limbs.

"Where are we?"

"The Red Briar Inn, my sweet. We'll spend our wedding night here. Come—or do you want to enter this place tossed over my shoulder?"

She ignored his proffered hand and stepped down from the coach. The landlord came to welcome them as they entered the half-timbered old building. They were led through the crowded public room by a serving girl whose white muslin blouse hung loosely off bare shoulders, showing off an ample bosom. After they were seated in a private dining room, the girl did her best to catch Garrett's eye as she busied herself around the table serving the meal. It was obvious that she was pleased to serve someone as young and good-looking as Garrett, and furthermore, he was enjoying her attention. He openly ogled the immense breasts thrust before him as the wench served the first course.

"Anything else, your lordship?" the girl queried.

Catherine fumed in her chair. "That will be quite enough!"

The girl bobbed to Garrett, oblivious of Catherine. "Need anything else, dearie, you just call out."

Garrett grinned after the retreating figure. "There goes an honest girl. She knows what she wants and goes out to get it."

Catherine remained silent. Perhaps he would prefer to spend his wedding night in the arms of the serving wench. She was filled with cold dread, knowing that when the meal was over, she was expected to walk up the stairs to their rooms and spend the night in her husband's arms. She reached for her glass of wine, drained it in one swallow and asked for more.

"Preparing for the ordeal that lies ahead?" He poured her another glass. Setting the bottle down, he leaned back in his chair and watched her.

"I don't know what you're talking about." She drank the second glass of wine as quickly as the first. Entirely too aware of him, she picked slowly at the food on her plate, putting down her glass to be filled again. Anything to delay the end of the meal.

Garrett finished his supper and sat back, watching her intently. Her fingers started to shake. Finally her fork fell to her plate with a clatter, and she spoke in a voice heavy with emotion. "I'll fight you, Garrett. I'll scream the house down."

"Catherine," his smile was indulgent, "do you think that I'll leave you alone now that you are legally mine?"

"You don't own me," she declared, the wine giving her a false bravado.

"Listen to me, Kate. You can either come up to our rooms willingly, or I will throw you over my shoulder and carry you. I've had enough of your protests, damnit! You won't deny me the pleasure of making love to you on our wedding night. You are my wife, and I'll have you in my bed whenever I choose." His speech was given in a voice that stung. His eyes dared her to try anything. She forced herself to look at him, her defiant eyes dark purple in her pale face. He pushed back his chair and stood up. When her shaking limbs refused to move, he came to her aid, slid one arm around her waist and practically lifted her out of her chair.

He guided her unwilling body, prepared for any rebellion. She was held so close to him that she felt the heat of his body through his coat. Her eyes darted across the dining room, searching for the landlord, preparing to scream. She nearly tripped when Garrett spoke softly against her ear. "I wouldn't, Kate. He will turn a deaf ear. Many brides prove unwilling their first night in their husband's bed."

"Why don't you go to someone who wants you? That girl made her invitation plain enough."

He laughed and swept her along. "I'm sure you will be as willing as she quite soon, kitten." They reached the landing. Tired of her resistance, he bent down and picked her up, climbed the few remaining steps and kicked open the door to their room. He set her down inside and shut the door behind him, turning the key in the lock.

The room was clean and pleasantly warm. A fire blazed merrily at one end; a huge four-poster stood at the other. A washstand stood before a large oval mirror that cast reflections of flames against the whitewashed walls.

Catherine kept her back to Garrett and stood stiffly. Her muscles jerked spasmodically when she heard the creak of the ropes of the bed and the first heavy boot drop. The second thudded loudly a few moments later.

She heard the soft rustle of material as he discarded his clothes, but still she stood there, her cheeks flaming and her knees shaking. She flinched when he spoke. "Come to bed, Catherine." When she didn't move, he ordered again, more insistently. "Get out of those clothes and come to bed, or I'll undress you myself."

Keeping her back to him, she started to unbutton her jacket. "Where is my trunk?"

"You won't need anything tonight. I'll fetch it in the morning."

She spun around. "I will not sleep completely un-clothed! It's indecent!"

"Catherine, come to bed," he said quietly.

Biting her lip, she again started to disrobe. When she was entirely naked, she turned to face him. Pride holding up her head, though her quaking limbs threat-ened to collapse, she walked as calmly as she could to the big bed. Only sheer will kept her from diving under the eiderdown coverlet. "You are beautiful; let me look at you." She closed her eyes in embarrassment as she felt his hand on her wrist. "Come here," he murmured, his voice husky with arousal.

She lay down, praying he would not stop her attempt to cover herself. A deep, burning blush covered her entire body. She drew the sheet and coverlet up to her neck and lay rigid. Squeezing her eyes tightly shut, she waited, her arms clenched to her sides. She felt him roll toward her and she held her breath. The covers slid down her breasts, her stomach, and came to rest against her shins.

An eternity seemed to pass, and still he did nothing. Her exposed body began to shiver and burn at the same time. Finally, her breath coming much too fast, she opened her eyes—only to find herself staring straight into his. He hadn't been surveying her nakedness but was waiting for her to overcome her shyness. His head was resting on one arm, his eyes filled with amusement. Her lips parted in surprise and indignation; his descended at once. He made no attempt to touch her, as if her soft lips were enough territory to explore, tantalizing her mouth with his questing tongue and waiting for her reponse. She found she wanted to kiss him, wanted to feel his lips and mouth. Her tense spine relaxed as she gave in to his demanding mouth.

When he attempted to move away, her lips moved beneath his, bidding him stay. He continued to draw her sweetness into himself until unconsciously her arms reached around his neck. She relaxed further when his lips moved to explore her ears and neck. By the time he brought his hand to one breast, she had long since wanted his touch.

He brought the nipple of her breast to taut erectness, and she was filled with a delicious longing for more. She pulled him closer, feeling the sinewy muscles of his back in wonder. The soft mat of hair on his chest brushed tantalizingly against her aroused breasts. Totally under his power, her body responded to his touch—to his lips that trailed liquid fire over her throat and breasts. She opened to him as a flower hungry for rain.

It was only by chance that she opened her eyes, dark violet with passion, to see the triumphant expression on his face as his blue gaze devoured the places she was willingly allowing him to touch. She stiffened in his arms, twisting to free herself from his embrace, his nearness suddenly appalling. She had almost given herself to him again! His expert hands had drawn such a strong sexual response from her that she could not deny him. She tried to escape from beneath him, squirming and tossing her head from side to side to escape his mouth. She heard the low, throaty chuckle deep in his chest.

"It's a little late, kitten." His knee parted her thighs. He entered her slowly, not satisfied until he felt her growing response. Unable to deny the spasms of pleasure that shot through her, she moved against him. She couldn't stop the contractions of her loins when he moved within her or control the moans of delight that were forced from her lips. They climaxed together, a perfect joining of man and woman.

She opened her eyes. He lay heavily across her, his head nestled against her neck, his lips warm against the skin of her throat. One hand was beneath her, cupping a rounded buttock, the other entwined in her hair. She felt his breathing calm as hers had when rational thought replaced floating languor. He raised his head and looked into her face, saw the love-softened lips, the flush of sexual excitement like roses on her cheeks, her eyes mirroring his reflection. He smiled at her curiously, as if surprised at the depth of emotion in their joining. He had experience, but to her, this world was new, this rapture totally alien.

She squirmed beneath him, unwilling to endure another moment of their intimacy, which represented her defeat. Her breasts ached from the pressure of his hard body. She pushed at his chest with her hands, moving her hips from side to side in order to escape from that part of him still within her. She was shocked when she felt him grow hard as her movement aroused him.

"Keep that up, my lovely, and I'll take what you are offering. I'm perfectly willing," he teased.

"You . . . can't," she whispered, stilling all movement. "Get off me! I can't breathe."

"Is this better?" he asked, rolling over and taking her with him. She was atop him, impaled and held fast by his hands on her buttocks. She held her chest away from his with arms that ached with the strain.

"No!" she denied, catching sight of their reflection in the big oval mirror, horrified at the picture she saw. Her small, ivory body arched away from his tan one, two brown hands holding her buttocks. Her breasts were temptingly displayed before his gaze.

"Let me go!" she screamed, then moaned as he began to knead her buttocks. She tried to get away by drawing up her legs to a kneeling position, but he took advantage of her change of position. He brought his hands to her hips and lifted her sensually up and down upon himself until she was aware of nothing but the hardness surging within her, filling her so deeply she felt she might die from the pleasure. A hot flood of sensation, unbearably intense, overcame her when he brought his hand to her and caressed her womanhood. She convulsed upon him, crying his name as he brought her over the edge, gained his own release, and brought her to culmination once more. Totally exhausted, she collapsed against him, his claim upon her senses clear to them both.

"You are my woman," he murmured huskily in her ear, cradling her gently in his arms as her racing heart began to slow. "Now you know."

Garrett awoke as the clinking sounds of glasses and silver in the public dining room downstairs reached his ears. He stretched his legs beneath the sheets and encountered a warm, soft, feminine leg. He reached out his hand and tentatively touched her. God, but she was beautiful. Once he had kissed away her inhibitions, she became wonderfully passionate as well. His smile was gentle, knowing that her strict Victorian upbringing had not prepared her for the overwhelming nature of lovemaking. He recalled the shock in her violet eyes when her own sensuality betrayed her. Willing or not, she had been swept away by a tide of passion that encompassed them both. She belonged to him as no other woman ever had.

Looking at her, her silver-gold hair arrayed wildly around her oval face, her breasts soft and warm, her legs curled underneath her like a baby's, he was filled with a feeling of protectiveness that denied that she had little need of it. Who would believe that this tiny, perfectly formed piece of femininity had a will of iron and a cutting tongue?

When she awoke, Catherine felt Garrett's hand, warm and caressing, upon her breasts. Her eyes flew open and she found herself staring into her husband's face. He dropped a light kiss on her parted lips. "Good morning, Mrs. Browning." He enclosed her breasts with his hand, teasing the nipple with his thumb as he leaned on one elbow. "I love the way you murder me, sweetheart," he teased, watching her face flame. "I plan to die every night."

He was sure of himself and of her. She bit her lip as she felt her body instinctively melt beneath his touch. She could not allow him to do whatever he wanted with her, whenever he chose. She concentrated on maintaining an icy calm, willed herself to feel nothing as his hands started a slow exploration. "I was drunk," she said coldly as he ran his fingers over her warm skin. His hand stilled.

"What did you say?"

"I said I was drunk. I would never have let you make love to me if I had been in control of my senses. I am unused to liquor, and I used it to get through that horrible ordeal as best I could."

"You're not drunk now," he bit out, furious with her for denying what had happened between them. He leaned over her, intent on having her writhing with need, begging for it. His confidence was swiftly replaced by fury when she remained stiff, her eyes wide and unblinking. His face became etched with tight lines.

"As I said, I am quite sober now." She hoped he didn't feel her releasing her pent-up breath, seconds away from giving in.

"Damn you!" he growled, getting up from the bed and pulling on his trousers. "You loved every minute of last night. If we had the time, I would prove it to you." He pulled his arms into the sleeves of his shirt, his muscles rippling with anger, his mouth tight.

Catherine savored the sweet taste of victory, her first over him. She had wounded his pride, and he was enraged. He charged about the room, pulling on his clothes. He had to feel something for her. If he didn't, her rejection wouldn't have evoked his anger, and he was livid. Heady with her small triumph, she pressed on. She stretched like a cat, letting the sheet fall away from a shapely leg. "Why don't you take time? I promise we won't miss the ship's departure if you make another attempt to seduce me. You leave me quite cold when I'm not the worse for drink."

He stopped in his tracks. His eyes darkened and his teeth clenched together as she beckoned to him with one hand. No woman had ever done this to him before. She was making fun of him—taunting him.

"There are many women who welcome my lovemaking, madam. You don't have to worry. I won't touch you again until you show me you want it. You have nothing to offer that I haven't had before. Get dressed. It's still a few hours before we reach London."

The mention of his other conquests made her seethe. She pressed on, not caring that she was treading on very dangerous ground. "Is that a promise?"

He was pulling her trunk in from the hall, but her question reached him. His face darkened with angry color. "You little minx! What do you want, a signed statement?" He stalked to the bed and pulled her up to her knees, his hands biting into the flesh of her arms. "The day I bed a woman who doesn't have the honesty or the guts to admit she loved every minute of it will be a long time coming."

She was terrified but nevertheless satisfied that at last she had some small power over him. He saw the slight glimmer of triumph in her eyes and raised his hand to strike her. His eyes blazing, he glared at her, dropping his arm in self-disgust when she proudly lifted her chin. "Very well," he said. "I shall find my pleasure else-where, sweet wife, but know this—you touch me at any time and I'll take it to mean you want me. Do you understand?"

She forced a brittle laugh. "Understood. I will find someone who knows the meaning of love; then we will both be happy."

"The hell you will!" he declared savagely, preparing to shake the life out of her. It took him several seconds to regain control, the fearful trembling of her lips and the terror in her large, beautiful eyes very real. He cursed under his breath, but his voice was without expression when he said, "You're bought and paid for, lady. When you have served your purpose, you can do as you like. Until then, whether you share my bed or not, you'll not share anyone else's. If I find you with another man, I'll break your neck." He threw her down on the bed and stormed out of the room, leaving her gaping after him and feeling strangely sick.

An hour later, they were seated inside the carriage and traveling toward London. Neither spoke. They avoided each other's eyes, holding themselves stiffly away from any contact as the coach bounced and lurched along the bumpy road.

Catherine stared out the window but couldn't see the beauty of the passing Kentish countryside through the mist of tears—tears she could not let him see. She was dressed in a pale pink traveling dress with a matching jacket and ruffles at the neck and wrists. A perky little hat sat jauntily on her golden head, but her pale face reflected none of the ensemble's impudence. She had too much pride to recall the angry words she had spoken and knew that her husband had no intention of doing so, either.

Garrett spoke for the first time as they neared the outskirts of London. The strong lines of his face were set, his eyes as cold as a winter sky. "I will expect you to behave as my happy bride in front of my grandmother and aunt. What lies between us should not affect them. They are fine people, and I won't have them upset."

"I am perfectly capable of conducting myself properly," she replied tightly, clutching her gloved hands in the folds of her dress. "I don't enjoy hurting people."

He looked away, disturbing her when he muttered, "You could have fooled me."

Chapter 6

The green, rolling countryside studded with quiet villages gradually gave way to squalor at the edge of London. It was midday, and the narrow streets were filled with every type of vehicle, from crude farm carts to the fashionable carriages of the elite. Their carriage was jostled innumerable times as the driver fought to pass through the glut of traffic. The air was filled with the voices of vendors hawking their wares and the clatter of wheels and horses' hooves on the cobbled streets.

London was the world center of culture and science, but the streets were fouled with all manner of human and animal refuse. The stench of rotting garbage assailed Catherine's senses. The smoke from factories begrimed the buildings, giving the old city a worn and tawdry appearance. At length, the squalor and filth gave way to increasingly better kept buildings and more affluent dwellings, until at last they began to circle a large, grassy square studded with trees and carefully arranged beds of flowering plants and shrubs. Large red brick town houses, each separated from the street by a low brick wall, faced the square. The carriage pulled to a stop in front of one of the gracious buildings at the end of a cul-de-sac.

"We have arrived," Garrett said, jumping down from the coach and helping Catherine alight. He took her arm as he walked through the iron gate and the small courtyard that led to the massive front door. When he pulled the thick bell cord, a stiff doorman answered. The man took their wraps and very properly escorted them through to a small sitting room. A middle-aged woman was seated working on a small sampler, her blue-gray eyes glued to the square of linen in her lap. A wide smile stretched across her thin face upon their entrance.

"Oh, my dears, I was hoping you would arrive soon." She came to Catherine and took both her hands, smiling down at her with kindly eyes. Catherine smiled back. "Forgive me," the older woman continued. "I am Garrett's aunt Estelle. I should have given my nephew the opportunity to introduce us properly, but when

Allen gave us the news, the conventions seemed much too time-consuming. My mother will take up most of your time, I am sure of that."

"Catherine," Garrett interrupted, "this lovely lady is my aunt Estelle, Allen's mother. We have plenty of time, Aunt; perhaps you could order some refreshment. It has been a long morning."

"Of course; traveling is so dreary." Estelle rang, and a pert, round-faced maid answered her summons, returning a few minutes later with a light luncheon tray. "Sit down by me, Catherine." She watched her nephew bite into a dainty sandwich. "Now, Garrett, how did you manage to marry the toast of London?"

"With some difficulty, madam." He looked more interested in his luncheon, but a veiled shutter over his eyes warned Catherine to agree with whatever he said.

"Think of it," Estelle said as she took Catherine's hand. "The dowagers will be talking for months. It is quite romantic."

Catherine's eyes widened. "Romantic" would not be the word she would use to describe her association with Garrett. "I am sure Garrett did not consider the gossips when he asked me to marry him," she said quietly, sensing his relaxation. "When he declared his great love for me so quickly after I met him, I did not know how to react. He can be very persuasive, and I found I could not turn him down."

"I am sure," Estelle agreed, smiling benignly at her nephew. "I am so glad you overlooked his impulsiveness. I was afraid he would marry someone whom he did not love merely to comply with that horrid will of his father's. Hasn't it worked out well? Allen is quite taken with your young brother; I'm sure we shall see him frequently. I was glad to hear that your father approves. Parental approval means so much, does it not?"

"Very true." Catherine's lips quirked. "In fact, if my father had not encouraged our relationship, I'm positive we would not be married today." She turned to her husband. She was finding it quite pleasant to talk about him with his aunt. So far he had offered no comment, but she could see that her barbs were reaching him.

"I doubt that," Estelle replied. "Your beauty alone would attract my nephew. I'm sure he pursued you relentlessly."

"Oh, yes." Catherine became dreamy-eyed. "They tell me that the strongest men fall the hardest. That's how it was for you, wasn't it, my darling?"

Garrett looked highly uncomfortable, listening to her darts and feeling the venom contained in every one of them. He was helpless to do anything about it without upsetting his loquacious aunt. Catherine was proving to be a very worthy opponent, which only increased his frustration. No woman had ever teased and tormented him as she did. "Our feelings for each other are mutual, my dear." He took another bite of his sandwich, cocking an eyebrow at her.

Catherine ignored his look and went on. "I must say, Garrett's stories about Texas are extremely compelling. If half of them are true, I shall be living in paradise." Her impish grin made him frown.

"Your wife is only teasing, Garrett." Estelle saw the frown and began to laugh. "Men do tend to brag, don't they?"

"I did not brag," Garrett stated. "Texas is a hard place to live. Catherine may be disappointed."

"Well, it cannot be too hard or you would not be taking this English rose back there." Estelle dismissed Garrett's rough tone. "My sister lived in Texas for many years before her death. She was as delicate as a flower, so don't worry, my dear."

Catherine saw Garrett stiffen and wondered at the

sudden dangerous glint in his eyes. Estelle began talking about their wedding, and the moment passed. Garrett was excluded, and he finally excused himself to go in search of Allen.

Catherine lifted her head as he walked out of the room, her eyes following him. When he was out of sight, she turned back to Estelle, a blush staining her cheeks when she saw the knowing look on the woman's face.

"My nephew is far too attractive." Estelle said. "Take my advice, Catherine—never let him feel too sure of himself. I believe he has met his match. I am delighted to see you don't fall all over yourself to keep his attention."

"Is your mother in good health?" Catherine changed the subject, not feeling safe discussing her husband without showing her real feelings.

"For her age, excellent. She has a heart condition, but it has improved vastly since Garrett's arrival. I am afraid that Allen is no match for her, whereas Garrett gives as good as he gets. Mother was outraged with his brashness at first, but he soon had her eating out of his palm." Estelle laughed with enjoyment. "She takes credit for his nature, saying he got his looks and character from herself and my father. Now that was a love match. I sometimes wonder how two such fiery people could have produced a daughter as dull as I."

"You are not dull, Lady Estelle," Catherine protested.

"That is sweet of you, my dear, but I am content with who I am. You look up to managing anything."

"Managing what?" Garrett came back into the room.

"You, my dear nephew. You!" Estelle laughed.

Garrett's grandmother was ready for their visit. Catherine felt as if she were about to have an audience with royalty, and Garrett's grin did not help matters as he ushered her up the stairs and into a dimly lit bedroom.

"Catherine, I take pleasure in presenting you to my grandmother, Lady Priscilla Parkinson, the dowager baroness of Andover." The Parkinsons were one of the most distinguished old families in England. Though he was without a title, her husband's blood was as blue as her own! Garrett raised one brow, acknowledging and enjoying her astonishment. He pushed her forward to the gigantic canopied bed where the regal personage of his grandmother impatiently waited.

"He does go on." The old woman spoke in a strong voice, belying her years. "So you are Garrett's bride. Come closer, child. I knew your mother and her mother before, very well. You favor them. I have been told you have some spunk. Why so quiet?" The blue eyes scrutinized her carefully.

Although the woman had to be at least eighty and her face revealed the natural ravages of time, she exuded aristocratic grace and authority with every gesture. At one time, she had probably been a great beauty. Beneath her white hair and piercing blue eyes, a classic bone structure was still evident under her creased pale skin. She was dressed in an elaborate dressing gown, the high ruffles of which concealed her thinness.

Catherine moved forward and dropped a short curtsy, much to Garrett's amusement, before taking the fragile hand in hers. "Leave us, Garrett, so we can talk freely," the baroness commanded, her sharp eyes never leaving Catherine's face.

He gave a short bow and reluctantly said, "As you wish, madam."

"He is afraid I will tell you all the family secrets," the baroness said with a wink. "At my age, I won't be ordered about by a young pup. Come sit beside me; I'm not the old dragon you think I am. I want to give you some advice, and we don't have much time. I'll get right to the heart of it."

Catherine's eyes widened. The lady had a way about her that did indeed resemble her grandson's. For some reason, Catherine wanted the dowager to think well of her and did not know what to say that wouldn't give this shrewd old woman a very good idea about the exact nature of her marriage.

"Now then, I can guess the details of your marriage. If I know my grandson, you had very little choice in the matter. Don't be a fool and think that this marriage is nothing more than convenience." As she had promised, the baroness indeed went right to the heart of the matter. "Garrett can come to love you and you him, if you set your mind to it."

"He will never love me." Catherine couldn't stand it. "He's incapable of loving a woman." The truth emerged before she could stop it.

"You are wrong, child. I was beginning to think you couldn't talk. I'm glad to see you are honest. I like that. It rankled him to have to choose an English wife. We will probably never know what was in Hunter Browning's head, but I sincerely believe he knew what he was doing. You are exactly what my grandson needs. You will give him a run for his money."

"Garrett does not need me or anyone," Catherine declared emphatically.

"Rubbish!" the baroness barked. "He doesn't trust women, and with very good reason. Celeste was my daughter, but I was not blind to her faults. Don't judge my grandson too harshly. His opinion of women stems from a legacy of painful memories."

"All we do is fight," Catherine explained. "We bring out the worst in each other."

"If I know Garrett, that is not all you do, is it? He is

too much like his grandfather." The baroness's eyes
sparkled in memory of her younger years.

Catherine didn't know what to say. Her cheeks were
flaming.

The shrewd eyes scanned her face. "At last. Now we
are getting somewhere," she said with satisfaction. "Is
he too much man for you?"

"No! I just resent his arrogance and his domineering
ways."

"Of course you do. Those milksops you are used to
couldn't inspire such reactions. Let the silly debutantes
land those weak types. Your marriage will be a constant
battle of wits to keep you on your mettle. Do not let
stubborn pride keep you from loving him."

"I don't seem to have been given a choice," Catherine said softly, not realizing how much she was admitting.

"Think about it," Lady Priscilla suggested, patting
Catherine's hand, highly pleased with her. "I want to
tell you one more thing before Garrett comes barging
in. He has two brothers. Jason, the middle son, is the
result of a liaison between my daughter and an English
nobleman, whom I won't name. When he came here,
Garrett found out that his mother had been unfaithful
to his father. You must never give him cause to think
you would do the same."

Catherine gasped, suddenly understanding her husband's violent reaction to her taunts. She had already
provoked him just the way the baroness warned against
doing.

"My grandson has suffered greatly in the past," Lady
Priscilla continued. "You can make all the difference.
Things may have gotten off to a bad start, but differ-
ences can be reconciled. It is your task to conquer the
memories . . . This is in strictest confidence, Catherine. Garrett will be angry if he hears how much I've

told you. He does a very good job of hiding his feelings. I'm sure he's cooling his heels outside in the hall, fearing I'm revealing every skeleton in the Parkinson closet. He will be quaking with terror if I don't let you go soon."

Catherine laughed at this mental image. "Somehow I doubt that." Sobering, Catherine hugged the fragile figure with genuine affection. "Thank you for telling me all this. I can only hope it helps me manage him."

"I think you will do more than manage." The baroness chuckled. "Give me a kiss and take yourself off. I want a few more words with my grandson before he leaves me. I won't live long enough to see him again, and I've discovered I love him deeply."

They were still embracing when Garrett came in, unable to control his impatience any longer. Catherine withdrew slowly from the baroness and turned to her husband. Her shining features were greeted by a suspicious smile as she went past him.

He turned to his grandmother, watching her eyes follow Catherine out of the room, her old face softly glowing. "What did you talk about?" he asked bluntly.

Ignoring his question, the baroness said, "Treasure her, Garrett. You have married a fine young woman. You are a lusty man, just like your grandfather was, but your prowess in bed will not hold a woman forever."

Dark color invaded his face. He could only imagine what the two women had discussed if this was his grandmother's advice. "Madam, you amaze me. I assume you are now going to tell me what else I must do."

"First, do you love her?" She gave him a piercing stare.

He grew increasingly uncomfortable under her scrutiny. "I don't know."

"You could have married any of these young debutantes; why this one?"

"She has more spirit than most."

"If you will admit it, she has a spirit to match your own. Before leaving, tell me if you love her."

Knowing she would not relent until he gave a suitable answer, he said sheepishly, "I admire her, Grandmother. I admire her very much."

"Good!" the baroness exclaimed joyfully. "That is a start. Don't be afraid to let admiration turn to love. If you handle her right, you could make a fine marriage out of what is obviously a shambles. Am I right, boy?"

"Yes. She's a stubborn little wench."

"As stubborn as you? Can't you see that she doesn't like being controlled any more than you would? Remember that, boy."

Not wanting to get angry with the old woman, he gave a noncommittal answer. "I'll try."

"Don't you patronize me, Garrett Browning. I don't want to see two fine young people suffer for mistakes made in the past. Trust your wife; she is not like your mother."

"Are you finished?" Garrett's temper rose, as it always did when his mother was mentioned.

"You will have to face up to it someday, Garrett. I hope Celeste doesn't keep you from loving that girl as she deserves." The baroness sat up straighter in the bed. "Stop looking at me like that. I'm finished with my lecture. I don't want you leaving here angry with me. These months with you have been the best I've spent in years. It was like having a little more time with your grandfather."

Garrett softened at the smile on her face. "I wish I had known him, Grandmother. I am grateful that at least I came to know him through you."

"You have only to look in the mirror. You are so like him, it is uncanny—arrogant, handsome, bad tempered. I loved him as well as a woman could ever love a man. Turn your devastating charm on your wife, and her defenses will crumble just as mine did. Now be off with you before I start blubbering like an old fool."

"I never thought to hear such flowery compliments from you." Garrett went to the bed and kissed his grandmother on the cheek, his throat aching.

"You are a devil, Garrett. How I wish I could be there when Catherine presents you with a son."

He gently wiped the tears from her eyes with his thumb. "I shall miss you, you old dragon." His smile brought more tears, and he had difficulty hiding his emotion.

A few minutes later, he stood in the hall outside her room, staring at the floor. He took a deep breath and wiped his eyes. It took several minutes for him to collect himself and search out his wife.

It was late afternoon when they arrived at the harbor. The tall masts of the ships could be seen long before the carriage arrived at the quay. The tangy smell of the sea mixed with less appealing odors. Large warehouses and miserable shacks lined the water's edge. Huge barrels and crates were being loaded and unloaded from the docks. Well-dressed gentility, sailors, ruffians and ragged beggars mixed together as they carried out their parts in the shipping industry. The carriage was continually jostled as the driver deftly avoided collision and made his way to Wharf Six, where the packet *Columbia* was docked.

Garrett did not speak until they reached the wharf and the carriage stopped. "Can I tear you away from the sights and lead you aboard our ship?" Catherine had been so engrossed that she hadn't noticed him watching her excited face. "By the look on your face, I would guess you have never been to the waterfront."

She was still looking up and down the quay when he escorted her up the gangway of their ship. They were greeted by the captain, a distinguished-looking gentleman dressed in an immaculate uniform, who gestured to a waiting steward to usher them to their cabin. Garrett made a cursory examination of their accommodations and then informed her that he was going to check on his stallion.

Catherine removed her hat and gloves, looking around at her surroundings with curiosity. The cabin was furnished comfortably. A small table stood in the center of the floor with two serviceable chairs. A washstand with a pitcher was next to one of the large wardrobes standing out from the paneled walls. A built-in bureau, railed by metal, stood between the two wardrobes. Burnished mahogany enclosed an alcove bed covered with a cream-color, down-filled comforter. Catherine shivered at the inviting intimacy of the bed, noticing how the waning light from a porthole streaked across the bed cover, enhancing its romantic appeal.

She pondered the details of her visit with Garrett's grandmother, wanting to believe that he would someday love her; but they had already hurt each other deeply. She could not deny that she enjoyed the glory of his lovemaking, but that was not enough. Her pride made her deny her response to him, and he had sworn not to touch her. They were embroiled in a battle of wills she could not afford to lose. No matter what the baroness thought, it was doubtful either of them would give in. She would not accept his role for her, and although she could better understand his contempt for women, he had no right to place her in the same category as his mother. She was determined to stand up to him and make him see that she wouldn't meekly submit to his demands.

A knock at the door interrupted her thoughts, and when she answered, several stewards began filling the room with her luggage. She looked at the tall pile of cases and grinned. When Garrett got a glimpse of this, he would react like a bellowing bull. The thought made her eyes sparkle as she began unpacking. She filled both wardrobes and the bureau, ordered the empty trunks removed and was left with several large pieces yet to be unpacked. She surveyed the cluttered space with satisfaction. Her husband wouldn't find one inch of vacant space.

"What in God's name is all this stuff doing in here? Good Lord, woman, don't you have an ounce of brains? What isn't necessary goes in the hold."

Catherine looked up from folding a petticoat and sweetly smiled. "I'm afraid I'll need everything I've unpacked."

"Let's just see how much you need when I start throwing it overboard." He reached for a hatbox and heaved it through the open doorway before she could stop him. Why hadn't she realized he'd react like this?

He threw another box and another, until she screamed, "Stop! I'll decide what I can store, you bully!"

"Good." He sat down on a chair and brought his booted feet onto the tabletop. Stretching his arms behind his neck, he watched her struggle with the mountain of luggage, cramming gowns and fripperies back inside her trunks. "If you won't do your duty in bed, maybe you'll earn your keep by seeing to my clothes."

"What?" She slammed the wardrobe door.

"Would you rather unpack my wardrobe or play the loving wife?"

She didn't say a word but began putting his things away. If he thought he could punish her for denying him his rights, he would find that two could play at that game. She wondered how he was going to like what she was planning.

At dinner, they sat at the captain's table and enjoyed their first meal with the other passengers. The conversation consisted of comments about the weather and questions concerning the voyage, but Catherine wasn't listening. When Garrett decided to stay behind with the captain to enjoy a cigar with the other men, she smiled. She needed time to arrange for his entrance.

Back in the cabin, she quickly donned a translucent nightgown. She brushed her hair until the silvery-gold strands shimmered. She heard Garrett's step outside the door and stepped in front of the glowing lamp.

Garrett caught his breath when he walked in and caught sight of her outlined figure before the light. He couldn't stop staring at her, drinking in the delectable shape of her breasts and hips as she brushed her hair. "Oh, God," he groaned, silently cursing himself. Why in hell had he let her get under his skin deeply enough to extract a promise not to touch her until she came to him of her own accord? Wanting was rapidly becoming physical agony. He forced himself to turn his back on her, discarding his jacket and jerking off his shirt. As he threw them on the floor, he could have sworn he heard a small laugh. He twisted around to look at her, but she was brushing her hair, looking the picture of innocence. He sat down on the bed, instantly imagining her beside him on the soft mattress. Another curse erupted from between his clenched teeth as he strug-

gled to remove his boots. When they fell to the floor
with a thump, he was compelled to look at her again.
She was sitting before the mirror, applying scent to her
throat and the valley between her breasts. He squeezed
his eyes shut and concentrated on other thoughts, but it
didn't work. His loins throbbed as he dropped his
trousers and flung himself onto the bed, tugging the
covers up with an angry jerk. He could hear her
humming softly, and he crushed a pillow viciously in his
fist. The witch meant for him to suffer every day of
their cross-Atlantic voyage, and she was beginning with
a vengeance. How was he going to keep himself from
ripping the gossamer gown from her body and making
love to her over and over?

She came to the bed. He was staring at the alcove
wall in front of him as if his life depended on it. She
inquired none too politely, "Where do you expect me
to sleep?"

"Get in here!" he growled.

Hiding her smile, she gathered the folds of her
nightgown about her and climbed onto the bed. Her
gasp was convincingly startled as she lost her balance
and fell headlong over his chest. Her twisting movements brought the nightgown up to her waist, and she
was deliberately naked beneath it.

"Sweet, holy heaven," Garrett moaned as a cascade
of perfumed hair tickled his nose and two soft breasts
melted against his burning chest. Every twisting effort
she made to prolong her exit increased his torture.
After what was to him an eternity, she dragged her
warm, quivering bottom over his naked belly and
landed safely on the other side. She waited for a
reaction, hoping he would admit how badly he wanted
her. The confidence she had lost on their wedding night
was coming back with each strained breath he drew. He
was a strong man, but she had plenty of time. Her lips

curled into a self-assured smile, and she relaxed into sleep.

That pleasure eluded Garrett for a long time. He willed his body to relax, but he couldn't, listening to the even pattern of her breathing and knowing she would not reach for him. She was curled into a tight little ball with her back to him, her silky hair fanned out on the pillow beneath her head. He raised himself up on one elbow and looked at her. Unable to resist, he picked up a long strand of shiny hair and drew it through his fingers. He had condemned himself to this living hell. It was too late to recall his promise without it looking to Catherine as though he couldn't do without her, but it was beginning to look like he couldn't.

Sometime during the night, she rolled closer to him, seeking the warmth of his body. When she woke up the next morning, she found herself snuggled against him, one arm thrown across his chest. He was still asleep, and she was afraid to move in case he woke up and found her almost on top of him. He could easily take it to mean she was offering herself, and she meant him to come to her. She hoped she could outlast him.

She gave him a sharp jab in the ribs and jumped back to her own side of the bed. "Move, you oaf, or do you want me to climb over you again?"

Garrett's eyes flew open as he woke with a start. He sat up abruptly and turned to his scowling wife. "Don't ever wake me up like that again. You're lucky I didn't come up swinging!" He bounded from the bed and crossed the small cabin, rummaging through the wardrobe to find a pair of trousers. She was treated to a full view of his virile body. "Why are you still in bed? You seemed hell-bent to get up a few moments ago!" He was like an angry bear as he stormed around the room.

"You really are a terror in the morning." She smiled at the jumble of curses he emitted before disappearing into the passageway. She began to laugh, remembering how ludicrous he had looked storming around the tiny cabin as naked as the day he had been born. "Well, Mr. Garrett Browning, we'll just see how much longer you can hold out. I'm certainly not going to make it easy for you."

She had just put on a low-cut lavender day dress when he returned. "If you don't mind, I'd like to shave." Ignoring the surly resonance in his voice, she blithely began pinning up her hair. Her breasts strained against the thin material of her bodice as she deliberately lifted her arms to her head. "There is only one mirror. Perhaps you'll be courteous enough to let me finish?"

Garrett threw up his hands, "Of course, milady. And what do you expect me to do while you primp for God knows how long?"

"Perhaps you could pick up the clothes you left all over the floor last night." A staccato of angry fingers beating on top of the table made her intentionally slow her pace. The insistent drumming got louder and louder until she finally pushed the last pin into place. With a wave of her hand and a broad smile, she said, "It's all yours. Patience is not your suit, is it?"

Stormclouds gathered in the sea-blue eyes. "Is that some kind of challenge?"

"Not at all; but I notice how fatigued you look. Did you have a troubled night?" Her violet eyes twinkled with enjoyment.

"I slept just fine, thank you!" He slammed out of the chair and began lathering his face. Each swipe of his razor was made in anger. She got the distinct impression he was imagining her throat beneath the blade's edge.

"I hope you don't bleed to death before I've eaten my breakfast." She reached for her shawl and began tapping her foot, pressing her advantage as far as she dared.

He smothered an oath as the razor knicked his chin. The small drop of blood brought a tiny giggle from the doorway. He would kill her! The first time she came crawling to him, unable to deny her desire, he would strangle her. In fact, if she kept goading him, she might not live until breakfast. Refusing to let her see his temper, he forced a smile to his face and finished shaving. He came to her, offering his arm. "Sorry to disappoint you, my dear, but I'm still alive. Shall we go?"

"I'm ready. Maybe your disposition will improve after you have eaten." She returned his false smile and placed her arm through his. She brushed against him briefly, felt his instant reaction and cast a knowing look up at him.

For days after that, he avoided her. He would enter their cabin far the worse for drink and crawl numbly into the bed. She continued to press her advantage at every opportunity. What a glorious and fitting retribution it was for his arrogant treatment of her. Unfortunately she had to fight her own yearning to turn to him each night when he passed out beside her. Her dreams were filled with images of their lovemaking. One night he groaned her name in his sleep, and tears filled her eyes. She cradled his dark head against her breast for long hours, sadly regretting that she was as determined as he.

One morning, after a heavy night of drinking, Garrett woke up to the sound of Catherine sweetly singing. He turned to the sound, staring mesmerized through the pained slits of his eyes, at her standing before the washstand bared to the waist. She was sponging her body, and her firm, round breasts stood out to taunt him while she ran the cloth over her glowing skin. His head felt as if someone were hammering inside his skull. Was she trying to drive him insane? He watched her slowly turn toward the bed and acknowledge his wakefulness with an impudent grin. She made no attempt to cover herself but enticingly replaced her chemise on dewy white shoulders, knowing he was suffering the pains of the damned. "You look terrible, Garrett. I had no idea I was marrying a man who could so easily turn to drink. Can I do anything to help?" She bit her soft lower lip with feigned concern.

"You know what you can do to help, you little vixen," he muttered. "How long do you think we can go on like this?" He was past caring that there was a defeated note in his voice.

She was moved by the rueful expression on his face. His black hair was rumpled and his red-streaked eyes were plain evidence of the strain he was under. Should she continue to resist him? The silence that hung between them lengthened until he got out of bed, dragging the sheets with him. He staggered to the washstand, where he poured a pitcher of water over his pounding head.

"Get out of here. I can't stand the sight of you." He turned his back on her, failing to see her stricken expression as she ran from the room.

He was desperate. There had never been a woman who haunted him as she did. He rarely thought about anything else, drinking himself into a stupor to ease his desire; but she was there even in his dreams. He clenched his fist and slammed it into his other hand. No more! He was not going to suffer one more hangover on her account. Two could play at the game she had started. He faced himself in the mirror and declared, "Prepare for the battle of your life, my little beauty. You are about to be charmed to quivering submission.

Let's see if you can deny that my body doesn't make you ache."

The first order in his campaign was to rid himself of the effects of his stupid bout with the bottle. He climbed back into the bed and fell into the first contented rest he had had since they left England.

Sometime later, Catherine reentered the cabin. She was startled to find Garrett dressed in a white linen shirt which he had not bothered to button and the tightest pair of navy pants she could imagine. The sight of him lounging casually against one wall of their alcove, his long legs encased in black leather boots stretched out before him, gave her a jolt. His hair was damp, as if he had just washed it. She stared at him, her gaze sliding down the naked line of his torso revealed by the open shirt. She swallowed the sudden lump in her throat when he turned the full brilliance of his ultramarine eyes on her. His molded lips quirked into a devastating grin. Her heart began to pound.

"Uh . . . you . . . look recovered." It was going to take a few minutes to whip herself back into a temper when he had blasted through her defenses completely. He had no right to look so attractive when she knew he had been drinking far into the night. His eyes practically smoldered a sensual invitation.

"I'll return the compliment, my love," he replied, displaying his appreciation of her appearance with a flash of even white teeth. "Have I told you lately what the sight of you does to me? I was sitting here thinking about my beautiful wife and wondering if she knows how much she would enjoy running her hands down my naked body."

She gulped and stepped back. "Well . . . I . . . I won't do that, will I?"

"No, unfortunately, but what's to stop us from

making the best out of this venture? After all, it won't be often that we will be able to enjoy the luxuries offered on board an expensive packet." He swung his long legs over the bed and walked across the room to the table. He uncorked a chilled bottle of champagne and poured the bubbling liquid into glasses that stood ready on the table. "Will you join me, Catherine?" His pronouncement of her name was a gentle caress.

She suddenly needed a place to sit down. It was not her imagination that his fingers lingered overlong at the back of her chair when he assisted her into it. She could feel them brush against the nape of her neck before he went to his own chair and moved it much too close for comfort.

"I . . . I would have thought champagne would be the last thing you desired today." She avoided looking at the captivating warmth of his gaze but couldn't help letting her eyes drift to the smoothly muscled skin she saw every time his shirt fluttered open.

He laughed—a regretful, short laugh that brought her eyes to his—and she was caught in the indigo net he cast. "Champagne is the least of my desires. What I desire is you, and you know it." He held out a glass, his tender smile the only evidence that he noticed how badly her hand shook as she took it. He hesitated before releasing it into her fingers, long enough for his fingers to touch hers and send a pulsating message of want from her hand to her heart.

She warned herself that she was in the midst of an all-out war and must shore up her defenses before he stormed the citadel without a fight. A quaking began in her legs and traveled up to her neck. She could feel his heated gaze lingering at the bodice of her dress, and her nipples sprang to life. "Don't look at me like that." She was deathly afraid that the tables had been neatly turned.

"It was touching, not looking, we agreed to dispense with, little witch. You are a witch, you know, for you have bewitched me. If you don't come to me soon, I may die of the spell you have cast. Would it be so terrible to admit you want me just a little bit? I am your husband." His voice was husky with passion.

Lord! How did she answer a question like that? She was out of her depth. She swayed toward him. The hard mahogany of the table brought her back to awareness of what she was doing. If he thought she was a witch, well, he was a devil. She didn't even realize she had said it out loud until she heard his amused laugh.

"The powers of magic and everlasting fire. We are a potent combination, are we not?" He saluted her and drank a toast to his own words.

"I know what you are doing."

"I'm sure you do." A devilish gleam was in his eyes.

"I'm going up on deck." She stood up and made a quick dive for the door.

"I'll find you wherever you go, beautiful," he promised softly.

Chapter 7

Catherine gripped the railing tightly. The beauty of the sunlight dancing on the blue waves beyond the ship did nothing to calm her nerves. Maybe I should try drinking myself into a stupor every night like he did, she thought. She wanted him, and he knew it. So lost in her thoughts that she was oblivious to her surroundings, she jumped when a voice spoke next to her. "Mrs. Browning?"

"Oh . . . you startled me, Captain."

"I'm sorry. The sea can be hypnotic."

"I . . . I was so caught up with the ocean's beauty, I didn't hear you."

"Beautiful she is today," the captain agreed. "At times like this, I can almost forget how powerful and destructive she can be."

"I believe that is why the sea is referred to as a woman," Garrett's deep voice cut in as he stepped between the captain and Catherine. "A beautiful woman who can be sweet and docile one moment and a vicious lioness the next." He turned briefly to Catherine, giving her a wide smile.

"You may be quite right, Mr. Browning, although I cannot imagine your wife being anything but the beautiful lady she appears."

"You would be in for a surprise, Captain. My wife and the sea have a great deal in common."

Catherine changed the subject. "When do you expect to reach Charleston, Captain? With the fair weather we are having, the ship must be making good time."

"The trip should take no longer than three weeks. We might gain a few days if this weather continues. I should think we will sight land in less than a week. You two will be on your way to Texas, isn't it?"

"That's right."

"You have property there?" The captain smiled as Garrett drew Catherine's hand through his arm.

"Yes, north of Austin." He kept his voice polite but didn't encourage further questions.

Captain Murdock was so used to passengers who enjoyed talking about themselves that he failed to notice Garrett's reticence. "Do you and your wife plan to live there alone? I've heard that some of the holdings are quite isolated. What with the war and all, it must be hard on the womenfolk."

"The war?" Garrett's sharp question made the captain draw his brows together in consideration.

"My, you have been away for a while. Yes, indeed. The United States and Mexico are finally at war. It was not a popular decision with Congress, but President Polk managed to get the declaration passed by both houses after the first confrontation between our troops and the Mexicans. It seems—at least the President claimed—that they fired on us first. Old Zack Taylor is down there and has taken some places called Matamoros and Palo Alto. America has war fever; volunteers are enlisting everywhere."

"Do you know if all the battles are being waged below the Rio Grande?" Garrett fired the question, damning himself for leaving Texas at a time when war was inevitable, cursing his father for giving him no choice.

"That is the last I heard. Is your property near there?"

"No. I'm much farther north, but all the same, I wish to God I were home. By the time I get there, who knows what I'll find." He felt totally frustrated. "What else have you heard? Any mention of *guerrilleros?*"

"I am truly sorry, Mr. Browning, but I have no further information."

Garrett nodded, losing interest in the conversation. "If you will excuse us, Captain, I have to speak with my wife."

"What does this mean, Garrett?" Catherine asked when, after returning to the cabin, he did nothing but pace back and forth.

"The hell if I know," Garrett growled. "If either Jason or Robert has left the ranch, I'll throttle him. Why on earth did I stay in England so damned long?" He shot an accusing glance at her.

She bristled. "Don't look at me like that. I would have been happy if you had not spent any time in England."

"I had no choice, as you well know." He resumed his pacing. "Damn! I knew it was a bad time to leave. It was only a matter of time before the Mexicans tried something."

"What are you talking about? I don't understand. Can't you tell me something, especially since we are heading into a war zone? Will we go to your ranch, or will we wait in Charleston?"

"Wait in Charleston? We won't stay in Charleston any longer than is absolutely necessary. I have to get to Tierra as soon as I can. As far as being in danger from the war, I doubt it; not the way we'll be going."

If there was no danger, why was he so agitated? She wanted to know more, much more. An inexplicable chill ran up her spine as she watched him. "How long will it take to get there? How do we travel from Charleston to Texas? I have only a vague knowledge of your country's geography."

He turned to her as if she had just walked into the cabin and interrupted his train of thought. He stared at her thoughtfully before replying softly. "Sit down; I'll try to explain. I assumed you didn't care."

"You assumed wrong."

He ran a hand through his hair, his mouth turning up at the corners. "So I see."

He began talking, clearly disturbed about the war. "I planned to book passage on another ship out of Charleston and reach a port in Texas called Galveston. That would have taken a week or so, but now this damned war may have ruined our chance of going home that way."

"If we can't find passage on a ship, what are our alternatives? How far is it?"

He leaned his arms on the table. "Texas is over fifteen hundred miles from the eastern shore of the United States." He grinned at her awestruck expression. "I hope we don't have to travel by land. It could take weeks, maybe months, by that method. We could travel by rail part of the way, but most of it would be done by wagon, and that's very slow. If we can get a ship to New Orleans, it would cut our travel time immeasurably. Then we would have another two weeks overland by wagon from New Orleans. It all depends on which route we are forced to take to avoid military action."

"How close is the fighting to your ranch?"

He saw anxiety in her big eyes and heard it in her voice. Though he felt apprehension himself, he did not want to frighten her and tried to sound reassuring. "The Rio Grande is a river over two hundred miles away from Tierra. It forms the border between Texas and Mexico. When I left, American troops were stationed down near the border with strength enough to protect the interior. The two towns the captain mentioned are across the border in Mexico."

Catherine studied her husband's face for a long moment, noting the lines of worry etched along his brow. "What aren't you telling me? You asked the captain about *guerrilleros*—what are they?"

She was too quick. He had hoped she wouldn't pick up on his question to the captain. He didn't want to frighten her any more than was necessary. "They are small bands of irregular Mexican army soldiers that sometimes attack isolated settlers in the interior. They usually don't go in very far. I seriously doubt they would raid as far north as Austin, and I doubt even more that they would attack Tierra. Does that reassure you?"

"I . . . I guess so."

"I'm going to question some of the other passengers and see if anyone has more information." He studied her, fighting off the desire to pull her into his arms and comfort her. She looked so tiny and defenseless, in need of more than words. He paused, hoping she would reach out to him, but she did not move as he exited.

Catherine sat at the table for a long time after he left. If he had only held out his arms to her, she would have thrown herself into them. His voice had been gentle and reassuringly strong as he explained everything. She had never felt so drawn to him; his concern for his land and family touched her deeply. His grandmother had been right; he was capable of loving. If only he could love her. She wanted him to love her. Why? She was desperately and irrevocably in love with her husband—a man who only weeks ago she had vowed she hated.

She went to the berth and lay down. She was in love with a man who didn't trust women, who had married her to fulfill the requirements of a will and who would kill her if he found her with another man. A man who ensured her brother's future one minute and tormented her the next with his steady blue gaze. Her eyes fluttered shut and she fell into a restless sleep—a sleep filled with images of her handsome husband, his tender lovemaking and a menacing sensation connected with their trip.

Above deck, Garrett began questioning the American passengers. Not one was able to offer more than Captain Murdock. Communications on the progress of the war were slow in reaching the East, and no one aboard was from west of the Mississippi. He did glean from a gentleman from Louisiana that there was a naval blockade in the Gulf that would prevent their securing passage on a ship headed for Galveston. All civilian vessels were halted in New Orleans, and the rest of their trip would have to be made over land; that is, if they were lucky enough to get passage that far.

Exhausting all sources, he reluctantly returned to the cabin. Catherine was asleep when he entered, and he quietly walked over to the alcove. How beautiful and vulnerable she looked, curled up with one hand resting beneath her cheek. Her long lashes formed a crescent of gold across the peach-toned skin of her cheeks, and he moaned inwardly at the familiar tightening in his loins. How easy it would be to join her on the berth and make love to her continuously for the remainder of the passage. He hoped she turned to him soon or he would break his vow and take her any way he could get her. She was his, and their celibate life was driving him crazy. From now on, he planned to be the most charming man she had ever met. He reached out with one finger and brushed a loose curl from her forehead. "Catherine," he murmured.

Her violet eyes fluttered open, and for a moment, she looked as if she would like to hold out her arms to him, but instead she slowly sat up and asked if he had been able to gather more information. He related all he knew. Determined to begin his campaign of charm, he quickly changed the subject. "Would you care to go to the dining salon or have our dinner brought to the cabin? If we eat here, I could describe Tierra to you."

She would like nothing better. Conversations of any kind, as long as they were not arguments, could only help their relationship. "Yes, I would like that. If you will order our dinner, I will freshen up."

"You look beautiful just as you are." His smile was tender. After he left, she jumped from the berth and raced to the washstand to splash cold water on her face. She ran a comb through her tangled curls and smoothed her skirts, wondering why she suddenly felt hopeful.

He entered whistling a merry tune and leading a white-jacketed steward carrying a large, linen-covered tray. "I was lucky enough to catch this good fellow on his way to the ship's kitchen." The steward placed the tray on the table and left. Garrett pulled out a chair for her. "Madam, may I assist you?" Catherine went along with his festive manner, accepting the wine and taking a long sip. "The steward promised that this champagne was of good vintage and chilled properly."

"It's delicious," was all she could mumble. She was terrified that she would do something to change the atmosphere. For reasons she could not understand, she felt that her future with him depended on this evening. She took courage from the amused grooves beside his mouth. "You promised to tell me about Texas and Tierra. How many servants do you employ, and where can I go shopping?" He was looking at her strangely, his eyes widening. She continued, excitement bubbling curiously inside her. "Will I get along with the house-keeper, the cook? At Bannerfield, Cook didn't allow anyone in her kitchen. Does yours?"

Her questions were interrupted by his burst of up-roarious laughter. He was soon nearly doubled over with merriment. "Will you explain what is so funny?" His laughter infuriated her. She threw her wine at him, desperate to stop his unexplained mirth.

"Forgive me," he began, but was then overcome with another burst of hilarity. "Oh . . . Catherine." He tried to compose himself, while she sat fuming in her chair. "I hadn't realized how completely unprepared you are for Texas. I thought you would know that marketing and buying clothes won't be a problem for you." His statement seemed threatening, and there was a decided glint in his eyes as he dabbed at the wine soaking his shirt. "I hate to think where that damnable temper of yours will take you when you hear that the closest shop is at least fifty miles away. There is no army of servants, my sweet; only our housekeeper and a young girl who helps her. You can cook any time you like. Hannah will probably appreciate your help." He couldn't hide the grin that tugged at his mouth as he continued to dab at the droplets clinging to his clothing. "Thank God your aim isn't good. You would not have liked what I would have done if this had hit me in the face."

Her glare increased as he told her about the conditions under which he expected her to live. Tierra Nueva sounded like a crude hovel in the middle of a vast wasteland. "But who will see to the house and the meals? Who will assist me when we entertain?" She couldn't conceive of a house with only two servants. He must be taking her to live in a shack. He was struggling with laughter but had the sense to hold up one arm for protection in case she started throwing things.

"I'm the only person you will be entertaining. You can do that by joining me between the sheets."

"What are you saying? You . . . you let my father believe you were rich!" she screeched. "Now you tell me that we will live in a hovel? I may be your wife, but I'm not going to any godforsaken wilderness and be a slave!"

The smile died in Garrett's eyes as he listened to her tirade. He reached for her with a grip of steel, hauling her up. "I've never hit a woman, Kate. Say any more and I might start." The deadly tone of his voice frightened her, so she fell silent. The fire of temper burning in her violet eyes was the only sign that she had not given in, only acquiesced to his greater physical strength. He felt his hand almost crushing the fragile bones of her wrist, felt her pulse beating wildly beneath his fingers.

He dropped her wrist and pushed her away. "I won't

say this again, Catherine Browning. You go where I go. Whether you like it or not is immaterial to me. Your father was in my debt, and I took you in payment. It looks like I made a bad bargain, but we're both stuck with it." Turning on his heel, he stormed out of the cabin, his hostility so strong she could feel it long after the door slammed.

She dissolved in tears across the berth. Her hopes for the evening were shattered completely. She was angry with Garrett, but even more angry with herself. If only she hadn't lost her temper and hurled all those awful insults at him. But what he had said was far worse. All she was to him was a bad bargain made to keep Tierra Nueva, his precious ranch.

Garrett had taken up residence in the ship's bar. He cursed himself for ruining the evening and cursed Catherine's sharp tongue. His grandmother's voice echoed in his mind: "She's not like Celeste." But damn the woman, she came so close to repeating word for word the taunts he had heard his mother make to his father. He ordered another drink and then another, downing them quickly as his thoughts shifted from Catherine to memories of his father and the cursed codicil to his will that had begun everything. His mind went back to a fight with his father. He remembered standing in front of him and listening to words he had heard a dozen times before.

"You must marry," Hunter Browning had said. "I want to know that Tierra is in safe hands and will always continue as Browning land."

"I don't plan to marry. Women are good for only one thing, and I don't intend to shackle myself to one of them for the rest of my life."

His father had glared at him, and his voice had grown

louder. "Listen here, son. You are the only one of my boys who can handle this plantation, and I want to see one of your sons ready to step in when you are gone."

"You'll never see one unless there are a few around that I don't know about. Want me to find out and bring them here for you?"

From that point on, as always, the argument had become a slanging match. It had ended with Hunter too furious to talk and Garrett riding off until his temper cooled down. One day, after another argument on the same subject, Hunter had suffered a stroke. Garrett had hovered outside his father's room for days, waiting for a chance to tell Hunter that he was sorry. He had been called to his father's bedside; he could remember it all so clearly—too clearly. His strong, proud father lay pale and unmoving in the large bed. His eyes, open and alert, were still able to penetrate through to his son and read his innermost thoughts. One large hand reached shakily from the bed to grasp Garrett's. Hunter struggled with speech. Finally he indicated that he wanted something from his desk drawer. Garrett found the notarized codicil, which was meant for his eyes only. He sat down on the bed to read it, choking back his rage. Hunter rasped, "You . . . will . . . do . . . it. I. . . ."

"Yes, you stubborn old man, I'll do it," Garrett muttered.

Hunter had died with a triumphant half-smile on his face.

Garrett raised his glass in a toast. "Well, old man, you won. I hope you are happy." He could still see the paper sentencing him to a marriage he didn't want. ". . . you deserve an aristocrat," it read. "Go to England and marry an English noblewoman within one year of my death. Only then will you receive full title to

Tierra Nueva." There had been no reason to tell his brothers about the codicil. He had promised, and even in death, Hunter held him to it.

He motioned for his glass to be refilled and then raised it again and offered aloud to the startled bartender: "Here's to beautiful English noblewomen. God save us from them all." He drank until he had to be carried back to his cabin. By the time the ship approached Charleston harbor, Garrett and Catherine had gone days without speaking more than a few syllables to one another. Both were unwilling to swallow their pride and apologize.

They were on deck, and Catherine saw her trunks being carried down the gangway to a very elegant carriage.

"Don't look so grim," Garrett said. "Charleston has a lot to offer. You will be able to take a proper bath. We are staying at a hotel equal to any in London." He hoped to prick her interest. Perhaps she'd unbend enough to abandon the frigid attitude she had adopted since their argument. She wouldn't find anything lacking at the Houghton House.

Catherine's interest picked up at the thought of a real bath. It would be delightful to feel truly clean after weeks of washing herself at the basin. In his own way, Garrett was attempting to ease the strain they were under, but she wanted an outright apology, not this obvious effort to divert her from what lay between them.

So this was America. It did not look nearly as uncivilized as she had been led to expect. The city looked clean and prosperous. Beyond the inevitable waterfront warehouses, she could see tree-lined streets, with colorful flowers blooming everywhere. She gave Garrett a suspicious look from beneath her poke bonnet, but he was too busy asking Captain Murdock questions about his horse to notice.

"Do you wish to wait for me in the coach or watch the unloading?" Garrett asked once they had walked off the gangway. It was quite warm, and Catherine felt it would probably be even warmer sitting in the carriage. She agreed to accompany him to the dock that received the stock.

Burly men were removing cargo from the bowels of the ship, carrying crates down a wide, fenced gangway that had been placed into the side hold. Catherine's eyes warmed to the sight of the high-stepping horses emerging from the darkness. "Are all those horses yours?"

Garrett smiled as if he had a secret. "No; I brought two. Many of my countrymen find that it is wise to introduce English bloodlines into their stock. We may be the ill-bred Americans you English claim, but we do recognize good bloodlines when we see them."

She ignored the encompassing look he gave her, concentrating instead on the unloading. She saw Trojan emerge and eagerly prance down the gangway. The great stallion seemed none the worse for wear after the voyage. The handler had difficulty keeping him under control once his hooves touched solid ground.

Garrett nudged her shoulder to get her attention. "Here's one you may be interested in." He pointed to the spirited golden-brown mare being led down the gangway.

"It's . . . it's Glory!" Her eyes widened until they were large amethyst pools. She forgot everything and threw her arms around Garrett's neck. She brushed her lips to his cheek, but he turned his head at the same moment, and their lips met. His arms tightened around her, and she found herself melting against him. For a brief moment, they were both lost in a sea of desperate

longing as the kiss intensified. Catherine was so overcome, she didn't realize that he had scooped her off of
her feet until he released her and set her down in front
of him. She opened her eyes and saw the light shining in
his and his mouth split in a wide smile. Only then did
she pull herself out of his arms. "I . . . I'm afraid I
have embarrassed us by such a display. Forgive me, but
seeing Glory was such a surprise."

His expression and the possessive arm around her
waist thrilled her. "I'm glad you like surprises." The
husky note in his voice told her that he felt she had just
made the first overture. Their impasse was over. The
past few days of tension had been miserable, and she
longed for them to end.

Not sure what to say, she asked where the horses
were going to be boarded. "At the hotel, until our
arrangements are made. Perhaps you can ride tomorrow. Until then, let's go to the hotel and get settled."
He allowed her time to croon to her mare and pet the
soft brown muzzle, and then she reluctantly walked
toward the carriage.

They rode through the streets of Charleston but had
not gone far when the carriage pulled to a stop before a
red brick building with a white pillared veranda stretching across the front. Chairs and tables were placed in
clusters, and many guests were sitting outside enjoying
the warm day while they played cards or sipped cool
drinks. Baskets of gaily blooming plants were suspend-
ed everywhere. "Houghton House" was inscribed in
gold letters across the portico.

"It looks quite elegant," Catherine declared enthusi-
astically, a tingling excitement making her voice lower
than normal.

"The best in Charleston, my love; and the food is
excellent. Let's get settled in our suite before we
venture into the dining room." The way he said "my

love" made her skin tingle. He escorted her through the lobby and checked in. Holding a large brass key in his hand, he pointed to the magnificent circular staircase that led to the rooms above.

"Will I have the chance to take that bath you promised?" Catherine slipped her arm through his as he informed her of his plans to check for passage on a ship for the remainder of their journey.

It was little more than an hour later when she stepped into a hot, bubbly tub set behind a screen in their suite. She sank into the steaming water blissfully, trying not to think about the evening ahead.

Their suite was as elegant as any in London. The sitting room was furnished in heavy mahogany pieces, and a Persian rug was laid upon the gleaming hardwood floors. Red velvet drapes hung at the wide windows, and several tasteful paintings stood out on the cream-colored walls. In the bedroom, a huge gilded mirror stood against one wall, reflecting a picture of a large brass bed covered with a royal-blue satin spread.

Catherine had unpacked a few things when a young black girl appeared to hang up her clothing while she made herself ready for the bath. The smell of lilacs caressed her skin as she sank beneath the bubbles. She used a large sponge to drip the perfumed water over her shoulders and down her back. It was heavenly! Her hair was pulled up by a pink ribbon, holding the golden tresses off her neck.

"That tub looks big enough for both of us." Garrett stepped out from behind the screen, his arms folded over his chest. His eyes roved her nakedness, tracing a line from her temple to the dark valley between her breasts hidden beneath the bubbles. She sank deeper into the water, blushing furiously.

"I did not expect you back so soon," she said warily,

watching his approach, her body quivering with both excitement and embarrassment.

"I need a bath, too, my sweet. Would you go to dinner in that elegant dining room downstairs with a man who hasn't had a decent bath in weeks?" He stood at the foot of the tub and bent to lift a few bubbles onto his fingers. He blew them softly toward the glowing skin of her shoulders and neck. A devilish gleam appeared in his eye as he scooped up another handful and walked behind her.

"Garrett!" she warned suspiciously. She could not turn to see what he was up to without disclosing more of her body to his gaze. When she felt the disentegrating bubbles fizz against her back, she gasped and tried to move away—too late—as he dribbled water across the back of her neck, which sent shivers down her spine.

"Shall I scrub your back for you, milady?" His voice was at her ear, his warm breath blowing the tendrils of hair at the side of her neck. The effect was devastating. Catherine felt warmth spread from her loins. "Or would you rather have me shampoo your hair? I've been told I have quite a knack for that."

She just bet he had! Probably innumerable ladies had been the recipients of his tender services. So she was just another in a long line of women! Forgetting that she was totally vulnerable beneath the surface of the water, she grabbed a soapy sponge and quickly threw it at his face.

He sputtered, water dripping from his chin and face onto the material of his shirt as she scrambled out of the water, lunging for a fluffy white towel. "Damn!" he cursed, having to keep his stinging eyes shut. He shook the water from his black hair and grabbed a towel from the bench, wiping his eyes. She made a dash to get past him, but he blocked her way.

"You asked for it." She backed one step, then two. There was a very calculating expression on his face, and the muscles of his arms rippled beneath his damp shirt. He snatched a trailing corner of her towel and began gathering the material in his hands, pulling slowly and steadily, forcing her toward him. If she tried to pull away, she would be totally exposed.

"You devil," she whispered.

"I told you I would act on the slightest sign of encouragement. You kissed me today, my sweet wife. You threw yourself into my arms. I found it more than encouraging." Desire darkened his eyes to the deep blue of the sea as his mouth quirked upward in a smile of pure enjoyment.

"You . . . you know I did not do that to encourage you. That . . . that's not fair!" She didn't dare drop the towel and run. He would catch her before she got anywhere, and she would be without even the tenuous safety of her towel. With one swift tug, he pulled her into his arms, letting the towel drop to the floor. His lips plundered hers while his hands roamed over her naked body. She squirmed in torment, not wanting him to know how deeply his touch affected her, turning her limbs to water and making her want to cling to him as if she were drowning.

His fingers played against her skin, burning wherever they touched. With no will left to withstand him, she pressed against him, needing to be closer. His mouth explored, drinking her sweetness, searching for more. When her hardened nipples pressed against his chest, he tore open his shirt to feel her softness against his flesh. The embrace was endless, a burning possession, as intimate as the final act of love.

When he abruptly pushed her away from him, a flush of triumph on his cheeks and the light of conquest in his eyes, she did not know how to react. She swayed before him, her breasts heavy with desire, her body burning, staring at him with eyes gone deep purple with longing.

"I knew you would appreciate any loophole I could discover in this ridiculous farce we have been playing," he said. "I should have found one long before this. Tonight we shall resume our honeymoon, and you will wish you could call back every damned frustrated evening of our voyage." He turned her around and gave her bare bottom an affectionate slap, then told her to get dressed for dinner.

Catherine ran into the dressing room and leaned against the door. It took several deep breaths to recover. His lips and hands had aroused her to such a fever pitch; she would allow him to take her in any way he chose. Nothing was worth another night of aching for his touch; not even her pride. She heard him splash into the tub she had vacated and start singing some outlandish ditty about the delights of love. She could feel the sensitive nerves beneath her feverish skin begin to quake. Nothing would stop their making love tonight; nothing.

She slipped on a lacy chemise and petticoat, then discarded gown after gown, finally settling on an aqua-blue silk. Her stomach seemed to be turning cartwheels as she dressed.

As the sound of Garrett's singing grew more triumphant, she brought her pulses under control. Well, my husband, it's not going to be quite that easy. You are going to have to woo me before I join you in that big brass bed. Although she had to admit that the first overture had been hers, she meant to find some way to dampen his crowing exultation to the extent that they could meet on common ground.

The many hooks up the back of her gown gave her a little trouble, but she finally managed to fasten them. A wide ruffle of ivory lace fell across her bosom, following a line just off her shoulders. Studying herself in the mirror, she decided it was just the right dress. Certainly not demure, but not overwhelmingly provocative, either. She brushed her hair until it gleamed and pulled it back from her face with gold combs studded with aquamarine stones. A matching necklace and ear studs completed the ensemble. After one last look in the mirror, she reached for the door leading to the bedroom. She quietly tiptoed past the screen where Garrett, hidden from view, still splashed and sang in the tub. She arrived in the sitting room and sat down to wait.

She heard him crossing the bedroom after dressing and struck an imperious pose before he entered. Garrett came in and caught his breath at the sight of her. A ray of waning sunlight fell on her hair, and her blue gown was spread on the chair like a cloud around her petite figure. She held herself stiffly in an attempt to appear unmoved, but that only made him smile. He knew he had better proceed carefully or he would lose the tenuous victory he had won with her today. The little witch was probably trying to figure a way out. He crossed the room and took her hand. Bending low, he brushed it lightly with his lips and looked deeply into her eyes. "You look lovely tonight, Catherine."

The expression in his eyes was disconcerting. Catherine tore her gaze away and stood up, striving to appear cool and calm as he escorted her to dinner.

They entered the dining room in silence, neither willing to chance ruining the evening by making a wrong remark. They were ushered to an intimate table by a window at the back, where they could enjoy a view of the pretty lawns. "Catherine, relax. Stop thinking so much and just react. We are going to have an enjoyable dinner and a leisurely stroll on the lawn, and then we will go back to our rooms, where a bottle of champagne will be waiting. I won't just leap on you like a rutting boar and take my pleasure. You know you will enjoy it, too, so stop looking like a martyr about to face the lions."

"I am not a martyr, but you misinterpreted my action this afternoon. It isn't fair, and you know it." She was quivering under the molten heat of his gaze.

Garrett raised his wine goblet and said huskily, "Whatever you say, my love. But you did touch me, and I'm willing to take that as an overture and begin again."

His sincere smile was almost her undoing, and she was relieved when their dinner arrived. She concentrated on the sumptuous meal but barely tasted it. She felt abnormally thirsty and quickly drained her wineglass. When a waiter moved to fill it, Garrett turned her goblet over. "Not tonight. I'm not going to allow you to claim drunkenness again." He smiled at her flaming cheeks.

"You never forget anything, do you?"

"Not when it's to my advantage to remember." He held her eyes, a smile lurking around his wide, sensuous mouth. She dropped her lashes and concentrated once again on her plate.

Chapter 8

In a tavern along the Charleston waterfront, several men took their seats around a large oak table. The circle comprised three military men: Colonel Thomas Moore, regular army; Commander Benjamin Little, US Navy; and Lieutenant Simon Mariner of the Texas Rangers on special assignment. They were joined by

two somberly dressed civilians. All of them drank ale
from tankards that were constantly kept full by a silent
old man who entered the darkened room from the
saloon out front.

Colonel Moore addressed the Ranger. "I think con-
gratulations are in order, Mariner. Today we received
the first shipment of the new revolvers from the Colt
company. Commander Little will load them on his
vessel tonight. You are in charge of their safety until
they reach the battle lines. Senators Whitfield and
Heets have assured me that you have the deepest
gratitude of the American government for this brave
undertaking. President Polk has been apprised and
sends you his personal best wishes for success. Are you
prepared to leave for the war zone?"

"I will need a few more days." Mariner was much
younger than the others assembled in the room. He was
of medium height, whipcord hard, and although no
woman would call him handsome, there was something
about the combination of sandy-color hair and mischievous green eyes that drew eager young women to him.
He felt contempt for the men he was with. Even the
President's message didn't excite him. They wouldn't
be facing Mexican guns. While he was moving the
shipment, they would probably be in some tavern
drinking ale and smoking fat cigars.

Mariner's casual disregard for authority rankled Colonel Moore, but there was nothing he could do about
it. The Rangers recognized no authority but their own.

"How many men are you taking? The more who
know of this, the less chance we have for secrecy."
Colonel Moore puffed steadily on his cigar, throwing a
reassuring look at the two senators through the smoke.

"I had a stroke of fortune today, gentlemen. The one
man who can ensure the success of our mission is in
Charleston. All I must do is convince him that he wants

to risk his life for the sake of a few boxes of guns."
Simon nodded to the guard at the door, and his tankard
was immediately refilled.

"Is this man a Ranger?" Moore asked.

"No, but he's the right man for the job. I'm just not
sure he will be willing to leave his new wife to help me.
I saw his name on a list of people wanting passage to
New Orleans. We go back a long way. I'll visit him later
tonight. Shall we get on with it?"

It was hours later that Simon obtained total agreement for his plan. He walked out into the night. He
could hardly wait to meet the woman who had trapped
an avowed bachelor like Garrett Browning. She had to
be someone special, Simon thought, with a grin that
gleamed until he disappeared into the dark shadows of
the waterfront.

Garrett and Catherine finished their dinner and took
a leisurely stroll through the flower-studded lawn behind the hotel. The strains of an orchestra floated
across the lawn. Garrett swept Catherine into his arms
and waltzed around a patio before he stopped to kiss
her tenderly. She melted into his arms and returned his
kiss, her fingers entwining in the hair at the back of his
neck. With a low groan, he raised his lips slightly and
whispered, "We had better go back to our room before
I drag you to those bushes and make love to you now."

She looked into the sapphire eyes of her husband and
thrilled to the tenderness she saw. The violet depth of
her eyes glowed with passion, and he was almost
overcome with need. He had waited much too long to
see that look in her eyes, and he cautioned himself to
guard every word he spoke between the garden and
their bed.

They reached their suite, and Garrett enveloped her

in his arms. His lips claimed her in a tender caress that deepened and became more demanding as she opened her lips to receive him. Every nerve in her body seemed to be on fire with longing. He released her mouth and brushed his lips lightly across her eyes, her temples, the tender skin of her throat. He gently unclasped her necklace, fingered the combs from her hair and ran his fingers through her freely flowing silken tresses.

"Spun gold," he whispered as his lips covered hers. His hands began roaming her spine, but she wasn't aware he had released the hooks of her gown until he pushed it off her shoulders. He held her close with one arm while his hand began a slow exploration of her breasts straining beneath her lacy chemise. Her gown slipped to the floor as his fingers deftly untied her petticoats, then returned to push her chemise down. It joined the growing mound of frothy clothing at her ankles.

He cupped her breasts. "These are glorious," he murmured, and pulled her to him. She knew nothing but him and the sensations of pleasure raging over her body. He pulled her tongue slowly into his mouth, and she found herself wanting to explore. She heard his moan of pleasure as she probed between his lips with her unpracticed tongue.

"Oh, Catherine . . . I . . ." He didn't finish but picked her up and walked swiftly through the bedroom door to lay her gently on the bed. His eyes never left hers as he removed his clothes. Her eyes were drawn to his flat belly and lean hips, and she could not look away when her stare brought his manhood to full prowess. She started to shake, but the minute he drew her into his embrace, she was aflame with her need for him.

He took his time, wanting to give her as much

pleasure as possible. He kept himself under tight control as he savored every inch of the willing body in his arms. He played with the white mounds of her breasts, bringing his mouth to one pink tip and then the other, watching her reaction as they rose and hardened. Her eyes were closed, but she was gasping for breath as he molded her pearly flesh with his hands.

Her hands brushed lightly across the muscles of his chest, reveling in the feel of the curling dark hair and smooth, burnished skin. Her soft hands descended down his chest and belly, but stopped when she heard him suck in his breath. He groaned at her lips, "Don't stop," but her innocence prevented her from going further. He grasped her hand and guided it to him. When her slender fingers enclosed him, he gasped, "Oh, God . . . yes . . . yes." He taught her how to caress him, then brought his hand to the golden triangle at the juncture of her thighs.

As his fingers stroked and caressed her womanhood, she strained closer, arching her back in response to his touch. He couldn't control his need for her any longer and covered her body with his, spreading her legs with one knee before joining their bodies. They were both swept away by the currents of desire that surged between them. Unable to withstand the stimulation of the soft body writhing beneath him, he drove deep within her, and she countered his every thrust. They reached the peak together. As she was swept away to a place she had never dreamed existed, Catherine's last thought was that she was going with the only man who knew how to get there.

Their ragged breathing returned to normal, and Garrett rolled to one side, pulling her gently into his arms, continuing to caress her almost absentmindedly as they lay intertwined. His fingertips traced lazy patterns down her back. Neither awake nor asleep,

Catherine felt as though she were floating on a warm cloud.

Simon sauntered into the Houghton House. The night manager looked at him with suspicious eyes, trying to decide if he had the authority to deny the unkempt man a night's lodging. He looked at the buckskin breeches, the muslin shirt, then made note of the leather holster strapped to the man's lean hips. The weapon looked large and dangerous, and suddenly the clerk knew he would not question the man's intentions.

"A friend of mine and his wife are guests of yours." Simon sized up the scrawny clerk with one glance. "The Brownings. Give me the number of their room."

"I . . . I don't know." Herbert Cook hesitated. He knew of the young couple. A gold coin dropped onto the desk, spiraling in circles before clattering to stillness. It was a twenty-dollar gold piece. Herbert no longer cared what business this man had with the Brownings. "Their suite is on the second floor. Number ten." He nodded toward the spiral staircase and palmed the coin.

"Appreciate it," was the terse response.

Simon walked up the staircase, the dimples in his tanned cheeks deepening as he thought about the surprise he had planned for Garrett. He thought of him as a brother. The day the Comanches had killed Simon's parents and Hunter Browning had brought Simon and his half-sister, Elena, to Tierra Nueva was the beginning of their friendship. Although Garrett was three years younger, they were well matched physically and mentally. Over the years, they had hunted, fished and fought with one another until Simon felt he knew more about Garrett than any man alive. Still, it was only Hunter Browning who could control Garrett's actions. Many times Garrett had proposed things so wild Simon had balked, but he had never been able to change Garrett's mind. Only Hunter had been able to do that.

Simon was saddened by Hunter's death. If he had not received a letter from Elena bemoaning Garrett's departure, he wouldn't know yet that the man who had been a father to him was gone. He knew very well that Garrett would forever miss the dynamic, granite-hewn man who had been his father.

Simon made no sound as he approached the thick door to Garrett's rooms and turned the handle. He knew it would be locked, but there was always the possibility that someone had forgotten to turn the key. He slipped his hand inside his shirt and withdrew a curious metal pick, which he placed into the keyhole. Seconds later, he silently pushed open the door.

He looked about the darkened room, trying to decide if his entrance had been discovered by his light-sleeping friend. His green eyes searched for the doorway to the bedroom. Garrett was certainly entertaining his wife in style. That surprised him. Garrett and his women were usually satisfied with a bed and an empty room. He hoped for the sake of the new Mrs. Browning that Garrett's womanizing days were over.

He stealthily crossed the sitting room and smiled at the pile of feminine clothing he encountered on the floor. Not too much had changed, he thought; only Garrett had married this one. He reached the door to the bedroom and paused to reach beneath his shirt to the sheath strapped below his shoulder. A gleaming blade flashed in the moonlight as Simon pulled his scarf over his mouth and nose. Crouching like an Indian, he entered the bedroom, waiting until his eyes adjusted to the darkness. He could see two figures sleeping peacefully on the bed. Luck was with him, for Garrett was lying on the side closest to him. Making no sound, Simon moved toward the bed, keeping his body low.

He was so close he could hear Garrett's steady breathing, the sound sleep of a satisfied man. Swallowing the laughter in his throat, he pounced. He pressed his blade to the side of Garrett's neck, pulling him up and pressing his knee into Garrett's back. He felt the instant contraction of the muscles along Garrett's spine but swiftly pulled Garrett's arm behind his back and jerked it up, pressing the Bowie knife at his throat. He could feel Garrett's hesitation. He had decided not to fight, probably because the tiny figure next to him might get hurt. Simon disguised his voice in a raspy whisper.

"Lady, you'd better light a lamp quick, or your man here is gonna die in the dark." He pressed the blade into Garrett's flesh as he felt him gear up.

There was a wild scrambling from the other side of the bed. When the lantern was lit, Simon saw Catherine standing by the bed, her tiny figure wrapped in a bed sheet. "Please, what do you want with us?"

Friend Garrett was a lucky man! The quivering voice held music.

Simon was so impressed with Garrett's petite blond wife, he wasn't concentrating on his captive, and before he knew it, Garrett had twisted out of his grasp and the knife was held at his own throat.

"You're getting rusty, Simon." Garrett was grinning down at him. Catherine's eyes widened in astonishment when the two men rolled off the bed and embraced, laughing. "What hole did you crawl out of?" Garrett hooted, reaching for his pants.

Simon pulled down his scarf, showing a flash of dimples.

"Couldn't believe it when I heard you got married.

Thought I'd better get a look at the gal." Simon bowed to Catherine, whose cheeks were flaming bright red. "Got a real beauty here, my friend. If I find a filly like this, I might take the plunge myself."

"Is . . . is," Catherine croaked, "this man a friend of yours? He . . . he tried to . . . he was going to kill us." The blood was finally rushing back into her arms and legs, allowing her to move.

Simon looked repentant. "Sorry, ma'am, for scaring you like that. Garrett can tell you I'm really quite harmless. Simon Mariner, Mrs. Browning. Pleased to meet you." He offered Catherine his hand, so honestly contrite that she took it. Discovering that she wasn't in any danger, she found she might actually like this outrageous man. He was shorter than Garrett, yet he, too, carried an aura of self-assurance and vitality. Were all Texans like this? So sure of themselves? So vibrantly alive?

Garrett and Simon grinned affectionately as they spoke, talking like brothers and remembering exploits of their youth with unbridled enthusiasm. Catherine was nonplussed. Simon's treatment of Garrett was a revelation to her. She had never seen her husband so relaxed or so boyishly pleased with anyone.

"Come on, Simon. Let's go outside and let my wife get dressed. This calls for a drink."

"Fine by me, Garr." Simon gave Catherine a less than brotherly look. "That outfit is fetching, but maybe your wife would like to return to bed. I doubt she's used to callers appearing at this time of night."

"There is a lot I'm having trouble getting used to," she said with a grimace, and then she relented at the rueful expression on Simon's face. He followed Garrett out of the bedroom but turned back for a second and threw her a wink over his shoulder. Unable to help it, she winked back. He nodded and grinned.

Simon was glad for Catherine's sense of humor, but still, he knew he would have been better off making a more conventional entrance. How the hell was he supposed to know that Garrett had married the most aristocratic-looking beauty he had seen in all his years? No wonder Garrett slept like a baby by her side. He had the damnedest luck.

Simon accepted the glass of whiskey Garrett held out. He gulped down the whole glass, while Garrett scooped up Catherine's clothing and tossed it into the bedroom. He needed something to quench the instant fire that burned in his loins. "Damn! What a looker, you lucky son of a bitch," he burst out. "You didn't find her in the places you usually look for women. By the sound of her, I'd say she's English. She sounds like your ma."

Simon saw Garrett's eyebrows shoot up. Why had he been fool enough to say something like that? Before he could attempt to extricate the proverbial foot from his mouth, Garrett said, "Yes, she's English, but there's a good reason for it. Let's drop it for now and talk about something interesting. What are you doing in Charleston, and what the hell is going on back home? I heard about the war on the damned ship coming across. If Pa had known what he was asking when he made me go to England at a time like this, he would never have done it."

"Hey, I was sorry to hear about Hunter, Garr. He was the best man I ever knew. Elena got word to me a couple of months ago, but it was too late to pay my respects."

"Thanks, Simon." Garrett paused for a moment, remembering. "What else did Elena say? Anything about how the boys were handling things? Did she mention the stock or the cotton crop?"

Simon made no comment about Garrett's abrupt

switch of subject. He knew Garrett felt his father's death deeply. The trip to England had probably done him a lot of good, helped him handle his grief away from the ranch and the memories. "She said everything was fine. She had gone into Austin with Jason and a few of the boys for supplies. You know how much she likes getting a new dress. That was the only news I got."

"How bad is it, Simon?" Garrett was pacing.

"We're doing well. A shortage of decent weapons and trained men is the biggest problem. The Mexicans are equipped with artillery from Europe, and they outnumber us, but they won't have the advantage long if we get some decent guns to our men." Simon gauged Garrett's interest. "You find passage home?"

"You know damned well I haven't. Galveston is closed except to naval ships. Private boats aren't allowed through the blockade, and the thought of going overland makes me cringe. The closest I can get is New Orleans. So what have you got, Simon, and what's my part in it?"

Simon burst out laughing. He would have begun his explanation, but Catherine joined them.

"Mr. Mariner. I apologize for my attire." She looked perfectly demure in the high-necked dressing gown, even though it was unlikely she had ever worn it in the presence of callers.

"I'm the one who is sorry, ma'am." Simon couldn't stop himself from staring. She looked sensational. "If I had known Garrett had married a lady instead of one of his . . ." Simon stopped, aghast. Good Lord! When would he learn to keep his mouth shut? He looked wildly at Garrett. Garrett seemed more annoyed with the interruption than with Simon's slip. "What I mean to say . . ." Simon stammered, "is that we don't find such beautiful ladies around here."

"I'm sure I understand what you were trying to tell

me, Mr. Mariner." There was no doubt that she was aware of Garrett's reputation. "Please call me Catherine," she continued politely in her soft, low voice, "since you and my husband are such close friends." Simon winced and felt like a complete heel.

He pulled at the collar of his shirt, uncomfortable in the extreme. "I guess you think we have a mighty strange way of showing it."

To his surprise, Catherine laughed. "I have often wished that I had the strength to confront him as you did tonight."

Simon returned her pretty smile, but he was aware of a strange tension that hung between the couple. Curious. Very curious.

"Simon would like to tell me a few things he's been up to lately. He's a Texas Ranger. You can go now." Garrett seemed to be ordering her.

Instead of following his terse command, she smiled provocatively at Simon and took a seat beside him on the settee. She glanced up at Garrett to gauge his reaction, and he couldn't quite hide his irritation.

"I'm sure you are tired, Catherine." He stared pointedly at the slight gap in her wrapper, drawing her attention to the glimpse of her legs she was affording Simon.

Catherine slid her fingers under the smooth satin and drew the edges together, but it didn't solve the problem and she wasn't about to reach down to cover her slightly exposed lower limbs. Garrett was behaving in a ridiculous fashion, and she didn't understand. Supposedly Simon was his best friend. "Tell me about yourself, Mr. Mariner."

Simon gulped, suddenly realizing that he was the cause of their unspoken battle. He tried to ease the tension by directing his attention to Garrett, but it had been a long time since Simon had shared a couch with a lovely woman dressed only in her nightclothes. He couldn't help letting his glance stray to the shapely legs beneath the thin wrapper. Unfortunately Garrett knew exactly how his wife was affecting his friend, and he was clearly annoyed.

"I'd better go." Simon stood up and addressed them both. "We can meet for breakfast."

Catherine stood, too, and held out her hand to him. Before he realized what he was doing, he had taken it and placed a kiss on the soft palm. A dull red flush crept up his neck when he saw Garrett's fist clench.

He hastily bid them good night and left, wondering what would happen when he was out of earshot. Neither the tiny, violet-eyed woman nor the tall, blue-eyed man seemed to notice his exit.

"Why were you so rude?" She brought up her chin.

"For God's sake, didn't you see the way he was looking at you? Even my best friend isn't immune." Garrett gritted his teeth. "Over here, if you so much as bat your lashes at a man, you'll be thrown into the nearest bush."

"It sounds to me like you were jealous."

"Just remember that I am your husband!"

Catherine flounced toward the bedroom. "I'll remember that you are my husband when you start treating me like your wife and not some doxie!" She slammed the door behind her.

Garrett winced and crossed the room. He grabbed the whiskey bottle he had shared with Simon and drained the contents with one swallow. Then, wiping his mouth with the back of his hand, he slumped into a chair. If she were a doxie, he wouldn't be jealous.

Chapter 9

As the naval ship steamed out of Charleston Harbor, Catherine watched the receding shoreline and wondered if she was seeing the last of civilization. Simon had promised a brief stay in New Orleans before they joined a wagon train heading west. The chosen route was supposed to keep them away from the battle lines and afford the fastest way to Tierra. The train would be filled with settlers bound for Oregon Territory, newly ceded to the United States by Great Britain. Promises of rich land free for homesteading were provocation enough for many farmers in the east to seek a better life for themselves and their families. Increasing taxes and the high cost of land were causing financial hardship to small landowners. The emigrants from the eastern seaboard were making their way in ever-increasing numbers through Nacogdoches in Texas to Bent's Fort in order to join up with other wagons from St. Louis and start over the dangerous Rocky Mountains on the Oregon Trail. The Browning wagon would separate from the train at Nacogdoches and proceed southwest to Austin and the Tierra Nueva ranch.

Their stay in Charleston was short because Simon procured passage for them on the naval ship going to the Mexican coast to unload supplies for the American army. Catherine had not been apprised of the details, but the strained look on Garrett's face indicated that he and Simon were keeping something back. As she leaned against the rail, she felt a shiver of fear. The war seemed closer, somehow. There were soldiers on board being transported to the American lines. Stacks of supplies and munitions lined the decks, making her feel like part of the war. Then she chided herself for letting her imagination get the better of her.

Soon the shore was but a distant line, and Garrett took her arm. "It's time to go below, Catherine. This is a military ship, and 'men are men. One woman on board is too much temptation."

They went to their cabin, and Catherine looked around in horror. "You expect me to stay here?" It looked more fitting for use as a closet. The berths extending out from one wall were the only furnishings. There was no mirror, washstand or wardrobe, not a single chair, and the walls were painted a dismal gray.

"This isn't a pleasure cruise. We were very lucky to get passage. It's a damn sight better than going overland. You'll find that out once we leave New Orleans." He grinned at her. "I can't say I think much of the sleeping arrangements. We'll have to figure something out."

"I will demand better accommodations. This cabin is no bigger than a horse stall."

"You'll demand nothing. You can sit on all those damned trunks. This cabin wouldn't be so small if we didn't have them to contend with."

"If I can't get satisfaction from you, then I'll go to the captain."

"If you so much as show your face outside this cabin without my permission, I'll drag you back by your hair. You'll do as I say."

"You can't expect me to stay in this black, stuffy hole for the entire trip. I'll go stark raving mad."

"If you behave yourself, I'll take you up on deck in the evenings."

Catherine intended a scathing retort, but just then Simon came in. The wide grin on his face disappeared when he saw their angry expressions.

"You could knock, Simon," Garrett declared.

"I guess I'm not used to having you married. Excuse me, Catherine. I'll try to remember next time that there is a lady in here."

"Yours is a welcome interruption. It's a relief to know there is one gentleman on board. Garrett would have me believe that every man on this ship is dangerous. He wants to keep me prisoner in this dismal cabin."

Garrett was distinctly annoyed when Simon answered, "Little lady, we'll just see what we can do. Garrett is right in saying you would be safer remaining below unless we accompany you. I'll be happy to escort you on deck whenever you wish. Commander Little will make things more comfortable in here. He also wants you to join him at the officers' table."

"How very kind of you both. I appreciate your concern for my welfare." She threw a venomous glance at Garrett.

"I'd appreciate it if you'd mind your own business, friend," Garret growled.

Unabashed, Simon asked Catherine if she'd like a tour of the ship. "Garrett can't expect to keep you all to himself down here." With a mischievous look, he offered her his arm, giving Garrett a blatant wink as they passed out the doorway.

Garrett kicked one of his wife's trunks in frustration. The pain that shot through his foot brought out a string of profanity that would have burned his young bride's ears.

Later that evening, Catherine dressed in a black gown shot with silver silk. Simon escorted her to dinner. He was enjoying his new role as her protector. Garrett seethed in angry silence. When he got Simon alone, he would pound the lovesick grin off his face.

"Commander Little," Catherine said graciously, "I

want to thank you for making our cabin more livable. I appreciate the washstand and wardrobe. Everyone is taking wonderful care of me." The audacious smirk she cast Garrett was intended to point out his shortcomings, and Simon picked up on it.

"Marriage to such a fine lady ought to smooth out Garrett's rough edges."

A glass broke, and Garrett emitted a muffled curse as a shard of his crushed goblet pierced his palm. The commander hastily called for a steward. Garrett wrapped a napkin around his hand and strode out of the room. "What an unfortunate accident. I'll see that the medical officer attends him." The commander's voice broke the shocked silence.

"Gentlemen," Catherine said, "if you will excuse me, I think I will make sure he is all right." She didn't want to venture within Garrett's reach any more than face the Mexican army, but her teasing had gone too far.

The commander escorted her back to their cabin, where they found Garrett soaking his hand in a washbowl. "Your wife was concerned, Browning. I trust your injury is not serious?"

"I'm fine, but I'll need my dear wife's assistance in bandaging this." He held up his hand, his eyes deep with temper. Commander Little nodded and returned to the officers' mess.

The silence dragged on for what seemed like hours. He finally beckoned to her with his injured hand. "Are you going to help me with this?"

She approached warily. He held out his hand, and she wrapped it with the torn strips of cloth he gave her. Her shredded cambric petticoat was discarded on the floor, and she knew he was just waiting for her to comment. "There." She finished the wrapping. "We had better return before our meal gets cold."

She moved to the door, but he had other ideas, grabbing her by the waist and swinging her around to face him. "You come between me and my best friend and you'll regret it."

Catherine stood shaking in his grasp, all the color draining from her face. She murmured in a strangled voice, "You don't scare me."

He looked incredulous, the black rage in his face replaced by open astonishment. He lay back his head and laughed out loud at her ludicrous comeback. "You may be short on sense, but no one would accuse you of cowardice." Before she could stop him, he kissed her soundly. She looked up at him, feeling bereft when he released her bruised lips. "Oh, no, don't use those eyes on me. I'm working up an immunity."

"I don't know what you mean," she said, still affected by his kiss.

"Heaven help me if you ever do," he remarked dryly, and took her arm. She was still bemused when they joined the waiting officers. Simon looked up and made a poor attempt to hide a knowing grin. She darted a quick look at Garrett, who didn't try to hide his smug expression. Coloring, Catherine remained subdued for the remainder of the meal.

The self-satisfied expression remained on his face as they returned to their cabin. She watched apprehensively as he began removing his clothes. He caught her look and judged exactly what she was thinking. "Go to bed, kitten. We've had enough excitement for one day. You can have the top bunk."

After she had undressed and slipped on her nightgown, she made several unsuccessful attempts to reach the upper berth. She was startled when he scooped her up from behind and tossed her into it. "I sometimes forget how little you are," he said as he disappeared beneath her and stretched out on the lower berth.

"I'm not little." She sounded petulant, not liking the cold emptiness of the berth.

"Are you asking for something, Kate?" She could hear the amusement in his voice.

"Of course not!" she snapped, hating herself for letting him know she missed him.

"Too bad." She heard him chuckle and turn over on his bunk.

In the middle of the night, she woke up shivering. It was June, but the air in the cabin was frigid. The vessel was rocking turbulently, and she could hear a high wind screaming outside, rushing the sea. A loud groan shook the creaking timbers of the ship, terrifying her.

"Garrett?" She whispered his name softly, then screamed when the next swell tossed her against the cold outside wall where the sea splashed fiercely at the porthole. When his hands slid underneath her shaking body and lifted her out of the bunk, she clung to him. "Are we going to sink?" She couldn't lift her face from the security of his chest.

"Just a storm, little one," he reassured her, taking her with him to his berth and settling her on top of him. She curled up in the safety of his arms, warming herself with his nearness. "I'm glad you don't weigh much." He struggled to get comfortable beneath her. "At least one of us will sleep tonight."

The next morning Catherine didn't stir when Garrett eased himself from underneath her and stiffly pulled on his clothes. He joined Simon on deck.

"Have you told Catherine you're leaving her behind, Garrett?"

"I plan to make that announcement when we get to New Orleans. Do you think the Mexicans will come so far inland as to stop us?"

"There's always that possibility. I've heard that our old friend Torres is leading a group under Canales. They've been raiding pretty far north. Torres's father still runs that spread up by Tierra. He could be using his pa's place as a base of operations."

"Why don't we just stay on board until Galveston? It would be a lot closer."

"We have to sneak those guns past our own army, and with communications so slow, I don't know where the Mexican lines are by now. For all I know, they could have regained ground, and we'd have their army to contend with, too."

"All the same, this seems the long way around."

"I know, but the way things are, there really isn't any other way. We'll be out on our own until Nacogdoches; then we'll pick up a Rangers escort."

Garrett shrugged his shoulders. "What were you going to do if we hadn't shown up?"

"I was lucky," Simon admitted. He gave Garrett a sidelong grin. "Hell, I don't know."

"Can you use another man in your outfit?"

"You know it. It might be fun having you under my command. If we had joined up together, you'd probably outrank me. Remember that day, Garr?"

They had sneaked away from the ranch at night so that Hunter wouldn't catch them. But he had followed and lassoed and dragged Garrett from his saddle as they rode past a line of trees. By the time Simon had dismounted, Garrett was sprawled on his stomach and Hunter was trussing him up like a calf for branding. The big man completely ignored his son's curses.

"You leavin' us, Simon?" Hunter had asked.

"I'm joining up, sir. Garrett and me thought Governor Houston's Rangers needed us more than the ranch." He mutely apologized to Garrett while Hunter plucked him up from the ground and threw him over the back of his horse.

"Fine, Simon. A noble gesture. 'Course, Garrett's got responsibilities at home." He had taken his leather quirt and lashed Garrett hard across the rump, which sent the well-trained horse galloping back to Tierra. Hunter turned to Simon and offered his hand.

"Please, sir. Garrett will kill me if I go without him."

Hunter had looked at him with affection. "Garrett's sixteen, Simon. He'll get over it. You are a man and can make your own decisions."

Simon rode off and heard later that Garrett had received a thorough dunking in the horse trough to cool him off.

"You never miss an opportunity to remind me of that, do you?" Garrett said as he shrugged good-naturedly.

"You have the same responsibilities now, Garr. Would you trust your brothers with Tierra for the length of the war?"

"That's a decision I'll make after I get back home." Garrett turned his back to the water and leaned against the rail. "Since when did you turn into such a mother hen?"

"Since when did you—" Simon broke off when Catherine spoke.

"Good morning, gentlemen. Were you waiting for me, or have you had breakfast?" Both men looked at each other; Simon smiled and Garrett frowned.

"What do you think you're doing up here? You are not to leave that cabin unescorted." Garrett ignored Simon's speaking glance.

"What were you going to do? Leave me down there

to starve to death?" Catherine turned to Simon with a devastating smile. "Simon isn't angry. As you can see, I arrived safely."

Simon returned her sunny smile but felt guilty that she was unaware of the facts. He wondered if she would accept being left in New Orleans until their mission was completed and Garrett could return to fetch her. She would be safe, but he doubted that she would appreciate Garrett's concern when it would mean a long, lonely separation. Before he could say anything, however, Garrett took Catherine's arm and propelled her below to the officers' mess.

The day before their ship reached New Orleans, Catherine noticed a disturbing change in the behavior of both men. Every word they spoke seemed laced with serious undertones. They were seated around the officers' table after breakfast. Simon and Garrett were drawing pictures of hills and rivers on pieces of paper. In their absorption, they ignored her completely. It wasn't fair. She would be as much a part of this journey as they were, and she was just as interested in the details.

"Garrett?"

"Mmm?" He barely gave her a glance, continuing to pore over the map in front of him.

"May I see that?" She reached for a corner of the paper he was drawing on. When her hand touched it, his brows rose. "I want to see that," she repeated.

"Why? You don't know anything about the routes we plan to take," he drawled absentmindedly.

"Well, I should know, since I'm going to be on them." She pounded her fist on the table.

"You'll be safe, if that's what's worrying you." Garrett's tone was dismissing, and he lowered his head back to his drawing. Simon leaned back in his chair and folded his hands over his chest, waiting for the next round.

"That is not what is worrying me!" She pulled the paper from under his hand. "I can read a map as well as you. What does this X mean by Nacogdoches? Isn't that where we leave the rest of the wagons and start toward Tierra? And then this trail you show leading toward Mexico and this line going toward that river. Who is going to Mexico?"

Simon answered her. "I'm going to Mexico, Catherine."

She wasn't satisfied. "Simon, why would you travel all the way up north with us when you could continue on with this ship and land at Matamoros, closer to your Rangers unit?" She heard Simon's sharp intake of breath and saw the strange exchange of glances between the two men. "What are you keeping from me? I demand to know right now! I have a right to know what you are planning."

"No, you don't." Garrett tried to dismiss her again by returning his attention very deliberately to the drawing.

His curt retort and furrowed brow made her even more suspicious. She spoke a trifle louder. "I am going with you on this trip." Her words fell into a pool of silence. She glanced at Simon and saw him lean back farther in his chair and begin to stare at the ceiling. "Garrett?" she demanded.

"You had better tell her, Garr." Simon's displeasure at having to make this request was apparent in his tone.

Garrett looked up slowly from the map, his face wry. He shot Simon a piercing glare and muttered, "I've no choice now." In a measured voice, he said, "For your own safety, Catherine, we are going to leave you behind in New Orleans for a while. We have gotten involved in a mission for the army that is too dangerous to drag you into."

"What kind of mission?" She took a seat next to Garrett at the table, looking him straight in the eye. He looked slightly uncomfortable under her scrutiny. "We are kind of smuggling guns to some Rangers in Nacogdoches."

"Kind of? You are smuggling or you are not. Are you involved in something illegal?" A chilling fear gripped her as she saw the speaking glance exchanged between the two men. "Garrett?"

"Catherine, the less you know about this, the better off you will be. I don't want to tell you any more. If anyone has reason to question you, you won't be able to tell anything." He stared at her with a hopeful expression. "Can you make do with that?"

"No. Whatever you are doing, I want to be with you," she said softly, trying to cover her apprehension. He took her hand, rubbing the palm as if unsure how much he should admit.

"Tell her, Garrett. We can trust her." Simon went to the door and checked outside. "There's no one about."

Garrett took a deep breath before he began. "A new, repeating, six-shot revolver has been developed. There is a shipment of these guns on board this ship en route to Matamoros. We plan to switch the crates of guns with others loaded with wood, and when our belongings are unloaded from this ship, the guns will be among them. Simon and I will join the wagon train, and we will deliver the guns to a troop of Rangers waiting outside Nacogdoches. Our green army boys are more familiar with plows than revolvers. These new weapons are going to where they can do the most good."

Catherine was stunned. No wonder they had both been exhibiting so much tension since leaving Charleston. They were stealing from their own army! She was terrified by the thought of what might happen to them if they were caught. Her expression must have been easy for Garrett to read, because he took her hands and squeezed reassuringly. "Some of the top men in the military know of the switch, Catherine. Even President Polk has given us his blessing. The Rangers can do more damage to the Mexicans in one week than the regular army could do in months. The best men are getting the weapons first, that's all. No one will suspect until we are well on our way to Texas. By that time, it will be too late to come after us, and our only concern will be to stay away from Mexican irregulars."

"As soon as they open those crates, they'll know it was the two of you who made the switch!" Catherine's voice rose, and Garrett warned her to keep it down.

"This is supposed to be a secret, Catherine. Commander Little knows all about it but is supposed to pretend surprise when the exchange is uncovered. It should look as if someone made the exchange on his own. Why should they suspect us? We're not the only civilians on board."

Catherine's expression was grave as she queried, "Everyone knows we are recently married and on our way home to Tierra, don't they?"

"Yes. So?" Garrett didn't look the least bit worried about the implications of her question. She pressed on, surprised that two such thorough men had not thought of the obvious.

"Why would a newly married man taking his wife home to Texas leave her behind while he joins a wagon train?" She chose her words carefully, making sure that her question sounded logical and not critical. She knew that Garrett was sincerely concerned for her safety. She had overheard enough conversations about the vicious bands of marauding *guerrilleros* to understand and appreciate his reluctance to involve her.

Both men looked incredulous. Garrett eventually tried to shrug off her question, but she could see the worry in his eyes. "I doubt anyone will check up on us after we leave the ship."

"What if the exchange is discovered sooner than Matamoros? The army commander on board this ship will force Commander Little to return to New Orleans, and all the civilians who were transported will be investigated. He would soon discover that you and Simon joined a wagon train heading for Nacogdoches and that I wasn't with you. How long will it take them to track me down? How many hotels will they have to search to locate me? My accent makes me stick out like a sore thumb."

"Not only your accent," Simon muttered grimly from the door.

"Catherine! I can't take you with us. You must see that." Garrett stood and began to pace. "No. It is much too dangerous. If we are attacked, they will . . . Simon, you know what they will do."

Simon came away from the door and stood staring down at the map on the table. "I don't want to endanger Catherine, either, but she would add more credibility to our trip," he said quietly.

"Simon!" Garrett shouted, then flushed when Simon rushed over to the door and looked outside. Garrett looked at Catherine, who was silently waiting for him to give her the only possible answer. Simon had already reached the right conclusion.

"The mission will be less likely to be detected if I go with you," she offered tentatively, waiting for the explosion of temper that never came. Garrett didn't say a word. His expression was harsh, and there was a savage anger in his eyes that was not directed at her but at himself. Catherine knew that she would not be left in New Orleans. The country Garrett loved was at war, and the fact that she was his wife and he wanted her safely out of it was not enough grounds to jeopardize their mission—a mission that might mean a shorter siege with the enemy and less loss of human life.

"No." There was restrained violence in his voice, and his eyes were like metal. "I don't want to involve you. Damnit, Simon, there must be some other way!"

"There's no time, Garrett. We arrive in New Orleans tomorrow, and the wagon train pulls out two days later. We could hire some woman to impersonate Catherine, but anyone who has caught a glimpse of her would be able to tell it wasn't Catherine in a second. She isn't exactly a woman you forget." Simon shrugged his shoulders and looked at Catherine solemnly, apology for once in his serious green eyes.

She wanted to erase the misgiving on their faces. She was an intelligent woman and would do her utmost to ensure their success. If anything did happen to them, Catherine wanted to be there, not hear of it from a stranger. "It will be all right. I know it will," she stated bravely. She knew they weren't ready to talk about this new twist in their plan, so she walked to the door. "I'll be in our cabin."

She waited for Garrett's nod, smiled weakly at Simon and left them to work out the frustration her logical suggestion had inspired.

Neither man spoke for several moments after she left the room. Garrett lit a cheroot and stared at the rising blue smoke with unseeing eyes. Simon sat down next to him, feeling helpless sympathy and a good deal of guilt for involving Garrett in the first place. Why hadn't he thought about the consequences of leaving Catherine in New Orleans? She was totally correct in her assessment of the situation. If she were plain and spoke with a Texas drawl, they might have pulled it off. If she weren't so intelligent, they might have convinced her to stay in New Orleans. "I'm really sorry, Garr. I ought to be shot with the damned guns that got you into this mess."

"Forget it." Garrett exhaled another breath of smoke, then ground his cheroot savagely into a tray. "She's too smart by half. Why in hell didn't I realize that? She's right! If I leave her behind, we'll be the first people they check. What are the odds that they'll discover the switch early?"

"We can't take any chances," Simon said, harshly condemning himself.

"If anything happens to her . . ." Garrett trailed off, a picture in his mind too painful to contemplate.

"Have you told her how you feel?" Simon asked.

"No, and I don't plan to. Don't change the subject. You think we have a good chance of getting through to the Rangers with no trouble?"

"Security has been tight all the way along. The Mexicans have agents all over, but I think we are in the clear on this one. They will never expect weapons to be hauled north when the action is south of the Rio Grande. We will make sure that even if we are caught— by our side or theirs—everyone will know that Catherine had no part in it."

"You don't know my wife. She's got guts, Simon. She may look defenseless, but you haven't seen how she's handled everything I've dished out." Garrett's voice grew husky, and he emitted a low laugh. "Thank God her brother isn't here. We would have both of them telling us our business."

"Hope to meet him someday. You said he was like Robbie?" Simon was sorry they had diverged from the subject of Catherine. It was strange that a man as intuitive as Garrett wasn't aware of his own emotions. He spoke about his wife with feelings that were apparent to everyone but himself. No, not everyone. Catherine seemed to suffer from the same lack of insight. Simon listened to Garrett's story of his first encounter with Colin Maxfield with amusement. "Sounds like your wife's an expert horsewoman. That should help her adjust to life on Tierra." Simon brought the conversation back to the topic Garrett wanted to avoid. "We've been friends a long time. Can't you see that you've finally met your match?"

Garrett looked pained, and Simon shook his head. "I think it's wonderful, pal."

"There is nothing wonderful about it," Garrett burst out. "I don't like loving a woman, Simon. It's eating me. Any minute now I'm going to get down on my knees and beg her to love me in return."

"She already does, my friend," Simon said seriously, pouring himself and Garrett a shot of whiskey. "Drink up. I can think of worse fates and don't keep comparing Catherine to your ma. I don't see any resemblance at all."

Garrett took the offered glass and gulped down the burning liquor. "I wish I could believe that," he muttered and stood up. "I'm going down to make sure she understands what she's letting herself in for."

Simon nodded, watching him leave before picking up his glass and pouring himself another drink. He solemnly vowed to stop flirting with Catherine. Garrett had enough problems without that.

Chapter 10

They docked in New Orleans. Catherine was glad to say
good-bye to the cramped naval ship, even if it meant
embarking on a dangerous trip. Garrett and Simon
deposited her like so much excess baggage in a back-
street hotel, with strict orders to stay put while they
made arrangements for the wagon that would carry
them to Texas. They would return when the guns had
been safely deposited in the false bottom of their
Conestoga. After waiting for two hours, Catherine
became increasingly desperate for freedom. She had
already endured weeks of confinement at sea, and she
could not bear to be cooped up a moment longer.

Rebelliously she picked up her reticule and walked
out of the hotel room. She was ravenously hungry, and
if they did not spare her a thought, she would fend for
herself. She walked into the dining room and brazenly
asked for a table. When the waiter looked askance at
her lack of escort, she pointed to a young man at a table
near a window and said, "I am expected." She walked
past the suspicious waiter and over to the occupied
table.

"Excuse me," she said politely. "I am afraid I have
done something very foolish, and I am wondering if
you would help me."

The man looked up, showing a pale, boyish face with
steady brown eyes. A smile broke over his pleasant
features as he stood up. "My dear young lady, your
voice is like music to my ears after months in this
country. Sir Randall Peyton, at your service." He rose
and bowed slightly as he introduced himself.

Catherine's eyes widened in astonishment—a fellow countryman! "Sir Randall, I cannot find words to express my gratitude. To think that I would find an English gentleman in New Orleans is quite beyond belief." She had not realized until this moment how much she missed her homeland. Sir Randall's clipped English accent and very correct manner were a welcome balm, but at the same time, they increased her feelings of homesickness. He invited her to join him.

The hours passed quickly as they shared a meal and several cups of fragrant English tea. Upon Peyton's admission that he had attended Eton, Catherine told him about Colin and how very much she missed him. Then their conversation shifted to reflections on America and Catherine's imminent trip to Texas.

Peyton was visiting a distant cousin but would be leaving soon to return to England. Realizing that she could send a letter home with him, Catherine asked him to come to her room. Seated at a small table, she quickly wrote down her thoughts about America, recollections of her voyage and reassurances about her health. Peyton slipped her letter inside his coat and reached out to kiss her hand as he stood up to leave.

"Who the devil are you?" Garrett's voice cut across the room. Catherine gasped, rushing to Peyton to protect him from the light of battle evident on Garrett's face. Simon came to a standstill behind Garrett.

"This is Sir Randall Peyton, a countryman of mine," she declared.

Peyton hesitated as Catherine politely walked him to the door, thinking she would introduce her husband, but she did not. She was eager to usher the Englishman out of the room before any violence occurred. She stood with Peyton in the hall, apologizing for her husband's lack of manners. Every word was heard by the men inside, and she tried not to flinch when she heard something crash into a wall. Assuring her that he would deliver her letter to Bannerfield, Peyton made short work of his leave-taking.

Simon swiftly shuffled out the door when Catherine came back inside, her face a picture of righteous indignation. "How dare you treat an English gentleman in such an abominable manner!"

Garrett's mouth was working, but no speech came forth. Catherine stood her ground, impatiently waiting for an explanation of his behavior. "Are you going to apologize or not?" she asked, her fists clenched at her sides.

"Apologize?" Garrett picked up a vase and threw it. "I'm not gone more than three hours and—"

"Six hours!" Catherine corrected vehemently. "If anyone has anything to complain about, I do." She fell back a pace when he made a grab for her, missing her by less than an inch. "I didn't say one word about our mission, so stop behaving like an enraged bull." He gave her absolutely no credit for being a sensible woman. She faced him defiantly, holding up her chin.

When her eyes locked with his, she realized that he had not been thinking about their mission at all. Her lip began to tremble, and she instinctively backed away. "I . . . we merely shared a meal and a pot of tea in a very public dining room."

"Just what else did you share, my dear wife?" He didn't give her the chance to answer before continuing his accusations. "You should have used more sense than to bring your lover to our room!"

"My lover! Garrett Browning, Sir Randall was in this room merely a few moments, waiting for me to write a letter to Colin. He quite kindly offered to carry it to England for me."

Catherine's eyes were flashing fire as dangerously as Garrett's. The two stood glaring at each other, neither wavering. Garrett's fists were clenched, and he looked as if he wanted to strike her. Instead, he slammed his fist into his palm, stalked out the door and violently jerked it closed behind him.

That night she refused to speak to Garrett, and he met her with a sullen glare. The atmosphere got even colder when Garrett tersely informed Catherine that her wardrobe was being given away because there was no room for it in the wagon. He replaced her trunks with a bundle of clothing and dared her to say something. She didn't give him the satisfaction.

When they climbed into the canvas-covered wagon the next morning, Catherine was wearing an ugly brown dress made of homespun cotton. A wide-brimmed straw hat was crammed on her head, and a cotton kerchief hung around her neck. She felt like some poor homesteader's wife. But her transformation was nothing compared to Garrett's. He wore a pair of leg-hugging breeches, a muslin shirt and a wide-brimmed hat. Slung about his lean hips was a leather holster and a lethal, long-barreled revolver. A knife was sheathed and strapped to his thigh. He looked untamed and dangerous, and she was both attracted and afraid.

"Ready?" he asked as he took up the reins, turning back to make sure Simon was ready to pull out.

She didn't answer, glaring at the mocking glint in his eyes. He knew very well what she was feeling. He had not said a civil word to her since the incident with Peyton, and she was surprised when he started talking about their surroundings and pointing out points of interest along the road.

"Stop sulking, Kate."

"You had no right to humiliate me with jealous

accusations that you know are completely unfounded." The hours of frustration pushed the hot words from her throat.

"Perhaps you're right." He gave her a grin that made the breath catch in her throat. "I should have made love to you instead. Someday I'll take you in a way you won't ever forget."

"I won't forget anything about you, Garrett Browning—not in a thousand years."

He threw back his head and laughed, but she sensed that her answer had touched him. His eyes softened, and his lips curled into a slight smile. She felt compelled to say, "You needn't look so sure of yourself."

"Catherine, with you, never being sure is half your attraction. The day I discover there are no more surprises is the day you'll have to worry about." He gave a light slap on the reins, and the mules quickened their pace. "I suppose you still want an apology for my behavior last night. I am sorry, Catherine."

A few miles before they reached the wagon-train encampment, Simon veered off to come in from a different direction. They would begin this journey like strangers.

It was almost nightfall when they drew the wagon within the circle of the others. Garrett jumped down and stretched his long body. "I'd forgotten what it feels like to drive a team of mules for any length of time. Climb down, Catherine."

"How many wagons are there?" The fading light made it difficult to discern more than shadows.

"About fifteen, twenty wagons, I think. Stay here while I go talk to the wagon master. You could arrange our blankets under the wagon. We'll be up at dawn tomorrow, and that means we go to bed early."

She had never risen at dawn in her life! She dared not complain, for she had volunteered to come, but she wondered what other surprises she was in for. Climbing into the back of the wagon, she found provisions stored there and tried to convince herself that she was going to enjoy this trip into the wilderness.

It wasn't long before she heard Garrett coming back. He had someone with him. She jumped down from the wagon and found a small group of people gathered around a newly laid campfire.

"Kate, these are our new neighbors from the next wagon." Garrett drew her beneath his arm as he introduced her to the weatherbeaten couple. Catherine winced when her hand was gripped tightly, first by the man, Charles Amory, and then by his wife, Abby.

"Glad to meetcha, ma'am," Mr. Amory volunteered. "You settlin' in Oregon, too?"

"No, we'll only be going as far as Texas. We have a place there. We were married in England and I'm taking Catherine home," Garrett answered, and the two men fell into a discussion of the ranch in Texas.

Abby Amory put a thin arm around Catherine and gave her a hearty squeeze. "You call me Abby, honey. Us womenfolk have to get close. My, but you're a pretty little thing. Ain't she pretty, Papa? My Molly ought to learn ladylike ways from you." She called out, and the girl she had mentioned came shyly forward. She was about fourteen, with carrot-color hair tied in two pigtails and a pert, freckled face with blue eyes. Molly was as thin as her parents, and her dress hung on her like a sack.

"Pleased to meetcha, ma'am." She didn't meet Catherine's eyes but traced circles in the dust with her toe.

"I am pleased to meet you, Molly, and you too, Abby." Catherine smiled at them, all the while wondering if she would look as old and worn out as Abby Amory someday. The only thing pretty about Abby was her eyes. They were a deep, sparkling gray with thick, curling lashes, full of warmth and good humor.

After they parted, Garrett walked Catherine back to the wagon. She could still hear the Amorys as they got ready to bed down for the night. "Don't you think we should move a little farther away from them?" Catherine whispered, sure the Amorys could hear them as easily.

"Why? Afraid our neighbors will hear us rolling around under the wagon and come to the right conclusions?" He grinned at her while he untied the horses. She followed him as he unhitched the stock and led them to the rope corral. She certainly did not want anyone to know what she and Garrett enjoyed in their private moments together. If anyone heard her moaning with pleasure during the night, she would die of embarrassment. Either he moved their wagon out of earshot, or she would sleep inside and he could sleep outside. As soon as they were far enough away from the wagon circle, she made her wishes clear.

"The wagons are pulled close together for safety. You'll soon get used to hearing the sounds of people living together. Believe me, ours won't be the only cries you'll hear during the night." He didn't look in the least disturbed.

He marched her back to the wagon after he had finished feeding the animals and told her she could undress inside if she wanted. She certainly was not about to strip off her clothes in the open. She searched and searched through the bag he had brought, but didn't find any nightwear. He couldn't mean for her to sleep outdoors in the nude? Could he? She almost burned her fingers lighting the lantern, but she still didn't find anything to put on. Garrett heard her shuffling through the wagon, pulling down boxes and reaching inside every bag.

"How long is this going to take?" He stuck his head inside the hole formed by the flaps of the white canvas stretched over the wagon.

"What have you brought for me to sleep in?" she demanded. He drew his brows together as he considered her question. When his brows shot up and his expression turned rueful, she sprang to her feet.

"Honest, Catherine, I didn't mean to do it, but I forgot you can't go to bed without one of those damn long gowns. You never wake up with them on, anyway. No one will see you under our blankets. It's hot in there; come outside."

She was very hot, but it had little to do with the stuffy interior of the wagon. When he saw that she had no intention of complying, he untied the flaps at the back and jumped up. "Listen, tomorrow I'll see if I can locate a nightgown for you. You can sleep in your underclothes for one night—there are certainly enough layers under your dress. It's late and I'm tired. I don't want to put up with any more of this nonsense."

Having little choice, Catherine pulled off her dress and left her chemise and petticoat on. "Isn't the ground hard?" she asked as he lifted her down. The cool night air felt wonderful compared to the hot, stagnant atmosphere inside the wagon, but sleeping on the bare ground seemed heathenish.

"Remember, you insisted on coming. Changed your mind?" When she shook her head, he said with a smile, "You'll get used to it." This seemed to be his answer for everything. He pulled her with him as he ducked under the wagon. Catherine lay watching as he took off his boots and pants and unbuttoned his shirt. They nestled under the blanket, trying to smooth out the wrinkles beneath them and pat down the lumpy ground that was their bed. Hard? Catherine felt as though she were lying on a bumpy, scratchy mattress filled with rocks.

"We'd be much better off in the wagon," she fumed, twisting and turning to find a place that didn't stab her. She gasped when Garrett pulled her bodice off her shoulders and down to her waist. "No . . . don't. . . ." she breathlessly murmured as his hands worked down her body and bared her completely.

"I told you, you wouldn't need a nightgown," he whispered back. As always, she succumbed to his special brand of magic, eventually unable to keep the moans of passion inside. He rolled on top of her and burst inside her with explosive desire. She lay panting, trying to regain her breath, when she heard footsteps pass alongside their wagon.

"Sorry, folks, just checkin' my mules. Got one with a bad leg," the voice said calmly as the footsteps receded.

"Oh!" Catherine brought her hands over her heated face. She felt Garrett's lungs expand and contract with silent laughter before he chuckled out loud in her ear. His laugh brought a chorus of additional good nights from the Amory wagon, and Catherine wanted to sink into the hard ground beneath her.

Garrett rolled to the side. "I promise," he whispered, "tomorrow we'll move farther off. This audience is more than I bargained for." He helped her pull her petticoat back up her legs but spoiled his own efforts to gain her forgiveness by slapping her hands away when she tried to bring the straps of her chemise over her shoulders. He slipped his hand inside her gaping bodice and closed it over one breast. "If I can't feel all of you, I'll settle for this," he said in her ear. "Now go to sleep, as I intend to do."

Catherine waited until his breathing became regular, then pushed his hand away, but before she could move out of his reach, he brought his arm up underneath her bosom and her chemise was caught by its weight. Her cheeks burned as a shaft of moonlight gleamed across her bare shoulders, but he wouldn't release her from his possessive embrace. Giving up, she drew the blanket up and went to sleep.

In the gray light of dawn, Garrett woke her, and they got ready to leave. Breakfast was a few bites of dried fruit, for, impossible as it seemed, they had overslept. The others were ready to pull out. Garrett shrugged off their comments about newlyweds, but Catherine couldn't look at anyone.

By mid-morning, the dust from the trail was coating her face like a mask. Her mouth felt gritty, and she longed to cool herself in the sluggish water of the Mississippi River that flowed lazily beside the road. The broad, grassy banks promised cool comfort as one hour passed to two and then three. She was beginning to feel like one condemned. Every jar of the wagon was an uncomfortable shock to her spine. Her fingers, clamped tightly on the seat, were sore and full of splinters. The sun beat steadily upon her arms, and her delicate skin was beginning to burn. Surely they would stop soon and have their midday meal.

"Garrett, when do we rest? It must be past noon."

He squinted his eyes at the sun and pulled down the brim of his hat. "The sun is high, so I expect we'll stop soon. The animals are tiring and will need to rest." It was a simple statement that expressed concern for the animals but not for her.

"Garrett, we have to eat. Stop now and let us at least have tea. The others must be as hungry as I."

"You should have stayed in New Orleans if you wanted to enjoy afternoon tea. This train is in a hurry to get West, and so am I. We won't be stopping any

more than we have to. Our midday stop will last long
enough to rest and water the animals. You'll be so busy
helping carry water for them that you won't have time
to brew tea. We'll grab something cold to eat and then
be on our way."

Catherine was to learn that human comfort was
always of secondary importance. The noon stop was
brief. Catherine's arms and shoulders ached with strain
from carrying the heavy water buckets to the thirsty
mules. She stretched out on some cool grass under a
willow tree and closed her eyes.

Garrett's voice roused her from her too-brief respite.
"Time to get moving. Come on, climb up here—unless
you'd prefer to walk alongside the wagon."

She pushed her damp hair back from her face,
brushed the grass from her skirt and slowly made her
way back. She was barely seated when the plodding
pace of the mules began again. She had never worked
so hard for so little reward.

Garrett tossed her a heavy cotton pouch and told her
it was their lunch. She opened it and inspected the
contents. "It's disgusting."

"It's jerky, and pretty good if you chew it slow. Get
me a cup of water from the barrel inside. Pour yourself
some, too, because jerky is salty. If you don't want
your belly to swell, don't eat or drink too much." He
grabbed a long strip and grasped it between his strong
teeth. He ripped off a piece and started chewing.
Catherine's hunger overcame her repugnance, and she
gave the leatherlike meat a try. It was not bad-tasting;
at least it would keep her from starving.

"Are you going to tell me what else I will be expected
to tolerate on this trip, or are you going to spring a new
surprise each day?"

He kept his face directed straight ahead as he enu-
merated. "Cook our meals, spread the bedrolls, wash

clothes, fetch firewood and water, help feed the stock, clean up after each camp. That probably covers it."

"You expect me to do all that? I've never done any cooking—we may starve."

"You'll learn. I'll see to it." He turned to her with a teasing glint in his eyes. "I tried to warn you."

"Hey, folks! I'm your scout on this trip—Mariner's the name," Simon interrupted their exchange. He whisked off the sombrero he wore with a flourish and nodded to Catherine, never once showing a flicker of recognition. Simon raced ahead to the next wagon and gave the same greeting.

"He looks very pleased with himself."

Garrett laughed and picked up the wagon's pace. Then his face became serious. "Remember what you've been told. Simon is a stranger."

"I'm sure you'll remind me if I forget."

He honed in on the irritable timbre of her voice. "I didn't realize when I married you that you had a tendency to pout."

"I didn't realize that this country was such a heat-plagued wilderness." She wiped her brow and frowned at him.

"There's a lot you didn't realize." There was a cutting edge to his tone that hadn't been there before. They lapsed into silence.

The heat of the afternoon sun and the constant sway of the wagon lulled Catherine into an exhausted stupor. Without realizing it, she leaned on Garrett until he complained, "Get in the wagon, Kate. Curl up and take a nap. I need both arms to drive."

She obeyed at once. What a relief to be out of the glaring sun. She sank gratefully between two flour sacks and was immediately asleep. Garrett turned around and observed her sleeping figure. He had wondered how long she would last, sitting on the plank seat. She hadn't done badly for someone totally unused to this kind of environment. She had gamely carried the water buckets, which were nearly as heavy as she. He had driven wagons for long distances, but he still felt the muscles of his back and legs protesting. He'd forgotten how long the hours seemed with six mules pulling at the harnesses, almost jerking his arms from their sockets.

At dusk, the wagons pulled into a circle. The men jumped down and unhitched the wagons, leading the teams to a creek to drink, then placing them on a lead rope to graze for the night. Garrett didn't have the heart to wake Catherine until he returned to the wagon, his arms full of dried wood for their fire. "Wake up, Kate." The gentleness of his tone denied the harshness of his earlier words. "The other women have already started cooking. You're falling behind, and it's only the first day."

She heard him as if in a dream. She opened her eyes to gray darkness and the smell of flour in her nostrils. Her stomach growled hollowly, and her legs felt weak as she stood up. "I'm up." She crawled to the back opening and stiffly dropped down to the ground. Seeing Garrett lighting a small cookfire, she walked over to him.

"Lesson number one, Mrs. Browning. After tonight, while I'm off watering the stock, you set up camp." He went to the wagon and showed her the pots and pans she would use, hauling out a tripod that he jammed upright over the fire. On that he placed a black kettle. Then he drew out a burlap sack and handed it to her. "There's water in the barrel at the side of the wagon. Peel those potatoes and throw them into the kettle. I'm going for fresh meat. You should find whatever you need in the wagon." He grabbed his rifle, slinging it beneath one arm as he started to walk away. "Hop to it," he ordered, letting her know she had lazed about long enough.

She felt a flush of guilt and moved hesitantly to the wagon, unsure of what to do. All around her were the sounds and smells of cooking. Everyone seemed to know exactly what should be done, but Catherine felt helpless. She found a knife and tried to get the skin off the vegetables she found inside the burlap bag, but she cut her fingers often. She eventually succeeded and tossed them into the bubbling water over the fire. She didn't know what to do next.

Simon came around the corner of the wagon and saw her staring at the pot over the fire. "Smells good, Mrs. Browning."

"Thank you, Mr. Mariner," she said, not at all politely.

Simon squatted before the fire. "Where's your coffee, Catherine? Garrett will be wanting a cup."

She gave the vegetables a vicious stir with a wooden stick. "Well, Garrett can just make it himself, then. He hasn't shown me how to do anything, so he can do without."

"Come on, Mrs. Browning. I'll show you what you have in the wagon and what it's for." He explained their provisions and showed her how everything was packed up after being used. "You are being tested, you know." Simon spoke softly so none of the other travelers could hear their conversation.

She hadn't thought of that, but it was indeed beginning to look that way. She was up for any challenge Garrett cared to make. He would see that she was as strong as any woman.

"Can you give me a quick cooking lesson?" Her smile was totally disarming. She was determined to prove to Garrett that she was capable of being part of their mission.

For the next half-hour, Simon showed her the basic rudiments of cooking on the trail. When he was satisfied that Catherine could prepare a meal and set up a makeshift camp, he decided it was time to go. "I'll be seeing you, ma'am," he said as he tipped his hat and sauntered away.

A few minutes later, Garrett strolled back into camp carrying a dead rabbit by the ears. "Tomorrow's supper," he announced, his lips quirking at Catherine's horrified stare. He dropped the animal, and his eyes traveled to the fire, noticing the bubbling stew and the smell of freshly brewed coffee. A pan of biscuits were sitting on a dropcloth she had laid with their eating utensils. Garrett's disbelief showed clearly on his face, and she almost laughed out loud.

"I'll clean the rabbit after I find out if this stew is any good," he growled. He curled his long body down to the ground and sat cross-legged by the cloth. Catherine handed him a plate of the steaming stew as if she had been serving meals all her life. He silently accepted it and couldn't hide his bewildered expression when the savory taste got through to his taste buds.

"How is it?" she asked smugly, knowing he had no cause for complaint.

"Simon never could make good biscuits," he said thoughtfully. "Seems to me he has enough to do without teaching you to cook."

"Oh!" She could have hit him. "Why must you be so hateful?" She was charged with hurt feelings and renewed temper.

"Look, Kate, I don't want someone else, especially Simon, doing your work for you. I expect you to pull your share like the rest of the women."

She had slaved over this meal, and he made it sound as if she had watched Simon prepare it without lifting a finger. She got to her feet furiously and abruptly started for the wagon, but strong fingers gripped her shoulders and pulled her around. Garrett's eyes glittered dangerously but then flicked to something behind her, and instead of making the scathing retort she expected, he planted a masterful kiss on her astonished mouth. He murmured a warning "Later!" into her ear and put a false smile on his face.

"Evening, Charles," Garrett said politely. "Want to join us in a cup of coffee?"

"No thanks. I was wonderin' what you knew about the scout, Mariner. You think we can trust him?"

Garrett didn't answer until he had poured the man a cup of coffee, acting as if he hadn't heard the negative tone. "He looks all right to me. I don't know much about scouting, but he rode out this morning and came back when we made camp, with water information. He must be doing his job."

"I guess so, but some of us were talking with the wagon master, and Mariner's not the man who was hired for the outfit. He showed up and said he'd be taking our scout's place just as slick as you please. I don't like the sound of it." Charles creased his leathery face into a worried frown.

"I wouldn't worry about it, Charles. The man seems thoughtful. He was with Catherine earlier. What did he have to say, honey?" Garrett sent silent directions with his eyes. Now was the time to prove she was halfway intelligent.

"A very nice man, Charles. He assured me that he saw no cause for delays. Traveling like this is quite new to me, and he was most kind."

"I saw him helping you, ma'am. It was that that kinda made me wonder if you-all were friends of his."

Charles looked relieved that Garrett was aware of Simon's visit to Catherine when her man was out of sight.

"Nope; just met him. I did ask him to keep an eye on Catherine for me, though. 'Course, if you think that'll cause gossip, maybe your missus wouldn't mind showing Catherine a few things. I didn't want to bother her when she's got her own family to tend. Catherine will get better when she's used to things. Won't you, honey?" He drew her under his arm and squeezed her shoulder. She could feel his anger in every taut muscle.

"I don't want to be a burden," Catherine tried.

"Don't you worry none, ma'am." Charles looked satisfied. "I'd be right proud to send my Molly to lend you a hand. That girl knows all her ma's got to teach." He smiled in a fatherly way. "I'll say evening to you. First light comes quick, don't it?"

"That's the truth." Garrett loosened his grasp on Catherine and watched Charles go back to his wagon. "I'm going to find Simon and pound some sense into his head." His low voice was seething with displeasure. "Hopefully you can get ready for bed without causing more talk."

Just before he left, he reached inside his shirt and pulled out a long white nightgown. "Here," he said as he threw it at her. "I bartered some meat for it."

Catherine watched Garrett walk away, knowing that Simon would be the next victim of his anger. After clearing up their dishes and restoring everything to the wagon, she reached for the bedrolls, then changed her mind. Garrett be damned, she thought. I'm not spending another night on that lumpy ground. She made up a makeshift bed on the wagon floor and donned her new nightgown.

She heard his footsteps approach the wagon and stop. "What the . . . ?" was his soft exclamation before he climbed into the wagon. He looked ready to drag her outside, but then he noticed the innocent appeal in her eyes and the virginal primness of the gown. He shed his clothes quickly and joined her. He slid one hand under her nightgown. "I'll give you credit for coming up with a good idea. We won't have an audience in here."

Chapter 11

The days dragged on. Simon had barely spoken to Catherine since Garrett had chastised him. He would pass by their wagon and nod once in a while, but he never stopped to talk. If Catherine hadn't seen the wink he cast her from under his hat every time, she would have felt worse.

They were traveling straight west. The scenery changed from the pretty, lush greenery bordering the Mississippi and Red rivers to flat terrain with less vegetation. The oppressive humidity of the bayou country was replaced by a dry heat that made her feel as though every inch of her skin might crack. She began dreaming of the cool green Kentish countryside she had left behind in England. She would have given anything for a bath and a decent bed to sleep in. She saw Simon riding toward them, and his wink as he passed their wagon.

"Damnit! What is it about you that makes a man lose the sense he was born with?" Garrett griped to her.

"Were you born with any sense?" Catherine returned waspishly. She was sick and tired of the wagon train and Garrett's moodiness.

He seemed to be taken aback by her quick retort.

"This has been rough on you, hasn't it?" He noticed her sunburned nose and the brown cast to her arms. "We're almost to the Sabine River. I figure we'll be there tomorrow, and after that, our cargo will be in the hands of the Rangers. We'll be able to let down our guard and relax. There's going to be a dance tonight."

Catherine was feeling much too sorry for herself to be elated at the mention of dancing. Her hair felt stringy and full of dust. Her nose was freckled, and her clothes were stiff with perspiration.

"Am I supposed to attend a dance in this ugly thing?" She took a bunch of the heavy material of her dress in her fist.

"You'll feel better after you've had a wash." He was smiling to himself.

She sat in silence, refusing to listen, until they pulled into the camp location. She declined to move—Garrett could get his own dinner for a change. She wasn't hungry. He shrugged his shoulders and climbed into the back of the wagon, then reappeared on the ground below her. He reached up, and before she knew it, he was carrying her over his shoulder. He carried something in his hand, but she couldn't tell what it was as her head hung dizzily behind him. "Must you manhandle me?"

He kept walking without responding.

"Evening, Garrett, Mrs. Browning," Charles said as Garrett strolled by the Amory wagon.

"Evening, Charles." Garrett returned, equally nonchalant, as if a man carrying his wife over his shoulder were an everyday event. Garrett stopped to greet Abby Amory and take the hot biscuit she held out to him.

"Abby, will you tell this big brute to put me down?" Catherine cried, finally finding someone who would side with her.

"Can't interfere with a man and his woman, honey."

Abby came around Garrett's back to smile into Catherine's reddening face. "I don't doubt he's up to something you won't be mindin' long. Be back in time for the dancing, young man."

Garrett readjusted Catherine on his shoulder. "Nice people, the Amorys." His voice was full of humor as he walked on, pushing away the branches in front of them.

"Where are you taking me?" She was unable to see anything.

"It's a surprise for you, but you were feeling too sorry for yourself to go anywhere I asked. I came by here once a long time ago and discovered something I think you'll appreciate."

Minutes later, she heard the sound of rushing water, and he put her back on her feet beside a small waterfall. Cascades of cool spray splayed the air and misted over her hot skin. She was removing her shoes and throwing her stockings on the ground before a word was said. "Oh, Garrett, it's beautiful. Doesn't anyone else know about this heavenly place?"

"Our secret. I'll tell the others when we get back." He pulled off his sweaty shirt and sat on the ground to remove his boots. "I brought some towels and soap."

"You thought of everything, didn't you?" She smiled warmly as she unbuttoned her gown, eager to immerse her body in the inviting water.

He grinned and said, "I tried."

By the time she stepped into the pool, he was in the water up to his waist. "Bring the soap?" he asked.

"Here." She reached out her arm and handed it to him. He took her hand and brought her gliding through the water to him. She saw his teeth flash in a grin before he began rubbing soap into her hair. She could touch the bottom, but he ducked her beneath the surface, laughing when she came up sputtering. As she tried to wipe the water from her eyes, he began lathering her skin. She felt his hands running over her breasts, and her nipples sprang to life.

"I'll do it myself." She tried to protest, but he ducked her again, rubbing her skin under the water until all the soap was removed and she was clean all over.

"My turn." He held out the soap when she emerged from the depths, her skin shiny and tingly, her hair wrapped in wet strands around her neck.

"Wh . . . what?" she said, eyeing the soap as if it had turned into a snake.

"Fair is fair, my sweet. You wanted to wash something, and here I am," he teased. A casual playfulness was flickering in his eyes. She reached for the soap and ordered him to sink down.

"Whatever you say." He complied at once, slipping down in the water until she could reach his head. She began washing the springy black hair. When she was done and he sprang like a seal to the surface, it was plain he wanted to continue the game he had started. "Don't stop now. I did you a good turn, and you owe me the same courtesy."

She laughed with delight when she saw the boyish tilt to his head and the pleading look on his face. "You're ridiculous." She began lathering the bronzed skin of his neck and shoulders. Somewhere between the time her hands ran down his sides and the time her palm passed across his flat stomach, the playful game changed to something else.

"My willpower is not nearly that strong." He pulled her to his slippery body and brought her hips against his belly, bending his dark head to lay claim to her lips. He leaned back, floating in the water, and she floated with him until he possessed her fully, reaching culmination beneath the shimmering depths of their private paradise.

He carried her out of the water and picked up the towels, wrapping one around his hips and her in the other. He rubbed her hair and her body with brisk strokes, and she stood quietly while he finished, enjoying their domestic intimacy. It would be lovely if they could always remain as in tune with one another as they were today.

He held out her clean clothes, something else he had had the surprising forethought to bring. He watched her step into her plain calico dress. "I doubt I'll tire of you for a long time, madam," he teased wickedly. "I enjoy it immensely each time you forget you're a lady and go wild in my arms."

She swayed toward him, and he caught her at his chest, tilting up her chin to place a tender kiss on the corner of her mouth. "Thank you for this, Garrett. I feel wonderful. I didn't think I'd ever feel clean again."

"I hope the bath was secondary in your enjoyment of being here." He nuzzled the skin of her neck, slipping his hand into the loose buttons of the bodice. "We won't miss much of the dance if we stay a little longer."

"Abby will be watching for us." She laughed, grabbing for his towel. He reached for his pants and pulled them on, his mouth turned down in a regretful frown, grumbling under his breath. He dressed quickly, and they started back to the camp hand in hand.

When they arrived, Garrett picked her up and placed her inside their wagon, following closely behind. He went mysteriously to a wooden chest and pulled out a paper-wrapped bundle. "I saved this for you." He offered her the package, and she eagerly unwrapped it.

Tears gathered in her eyes as her fingers found the pale blue silk of the dress he had kept for her. She looked up at him in wonder, unable to express what she felt. He was always disarming her. This gesture was totally unexpected.

"I thought I'd get more out of this than tears. Come here." He held out his arms and she melted into them.

The twirl of heavy skirts moving in never-ending circles brought a smile of pleasure to Catherine's lips, as dancing always did. The dance floor was the hard-packed earth in the center of the encampment and the musicians were poor, but the couples who pranced around the fire didn't notice or care.

After the first dance with Garrett, Catherine whirled from one man's arms to another amid the clapping of hands and the joyful laughter of everyone. The older women eventually tired of the exhausting romp and collapsed on the sidelines. The absence of available female partners increased Catherine's popularity as her youth and love of music kept her on her feet. Someone brought out a jug of corn liquor, and the effects rapidly took their toll. There were many missed steps and much ribald laughter. The compliments Catherine received from her partners became more and more sugary.

Her enjoyment swiftly fled when a red-faced giant of a man named Jake Snyder became her partner. He stared blatantly at her bosom and held her much too closely. She tried to squirm out of his grip without causing a scene, but the man was too drunk to notice that she wasn't enjoying his company.

When the next dance was called, the man refused to let her go, and she was swung into another vigorous folk dance. She was breathless and had no idea that she had never looked more lovely. Her blue gown caught the light from the campfire, and the skirt swirled in an arc to show slim ankles and a tantalizing glimpse of shapely legs. Her face was flushed and her violet eyes were shining in the flickering light.

"May I?" Garrett's voice was a welcome interruption. Jake Snyder grudgingly gave her into her husband's arms, and before she could express her relief, Garrett took her by the hand and pulled her away from the other dancers. "Let's get out of here," he said tersely, walking so swiftly that she almost had to run to keep up with him. She was startled to discover that they weren't heading for their wagon but for the rope corral, where Trojan and Glory were tethered for the night.

"Where are we going?" she asked as he lifted her onto Trojan's back and swung up behind her. His arms imprisoned her in a possessive grip that made her gasp. "What's wrong?"

She felt the granite hardness of his thighs and the sinewed muscles of his chest and arms as she leaned back against him. "You know exactly what's wrong," he said through gritted teeth as the horse swiftly carried them away into the darkness. In the moonlight, she caught a glimpse of his face and saw his dark, fathomless eyes glinting, his features glacial. When they neared the waterfall where they had bathed earlier in the day, he pulled Trojan to a stop.

Garrett slid from the horse's back and pulled her down into his arms. He covered her mouth, devouring her lips, branding her as his possession. He released her just as abruptly. "God," he groaned, "why did you have to be so damned beautiful?"

She heard the raw pain in his voice. "Garrett, please."

"The first time I saw you, surrounded by men, you were enjoying every minute of it, just like tonight. How many men do you need? It took you an hour to take up with some stranger in New Orleans, and tonight you had Snyder slobbering like a dog." He turned his back on her, as if the sight of her sickened him.

"How can you think there has been any other man in

my life?" Catherine ran to him and placed her hand on his arm, but he jerked away from her touch.

"Wasn't there?" he spit out. "What about that English nobleman you hoped to marry? Have you forgotten him?"

"There was never anyone." She explained that she had let him believe she was interested in someone else because she thought then he might back out of their arranged marriage, and that at the time, that was what she wanted.

"What about Longley and that young officer in the garden?" He demanded a fuller explanation.

"David?" she asked increduously and burst out laughing. Garrett turned to face her, a glimmer of comprehension softening the ice of his features. "David Longley is a pompous fool. I was bored to distraction whenever I was forced to endure his company at one of those wretched parties my father dragged me to. As for the officer you saw escorting me at the Strathmore ball, I forgot him the instant you kissed me." She gave him a shy smile.

"You never wanted Longley?" he demanded, and she shook her head, smiling wider. He reached for her hands and pulled her close. "I've had an image of that fop haunting my bed for weeks. The thought of you with another man has been churning my insides from the day we got married."

"I much prefer you to ghosts, Garrett Browning."

Catherine pulled down his face and kissed him soundly on the lips. Their embrace became a tidal wave of sensation that carried them both away. He brought her down to the sweet grasses beneath them, swiftly removing her gown. His eyes roved her nakedness like burning flame as his hands caressed her silken skin with an urgency she had never felt from him before. It was as if he was compelled by an emotion he could no longer control. Moonlight shimmered over her body, glistened upon her ivory skin and turned her fair hair to a silvery cloud. She held his warm gaze as he removed his clothes. He groaned huskily as he dropped down beside her and crushed her to him.

She moved with him, giving him whatever he wanted. She wanted him as much as he wanted her. His lips moved down her body as he knelt between her thighs. He brought his hands to her breasts, kneading the soft skin until he heard her moaned response. He played with her nipples until the sensitive tips stood up, aching for his touch. "Oh . . . Garrett . . ." She caught her breath when his face lowered between her thighs and his tongue seared her, his lips tasting the sweetness within. She cried out with sensual delight as her body writhed with unbearable pleasure. His tongue teased the delicate skin until she was mindless with need. He brought her to helpless release again and again, taking her to ever higher plateaus of sensation. Her breath came in ravaged gulps as he covered her softness with his hard body, pushing the rigid shaft of his manhood deep inside her. His mouth returned to hers, and his tongue thrust deeply with the same pulsing rhythm that pounded between her thighs. She met every powerful surge with the seductive dance of passion he had taught her as waves of liquid fire passed through her body.

An eternity later, Garrett raised his head from her breast and looked into her face. "We've wasted so much time," he whispered gently, brushing the silver tangles of hair away from her face. He kissed her with a tenderness born of love. He might never be able to admit his love to her, but this night she was his and he was hers.

He brought his lips to her throat and down the curve of her shoulder, muttering her name without hearing himself, lost in the wonder of her yielding flesh and his love for her. She rolled on top of him, returning his kisses, filled with the ecstasy of his ownership and reveling in it. She felt his rising desire as she moved against him, and her lips wandered down his throat to his chest. His heart beat wildly, and she heard his unrestrained gasp as she moved lower. Taking courage from his response to her tantalizing kisses, she ran her hands lightly down his sides and across his flat belly. She was filled with awe when she felt the hard muscles quiver and his breathing become ragged. A great joy welled within her with the realization that she could demonstrate her love by giving him so much pleasure. She brought her lips to his manhood and he spread his legs involuntarily, just as she had done when he had loved her this way. She waited, tantalizing him with her lips and tongue, until he was totally throbbing and groaning with need. She slid up his body and covered his rigid length with her softness.

As the last shudder shook him, he hugged her fiercely to his chest. "My God!" His voice was husky with emotion. "There was never a woman like you."

She laughed in delight. He heard the new note in her laughter and rolled her beneath him, growling softly down at her smiling face. "And there was never a man like you," she returned, elated with their new closeness, until his lips closed over her mouth and thought disappeared.

Chapter 12

Alejandro Torres sat quietly on his horse, staring down at the wagons gathered in the valley. Hidden behind a patch of live oak, he was invisible to the people encamped below. He and fifty men, each more deadly than the next, had been watching for hours after his scouts had reported the train crossing the Sabine. He had driven his men hard to arrive at this location before nightfall. There was still enough light to study the wagons and determine which was the one he sought. Mexican-government spies had reported that a shipment of new weapons was to be spirited into the war zone, but it had only been by chance that they had discovered how. Spies had reported sighting Simon Mariner in Washington, Charleston and then New Orleans. It was his appearance on the wagon train that had tipped them off that guns were being transported via the Old San Antonio Road.

Torres smiled maliciously. He was especially glad that Mariner was the escort. He would have the satisfaction not only of capturing the guns but also of inflicting a slow, painful death on Mariner, one of the two men Torres hated most in the world. His evil smile broadened as he recognized another figure strolling through the encampment. Garrett Browning! What luck! He could barely suppress his desire to order the attack instantly, but the personal pleasure he would derive from the certain capture of both his enemies checked rash action. He wanted to enjoy every moment of the torture he had dreamed about for so many years.

The guns would be easy to find. Discover which

wagon belonged to Browning and Mariner, and the weapons would be there. For now, Torres was content to watch his enemies prepare themselves for a rest they would not long enjoy.

Eyes black with remembered hatred, his thoughts turned to the past. He had been twenty, and the girl perhaps thirteen. Elena Mariner, ripe, black haired and full breasted already. Torres had caught her alone one day by the little creek that cut between his father's cliff-ridden land and the great Tierra Nueva Ranch.

He ran his finger along the scar that marred his cheek from ear to chin, a constant reminder. He had crept up and grabbed her from behind. She had seemed to turn willingly in his arms, and it had been the girl who had brought his hands to her breasts. She had even helped him undress. He had just thrust his hand between her legs when Garrett Browning had appeared out of nowhere.

At the sight of Garrett, the girl had begun to scream hysterically and push Torres away as if she were fighting him off. Torres would never forget the sight of young Browning or the gleaming knife that was suddenly part of his hand. He had dived for his own knife, but he hadn't been fast enough. At eighteen, Garrett had the skill of a Comanche warrior. He twisted, turned, parried—in for the attack, then back out again—until Torres was reduced to a whimpering mass of bloody cuts. He remembered the girl's laughter at the sight of him, naked before her, bleeding, pleading with Browning for his life. Elena had finally made Garrett relent, and the two of them had left him to nurse his wounds. Later, Elena's brother, Simon, on leave from duty, had come to his place and beat him badly, but not so badly that his own father hadn't continued where Simon left off. That was the last time he had seen any of them— Browning, Mariner or his father. He had left to become a soldier in the Mexican army, eventually becoming the leader of a vicious gang of *guerrilleros* under General Canales, but he never forgot his vow to get revenge.

His thoughts were interrupted by a question from one of the half-breeds who rode with him. "They may fight us if they have many guns, *Capitán*." The man sounded as if he hoped the train would put up a fight so he could kill the settlers. "We will slit their throats even as they sleep. The gringos will not see tomorrow's sun."

Torres laughed at the blood-thirsty plan but held up his hand. "Ah, Sanchez, it is not our plan to kill all of them, even though we would like to. We have orders to let the settlers go and capture only the guns." As he watched his companion's joy disappear, he smiled and said, "But it would not be so very wrong to kill the two men in charge of the guns, eh? We will kill them so slowly you will not miss the joy of slitting the throats of the others. Come, we must give the men their orders. Remember, we must not fire a shot, for the scouts report American Rangers in the area, and we do not want them to learn of us."

Below, Simon and Garrett were having difficulty convincing the men of the train that they might be in danger from Mexican attack. They insisted on retaining sentry posts until another day or two of traveling had passed. The night's first watch was grudgingly taken by four green farm boys who were more likely to fall asleep than remain alert. Garrett and Simon exchanged meaningful glances and volunteered immediately for the second watch, when an attack would most likely come. They didn't want to arouse suspicion, but if any attempt to seize their cargo were to be made, it would be tonight.

"By this time tomorrow, Garr, our mission will be accomplished, and you and I can quit looking over our shoulders." The two men drank a last cup of coffee before turning in for the night. "We'd better sleep now, while we can."

"I hope your Rangers are where they are supposed to be. I don't mind admitting that I've been uneasy ever since crossing the border. Are you sure you saw nothing suspicious when you scouted around this afternoon?"

Simon was as worried as Garrett and took no offense. "I wish you could have ridden out, too. Two men are more likely to spot trouble than one, but that would have caused too much talk. I don't think Gibbons ever believed my story, and a few others have asked some pointed questions. You'd better climb into your wagon and reassure your wife. I plan to roll out my blankets near the corral."

They went their separate ways. Garrett stood outside his wagon for long moments, listening to the sounds of the night beyond the ring of wagons. He didn't want to alarm Catherine about their possible danger. He knew she had been valiantly trying to hide a growing fear as they crossed into Texas.

He had to admire her—she'd tried very hard on this trip. She had learned to cook over an open campfire, had kept her complaints to a minimum and had even learned to handle the stubborn mules that pulled the wagon. He smiled as he remembered her first attempts. The beasts had balked, and she had gotten so mad that she had grabbed the whip and cracked the leaders as hard as any mule skinner. The animals had started up so suddenly that she had been thrown off balance and landed hard on the wagon seat, but she had gamely held onto the reins and brought the team under control. Yes, he thought, she was some woman, his woman. He climbed into the back of the wagon and lay down beside her.

"Garrett?"

"Were you expecting someone else?"

"Of course not! I . . . I . . . are you expecting trouble?" she whispered.

He pulled her into his arms and answered as truthfully as he could. "We'll join up with the Rangers tomorrow. Simon didn't see anything earlier, so I think we're safe. He and I are splitting the late watch, so don't be surprised when I leave. Try to sleep now." He nuzzled her ear with a light kiss and fell quickly asleep.

Catherine didn't know how he could be completely alert one minute and sound asleep the next. She studied his handsome features as he slept. She wanted to tell him how much she loved him and how afraid she was. She had tried to shake off the feeling of foreboding that had begun when they neared the river. The crossing had been arduous, for the Sabine was higher than they had expected. Although no one had been hurt or lost, it had been dangerous.

Catherine, like most of the women, had driven the stubborn mules while Garrett pulled the leader across, up to his chest in the swirling water. He had lost his footing once, and she had been terrified that he would be swept downriver, but he had quickly bobbed to the surface and retained his hold on the mule's halter.

Finally exhaustion overcame her apprehension, and she fell asleep in Garrett's arms.

As soon as the camp quieted, Torres and his men began their approach, crawling on their bellies through the darkness. The inexperienced sentries were quietly overcome, bound and gagged. At a signal from Torres, when all his men were in place, the *guerrilleros* leaped into each wagon. Others surrounded the camp with drawn guns.

Simon woke up at the first sound of the stock's

unrest. He silently rolled out of his bedroll, knife in hand, but it was too late. He was hit over the head from behind. He slumped forward, unable to sound an alarm.

Catherine's gasp of terror woke Garrett. He grabbed for his weapon, but a grinning Mexican was already holding a knife to Catherine's throat. Garrett was forced to drop his gun.

The frightened cries of women and children echoed through the night as one by one the settlers were dragged to the center of the camp and held there by the dozens of guns pointed at them. When Catherine and Garrett were pushed into the circle of frightened people, the capture was complete. Catherine threw herself into Garrett's arms, sobbing with terror. His arms encircled her securely, whispering reassurances into her hair. "Shh, shh, they only want the guns. They'll let you go. Show them how brave you are, my little one."

She tried to stop her frightened crying, knowing that her worst fears had been realized. These men were not regular Mexican army soldiers but something far worse. Every one of them looked capable of murder. She heard a harsh order given in Spanish, and Simon was dragged out of the shadows and left unconscious on the hard ground before the embers of a dying campfire. A minute later, three men came to Garrett and dragged him, his arms behind his back, forcing him to move to where Simon was lying. Catherine wouldn't let go of him, trying to keep him with her as he was pulled along. "Go back with the others," Garrett ordered sharply, but she couldn't obey.

Torres stepped from the shadows and nodded to the three half-breeds who held Garrett. They pushed him forward, restraining his arms so he couldn't move. "So, we meet again, *amigo mío*. It has been a long time, and

I have longed for such a meeting for many years. Now you will know how it feels to be on the receiving end of a whip and a knife." Torres was overcome with exultation. Then he noticed Catherine. "Who is this woman?"

Garrett's controlled reply showed no fear. "She's only along to warm my bed. Just a little gal I picked up in New Orleans." He heard Catherine's shocked gasp and tried to warn her to say nothing.

"We shall see, *señor.*" Torres issued a curt order, and Garrett was forced backward against the closest wagon and roughly tied to a wheel. Seconds later, Simon was similarly tied to another. Torres returned his attention to Catherine.

"*Señorita,* may I know your name?"

Remembering Garrett's exhortation to be brave, Catherine straightened her spine and lifted her chin. She assumed the regal mantle of her birth and announced imperiously, "I am Lady Catherine Maxfield, daughter of the earl of Brockmere. If you or your men harm any of these people, the British government will seek a grave restitution."

Torres was taken aback for only a moment; then he began to laugh, a cruel, guttural cackle that sent shivers up Catherine's spine. "But, *señorita,* you were found with Señor Browning. You are more than what you say, my fine English lady." With lightning speed, he reached out and grabbed her by the arm, pulling her close to his face and snarling, "What else are you, eh? You are not the little whore *mi amigo* claims. Answer me, now!"

Catherine began to shake in his grasp, the carnal gleam in his eyes terrifying her. "I . . . I'm his wife." She couldn't see the sick look that passed over Garrett's face. Torres's triumphant laugh reverberated through the camp, making Garrett struggle desperately in the ropes that held him. Torres now had the ultimate means of torture within his grasp.

"Tie her, too," he ordered his men. "We will deal with these three later." He walked toward the settlers standing helplessly within the circle of guns and shouted, "Who is in charge of this wagon train?"

Chester Gibbons stepped forward and replied, "I am. Why are we prisoners? We are only farmers on our way West. We have nothing to do with the war."

Torres laughed as he answered, "You show much courage to question me, *señor,* but you are stupid! You have been hiding weapons for the Americanos on this train, and yet you try to claim no part in the war."

Gibbons's shocked denial seemed to convince Torres of his innocence, for he continued, "You and these others, we will let go. I want only Mariner, Browning and his woman. Which is their wagon?"

A startled Gibbons slowly pointed to the Browning wagon, knowing that if the guns were found inside, he had sealed their fate. He had suspected their peculiar last-minute joining of the wagon train, but he had come to like them and did not want them harmed. Still, his first responsibility was to the larger group of endangered settlers.

Torres sent two of his men to the appointed wagon. The sound of ripping boards and splintering wood was followed by shouts of triumph. The incriminating crate of guns was dragged out to the waiting Torres.

Gibbons tried to save the bound threesome. "You've got the guns now; take them and leave us. We will do nothing to stop you."

The cold-blooded malevolence on Torres's face showed that it was hopeless. There was far more than guns involved here. Gibbons's only hope was that Torres's hatred would not lash out to the other settlers.

The Mexicans began loading the guns into a flatbed

wagon, lashing the crates to the wood floor with thick hemp ropes. Torres watched his men for several seconds, satisfying himself that the guns were safely in his possession. He designated two of them to drive the wagon to the rendezvous, where he would join them after taking care of Garrett and Simon. As soon as the wagon rolled out of sight, his attention returned to the wagon master.

The Mexican swaggered back and forth as he said with a sneer, *"Señor,* you and the others may leave immediately. On foot. You will have no weapons and little water. If you start now, you may get a few miles before the day grows warm."

Catherine caught Abby Amory's silent look of despair as the men, women and children of the train slowly began their long walk. She tried to give Abby a reassuring smile, but in her mind she prayed for a quick death.

She looked at her captors with dread. They were a mixture of Mexicans, Indians and criminals. She tried to hide her fear as the scar-faced leader came to stand in front of her.

"Ah . . . Señora Browning, you cannot know how pleased I am to meet you." His grin was evil, vile. He knelt down and insolently ran his eyes down her cringing body. "Your husband and I are well acquainted. Alejandro Torres at your service. I am an old family friend. Unfortunately we have not seen each other in many years, and it is now my unpleasant duty to punish your husband for his past mistakes." He laughed cruelly. "Perhaps your screams when I take you will be the last sounds he hears before he dies."

All color drained from Catherine's face, and she saw Garrett strain against his ropes. She knew with a cold certainty that they would die in agony. Torres followed her fearful eyes. He walked to Garrett and stood before him with his legs spread apart. "And now, you, *mi amigo,* the high and mighty son of the famous Hunter Browning." He locked his hands together and dealt Garrett a vicious blow to the stomach. Garrett doubled over in agony while Catherine screamed and the watching crew of outlaws laughed in enjoyment.

Garrett recovered slowly, gasping. "You've come up in the world, Torres, from rapist of little children to leader of scum." A back-handed blow across his face brought blood.

"Garrett?" Simon said. He opened his eyes and closed them again when he recognized Torres.

The Mexican walked to him and grabbed him by the hair. "I am glad you have returned in time for the festivities, my friend."

Simon remained silent, knowing it would do no good to goad Torres. From their position, there was no escape, and Torres held all the cards. Torres released Simon and stalked back to Garrett. "You have the best audience I could provide. Your wife and your best friend will witness you begging me for your life."

Catherine was terribly afraid, for it was obvious that Torres wanted Garrett's defeat far more than hers or Simon's. She tried to speak to her husband with her eyes, willing him to see her love when it was no longer possible to speak of it.

"The stakes!" Torres ordered gleefully. "Put them over here. I want the woman to have a good view."

The men surrounded Garrett and Simon like swarming locusts. They stripped both men of their clothes and spread-eagled them on the ground, tying their wrists and ankles to the stakes. Torres stepped forward, carrying a long black whip that he cracked in the air. "We will soon see what brave men you are, *mis amigos.* You will beg to die when you feel the sting of my whip and the sun comes up to bake your bleeding flesh. Just before you die, Browning, I will make your wife mine. A pleasant picture to take with you to hell." He raised his whip to deliver the first blow. Neither man uttered a sound as the whip descended, first on one, then the other. Catherine's sharp scream pierced the air as Torres's bestial laughter followed the lash.

Catherine was never allowed to look away, her head held in place from behind by a man's hand twisted cruelly in her hair. The whip cracked again and again and again. She fainted into oblivion the first time Garrett screamed.

When she next opened her eyes, Torres had paused in his torture. The first streaks of sunlight were beginning to break on the horizon. She saw the outlaws throwing buckets of water over the bleeding bodies of both unconscious men. Her husband opened his eyes, searching and at last finding her. They shared a gaze of deep longing before Torres stepped out and blocked their view of each other.

"Are you awake, my brave *amigos?* The best is yet to come." He swaggered to Catherine, enjoying her tears and fruitless struggles to loosen the bonds at her wrists. With one swift motion, he ripped her nightgown from neck to hem. A cheer went up from the leering gang around him. "My compliments, *amigo.* Your wife is a woman to enjoy."

Catherine steeled her mind to the assault she knew was coming and tried to will herself into another world. She was brought back to reality when Torres squeezed her breasts painfully. He continued to abuse her, bringing his face close to hers as he began to loosen his trousers, enjoying her screams of protest and pain.

Suddenly, before he could go further, his men mounted their horses and pointed to a ridge beyond where a cloud of dust was rising. Torres turned to look in the direction his men were pointing and muttered,

"Dios!" He hastily fastened his trousers and shouted for his mount. Before it arrived, he ran to Garrett and delivered several kicks to the helpless man's side and head.

When Torres's horse was brought, he mounted quickly and started to follow his retreating men, but after a few yards, he stopped and turned in the saddle to hurl a knife at Garrett. "We will meet again, Señora Browning," he told Catherine menacingly. Then he spurred his horse away from the approaching riders.

Chapter 13

It was dark in the fruit cellar. The little boy pounded and banged against the bolted wooden doors that closed out the light until his knuckles bled. Hot, salty tears trickled down his dirty face, but he couldn't keep from crying. Boys don't cry, he kept telling himself. Filled with dread, he gave up trying to escape from the dank hole of the cellar and tried to hide, curling up behind a bag of dried fruit. He huddled in terror as he heard the scratching of the rats along the dirt walls.

Mother told me I deserve to be bitten because I defy her. She locked me in the cellar because I'm bad and more fit company for the rats than I am for the family. He tried to swallow his horror. Boys don't cry, boys don't cry . . .

"Garrett Andrew Browning! I will have your apology now!" He heard his mother's step on the wooden planks leading to his musty sanctuary behind the burlap bags. He didn't move and tried not to breathe, clinging to the rough material of the sacks in desperation. Maybe she'll leave and forget to barricade the cellar doors. He felt her hand grab his collar, and he was dragged out of his hiding place. He struggled against the clawing hand, whimpering at the sight of the leather strap she raised. *Boys don't cry! It hurts . . . she's hurting me.* Why was it so hot in the cool cellar? Why did each stroke of the strap against his legs make his whole chest hurt and burn? "Stop! I'm sorry, Ma. I'm sorry. I won't do it anymore."

"That's enough, Celeste! Look how you've hurt him!" It was his father; the whipping stopped. What was he saying? There were too many voices to make out what Pa was saying. "Hannah? Give me something to drink." *Hannah always heals my hurts and makes them better.* Cool drops of water in his throat. "It feels better now."

"God, they'll pay for this!"

Burt? Was it Burt who sounded so angry? Garrett felt himself being lifted by hands, hands everywhere, hurting him. A woman was crying out his name. He tried to see her, tell her he'd be okay, but when he opened his eyes, he saw who it was. "Make her go away, Burt. I hate her! I hate her!"

Why does Ma look like she's sorry? She hurt me. She's not sorry. She's never sorry. A black cloud passed over his eyes, and he couldn't see her anymore.

"He'll need rest." It was dark again, and Garrett sank beneath the fog that swirled around him. He didn't want to feel any more.

Grief shone in Catherine's tearful eyes as she looked at the doctor. "Can't we do something for his pain?" She turned to the man who lay in unconscious torment upon the examination table.

"I have to determine the extent of his injuries first, Mrs. Browning." Dr. Griffith beckoned to the Ranger stationed at the door. "Would you take Mrs. Browning outside? You must leave him now, so I can do my job. Please."

She let herself be drawn away from the prone figure on the table. Abby Amory waited for her in the sitting room. Catherine ran into her waiting arms and sobbed.

"He'll be fine, honey," Abby crooned, rocking from side to side, wishing there were more she could say. Thank God their walk had led them quickly to the Rangers' encampment, so they could enlist help before Garrett, Simon and Catherine were killed. Catherine had escaped harm, but Garrett and Simon had not been so lucky. Abby hated to think about the agonies the two young men must have endured that long night before the Rangers arrived.

When the Rangers returned, escorting the wagons of the settlers, Abby had been overjoyed to see Catherine emerge, looking well except for her pale face and drooping shoulders. It took only minutes for her joy to be replaced by horror as the Rangers lifted out the still bodies of Garrett and Simon. A swift transfer was made. The two men were placed on makeshift stretchers and carried to a flat-bottomed wagon drawn by fast horses. Abby had scurried aboard in order to accompany Catherine and the injured men to Nacogdoches.

It was fortunate that one of the Rangers knew where the town's doctor was located. They had reached the doctor's home not a minute too soon. Garrett's groaning had become louder and louder throughout the fast ride, and every time he opened his mouth to cry out, his wife suffered.

Simon had regained consciousness immediately after setting out. Although he had tried to reassure Catherine that Garrett would be all right, he had to sink back in silence when the jarring wagon set his own teeth on edge with pain.

The doctor's wife was capable of seeing to Simon, so

he was carried to a cot in the infirmary while Dr. Griffith concentrated on Garrett.

Catherine lifted her head from Abby's shoulder and wiped her eyes with the back of her hand. Abby helped her to a chair, and the two women stared at the door of the examining room, waiting for word.

Inside, Dr. Griffith carefully lifted the blanket from his patient. He was faced with a mass of bloody stripes reaching from the young man's chest to his knees. Several bruises were darkening along the ribs, but what got his immediate attention was the oozing blood dripping from the bandage wrapped around his patient's thigh. His mouth set in grim lines as he removed the tight cloth and cleaned the knife wound he discovered.

He had just finished suturing and bandaging when his wife emerged from the infirmary. "That young fella in there got a pretty good working over, but his cuts should heal well. He wanted to get up and see about his friend here, but I dosed him with some laudanum, and he's sleeping," Cora Griffith explained to her husband, coming to stand beside him. As soon as she saw the seriousness of Garrett's injuries, she gasped and covered her mouth. "Oh, my God, John, this boy received twice the whipping the other one got. How bad is he?"

"He'll pull through, Mama, but I'm going to need your help. Bring me some more salve. He's in bad shape and already burning with fever. He's got some broken ribs. As soon as we get his ribs strapped and this salve on, I must talk to his wife. She's scared to death."

Cora nodded, unable to keep compassionate tears from her eyes as together they cleaned the multiple lacerations. "Whoever did this should be shot! I hope those Ranger boys catch them and hang them."

John Griffith looked down at his wife's white head. "I

know it's hard to see a fine young man like this tortured so brutally."

They worked together until Garrett's torso was swathed in heavy bandages. "You go on out and reassure this boy's little wife. I'll join you as soon as I've cleared up the mess in here." Cora began to cover Garrett while her husband washed his bloodied hands.

The elderly doctor paused to listen to his wife's motherly crooning before he left the infirmary. "Mrs. Browning? Your husband appears to be a healthy young man. I should think with rest and proper care, he will recover. Of course, he risks infection, but if we keep a close eye on him, he will get on fine." Dr. Griffith smiled encouragingly.

"Can I go to him?" Catherine stood up and looked anxiously into the examining room, unable to see Garrett.

"I'll let you go in soon. Be patient." He turned to Abby Amory. "You look pretty tired, ma'am. I suggest you get back to your family. I understand that you took a mighty long walk last night, and I don't need another patient."

His voice was kind, and Abby nodded, putting her arms about Catherine. "Are you going to be all right, honey?"

"You go along, Abby. Charles and the children need you. Thank you for coming with me, but the doctor is right. You're exhausted."

Abby didn't want to leave, but they finally persuaded her when she was told she could come back the next day. She gave Catherine one last hug and then instructed the doctor, "You take care of this little lady, too, Doc. She's had an awful time of it."

A few minutes after Abby left, Catherine was allowed into the examining room. She ran to Garrett's side, stunned by his paleness. He looked as though he was sleeping peacefully, yet his shallow breathing frightened her. She felt sick, remembering his suffering.

"He's so quiet." She took one lifeless hand within her own, willing the silent man on the table to respond. He should not be lying there so still, she thought. He should be standing up, laughing at her, drawing her into his strong arms and planting demanding kisses on her lips.

"He's been sedated, Mrs. Browning. It's the best thing for him." The doctor saw Catherine blanch. "I think you should rest, too. He's going to need you."

Cora enveloped Catherine in her arms and pulled her close. "My John is a good doctor, honey. If he says your husband will recover, he will. Now, what you need is a nice soft bed and a hot cup of tea."

Catherine pulled away from the gentle comfort of the old woman's arms and went to Garrett. She brushed a stray lock of hair from his forehead and bent to kiss his brow. "I love you," she whispered, tears gathering when she realized he couldn't hear her.

Catherine was put up in the doctor's home while Garrett and Simon recovered. Two days after their arrival, she found Simon in the infirmary, strapping on his guns. "Simon Mariner! You're not leaving? You can't be well enough yet."

"I can't waste any more time, Catherine. The Rangers are pulling out tonight and heading south to find Torres. He's not going to get away with this, Catherine. You worry about Garrett and not about me."

Her gaze turned to Garrett. "Oh, Simon, I can't bear to see him so helpless."

"Sit down here for a minute, Catherine." Simon grimaced at the look of profound pity on her face. "He's tough, Catherine." He reached for her hand.

"You can't let him see you like this. He won't want your pity. He's never let anyone feel sorry for him. I think I'd better tell you what you'll be up against."

He began talking about Celeste Browning, reinforcing what Catherine already knew from Garrett's delirious ravings.

"When we were boys," Simon said, going back in time, "I walked in on Garrett when Celeste was slapping his face. She knew I was watching, and she was hoping Garrett would react. I felt terrible, knowing she wanted him humiliated in front of me. We went outside and got our horses. Garrett almost rode his mount into the ground. I told him how sorry I was, and I got a fist in the mouth for my trouble. He didn't mean to hurt me, but he couldn't stand my knowing." Simon completed the story. "You seem to remind him of her. Probably because you are English. She was small like you and talked the same way."

He saw the anger and compassion reflected in her face. "He will kill me if he knows I told you any of this. You have to show him you're not like her, and it won't be easy. He thinks all women are alike. Even I didn't know how bad it was when he was small. Not . . . not till now."

"Maybe he'll always think like that." Catherine bent her head, her eyes filling with tears. "I love him so much, Simon."

"Catherine," Simon's voice was raw with feeling, "I've seen you two together. He might never admit it, but I know he loves you, too. No woman has gotten under his skin like you have. He'll be ornery when he gets better, but it will be because he feels guilty about involving you in this."

Catherine tried to smile. "Thank you, Simon." She crossed the room and put her arms around him. "Promise me you won't do anything foolish?"

Simon held her tightly, brushing a soft kiss on her forehead, oblivious to the burning skin beneath his shirt. His voice was choked as he gently pushed her away so she wouldn't hear his heartbeat quicken. "I'd better be going."

He reached for a polished walnut box. "I know these aren't much for what he's done, but give them to Garrett when he's better." He held out a matched set of Colt-Walkers. Abruptly he turned and left before Catherine could see the emotion on his face.

Later in the day, the Amorys came to offer their best wishes and say good-bye. Abby had come to visit again, but the wagon train had located a new scout, a volunteer from the Rangers, and they were ready to go on to Oregon. The leave-taking was momentarily painful, but Catherine's mind was mostly occupied with the man who held her heart. The Griffiths tried to cheer her, and Catherine began to respond to their warmth. Cora treated her like a daughter, and John showed her an affection she had never received from Lord Maxfield.

It was a full three days more before Garrett returned to reality. Catherine had listened to his tormented ravings until her heart ached and her mind burned with contempt for Celeste Browning. Garrett's memories seemed even more painful than the wounds he had suffered in Torres's attack. Catherine could sense the change in him when he finally struggled to open his eyes.

"You're alive," he whispered, trying to focus on her face as she fought to hide the compassion she felt. She reached out and brushed her hand across his forehead, smiling with relief that he had spoken. His eyes closed again, and then his whole body stiffened as they shot open, studying her face. "Torres . . . he . . . he didn't . . . ?"

"No!" Catherine denied instantly. "He was stopped

before anything happened." She could see he wasn't going to get any rest if he continued his questioning. He hadn't had more than a few spoonfuls of broth since he'd been brought in, and now that he was awake, he could take some nourishment. She slipped one arm beneath him and dipped a spoon into the bowl of broth Cora had made. When he turned his head away, she put the spoon down in the bowl.

"I can feed myself. I'm not helpless," Garrett asserted in a voice growing weaker by the second.

"Oh, yes, you are," she insisted, and held his jaw firmly while she spooned the broth between his lips. He closed his eyes, and Catherine kept slipping the spoon into his mouth, grateful each time he swallowed the warm liquid.

"I'm tired," he muttered, hoping the soft, warm hand behind his neck would go away and let him sleep. A gentle voice said, "Just a little more, then you can sleep. Just a little more." He smiled. Catherine had such a pretty voice. Musical, somehow. Sort of like a saloon singer he knew once in Austin. Strange, he couldn't remember her name. Every girl he could remember was called Catherine.

Chapter 14

Catherine woke up screaming. Once again her nightmares brought back the horrible night of the Torres raid. Would she ever forget how Garrett had suffered that night? She always woke up filled with fear, not for herself but for her husband. When she didn't dream of Torres, she dreamed of Garrett as a child. All the hours of listening to his tormented ravings returned to haunt her as she slept. He would appear as a small, dark-haired boy, alone and afraid, and she would wake up screaming.

She lit the lamp at her bedside and focused on the window across the room. Outside, the stars were shining in a vast sky and a soft breeze was blowing the sheer white curtains at the window. She thought about how much she had changed since leaving England. Colin's idea about adventure was true. In a few short weeks, she had discovered how much adventure she could endure. Nothing had been easy—neither trying to understand the man she loved nor adjusting to a wild country she knew little about. Would she ever feel totally secure with Garrett? Would he ever learn to trust her? Would he someday return her love?

She wished she could tell him how much she loved his strength, his loyalty to land and country and even the pride that so often tore them apart. If only he knew what effect his blue eyes softening to indigo when he wanted her had on her. His easy smile and demanding kisses melted her resistance completely. She shook her head and tried to think about something else, but Simon's words came back to her. "You'll have to prove you're not like her." He was right. She was being compared to the wife and mother Celeste Browning had been.

She shut off the lamp, her mind engrossed with plans to win her husband's love. When he was stronger, she would take up the battle again. She had convinced him that he was the only man in her life that wonderful night by the waterfall. Now she would conquer every last terrible memory that kept them apart, until he couldn't help but return her love. With that hope planted firmly in her heart, she turned on her side and fell asleep. She didn't have another nightmare that night.

* * *

"Garrett! You can just stop fighting me, because it's not going to do you one bit of good." Catherine tried to maintain a cool authority, but Garrett was making it extremely difficult. There was a definite light of defiance in his eyes.

The bandages around his chest were difficult to change, because he had to help her by rolling over. His face was gray by the time she had finished, but he hadn't tried to stop her.

Now, however, he had a grip on the sheet that covered his legs and belly, denying her access to the last few spots requiring treatment.

"You are acting like a child! Do you want to get well or not?" She tugged at the sheet, her temper overcoming her promise to be composed and calm.

"Just get out of here! Damnit, I can do the rest myself." His face was stubbornly set, his teeth clenched together. His navy eyes were unrelenting, prepared to do battle.

"Garrett, the risk of infection is still there."

"No! I don't want your help and I don't want your pity."

It was a standoff. Catherine was going to have to overcome his reluctance physically and close her ears to his verbal abuse.

"Pity you?" She released the bottom corners of the sheet. "I don't pity you, but for the time being, you are in no shape to stop me from taking care of you. I believe I was forced to make a vow a few months ago about better and worse. This is definitely 'worse.'" She whisked the sheet up and away, baring his lower torso and limbs.

"Damnit!" Garrett hissed, trying to twist away until he was too weak to continue fighting. She applied the medication as he tried to regain his breath. She was pleased to see how well he was healing. She looked up when she had finished, to find him staring bleakly at the ceiling. His pride was badly damaged, but what could she do?

"You're much better."

No answer.

"Dr. John says it won't be long before you're well."

He glared at her for a second and then returned to stare at the ceiling. The stubborn set of his chin looked so boyish that she had an irresistible urge to laugh. This man was no boy. A small giggle escaped before she could stop it.

"Ha ha ha. When I get out of here, I'm going to make. . . ." He paused, not able to think of a threat harsh enough.

"Make love to me? I know." She laughed again. "You just have to be patient for a while." She peeped up from underneath her lashes to gauge his reaction. Surely he wouldn't let that pass.

"Very funny." His voice was sullen but less charged with anger.

"Oh, it is." She placed her hand on his arm and ran her fingers lightly down his skin. He groaned.

"Someday, Kate, you'll pay for this." She noticed that he was beginning to relax. She pressed lightly against him, making sure she didn't cause pain. "I'll hold you to that, my husband," she crooned.

"You little wretch." He tried to smile. "I suppose I deserve this." Whenever she was near, he was no longer aware of the pain that constantly plagued him. The smell of her silver hair was like wild flowers in his nostrils, and her skin felt like silk against his arm, her breath warm against his neck. He closed his eyes and relaxed.

"Since I'm stuck with you, Garrett, I intend to make the best of it. Your expert ability as a lover is by far your best quality. So I'm going to make sure you regain your strength."

"I see." She heard the silent laughter deep in his chest. "I guess I'll have to let you have your way with my body, then, won't I?"

"I think that would be wise," she agreed, and felt the tension in his muscles seep away. She held his hand until she felt him drift off to sleep. She kissed his brow before tiptoeing out of the room.

Little more than a week later, Catherine cracked a whip over the heads of the mules and the wagon pulled out of Nacogdoches. Cora stood on the front porch, wiping her eyes with her apron before calling out one last bit of advice. "Garrett! Don't stay up on that wagon seat too long." John put his arm around her shoulders and drew her back into the house.

As soon as the wagon was out of town, Garrett reached for the reins, his mouth folded in a determined line.

"What do you think you are doing?"

"What does it look like? You can't handle these mules all the way across Texas. I'll be damned if I'll let a woman drive me anywhere."

Her eyes violent, Catherine shouted, "You stubborn mule! Dr. John said it was too soon. You're acting like an idiot!"

"Blast it, Kate, get off my back. I've wasted enough time lying around." His face was taut with barely suppressed anger.

"Can't you use your head for once instead of allowing your masculine pride to goad you into doing something stupid?"

"Like marrying you, for instance?" Garrett charged

without thinking, irritated that she was probably right but needing to reestablish his authority. After all, he was her husband and no longer a bedridden invalid.

"That was typical of you! But that isn't important. You have no right to kill yourself and leave me alone in this godforsaken country."

"Aah . . . so that's it." He flashed his grin of real amusement, the kind she hadn't seen since Torres's attack. If only he knew how much she needed him safely by her side, how much she loved and wanted him. She reached out a hand to him, hardly knowing what she was doing until he jerked back and raised the whip to the mules. He bit off his words. "Come on, Catherine. We don't have time for arguing. Let's get going."

The sun beat down upon their heads as the morning lengthened. Catherine watched through squinting eyes the prairie grasses waving forever away over each hill. Once in a while, a startled rabbit would scurry out of their path, but other than that, it was as if they were alone in a vast sea of prairie. The terrain rarely changed, so every hill, every gully, looked the same as the next. Eventually Catherine felt fatigue seeping into her bones as the hot sun parched her lips and burned through the muslin shirt she wore. She rode in a kind of stupor, concentrating dully on Garrett's straight back until she saw the unnatural slump to his shoulders.

"Garrett?"

"One more hour," he answered, not bothering to turn to her, his eyes on the trail.

"This is ridiculous. Let's stop before you lose consciousness completely." He was impossible!

"I'm all right. If we stop now, we'll just have to make a longer drive tomorrow." He tried to focus on her but failed. For hours, he had been allowing the mules to make the decisions, knowing they would stay on the well-worn San Antonio Trail.

Catherine glared at him, becoming increasingly alarmed when he swayed on the seat. Enough was enough! She reached over and grabbed the reins. He was beyond caring when she guided the wagon to a spot under a nearby tree. Fortunately they had been following a creek, and it was an ideal place to stop.

"Get in the back and lie down, Garrett. We're stopping, no matter what you say." She went to help him, but he was already crawling inside the wagon. He was clutching his thigh, his face ashen. "Oh, you fool, you're exhausted already."

"So it seems," he answered almost sheepishly, his voice weak. She made sure he was comfortable on the makeshift bed Cora Griffith had prepared for their wagon and then ran to the creek to fill her canteen with water.

She returned to the wagon and began bathing his face with cool water. "Oh, you blithering idiot," she grumbled, but the words held little anger. "How long have you been hurting?"

"Don't start; I'll be fine in a little while." He gritted his teeth through the pain, the flesh of his chest a mass of gooseflesh. She immediately covered him with a quilt. He was barely conscious. She sat back on her haunches, her eyes accusing.

"Do you know where we are?"

"Sort of." His eyes became guarded.

Catherine looked around her. The terrain looked identical to what she had seen all morning. She had no idea how far they had come. It was midday and a good place to rest. She held a canteen to his lips. "Here, drink some water, then I'll go and see to the other mules."

"The horses. . . ." His voice trailed off, missing her sarcasm. He was asleep.

She unhooked a bucket and went to fill it in the creek. She brought water to each mule and then led the horses to the creek to drink their fill. By the time she was finished, she was exhausted and wet with perspiration. She sank down on the grassy creek bank, not knowing if she could handle the chores for the remainder of the day, let alone the many days it would take to reach Tierra.

Her insides felt hollow, and she went for the basket of food Cora had provided for their lunch. She ate a piece of cold chicken and a large slice of bread. Garrett had to eat, but it was obvious he needed rest more than food. She didn't want him demanding to drive again, so she didn't disturb him. Feeling slightly overwhelmed, she climbed back on the wagon seat and started the mules.

When she stopped again, dusk was falling, casting long, dark shadows on the vast and lonely landscape. She swung around and looked at Garrett, asleep behind her. "Garrett, can you hear me?" She begged him to open his eyes and tell her he was all right.

She saw his lids lift wearily, a smile not quite on his lips. "Don't worry, Catherine."

She dropped into the wagon beside him. "You knew all along how hard this would be. Am I supposed to do this by myself?"

"Just follow the trail," Garrett insisted. It was too much effort to talk and his voice drifted away.

The night closed in around them. With no help from Garrett, Catherine did what she had been taught to do on the wagon train: gather wood, make a fire, feed and water the stock, make a meal. She couldn't get Garrett to eat. It was pitch black by the time she had done all that she had to do, and cold and getting colder. She climbed inside the wagon to find that Garrett's teeth were chattering. He rolled restlessly. She was frightened that he would die of fever before she could get him home. He was alternately hot, then cold. She sat with him all night, unable to sleep. By first light, he was delirious, and she was beside herself with worry.

"If you live through this, I'm going to give you so much trouble. . . ." She began to talk out loud, with no one to hear. "Garrett, you have to eat." She grasped him under the shoulders, her heart sinking when she heard his muttering.

"I'll check fences, Jason . . . Burt. . . ." Tears slid down her cheeks as she let him sink back on the bed.

"Hang on, my darling. Just hang on." She climbed stiffly onto the wagon seat and took up the reins. Cracking the whip, she hollered, "Gettup, mules! Get us home!"

The sun beat unmercifully. By noon, the trail veered away from the creek and started toward the distant hills, a hazy vision on the horizon.

The landscape got rougher and rougher the closer they got to the Trinity River. Tumbleweed replaced trees; rocks and jagged cliffs replaced the rolling hills of the prairie. It was starkly beautiful, but Catherine had no time for appreciation. Every ounce of her strength and all her concentration were spent keeping the mules on the trail.

Tears made dusty trails through the sweat and grime on her sunburned face. She wondered in self-derision how her aristocratic friends would react to this new Lady Catherine. The hours of driving brought aches to muscles she didn't even know she had. Nowhere was there any sign of human life. Only an occasional roadrunner or strange, long-eared rabbit crossed the trail. She didn't know how much farther they had to go or even if she was heading in the right direction. She bit her lip, feeling increasingly hopeless.

At mid-afternoon, she pulled the team to a stop. She was faced with the muddied waters of the Trinity River, and she couldn't cross it alone. Long legs appeared on the seat beside her. "Why did you let me sleep so long? I'm starving. Where are we?"

Control snapped. "How should I know? You've been sleeping for twenty-four hours, you brute! If you think I'm crossing that river by myself like I've had to do everything else, you're out of your bloomin' mind." She burst into tears and jumped off the wagon, ran to the river's edge and splashed cold water onto her hot face.

Garrett was dumbfounded. Was it possible that he had slept a whole day and night? It was indeed the Trinity. He scrambled off the wagon and went swiftly to his wife. He pulled her into his arms, ignoring the pain, as she sobbed against his chest. "I ought to be hanged," he murmured into her hair, taking a long, harsh breath. "I'll take over from here, little one. You are one hell of a woman, Catherine. One hell of a woman."

It was wonderful to be in his strong arms, wonderful to hear the tenderness in his voice. She cried until she had no more tears. "Oh, Garrett, I've been so afraid. Hold me." It was several minutes before she had recovered enough to return to the wagon.

They ate the leftovers from Cora's basket while Catherine told him of her long night. Finally they faced the river. Garrett manned the wagon, and Catherine mounted Glory. The water swirled around the mare's belly as she waited for the lead mule to follow. Glory kept her footing, and they made it slowly to the other side.

"I'm proud of you, Catherine," Garrett declared as

she got back aboard the wagon. "There aren't many women who would have been as brave as you or who could have done the things you've done."

Her blond head lifted. "That's the first genuine compliment you've ever given me."

"Oh? I think I've told you a number of times how beautiful you are—all of you." His eyes wandered down her curves. "Even with a dirty face." He winked at her and then nodded his head toward the back of the wagon. "Climb in the back and get some rest; I'll take over." He spun the words out in a soothing drawl.

"Oh, no, you don't! We'll end up the same as yesterday, you lummox. You're not passing out on me again. Give me those reins." She held out her hand, her chin tilted at a stubborn angle.

"You win, sweetheart. If I wasn't so damned tired, we'd use Cora's featherbed for something besides sleeping."

She swallowed the huge lump in her throat and muttered, "Sometimes I believe that's all you ever think about." She meant to sound cutting, but his suggestive glance at the open collar of her shirt quickened her pulse. Would she always yield to the invitation in his eyes and voice?

She was too weary to break the deceptively calm truce they had mutually declared. The days wore on, melting together. It was an endurance test neither of them was sure they could pass.

They traveled through miles of pine-covered country before the trail took them across the Brazos River. With no stopping in the little hamlet of Washington, they turned, at last, onto the trail that would end at Tierra Nueva.

Chapter 15

Elena Mariner raised herself up on one elbow and eyed Jason Browning with distaste. Since Garrett had left for London, Jason had become increasingly demanding of her affections. At first, she had tried to imagine it was Garrett who held her in his arms, but her memory could no longer envision the details of his sleek body. She kept confusing Jason's stocky physique with Garrett's tall, lithe one. Jason's was well known to her after all their nights together, and she knew Garrett's body only by sight—not touch.

She had watched Garrett swim naked often, but not once had she ventured out of her hiding place. If only she had—if only she had really been made part of the bronzed body that frequented her fantasies. Her dreams were more satisfying than the reality of Jason's clumsy lovemaking.

The morning began as it always did, with the clang of Hannah Kane's breakfast bell. Dressing quickly, Elena glared with disgust at Jason, asleep in her bed. His mouth hung open, his dark sandy hair and ruddy face pressed against her lace-edged pillow. He looked terrible. How could she have given in once again to his slobbering and pawing? She wouldn't have given herself to Jason at all if he hadn't discovered a means of blackmail.

"Get up, Jason, and get out of here. Robert will guess soon enough what you've been doing while he's out working." She tossed his boots on the bed, hearing his grunt when they hit him.

"Jeesuz! What's the rush?" He rolled onto his belly

again, his bloodshot eyes reflecting the amount of whiskey he'd consumed the night before. If Garrett had been home, Jason would have been at work hours ago and ready for a big breakfast. But Garrett wasn't home, and Elena was beginning to dread what would happen when he came back.

It was going to be soon. He had meant to stay away less than a year.

Burt Kane was doing his best, but with Jason overriding his orders at every turn, the ranch was becoming a place where little got accomplished. Hannah's disapproval of Elena's liaison with Jason was another problem. The older woman barely spoke to her, accusing her with soft hazel eyes all day. Elena avoided her whenever possible. It was lucky that Hannah wouldn't risk telling Garrett what was going on for fear of hurting him.

Elena meant to answer the bell. She was hungry. "Suit yourself; I'm going to breakfast," she snapped at Jason and left.

She sat in the big dining room alone, as she had many times since Garrett had left home. Celeste had reigned in the same chair Elena occupied and the ranch had been without a mistress ever since Celeste's death. But Elena intended to change that. She told Hannah to serve her meal and almost slapped the woman's face as she begrudgingly thumped the plates onto the table.

"Hannah! This coffee is cold," Elena complained loudly to the closed kitchen door. She stared sullenly at the woman as she came out with a pot of coffee and placed it noisily down in front of her.

Hannah was a tall, big-boned woman of Swedish ancestry. Approaching her fiftieth year, she had spent the last twenty on Tierra. Her husband, Burt, was foreman. They had a good life here, but it had been difficult managing in Garrett's absence. If they hadn't felt responsible for young Robert, they would have packed up and left the ranch in Jason's hands until Garrett got back.

Hannah, up since dawn, had been baking. A smudge of flour stood out across one plump cheek, and her almost-white hair fell over her forehead untidily. She pursed her lips before pouring Elena's coffee.

Elena was young in years, but her ripe body—high, full-blown breasts, dark olive skin and a mane of black hair—bespoke maturity. She had the dark eyes of a temptress, but Hannah was pleased to note that they were far less attractive when red-rimmed and shadowed from drink and lack of sleep.

"You done?" Hannah asked, anxious to get on with her work, knowing no help was coming from the haughty Miss Mariner.

"Yes, Hannah." Elena shrugged indifferently. She watched the stiff back retreat and told herself she would be able to deal with the woman as she wished when Garrett got home. Right now she had to be patient.

Jason was another problem. Somehow she was going to have to convince him that her marriage to Garrett could benefit them both. Perhaps she could convince Garrett that Jason had forced himself on her, and then Garrett would kill him. She had seen him almost kill a man for her before.

The morning grew warmer, indicating another hot summer day. She decided to go to the creek to while away the hours. She got her horse, mounted and headed for the cool stream. If she stayed long enough, she would evade the housework. Hannah and her Mexican serving girl would have to do it all.

"That's not Tierra Nueva?" Catherine asked in a shocked voice, staring at the valley below. She pulled the mules to a halt. Garrett was clinging to the wagon seat, his face gray as he gazed at his home. If he hadn't been so exhausted and aching, he would have jumped on the lead mule and sent the wagon hurtling down into the sheltered valley, screeching his arrival at the top of his lungs. As it was, he could barely stay put on the wagon seat and knew that if he let go, he'd fall off and not be able to get up.

"That's it. I've never been so glad to see any place in my life. Get these mules going!"

His temperature was up, and his throat burned. His eyes felt like sandpaper rubbing the insides of his skull. He could see the dark circles under Catherine's big eyes and could sense the sharp ache she must be feeling in her slender arms after days of driving. Why had he ever considered her delicate?

"But it's not a farm at all. It's more like a town! You deliberately misled me! Why?" There were at least fifteen buildings below them. Small adobe houses were arranged around a common well, and several large wooden buildings stood beyond. Set some distance away and surrounded by a high wall was the main house and stable. The large, Spanish-style villa was a fitting backdrop for the obviously prosperous ranch.

"Get going. I'm not in any condition to talk. Get those dumb mules on the road." He gritted his teeth when she raised the whip and started the mules down the winding road. She was in high temper, but he was too tired to care.

Biting her lip, Catherine managed to stay on the road and guide the mules through the open gates. She watched through blurring vision as a tall man came running out of the adobe structure and grabbed at the leads. She hadn't realized that she wasn't slowing down when she got to the house. An enveloping fog was descending, and the last thing she noticed before crumpling on the seat was a large woman running to the wagon and shouting, "Lord have mercy! It's Garrett!"

Hannah and Burt scrambled up on opposite sides of the wagon. "Get Catherine," Garrett gasped before he fell onto Burt.

"Good God, boy, what happened to you?" Burt helped him off the wagon, calling for help to Garrett's brothers. Robert came and put his shoulder under Garrett's arm and helped Burt support Garrett into the house. Jason went to help Hannah with the other passenger.

Inside the house, Garrett was let down on a low couch. "What the devil is this all about, Garr?" Robert asked. "Who is that girl?"

"Get her to bed," Garrett croaked before he was oblivious to everything.

Robert looked anxiously at Burt, wanting answers. His mobile mouth dropped open in bewilderment. Burt Kane's weatherbeaten face was as bewildered as Robert's. The big, barrel-chested man was not smiling when he took off his sweat-stained hat and ran a gnarled hand through his graying brown hair. "I don't know what to make of it, Robbie."

Hannah followed Jason as he carried Catherine inside. "Best get them both to bed." She took command as usual. "Jason, you carry her to the guest room. Burt, you call for help and assist Garrett to his room. We'll get our answers later."

Hannah called for Elena but got no answer. She sent Robert for Maria, the young Mexican serving girl. Inside the guest bedroom, Hannah undressed the angelic figure, wondering why on earth the child was driving Garrett's wagon. Who was she? Her curiosity went unsatisfied as she slipped the girl into one of her own nightgowns. The tiny figure was completely lost inside the voluminous gown. She brought a glass of fresh water to the rosebud mouth and clucked with dismay at the dried cracks she saw on her soft lips. "Garrett has some tall explaining to do this time," Hannah muttered to herself.

She turned to give rapid orders in Spanish to Maria. Together they sought to make their charge more comfortable, wiping the dust and grime from the sleeping figure with tepid water and mildly scented soap. Throughout, the girl slept, her soft breathing occasionally broken by a small whimper. She lifted her long lashes for a second and Hannah asked, "What's your name, honey?"

"Catherine . . . Catherine Browning," the girl whispered, and sank back into unconsciousness.

"Saints preserve us! This little bit of a thing is Garrett's wife. He brought back a bride, and there'll be hell to pay when Miss High and Mighty finds out!" Hannah's plain face lit up with pleasure. She had wished for a girl like this for Garrett but had lost hope that he would ever find one. Elena wasn't going to like this one little bit. Maybe she would settle for Jason, and the two of them would leave Tierra for good. Hannah was sure that if Garrett ever found out about those two, he would force a quick wedding on them.

Hannah left Maria to sit with the new Mrs. Browning while she went around to Garrett's room. She hoped he was in better condition than his bride. This was a story she couldn't wait to hear. Disappointed when she found him sleeping soundly, she turned toward the stairs, determined that neither would be disturbed.

Hannah walked down the stairs and met Elena racing toward her. "Where is he? I want to see him. Get out of my way!"

Hannah maneuvered herself directly in Elena's path. "No you don't, missy. You will stay out of Garrett's room until he recovers. Go back downstairs, and don't you let me catch you disturbing them."

Inquisitive black eyes noted her last word. "Them? Who's with him? Simon?"

Hannah placed her hands on the girls's shoulders and propelled her down the stairs and into the kitchen. "I'll tell you in here . . . He brought home a wife, Elena. Wait till you see her—she's adorable. Just like a little china doll."

"Wife?" Elena spat, attempting to leave the room to get direct verification.

"No you don't." Hannah grabbed her arm and spun her around. "Garrett will explain everything in his own good time. You will wait like the rest of us."

The Browning brothers and Burt were pacing the veranda when Hannah called, "What are you standing out there for? Go unpack their wagon and unhitch those mules. Those poor animals look ready to drop in their tracks. Get their horses to the stables."

Jason, burning with curiosity, asked, "Who's the girl big brother brought home? He's never brought one of his women here before. You must have found something out."

She shooed them toward their chores. "I don't know anything for certain. She says she's Catherine Browning, and she's wearing a wedding ring. Seems to me she's Garrett's wife. You get along and see to their belongings. We'll all get our answers later."

It was Hannah who was sitting with Catherine the next morning when she started awake. "Garrett! Garrett?" The hands that held her were not Garrett's but those of a gray-haired woman whose face was lit by a delighted smile. Catherine tried to say something but found her throat painfully tight. Her voice was a mere croak.

"Here, honey. Drink this up; you'll feel more like talking." She held Catherine's head and a glass to her lips. The fruit juice, cool and sweet, tasted delicious going down her throat. Catherine smiled in gratitude.

"I'm Hannah Kane."

"I'm Catherine Browning. I . . . I'm Garrett's wife." Catherine struggled into a sitting position and immediately got dizzy. She closed her eyes and waited for the fuzziness to pass.

"Bless my soul. That beats all." Hannah was nearly bursting with delight. The girl's huge violet eyes almost mirrored her innocent soul. Not like Garrett's usual women, that was for certain!

"Honey, I surely would like to hear how this all came about, but however it did, I'm very glad. How did Garrett get hurt so bad? Here, drink some more. It will help the talking. I know it must hurt some." Hannah perched on the bed while Catherine sipped the rest of the juice.

"Is Garrett all right?" Renewed panic was mirrored in her overbright eyes.

"He'll be fine, girl," Hannah clucked. "He's back home where he belongs. He has a fever, but it just looks to me like somebody let him out of a sickbed too soon. He's plain wore out." Her voice was calm, and Catherine immediately relaxed.

"Thank God. I didn't think we would ever make it. He was so tired, and he said the mules would lead us here, and I didn't know where we were. I was so bloody scared!" The words came tumbling out as Hannah's sympathetic eyes encouraged her to go on. She gave a hasty explanation of her marriage, leaving out the more painful details, and finally related the terrible events that resulted in Garrett's injuries.

"My dear child! An English lady! Well, you've had quite a time in this country, haven't you? This is a wonderful surprise. I was afraid he'd never marry. It's a relief to me, I can tell you. That boy hasn't been too particular about women up to now. But I guess that's why his pa sent him to England for a wife. I can see by the look of you that he picked out the cream of the crop. For all we knew, he went to England to visit his ma's family. Some promise he made to his pa. The truth is going to surprise some folks, that's sure. Fact is, though, if he married you, will or no will, he must have wanted to."

She surveyed Catherine from head to toe, shaking her head. "Don't surprise me none that that rascal Simon would drag Garrett off on one of his escapades. Neither one of them uses the sense God gave 'em. If he were still a boy, I'd take a stick to him for taking a girl into danger like that. Not sure I shouldn't anyway."

Catherine's lips quirked at the thought of Hannah chasing Garrett with a stick.

"Now, honey, you need more rest. I've been taking care of your man since he was a littl'n. A few more days won't matter a-tall. I can hardly believe you dragged that big brute all across the country." Smiling broadly, she pulled the covers around Catherine's fair head.

Garrett lay in bed, his chest bare except for the stark white bandages wrapped around his middle. Elena sat at his side, talking softly to him as Hannah walked in. Garrett gave Hannah a sheepish smile that pulled at her heartstrings. He was like a son to her, and now she could show her real feelings without fearing for her and Burt's positions. Celeste was no longer able to threaten her for interfering. Hannah had continued treating Garrett like an overgrown boy as he grew up, leaving everyone else to wonder how she got away with it. To them, Garrett had always been the unquestioned master of Tierra: first, as the heir-apparent and then the owner. No one crossed him—no one would dare. No one, that is, except Hannah, who knew his weaknesses and strengths better than anyone on earth. She was the person who had been privy to his innermost feelings. He had run to her as a child when his mother's wrath was running high. Her arms had been his refuge, her rooms his hiding place.

"I see you still can't stay out of trouble when you're out of my sight."

"I guess you'll have to keep a tighter rein, Hannah." He grinned as he took his hand from Elena's in order to sit up. He didn't see the flash of irritation Elena shot Hannah or the disapproving glance she got in return.

"He's going to be fine, Hannah." Elena patted his arm. "I'm here to take care of him."

"I want to talk to you, Garrett." Hannah glanced pointedly at Elena.

"Go get some breakfast, princess." He shooed Elena off.

Hannah waited until Elena was out of the room before she took her place on the chair by his bed. "So! Just what have you done this time? That pretty little girl in the other room is about on her last legs. Where did you leave your brains?" She tried to sound angry, but they both knew she felt only joy at his homecoming.

"You know patience was never one of my virtues." He laughed, then winced at a stab of pain as he struggled higher up on the pillows. "Damn!"

"Don't you start swearing, mister," Hannah scolded. "You know you're a crazy fool for traveling around with a chest full of broken bones. I thought you knew better."

He didn't look repentant. Hannah continued on a different vein, her features softening. "She's beautiful . . . so tiny. Looks just like an angel." She searched his face and didn't like what she saw. His dark blue eyes were hiding something. "Trouble already? I'd think that you could handle a little bit like her."

"Handle her? That's a laugh," he said, totally surprising Hannah. "She's more stubborn than one of those mules she drove, and little or not, she's got one hell of a temper. She's a lot tougher than she looks."

"Good for her! Just what you need!" Hannah declared, pleased. "A woman who can handle you for a change."

He looked offended. "What do you mean by that?"

"Just what I said. You've gotten away with your shenanigans far too long, wrapping women around your little finger, then casting them aside."

"I'm not wrapped around her finger, if that's what you're thinking!" he scoffed, hitching his shoulders up and wincing.

Hannah decided to change the subject; his color was poor. It would be a few days before he was up and around, and there was plenty of time to put things right now that he was married. "Don't get all riled up. You'll wear yourself out. I've no mind to keep neglecting my work to look after you all day. We both know if it wasn't for your wife, you wouldn't be here at all. Now think about that and start treating her right. Otherwise I'll sure know where to place the blame."

"Goddamnit, Hannah! She's already got you on her side, doesn't she? You don't know one damn thing about it—or do you?" His eyes narrowed suspiciously. "Just what has Catherine been telling you?"

Hannah stood up and pursed her lips, avoiding the question. She began tucking the blankets around him, not liking the fact that he still slept in the raw—not with Elena capable of snuggling in close before Catherine got her things moved into his room.

"Hannah? Answer me!" He shook his head, making the dark curls fall over his forehead. He was so handsome it was a wonder some female hadn't snared him before now. At least Elena was out of the running and couldn't get her hands on him.

"She told me why you married her and that the two of you don't always see eye to eye." She went to the dresser and pulled out a long nightshirt, never used but always provided. A determined look deepened in her eyes. "Here, you put this on."

Garrett stared at her, then at the nightshirt. "Good God, Hannah. I've always slept without one."

"And that's stopping, right now," Hannah snapped. She set her mouth and swooped over to the bed. Garrett fended her off as she tried to draw the shirt over his head.

"Now that I'm legally allowed to sleep with a woman, you want me to respect the proprieties. Catherine has seen me without clothes." He was too weak to keep Hannah from drawing the sleeves roughly down his arms. "Be a little gentle, for God's sake."

She pulled and tugged at the nightshirt until it was covering his bare legs. He was a full-grown man, not some little boy. A blush of embarrassment stained his cheeks.

"This isn't on account of her," Hannah blustered. "I've seen Elena looking at you, and Catherine doesn't deserve that, no matter how things stand between you."

His eyes widened in shocked amazement. "Elena? Why, she's like a sister to me."

Hannah briskly tucked in the sheets, taking no caution with his tender sides. "Ouch!" He blanched white under his tan. "Will you take it easy?"

"You hear me well, Garrett Browning. There's a lot you don't know about your so-called sister. That's all I'm going to say on the subject." With that, she walked to the door until his voice called her back.

"About Catherine, Hannah. It's no one else's business how or why we got married."

"I'm not as big a fool as you. I can keep my mouth shut without the likes of you reminding me. She told me because she needs a friend. Don't you holler at her for it, neither. You try to think on what I told you."

"Some homecoming!" Garrett shouted at the slammed door. Jason wouldn't answer the simplest question about the ranch. Burt kept putting him off until he felt "stronger," and now Hannah was making him feel guilty for dragging Catherine willy-nilly about the country. His young wife had Hannah eating out of her hand and had confessed everything before he got the chance to defend himself. Robert, at least, was pleased to see him, but he couldn't or wouldn't tell him much about the ranch, either. The only one who was genuinely sympathetic was Elena. Hannah's suggestion was ridiculous, and he dismissed it as rivalry between two women who had shared the same house too long.

It was Catherine's first day out of bed. She was eager to explore her new home, though her legs were still a bit shaky. Her bedroom was large, airy and sun-filled. It gave her a feeling of warmth and openness. The white chintz curtains and pale pink walls were delicately feminine, and she quickly felt at home. There was a writing desk, a beautifully carved walnut wardrobe and a spindled four-poster that held a soft down mattress that made sleeping a pleasure.

She crossed the room and opened the large oak doors of the wardrobe, the most likely place to find her meager belongings. Gasping in disbelief, she stepped back. There, hanging from satin-covered hangers, were all her clothes—not just the ugly garments Garrett had purchased for the wagon train, but every gown she had brought with her from England! Somehow Garrett had managed to get them delivered to Tierra. He had not given them away, after all.

She fingered the gowns with delight, finally choosing a favorite cream-colored morning gown for her appearance downstairs. She pinned up her hair and slipped her small feet into matching slippers. Spinning with happiness, she viewed herself in the large oval mirror at the door to the wardrobe. Pleased with her appearance, she went out.

She ventured down the carved staircase, her eyes alive with curiosity. She could smell coffee brewing and followed the rich aroma to the vast kitchen. "Good morning, Hannah," she said, startling Hannah at the massive black stove.

"Goodness, honey, I didn't expect you down so soon. Don't you look purty in that gown. I figured all them pretty things must be yours when a wagonload of trunks arrived yesterday from Austin. You was sleepin' so hard, you didn't even flicker an eyewinker when Maria and me put everything away for you." Hannah turned the spoon in her hand over to a thin, sloe-eyed girl who came to stand beside her. "This here's Maria."

"Hello, Maria." Catherine smiled encouragingly at the shy girl. Maria nodded, then quickly turned away with a murmured, *"Patrona."*

"You can say what you want, Catherine. She only speaks Spanish. Most of the families don't speak our language, so you gotta learn theirs."

"What did she call me?" Catherine asked as Hannah told her to sit down at the table where a place was already laid.

"On Tierra, you are *la patrona,* and Garrett is *el patrón.* To these people, Garrett is like a king. He decides their squabbles and provides for them. They will love you as well." Hannah nodded, and the dark-skinned serving girl brought a plate to the table and placed it almost reverently before Catherine. Catherine was disconcerted. No wonder Garrett acted like an arrogant ruler at times; to these shy people, he was almost a dictator. She had never expected anything remotely like this. Tierra Nueva was like a self-supporting kingdom, and her husband, the man she had called a dirt farmer, was the feudal lord. She didn't realize that she had said as much out loud until Hannah began chuckling.

"He bent the truth a bit, I gather." She sat down next to Catherine and ordered her to eat. "You must be fair starving."

"More than a little." Catherine attacked her bacon and eggs with relish. She swallowed a mouthful of steaming hot coffee and gave Hannah a demoralized frown. "If you had only heard some of the things I've called him. I feel like a complete idiot."

"Nonsense. I s'pect you took him down a peg or two and he didn't like it."

"Tell me about the rest of Garrett's family. He says so little."

"Jason—he's the middle brother—is a different man from Garrett altogether," Hannah explained, her brow furrowing. "Enough said. Now Robbie, he's the youngest and a good boy. Then there is Miss Elena Mariner, she's a ward of the family. There's Burt and me, of course, the ranch hands, and then the Mexican families. You'll meet everybody in due time. The boys eat here in the kitchen, and I s'pect they'll be down soon. Miss Elena eats in there." She nodded toward the dining room. "Thinks she's a queen or something."

"Isn't she Simon's sister?"

"Half-sister," Hannah corrected swiftly, and implied her dislike with her tone of contempt. Nevertheless, Catherine hoped to make friends with the girl, who was supposed to be near her own age. If she was anything like Simon, she'd be charming.

"Why aren't you carrying a babe yet?" Hannah's bald question made Catherine choke on a bite of bacon. She groped for an answer, spluttering, "I . . . I beg your pardon?" In England, no one would have asked such a personal question.

"Listen, honey. A big belly's just about the onliest thing I can think of that you can defend yourself with. There's trouble brewing here. You'd better get your man to breed you quick or you'll suffer for it."

Catherine's breath lodged in her throat. What on earth was Hannah talking about? She wasn't about to beg Garrett to bed her even if she missed his lovemaking so much it was almost a constant pain. "I . . . I don't understand," she managed to croak.

"Trust me, missy. You move into Garrett's room pronto, before someone takes your place." Hannah's earthy rhetoric continued. "You are what this place needs, but you may not be what it gets if you don't give in to your husband pretty damn quick, lady or no."

"Give in?" She was nonplussed. Garrett wasn't completely healed. As far as she knew, that was the only thing stopping him from seeking her bed.

"It's obvious you're not sleeping together. If you were, you'd be heavy with his child by now. Holding out on your man isn't wise, child. You'd best work your problems out some other way." Hannah sounded so concerned that Catherine wanted to laugh, but she was more shocked than amused.

"Hannah, I don't know what to say. We have very good reasons for sleeping apart. He's been hurt. I am his wife in more than name." Catherine blushed, not understanding why she had to defend herself and admit to the intimate details of her marriage.

"Good." Hannah beamed her approval. "I knew there was something between you. You're far too pretty for him to resist long. Now, that's all I have to say on the subject."

"Thank you for breakfast, Hannah. I think I'll go see if Garrett's awake. I'll be back down to meet the rest of the family a little later," Catherine said uncomfortably. She wiped her lips quickly and escaped from the kitchen. Barely outside the door, she ran smack into a thick, masculine chest.

"Ahh. . . ." the man said with a laugh, "my brother can sure pick 'em; always could." He ogled her from head to foot. She stepped back and tried to force a smile.

"And you are?" she queried politely, loathing the open desire she saw in his eyes.

"Jason Browning, fair one. Big brother's just surprising us all over the place. Showing up with a wife instead of a. . . ." He stepped closer, and she stood stiffly as he hugged her in what was decidedly not brotherly fashion.

She was thankful to see another figure come upon them, causing Jason to release her.

"You must be Catherine."

"You must be Robert." Taking no chances, she held out her hand. He grasped it tightly and shook it up and down. He was a younger and thinner version of Garrett. Jason, on the other hand, was shorter and thick-chested, round-faced, with dark blond hair. Of the two, Catherine already preferred Robert.

"Come into the *sala* and tell us all about yourself, Catherine." Robert smiled at her with warm blue eyes—the same color as his oldest brother's. "We're anxious to hear all about you." He gave Jason a playful shove aside as he escorted his new sister-in-law to a horsehair chair in the sitting room. "Forgive Jason. He has no manners at all with a real lady."

Catherine laughed. "You do, however?" She warmed to Robert as she saw how the youthful Garrett must have been. She gave Jason a wary glance, not sure if he had been teasing her with his familiarity or not.

"I beg your pardon, Catherine," Jason interjected, his eyes flicking up and down her body. "It's difficult to remember that cultured ladies like soft words—first."

She didn't like his words any more than his leering. He was not what she had expected. There was something about Jason that made her distrust him. Robert, though he was young, showed promise of becoming a man to be trusted and respected. His resemblance to Garrett was striking, but he projected a gentleness and sensitivity Garrett lacked.

Robert plied her with questions, showing no resentment over her unheralded entrance into the family. Jason remained silent, but his eyes crawled over her until she couldn't take it any longer.

"We will be able to talk more later," she said as she stood. "Right now I'd like to make sure Garrett is all right. I haven't seen him since we arrived."

Robert rose with her and took her hand, gently squeezing it. "It's nice having you here, Catherine. This place could sure use a woman's touch again. A lady's." She saw his dark flush when Jason glared at him from across the room. He didn't have to say it. Jason welcomed her because she was a healthy feminine body, pleasing to the eye.

She tried to shake off her feelings of repugnance as she entered the large foyer. She concentrated on her surroundings, looking forward to touring her new home later. After what Garrett had led her to believe, Tierra came as a pleasant surprise.

The house was immense and infinitely more sophisti-
cated than she had imagined. It was a sprawling adobe
structure, styled in the Spanish manner, with a tiled
roof and a covered veranda stretching across the front
on both the first and second floors. The sitting room—
Robert had called it the *sala*—was furnished with
masculine pieces, dark yet not austere. She had a
feeling of being outdoors and could actually smell the
arid breeze and feel the warmth of sunshine on her
face.

The stairs leading to the second floor were wide and
gracious, beautifully carved from mellow oak. The soft
cream walls were adorned with colorful tapestries and
subdued, earth-toned paintings. Bright rugs were scattered along the stone floors of the first floor, adding
splashes of color. Later, she would be told how they
were woven on looms by the Mexican women who lived
on Tierra. She was impressed with the aura of under-
stated wealth. Where Bannerfield had been stiffly formal, Tierra was warmly comfortable. She knew she
could be very happy within its sturdy walls.

Chapter 16

Catherine turned the heavy knob of Garrett's bedroom
door and peeked in. He was asleep, but he was not
alone. A dark-haired girl, who had to be Elena, was
curled up in the chair beside his bed. One of her hands
rested possessively on his chest. She wore a dark red
silk robe that clung to every curve of her body. It was
obvious that she wore nothing underneath the garment,
which was loosely wrapped around her body and tied at

the waist. The front gaped open, exposing a considerable amount of her large, full breasts. It was indecent, and Catherine felt unaccountably angry. Adopted sister or no, Garrett's first sight in the morning should not be this half-clad beauty. The girl opened dark, sultry eyes and stared openly at Catherine. She made no attempt to adjust her robe or introduce herself. There was naked hatred in her eyes. Startled, Catherine remembered her conversation with Hannah. "I'm Garrett's wife, Catherine, and you must be Elena Mariner," she stated quietly.

The girl sinuously uncoiled herself from her chair and stood up. Her breasts nearly fell out of the robe before she leisurely pulled the edges together and smiled at Garrett like a satisfied cat. She turned to Catherine. "Garrett's exhausted. The smallest exertion wears him out. You see how soundly he sleeps?" Elena whispered. "I'm afraid we won't be able to resume our relationship until he has completely healed."

The color drained from Catherine's face. "What do you mean?" she asked, stunned.

"We can't talk here, Mrs. Browning; but come with me and I'll tell you how things will be for you." Her voice was full of malicious meaning.

Intending to put a stop to the girl's highhandedness, Catherine returned, "I will wait in my room until you are properly dressed." She was gratified to see the surprise on Elena's face.

Catherine had to wait about five minutes for Elena's arrival. She didn't have a chance to say anything before Elena hissed at her, "You may be his wife, fair Catherine from England, but it is me he loves." Elena had discovered some interesting news about Garrett's marriage as he muttered in his sleep. Catherine had married him under protest. Perhaps it wouldn't be so difficult to get rid of the pale beauty who claimed the Browning name.

"Is that what you came to tell me?" Catherine asked, sickened.

"Tell me, Lady Catherine, what will it take to make you run back to England? He only married you to salve his pride, as you thought yourself too good for him. Now he regrets his rashness and wants to be rid of you," Elena said.

Could that be true? Had Garrett discussed her with Elena? Did all the months of traveling, the nights spent in each other's arms, mean nothing to him now that he was back with this brazen beauty? Elena was smiling as if she pitied her.

"Is that what Garrett told you?" Catherine immediately sensed her error. She had lent credence to Elena's statements, and a self-satisfied smile crossed her rival's face.

Elena laughed insolently. "Believe me, he has tired of you." She spat out the words venomously. "Oh, he wanted your body, all right, just as he's wanted a lot of other women's, but he always comes back to me."

"Strange, he barely mentioned you to me." Catherine kept her voice calm, not revealing her rising rage.

A dark flush suffused Elena's features, making her seem dangerous. "It would be stupid to mention your lover to a new wife, would it not?"

"I think I've heard enough. If Garrett wants me to leave, he knows I would be more than happy to oblige. I never wanted to be his wife in the first place; that was his idea. Perhaps he has been no more forthright with you than he has been with me."

"Where is your stiff English pride? If you leave now, I can help you. Garrett would never know how it was done."

"I don't think so, Elena. You can tell Garrett that he can have his freedom anytime he wants, but the request will have to come from him, not you."

Elena flounced to the door, her face twisted. "I think you must be even more stupid than Garrett says. I hope you are happy in a place where you're not wanted." The door slammed behind her.

"Oh!" Catherine fumed. "The nasty little schemer."

Had Garrett sent Elena to do his dirty work? He hadn't touched her since their encounter with Torres, but she'd thought it was because of his injuries. Hadn't he jested about saving his strength so he could make love to her? To find out he had already been with Elena, made love to her and told her intimate details about their relationship was disgusting. But—was it true? Elena had looked sexually fulfilled as she lingered by Garrett's bed. What kind of family was this? Jason openly ogled his brother's wife; Garrett slept with the girl he called his sister. They were all immoral! Only Robert and the Kanes seemed honest, but perhaps she didn't know all there was to know about them yet. How could Hannah live in this house and not know what was going on between Elena and Garrett? She did know. Her warnings to Catherine proved it. Catherine resolved to find a way to escape this depravity and get back home.

How could she have thought she was in love with Garrett—that he would return her love one day? She would never allow him to touch her again. How utterly stupid she had been! Still—there was the possibility that Elena was lying. But why should she lie? If she and Garrett were like brother and sister, she would never have said she was his lover. It was almost incestuous, and who would admit to such a thing?

For days, Catherine kept to her room—only venturing out at mealtimes and for a few trips outdoors. The ranch house contained a well-stocked library in which she found many of her favorite books, much to her surprise. At least she had something to do during the long days and even longer nights. She was not going to pretend to be part of this household. She made no show of seeing how it functioned. When she did leave her room, Elena's saucy smirk made it clear that things were back to normal in her love life. Catherine was well aware that the girl spent the majority of every day in Garrett's room. She assumed she spent her nights there, as well.

Seeing Jason pawing Elena outside Garrett's door only further convinced Catherine of the family's decadence. She saw Elena's slight resistance and heard Jason's angry retort, "So now you warm his bed, too." Catherine was sickened. Elena must have a difficult time dividing her favors between the two brothers. Catherine's pride kept her from barging in on Elena and Garrett to tell them exactly what she thought of them. Eventually she would demand passage back to England.

The only bright spots in her life were Hannah and Robert. Her original impression of them had been correct. Robert had no idea of what transpired in Garrett's room, and Hannah was an employee, with no right to judge. Robert tried to pry Catherine out of her room to show her the ranch, but she gently refused. She wanted to prevent herself from becoming too attached to Garrett's charming little brother in order to spare herself the additional pain of separation. She attempted to ignore the confusion she saw in Robert's eyes whenever she turned down his invitations. She kept telling herself it was better to hurt his feelings a little now than to hurt him worse later.

But Hannah had not taken no for an answer. After Catherine had skipped breakfast for two days, Hannah had searched her out. "Catherine, please understand that I don't approve of what goes on here. I have no right to interfere. I am paid help. I try not to see anything."

Catherine had snapped back, "You must walk around with your eyes shut." She had relented only when the older woman's plain face had crumpled with pain. Catherine apologized for her outburst, and after that Hannah came often to talk. She talked about Garrett. Hannah had been like a mother to him, as much as was possible with Celeste around. She had loved him no matter what his faults were. Catherine could understand. Hadn't she felt that way herself not too long ago? But under the circumstances, she could not overlook Garrett's faults any longer. His tomcat morality was abhorrent. She could not explain to Hannah why she was shunning Garrett. Though the two women became friends, Catherine preferred to be alone.

Once she heard Garrett's voice raised in anger and thought she heard her name. She waited, but he did not seek her out. It was obvious he had much more ardorous things to do with Elena.

She was perched on her bed, her book unread in her lap, when the door burst open, almost creaking off its hinges as it banged against the wall. "Just what do you think you're doing, sitting around all day doing nothing?" Garrett was more angry than she had seen him in a long while. He wore a tight pair of blue pants, but that was all. His chest was still tightly strapped, his feet were bare, and from the tousled condition of his hair, he had come directly from bed. Catherine was ready with an angry retort, but Elena came running in before she could make it. She grabbed Garrett's arm and tried to get him to leave.

"Garrett! Come back to bed. She isn't worth your risking another fever." She condemned Catherine with her eyes. "Lady Catherine is so used to lazing about, you can't change her. Don't waste your energy. God knows, my attempts have done no good!"

Catherine sat gaping—the girl lied so convincingly almost anyone would believe her.

Garrett was not to be persuaded. "We'll see about that! Elena, leave us!"

"But Garrett. . . ." Elena started, but when she saw his face, she knew she had no choice. She tossed Catherine a triumphant smile over her shoulder as she passed through the doorway.

Garrett locked the door. He was at Catherine's side in three long strides. His grasp on her shoulders was like iron as he lifted her bodily from the bed and towered over her, setting her down in front of him. "Get your things; you're coming with me."

"I'm going nowhere! Especially not with you! You are not *el patrón* to me." Her body was shaking with rage.

"We'll see about that," Garrett said grimly. Before she could protest, he hoisted her over his shoulder and carried her to the master bedroom, where he dumped her unceremoniously on the bed. "I'll be back later. I have to clear up a few things." She heard him lock the door and descend the stairs.

She was left to wait. There was no way to escape the locked room. Each hour that passed increased her tension. The sun was setting when Garrett finally returned, relocking the door behind him and placing the key under a bedpost. Catherine faced him defiantly, trying to hide her fear.

"Everyone has cleared out. The place has gone to hell, and Jason and Robert are out with Burt, gathering every stray they've lost. Elena's staying with one of the Mexican families. Hannah has been given the night off. You and I are now going to get our marriage back into proper perspective." He ducked under her swinging fists and tackled her around the waist, his momentum sprawling them both across the bed. "I haven't forgotten how beautiful your body is or how wild you can be in my arms. It's time you remembered what I can do for you. You have much to relearn." He pinned her beneath him.

"You can't teach me anything. I loathe you. I despise everything about you! You can kill me right now, because it's the only way you can stop me from leaving you." She tried to keep her voice as calm as his, willing him to feel her disgust.

"You're threatening me?"

"It's not a threat, it's a promise."

"I see. I've made some promises, too. Do you remember? Like control that temper or pay the consequences? Or—I keep what I pay for?" He grasped her by the shoulders. "Kate, nothing has changed. If you dislike it here, that's too bad."

"Everything has changed! I thought once it might work, but after arriving here, I've found it never will. You don't want me, Garrett. Why won't you let me go?"

"I've always wanted you. You knew that from the beginning. Why don't you admit you want me? You did once before." As he slowly stripped off her clothes, she stiffened to marble.

"Never! Why don't you go to Elena? You seem to love the time you spend with her."

His eyes widened in surprise. "How could you be

jealous of the time I spend with Elena? I told you, she's like a sister to me. Or is it that you don't like the thought of dirtying your hands the way Elena does around here?"

"I think both of you are disgusting. Your lecherous brother, Jason, too!"

A dark anger came to his face at her near-hysterical remarks. "If Jason has touched you, I'll kill him. Has he?" Garrett demanded, his fingers digging into her skin.

"Not for lack of wanting to. But he's scared of what you would do. All of them are scared of you—*el patrón!* I'm not afraid of you, and I won't jump at your commands! Anything you get from me, you'll have to take." She hoped she sounded braver than she felt.

Her words did not delay the inevitable. He removed his own clothes while still holding her in place with one hand. It was the first time she'd seen him completely naked since she had helped nurse his wounds. Only faint ridges of scar tissue and the white plaster on his thigh remained. Tears welled in her eyes. She could not accept the place in his life he had chosen for her: a bedmate when he tired of Elena. The tears rolled down her cheeks, tears she could not stop.

"Ah, *mi querida.*" His voice was soft and husky. "Why do you punish yourself like this? You know your body wants me even when your mind says no. Can't you give in and enjoy yourself? I've only to touch you and you'll respond. You always have."

"No!" she almost screamed.

He ran one finger down her bare skin from neck to flank. "It's a lot more pleasurable when you are willing."

"I'll never be willing for you again." She flinched from his touch.

He smiled at her tenderly, his lips curled in amusement at her struggling. "Why should this time be any different?"

"You can't keep me locked up forever," she challenged.

"That's not my intention," he answered easily. "I'll give you one more chance to say it, Catherine. Tell me you've missed me and want me to make love to you."

"Go to hell!"

"I doubt that's where you really want me."

She almost shouted her frustration. "What's that supposed to mean? That after you make love to me, I'll be ready to cling to you forever? Be your slave? You are blinded by your own conceit!"

"Not at all. I intend to get you pregnant," he stated quietly, his eyes intense.

Shock made her momentarily speechless. Would his treachery never stop surprising her? "I can still run away," she managed at last.

He turned his face to her, and she read in his eyes how far he was prepared to go. "If you leave our child behind, you can go if you wish," he said grimly.

This was what he was keeping her for—an heir. She meant no more to him than a brood mare. "I'd never let you raise a child of mine. Never! I will raise my child even if I have to stay here to do it!"

He turned his face away, and she didn't see the sudden relief in his eyes. "That would be up to you, but any child you produce will stay with me." His voice was totally devoid of feeling. Catherine closed her eyes, trapped as surely as a fly pinned to a wall.

"I pray to God I am barren, Garrett. That seems likely, too, since I haven't conceived yet under your onslaughts." She hoped it would be so, for if she bore a child, she would never leave this prison. She gritted her teeth, preparing for his assault, admitting, at last, that no matter what she said, he would not be denied.

"You are the most frustrating woman!" he declared. "Before I'm through with you, you'll be begging me to take you."

"Never!"

His deep blue eyes darkened, never leaving hers as he began running one finger slowly down her throat and between her heaving breasts, circling their softness with a tantalizing caress. His dark head lowered, and his lips followed the same path as his fingers. "I love the taste of you." He drew his tongue along the shadowed valley between her breasts, slowly ascending the quivering curves until he reached her throbbing peaks, where he enclosed her nipple with his mouth until it hardened and swelled.

Catherine moaned in torment, unable to withstand his intimate devastation without feeling desire rise up to overtake her. He raised his head to gaze deeply into her eyes, his mouth curving in a teasing smile. "I've just begun, and you're already ready for me, aren't you?" When she shook her head wildly, denying his words, he gave her a brief, sideways smile before lowering his head again.

She trembled beneath the onslaught of his lips, which made claim after claim on her treacherous body. She moved to his commands, no matter how hard she tried to prevent it. His fingers slid to her belly and paused until the insides of her thighs tingled with expectation. He knew he was driving her to a frenzy, but he continued tempting her, his fingers sliding lower.

Catherine squeezed her eyelids shut and tightened her lips to prevent the cries of pleasure from escaping. He meant to bring about her complete surrender before granting her release from the torture he was inflicting. "Do you want me, Catherine?" he said huskily, his cheek resting against her thigh.

She averted her head, unable to answer. He laughed softly, accepting her weak defiance, unremitting in his determination to force her willing acceptance. He began a slow trail down her legs, flicking his tongue along the sensitive insides of their smooth curves until she thought she would die of the exquisite torment. As his mouth explored her burning skin, his fingers moved between her thighs. With tears trickling down her cheeks, she gasped, "Please."

"Please what?"

"I want you." Catherine wept, her body clamoring for his possession. She felt his palms traverse her straining body, stimulating the fluttering nerves beneath her skin, still delaying the moment when he would enter her and brand his ownership upon her flesh. He could bring her to such a pinnacle of ecstasy, it was like falling from the highest cloud in the heavens before coming to rest in the enveloping safety of his arms.

Her fingers were clutching his head, grasping the black hair as she drew his face down to her lips. She opened her mouth, gasping his name over and over as he kissed her. The violence that governed her movements brought her breasts against the crisp dark hair on his chest as she reveled in the feel of him against her. She arched her back and moaned her need beneath his lips as he plunged inside her. Thunder throbbed within her with each driving thrust of his pulsating manhood. Catherine returned each movement and surrendered completely to the passions he aroused in her. She was as much the victor as the vanquished as they reached their tumultuous climax, soaring together, each as necessary to the other as the winds to the tide.

Her breath came like a native drumbeat, answered by the pounding rhythm of Garrett's heart upon her breast. Her skin gleamed with moisture as she plummeted back to earth and sanity.

"Deny that you are mine," Garrett groaned, pulling her with him as he rolled onto his back. Her cheek found its resting place on his broad chest under his chin, and her hands nestled on either side of his neck.

"I . . . I can't," she whispered softly. Her lashes fell and she slept, completely satiated and entirely his. He waited until her feathery, warm breath told him she would say no more. He brought his hand to the golden head snuggled beneath his chin and left it there. Relaxed in his ownership, he wrapped his long legs about her slim ones and closed his eyes. Nothing would ever separate them again.

Chapter 17

Catherine stretched her legs and reached out an arm to discover that she was alone in the vast bed. The sheets were cold to her touch, indicating that Garrett had left their bed some time ago. She looked at the empty space beside her and saw a white envelope lying upon the pillow. Puzzled, she picked it up. Her eyes grew moist when she recognized the seal. She propped herself up against the headboard and tore open the envelope. Garrett had left Colin's letter as a surprise for her.

It took some time for her blurred vision to clear enough for her to read the scrawled pages.

Dear Kay,

Ego amo te! That is Latin for "I love you." As you can see, I am mastering that language. I am doing better in all subjects, and Allen says he is proud of me. Because of my improvement, Allen invited me to London for a fortnight. I met the baroness, who is jolly good fun. Lady Estelle babies me, even though Allen told her I am almost a grown man. She is a nice lady, and I do not mind too much.

Allen tells me the news about your war. Have you seen any fighting? I wish I were there to join in the excitement. The baroness was worried, but I told her that if Garrett could fend off Indians, he could fight Mexicans, too.

Let me know when I can come for a long visit. I still want that horse Garrett promised.

Love,
Colin

Catherine read and reread the letter, wishing Colin were already on his way for a visit. How he would love Tierra! She folded the letter and placed it on the bedside table. Hurrying out of the bed, she put on a pink silk gown styled with a high neck, short sleeves and a deep ruffle at the hem. She wanted to look beautiful for Garrett this morning and thank him for the thoughtful gesture of leaving her to enjoy Colin's letter in privacy.

Slowly Catherine descended the stairs and crossed the foyer to the dining room. She heard voices coming from the kitchen beyond. The sound of Elena's throaty murmur stopped her in her tracks. Unashamedly she stopped and listened to the exchange taking place between her husband and the sultry beauty.

"I can see why you want to bed her, but why marry her? She is useless! She doesn't do one thing around here, though she is supposed to be *la patrona*, the new mistress. You had to send your family away from the house to make up to her. Doesn't that tell you what she's like?"

"Elena," Garrett's deep voice was gentle, "I'm sorry you and Catherine don't get along. But she is my wife, and she is *la patrona*. Give her time. She will adjust."

Catherine began to open the door, believing her husband innocent of all she had thought, but then Elena's angry voice stopped her.

"She will never fit in here! Did your mother adjust?" A malicious note entered the husky voice. Catherine heard a chair scrape across the stone floor.

"I want a son, Elena. Tierra will pass to a child of mine. Catherine can give me well-bred, spirited children who will be taught to love this land as much as I do."

Catherine's heart turned to stone. She didn't want to hear any more. He had been using her last night, using her to gain an heir. She ran on silent feet back to the master bedroom, where she stripped off her gown and put on a pair of pants and a shirt. She crept down the stairs and out the front door to the stables.

Minutes later, she was jumping Glory over the paddock fence. She had gotten here by wagon; she could get back to the Griffiths' on horseback. She had stolen a water flask and a cloth-wrapped bundle of sandwiches that had been left for the men who rode the fence line. She didn't consider the danger as she galloped like the wind along the winding trail.

She was almost on top of the rise when she heard the sound of a horse behind her. Looking back, she saw Garrett on Trojan. Memories of the steeplechase course at Bannerfield replayed in her mind as she whipped Glory to a furious gallop. As before, months ago, the horses ran neck and neck and she was scooped from the saddle.

"Where do you think you are going?" She slid off Trojan's back, and he joined her on the ground.

"Back to England." She didn't care how he felt about it; she was not returning to Tierra.

"How? With no money? Were you planning to ride your horse across the ocean?" He reached for her arm and spun her to face him.

"I can get to the Griffiths'." She tried to wrench her arm free.

"I always said you were long on courage and short on sense. Now what's this all about?" He pulled off his hat and wiped his brow.

"I won't be your brood mare. I'm leaving." Her chin lifted defiantly. "Get that through your head!"

His stunned silence grew dangerously long as they stared at one another. Without saying another word, he lifted her onto Trojan's back and swung up behind her in the saddle. She made no attempt to fight him, for she saw a violence in his eyes that frightened her.

They rode back to the hacienda without exchanging a word. Once they were inside, he placed a hand at the small of her back and marched her up the steps to the master bedroom.

"Let's get something settled, Catherine." His words broke the tense silence as he pulled up one chair and pointed to another. She had never seen him look so forbidding, and she sat down as ordered. She waited for him to continue, but he seemed to be struggling for words. His voice, when it came, was without expression. "Torres can't be allowed to distribute those new weapons. Simon will be tracking him down, and I plan to join him." He looked at her but was not seeking her approval, only giving her the facts. "It is possible that you could be pregnant. If I don't come back, I want your promise to make sure my son gets his share of this place."

She raised shocked eyes to his set face, terrified by the resolve she saw there. She didn't want him to go after Torres. He could be killed, and she didn't want that, had never wanted that.

"No," she said. "Torres will kill you."

"You expect me to believe you would care?"

"Yes, I care! You may prefer Elena to me, but I don't want you dead!" she cried out, standing up to take him by the arms, her fingers digging into the material of his shirt.

He stood up, too, and her feet were no longer touching the ground as his hands crushed her arms to her sides. "What did you say?"

"She told me she was your lover. I . . . I heard you tell her you married me to get an heir. I . . . I heard you, Garrett. And I heard Jason admit he slept with her, too. How could I stay married to you after that?"

He put her on her feet and grabbed her wrist, pulling her out of the room. "And you believed it?" He didn't wait for her answer as she was half-dragged out the front door and over to the Kanes' rooms. Inside the main room in Hannah's place, he pushed her down on the chair. "Don't move an inch or say a word. Hannah!"

Hannah was thoroughly nonplussed, staring at them both.

"How long was I too sick to lift a finger when I got home?"

The beginning of an understanding smile lifted Hannah's mouth. "'Bout three days, I reckon."

"Could I have bedded a woman in those three days?"

"Lordy, no." Hannah laughed. "Surely, Catherine, you didn't expect him to?"

Garrett shot her a triumphant grin, and Catherine blushed. A warm happiness was seeping into her body as she realized where Garrett was going with the conversation.

"Is Jason sleeping with Elena?" he shot out, the look on his face hard and unrelenting.

"This isn't necessary, Garrett." Catherine saw the look of horror on Hannah's face.

"I'll decide what's necessary. Answer me, Hannah."

Hannah hung her head. "Yes."

"Christ! Why wasn't I told?" Garrett exploded.

Hannah lost her temper. "You wouldn't have believed it. She had the wool pulled over your eyes. She's always been a sly one, and she's always wanted to be *la patrona.*"

Garrett reeled backward as if from a blow, then turned on his heel and left them sitting there staring after him.

Catherine rushed out after him, but he was already disappearing into the house when she got out of Hannah's place.

Garrett was strapping on a knife when Catherine flew into the room. She saw the saddlebags laid out on the bed. "You can't be leaving?" She pulled at his arm. "I thought . . . ?"

"I know what you thought," he spat harshly, shaking off her hand.

"I was hurt, Garrett. Don't go. I thought you were using me." His snort of disgust filled her with pain. "I made a mistake about you."

"How like a woman. Should I be grateful that you have changed your mind about me?" His anger was almost a living thing, and she stepped back from the force of it. "What's to stop you from changing your mind again?"

She felt a terrible sense of loss grip her. "I won't because I love you." The words were out before she could think. She was desperate to keep him with her at Tierra and resolve their problems. "Would it be so terrible to admit that you love me?"

Her question unleashed something inside him, snapping his control over something he had controlled all his life. "Yes, it damned well would! I've seen what love does to a man. It makes him weak and miserable. He can't think about anything but her, even postponing what he knows he's got to do, in order to show her he loves her. He can't work or sleep, can't do one damned thing without wondering if she still wants him, will ever want him. Then . . . then she's got him, crawling on his belly for the privilege of holding her hand."

He had almost said it. She cursed the woman who had made him so afraid of love. She wanted to rush into his arms and comfort his pain, make him believe she would never betray him, never make him crawl to her. Her voice was quiet when she spoke. "And is that how you feel about me?"

He took a deep breath and threw the saddlebags over his shoulder, surveying her as if trying to memorize everything about her, as if he might never see her again. "Yes! Damn you, yes!" he jerked out, his face full of pain. He pulled her to him, kissing her mouth, pressing her to him until she thought her bones might snap. She lost her breath, all sense of time, as she drowned in the sensations his lips and body created within her. She tried to respond as fully as she could, praying he could feel how greatly she loved him.

He pushed her away before she could convey anything at all, though, turning his back on her. She lost her balance and hit her head on the corner of the bed. The room swirled dizzily.

"Good-bye, Catherine. Here's your passage back to England. I won't hold you to our marriage if you want out." He threw a bag of coins on the bed. She heard the dull clink, and Garrett was gone.

It took her a few minutes to move, but finally she was able to run after him. By the time she rushed down the stairs and out the door, he was on Trojan's back and galloping away. He never looked around or heard her sobbing, "Garrett! Please . . . I love you. You fool . . . I love you!"

Chapter 18

Elena watched Garrett gallop away from the ranch. At last, he had left his aristocratic wife alone. From her vantage point inside the doorway of the Morales family's cottage, Elena could see Garrett's full saddlebags and rifle in its holster. His saddlebags were never so full unless he meant to be gone far longer than a day. Now was her chance to get close to him; to show him that Catherine had no business in Texas; that she, Elena, was the kind of woman he needed.

She called to Señora Morales that she was leaving and raced to the stables. A few minutes later, she was on horseback, following the path Garrett had taken. When she passed the grassy trail that led to the line shack, she saw the trampled reeds and knew that he had taken it. Disappointed that he wasn't leaving Tierra, she turned her horse to follow. The small cabin was only a few miles farther ahead. It was used by Tierra crews who were either herding or feeding stock. She supposed Garrett was checking on Jason and Robert.

As she passed through a section of the trail that was

lined with virgin firs, she halted. Garrett blocked the trail with his horse, somehow knowing he was being followed. "Garrett. It's me, Elena. You looked upset and I wanted to find out if I could help." She didn't understand the way he was looking at her.

"As a matter of fact, you can. I'm going to the line shack to find Jason. You should be there when I talk to him."

"Is something wrong?" she asked innocently, wondering why he wanted Jason.

"You're damn right there's something wrong," he growled, kicking Trojan's flank. She followed him up the trail, more curious than ever.

They passed around a rock-strewn cliff, and the wooden shack came into view. Robert, Burt and Jason were probably inside, enjoying a meal before going back to work. Their horses were hitched outside.

They reached the rail in front of the shack, and Garrett dismounted, not waiting for Elena. He walked up the steps to the ramshackle building. The slatted door almost broke off the hinges as he burst in. Elena quickly followed, eager to find out why he was so angry.

Burt was pouring coffee into three large tin cups that were standing on a crude table in the center of the room. Jason and Robert were seated, their hats tossed on the floor. They were sharing a joke of some kind but the laughter stopped when Garrett interrupted them.

"What's up?" Burt was surprised to see him after their morning meeting.

"This is between Jason and myself, Burt. Stay out of it." Garrett rounded on his half-brother. "Hannah tells me that you and Elena are lovers. Is that true?"

Jason slowly looked up, his complexion tinged with red. "And if it is?" he asked challengingly.

"If it is, you are going to marry her!" Garrett was almost shaking with anger.

"Why should I marry her? You've been using her and never thought of it."

Elena burst into tears, knowing her only chance was in acting innocent, as innocent as Garrett had always believed her to be. "Oh . . . you vile snake! You know Garrett would never touch me. Jason came to my room and raped me, and you weren't there to protect me. He said if I told anyone, he'd have me thrown off Tierra. I . . . I have no other home . . . What could I do?" She collapsed to the floor in a fit of weeping.

In the grip of deadly rage, Garrett reached for Jason and hauled him up bodily. He meant to beat him senseless. Elena's explanation was like a stab wound. Jason would pay for his debauchery.

They faced off, two snarling animals. Jason threw the first punch, and then they went at it, each delivering bone-cracking blows. Garrett was much stronger than Jason, and eventually he delivered a straight-armed fist to the midriff that sent Jason down on one knee. Seeing that Garrett had no intention of stopping, Robert and Burt ran over and held his arms.

"Stop it, Garrett! He's down!" Robert's voice was shaking. Neither he nor Burt was prepared for Jason's quick recovery. Two fast jabs and Garrett was doubled over while his arms were still held fast. Burt charged Jason like an angry bull, grasping him about the middle and squeezing.

"Kill him!" Elena's penetrating scream had all four men looking at her in disbelief. "Where's a knife? I'll kill him myself!" Seeing their faces, she stopped, trying to revert back to the innocent maiden, but it was too late. Her voice had been crazed with blood lust and her black eyes gleaming with enjoyment. She ran to Garrett and pleaded, "He deserves to die for what he's done to me. He came to my room night after night. Hannah is a vicious liar if she thinks I asked him to come. She's always hated me. She's been so cruel." Large tears dribbled down her cheeks.

Burt looked murderous; his gray eyes sparkled at Elena. He let go of Jason and turned to her. "You hold your tongue, girl—" he started, but Garrett regained his breath in time to hold him back.

He faced Jason. "You landed a couple of dirty punches, but you know damned well neither Rob nor Burt will hold me back again. If what Elena says is true, I'll beat you from here to the Rio Grande."

Jason pulled up his head and looked contemptuously at Elena. She quickly moved closer to Garrett. "Are you blind, big brother? She's lusted for you so bad that she took me into her bed as a substitute. When you came back, she came right out and told me she was sleeping with *el patrón* and no longer needed me. It will be a pleasure to prove what a fool you are about her." Jason drew a chair across the dirt floor and sat down. Garrett did the same.

"I'm listening," he said smoothly, waiting for the next surprise. It had been a hellish day, and it was rapidly getting worse. He wiped a dab of blood from his lip. "Sit down, Elena. I want to hear Jason's side." He asked Burt to keep the weeping girl quiet. Rape was a serious charge, and he needed the facts.

Jason began, forcing his bravado, for Garrett had the power to send him away from Tierra without a cent. Still, Jason had a malicious craving to show him how stupidly blind he was where Elena was concerned. "Don't go high and mighty on me, Garrett. You're such an expert with women, but you sure as hell didn't read this one right."

"Elena is no more than a child, Jason. I've known her since she was twelve. This had better be good, because as far as I'm concerned, you are the one to blame. If you have ruined Simon's sister, I'll make it right if I have to arrange a shotgun wedding."

"Ruined her? By God, you really are dumb. Tell me, big brother, why did you have to cut up Alejandro Torres? Remember the Rodriguez boy? How his whole family fled in shame because Elena accused Eduardo of attacking her? She remembers, don't you, sweetheart?" Jason gave her a scathing glance, seeing with satisfaction the fear in her eyes.

"Don't listen to him, Garrett," Elena cried. "He's lying."

Garrett frowned.

"Remember that day, big brother? Think back. About an hour before Eduardo was supposedly attacking our sister, you were taking a swim. Elena was your appreciative audience. She knew you wouldn't touch her, but she had unwittingly lit a fire in her loins. Luckily for her, Eduardo was dumb enough to fall into her trap. I saw the whole thing. She was naked when the boy got there, and she practically begged him to take her. Worked out rather well for me, since after that, all I had to do was mention Eduardo's name and she would lie down and spread her legs." Jason began enjoying himself, watching Garrett's stunned reaction and carried away by feeling superior to his virile big brother.

Garrett's face looked tortured, every word he heard filling him with revulsion. "You are telling me that you have been using Elena for years? You bastard, don't you have any moral scruples at all?" He felt like leaping across the table and wrapping his hands around Jason's throat.

Jason spewed the anger he had kept pent up for years. "That's right. I'm a bastard, but I know full well my father was better than yours—an English aristocrat.

Mother and I had to put up with living on Tierra, where
we should have been living in an English mansion in
splendor. She told me what my life should have been
like. I should have had the best of everything. Instead
I've had to live in your shadow all my life. Hunter hated
me for being who I am. You were the one he took with
him wherever he went. You inherited this ranch, became *el patrón*. Robert and I are doled crumbs from
your table."

Jason looked at his younger brother. "Don't look so
shocked, baby brother. Consider yourself lucky that
you were too young to realize what was going on.
Maybe it would have been better if you had seen
Garrett crying into Hannah's skirts after Mother gave
him a beating. Then you wouldn't think he's such a
fearless paragon."

"Stow it, Jason!" Garrett shouted. "I've heard
enough. Pa gave you his name and treated you like his
own. I was left the ranch because I'm the only one who
knows how to run it. That is past. What's going on now
is what concerns me."

Seeing her chance, Elena plunged into the conversation. "See! He hates you, Garrett. He told me how he
enjoyed making it look like you had done something
wrong so your mother would punish you. He told me
that the scar on your hip is from the time he spilled all
his mother's perfume out and made it look like you did
it. The whipping you took should have been his." She
paused to see how her words were affecting him.
"Why . . . why are you looking at me like that?"

"I don't recall showing you that scar, Elena." His
eyes were frigid.

"I . . . I saw it when Catherine brought you home
and you were delirious."

"That won't hold water, Elena. Hannah made sure I
was in a nightshirt. Maybe it's lucky she did. It doesn't

sound like Rodriguez or probably even Torres had much of a chance. I'll carry the scars from Torres the rest of my life to remind me of your deceit! No wonder he hates me so much."

Garrett stood up and walked to a window, staring outside, his shoulders slumped. There was silence in the room; everyone waited. Without turning, Garrett said quietly, "Pack your things. I want both of you out of here."

"Oh, sure!" Jason laughed harshly. "Kick us out because we've damaged your damned pride. I've got pride, too. Why should I leave when all I've done is bed a slut?"

Garrett turned around, his brow creased in a pained frown. "You'll leave because there's nothing left for you here. Catherine believed I was as corrupt as the two of you. She's going back to England where she belongs, but before she leaves me, I'm going to prove to her that I know the difference between right and wrong. I could have forgiven just about anything, but not this—not finding out that the girl I thought of as a sister is a lying whore and that my brother is a blackmailing coward who hates my guts. I lost. . . ." He spoke so softly it was difficult to catch the words. When no one moved, he yelled, "Get out! Damn you! Take whatever you think you own and get off my property. I hope to hell I never have to lay eyes on either of you again."

"You don't mean it." Robert came up and placed his hand on Garrett's arm, trying to keep his voice from shaking. "Jason and Elena can get married and make things right. He's been jealous of you. I can sort of understand."

Garrett pushed Robert away. "You can? Would you have lied to Catherine about me? Would you have tried to sleep with your sister? Just what would you do, Rob, if you had lost the respect of your wife? I'm not losing anything else that's mine. As far as I'm concerned, Jason and Elena can do whatever the hell they want— as long as it isn't on Tierra."

"And that is what this is all about, isn't it?" Jason growled, "your precious wife. She thinks she's too good for you, and it's eating at your guts. Are you afraid that when she finds out my father was an earl, she'll turn to me?"

A deadly silence lengthened to minutes. The impact of the day's revelations was in both brothers' eyes. "I'm taking enough money to get as far away from here as I can," Jason finally said. The brotherly bond had been completely severed the instant he had referred to Catherine. "Who would have thought a woman could bring the big honcho to heel? I can actually feel sorry for you. I can start over someplace else, but you're chained by the balls to a woman who despises you. Like father, like son, huh?" Jason dodged out of the way when Garrett lunged. "Hold him back. I'm going." Garrett began another charge like a wounded bear, but Burt and Robert grabbed hold of him and held on long enough for Jason to get out the door.

"He isn't worth it," Burt said grimly, his face set as he pulled Garrett away. "Robbie, don't let go."

Elena edged away. She knew she was in no better position than Jason. It was her lies that had been at the bottom of this whole thing. Garrett's eyes burned on her, making her sure she had no chance left with him, just as, minutes before, she had been sure he would kill Jason.

"Jason!" she shrilled. "Take me with you, please. Garrett is insane. He'll kill me if I stay here." She ran outside, continuing to plead with Jason. A few minutes later, the departing sound of galloping horses faded away.

"Let go of me." Garrett shrugged away the constraining arms. He brought one hand up to his forehead and tried to press away the stabbing pain in his head. "I'm sorry you had to hear all that, Rob. Burt, were you aware of any of this? Have I been completely blind for years?"

Burt reached into a curtain-covered cabinet and brought out a bottle of whiskey. "Come, Garrett. Let's have a drink. I think we need one. Robbie, get some glasses."

Robert walked over to a shelf and took down three glasses. "I don't understand. Isn't Jason our brother?"

"Calm down, son." Burt poured the amber liquid and passed out a shot of whiskey to each man. "Garrett, how long have you known?"

"Our grandmother, the baroness, told me when I stayed with her in England. Why didn't someone tell me before? Jason obviously knew it. My God, when I think how he felt all those years . . . I knew he was jealous of me, but I didn't know how much." He shook his head, drained his glass and poured himself another.

"Hunter didn't want you to know until after he was gone. Until today, I didn't know Jason had been told who his real pa was."

Garrett poured more whiskey and drank it as quickly as the first two rounds. The burning liquid was much easier to swallow than the last few hours' events. "Why didn't Pa let her go? None of this would have happened if he had let her stay in England when she went back that time." Garrett's voice was becoming more strained, his words slurring. His defenses were down, and the alcohol didn't seem to help. "I . . . I loved him, Burt. He knew . . . he knew how she felt about me, and he didn't stop it. That's what love is like, isn't it? A huge hurt that keeps getting worse."

"You're wrong. I know it must look like that to you,

but it doesn't have to be like that. Look at me and Hannah. Your pa couldn't stop himself from wanting Celeste. It was a sickness in him."

"Supposedly I'm like him," Garrett said darkly, scowling into his empty whiskey glass.

Robert looked bewildered, then scared, as Garrett kept downing one whiskey after another. Garrett looked different. In Robert's eyes, he had been a hero, his ideal. Seeing the pain on his face, listening to him talk in a defeated, expressionless voice, made Robert afraid.

"Don't end up like Pa and me, Rob. Don't ever love a woman; it'll kill you."

Burt sat down at the table and tried to take Garrett's drink away. "That's liquor talking. It's not your fault that Jason and Elena have been carrying on. Catherine will understand, and you can start over." He shook his head sadly when Garrett pulled his hand back and poured himself another drink.

"It's over between Catherine and me." He wiped his hand over his eyes, trying to erase a vision of the disgust Catherine had shown. He shut his eyes. "I'm going to find Simon and help him run down Torres. At least I can make up to her for that. She could have been killed. If I hadn't dragged her out here, she'd still safe on her English estate. . . ." Garrett rambled on, talking to himself as if Robert and Burt had ceased to exist.

Robert was going to shake him, but Burt shook his head. "He needs to get it out, Robbie. All these feelings have been festering inside him. He's never told 'em to a soul. When he's sober, he'll start dealing with things again."

"But . . . but, Burt, he's not like he thinks he is. He's been good to both me and Jason. Garrett, don't be so hard on yourself." Robert put his hand on his brother's and tried to get through to him.

"Leave him be, Robbie. You were too young to be told these things, but now you're a man, and it's time you realized that your brother's got feelings the same as you and me."

Garrett threw his whiskey glass on the floor and attempted to stand up. "Don't talk like I'm not here. What kind of rotgut is this? I feel like I've been kicked in the stomach."

"You've downed almost the whole bottle in less than half an hour, you young fool," Burt stated baldly, glad Garrett was still able to talk. "You won't be going anywhere until the effect of all that liquor wears off. Maybe by then, you'll talk sense. You don't have to prove anything. The Rangers will take after Torres."

"Maybe." Garrett frowned, running his tongue along the inside of his mouth and grimacing at the taste. "We both know I'm going, though, don't we, Burt?" He focused on the older man until he got the unwilling agreement he was looking for. Then he turned to Rob, the only family he had left. "Promise me you'll see Catherine safely back to England?"

"Don't say things like that. Catherine loves you. You love her." Robert hoped it could be that simple.

"Haven't you heard anything I said? I don't want to love her. I don't want to see her ever again. Promise me, damnit." Garrett stood up, swaying. He tried to move toward Robert.

"I . . . I promise." Robert caught him, taking the full weight of his falling body on his chest and holding him until Burt came to help. They dragged him to a cot and laid him over the covers, pulled off his boots and threw a blanket over him. Robert stood, miserable, looking down. "What do we do, Burt?"

"We let him go, Robbie. We let him go until he works it out. While he's gone, we take care of his land and his wife like they were our own. It's time you were told what he's been carrying all his life. But if you ever breathe a word of this to him, I'll string you up and flay the skin from your back. Come on over here. We're going to talk."

For hours, Burt talked and Robert listened. By the time the sun went down, Garrett was still sleeping off the huge amount of whiskey he had consumed. "He'll sleep till tomorrow. We best get our work done." Burt stood up and reached for his hat.

"I want to sit with him," Robert said softly.

"That'll mean a lot to him, boy." Burt smiled, seeing how strong Robert was going to be when he matured. "I'm proud of you, son. As proud as I've always been of your brother."

"Go on, Burt," Robert said with a grin, "before you have me bawling like a baby. He's going to have one hell of a hangover. This might be my only chance to be near him."

"Might be, at that. It will be a while before he lets anyone get close to him again. I know him, and I've seen him come to grips with a lot of things. He's strong, Robbie. More of a man than your pa ever was.

"I've only got one more piece of advice to give. In the morning, we're not going to talk about this. If Garrett has more to say, let him say it. But you and I aren't going to fight him on anything. Agreed?"

"Agreed." Robert nodded and brought a chair up to Garrett's cot.

Garrett woke up with a gigantic hangover, but no one mentioned it as he drank a last cup of coffee and passed on Burt's breakfast. He sat tight-lipped and silent, staring off into space, as if he were already gone from the line shack and Tierra, gone from everything and everyone who meant anything to him. Robert kept giving Burt anxious glances, feeling that his brother had turned into a stranger, a man he didn't know and was afraid he wouldn't like if he did.

"I'll be leaving now." Garrett put on his hat, drawing the brim down to shade his red-streaked eyes. He held out his hand to Burt; not a flicker of emotion showed on his face as Burt shook it. He turned to Robert, and for a minute, something flamed in his eyes, but it was quickly gone.

"Take care, little brother," he said as he went to the door. He paused there for a few seconds, looking around the shack until his jaw tightened as if it were stone. He cleared his throat, and his words were thick. "If I don't come back, see that Catherine gets . . ." He shook his head and looked at the floor. "Tell her I . . . Oh, hell, she already knows." He went outside. Burt and Robert followed silently behind him as he mounted his horse and pulled the reins through his gloved hands.

Robert's mouth worked furiously and Burt's eyes were moist as they watched the tall figure ride out of sight. They called good-bye, but Garrett didn't turn to wave. Maybe he didn't hear.

"God, Burt. I don't think he's going to come back. Did you see the look on his face?"

"He'll come back," Burt insisted, but he couldn't swallow the huge lump in his throat. "We'd best get things cleaned up and head for home. Catherine has to know."

"I hope I can tell her."

"You will," Burt assured him, throwing his arm across Robert's shoulder. "Garrett is counting on you."

Chapter 19

"Still don't see why in the Sam Hill you came down here to chase after a bunch of scurvy bandits." Simon filled Garrett's glass with whiskey. "This hunt for Torres is strictly army business."

"If Torres is alive, it's my business," Garrett replied in a firm voice. His eyes never wavered from their scanning of the small *cantina* in Camargo, which was overflowing with heavily armed Americans. He and Simon sat away from the others, who were enjoying a last night of camaraderie before the start of a campaign to capture Antonio Canales, known as the Chaparral Fox, whose irregulars had plundered the Texas frontier for most of the past ten years. The main group of McCulloch's Rangers would be moving out early the next morning. Simon's group, which Garrett had recently joined, was breaking away from the rest of the Rangers in order to go after Alejandro Torres and recover the captured Colt-Walker revolvers.

Simon watched the back stairs of the *cantina,* where young prostitutes were leading a steady flow of customers. "Canales's woman should be able to tell us why Torres broke away from his general, and if we're lucky, she'll know where that scum went." The men exchanged knowing glances when Rosa Martinez walked down the back stairs and paused to survey the crowded, smoke-filled saloon. "Looks like we won't have to wait any longer. That should be her now. She sure fits the description the bartender gave us."

The object of their intense interest scanned the room, looking for another likely conquest, and spied

Garrett and Simon at the back table. The two men stared boldly at her scantily clad figure, and she sauntered seductively over to them."

"You buy me drink, *señores?*" She leaned toward the taller of the two men, drinking in his handsome features while a flirtatious smile pulled up the corners of her generous mouth. "Tonight is the last you will see of good drink and pretty women, eh?"

"What's your name, *chiquita?*" Simon smiled at the girl, summing up her assets with a sure gaze. "You look a mite young for this place."

Rosa laughed and sidled between the two men, offering then both an equal view of her full breasts, which spilled over the edge of her gaping bodice. She hoped that the black-haired man with the smoldering blue eyes would show his interest soon, for she preferred his dark good looks to those of his comrade with the laughing green eyes. The sandy-haired one asked too many questions.

Garrett saw the gleaming pendant the girl wore around her neck and caught Simon's eye. "Sit down, honey. We don't have time to take you upstairs, but we'll pay for a little conversation."

Rosa looked startled. *"Es verdad?* You wish to talk?" she asked incredulously, smiling happily when a gold coin was tucked into her bodice. These men were not like the others, that was for certain. Still, they didn't find her unattractive, for she could feel their eyes on her. "You leave before the others?" She decided that was the only reason she wasn't being taken up on her offer.

Simon pulled his chair closer to the girl, effectively blocking her view of the front of the saloon and the bartender, who kept his eyes on the circulating prostitutes to make sure they weren't wasting any time. When the young girl gave Simon a suspicious glance from flashing black eyes, he held out another gold coin, and she obediently stayed in her seat. "I am called Rosa."

Garrett reached out and picked up the lovely cross that hung between Rosa's breasts. "You do well here, Rosa? Would you like enough money to buy another pretty piece like this?"

"*Sí, señor.* I like pretty things." Rosa made no attempt to draw back from the warm fingers that rested on her bosom. The gringo had a way of speaking that made a woman listen, eager to hear a few compliments and have his complete attention. "What must I do for so much money?" She captured his hand and placed it over her breast, her dark eyes growing soft and limpid. She really didn't care what method of lovemaking this man preferred; if the price was right, she would agree to most anything. When he withdrew his hand and the other man laughed at him for his retreat, her curiosity grew. He did not seem the type who was shy of women.

"You haven't lost your touch," Simon teased.

"Just the inclination," Garrett returned in self-derision. Both men took a swallow of whiskey before they started interrogating Rosa again. Garrett was fast losing his patience. "Look, sweetheart, we know you're the girl who sees Canales from time to time. We need information about one of his lieutenants. The name is Torres. Have you heard of him?"

Rosa felt a good deal disappointed, but she didn't show it. The twenty-dollar gold pieces inside the bodice of her dress were warming her skin and were enough to loosen her tongue. "*Sí.* That one is known to me."

Their reaction was instantaneous. Garrett shot the next question rapidly and followed it with two more. "When did you see him? Where was he heading, and how many men were with him?"

"It is important?" Rosa asked slyly, wondering how

many more gold pieces she could earn so easily and if she could keep the amount unknown to the watchful bartender. She glanced in the direction of the long, polished bar at the other end of the room and was satisfied that the man behind it had not seen the exchange.

Simon swore under his breath and gave Garrett a disgusted glance from beneath his sombrero. "Keep it up, pal, and you and I will be traveling light."

He knew that Garrett had good reason to be concerned about Torres's whereabouts. The Mexican scum had given them notice that he intended to meet up with them again. The alarming words had been directed to Catherine. Simon's green eyes turned cold, flickering harshly at the Mexican *puta* who was bartering for more money in exchange for whatever information she had. "One more gold piece, Rosa." He tossed the coin on the table and watched her grab for it. "Tell us what you know."

"Torres is not with Canales. He brag about taking a shipment of weapons away from the Americanos, but when Canales see him, there are no new guns. So, my general is very angry. He thinks Torres is keeping the guns for himself and his own men. They argue, and Torres, he sneak away. He tell Canales that he would bring much gold instead of guns. He say there is a *rancho* where his enemy has many riches. Canales will only let Torres ride with him again if Torres can deliver many horses and goods."

"You actually heard all this?" Simon demanded.

"*Sí!* I am there with my Antonio when Torres come. He is mean *hombre.* He hurt my friend Teresa, very bad. You hunt him, yes?" Rosa was far too shrewd to miss the tall man's smothered oath when she mentioned Torres's intentions. She hoped these two men would find him and kill him. She did not trust Torres to stay loyal to the Chaparral Fox and thought Torres might even gather enough courage to kill the general one day. She could not afford for that to happen. Canales stirred her blood above all others and, more important, paid very well for her favors. It was Rosa's hope that someday Canales would become her protector and provide for her so that she would no longer be forced to ply her trade in the *cantina.*

"Did he mention the *rancho* by name?" Garrett waited with pent-up breath for the answer, a cold fear gripping his belly.

"Tierra . . . I'm not sure. It is north of the border. He say something about the *río* Brazos. Torres brag he raid this great *rancho* come spring and disappear again very quickly. If you take many men, perhaps you can catch him. He was here only a day before you come. My friend Teresa is still suffering from his visit." Her next words intensified the fears that both men had. "You ride fast and kill that mad dog before he hurt more women!"

Their questioning became even more demanding, until both men were certain that they knew where Torres would be heading and just how he could think that he could disappear after raiding Tierra.

At first light, Simon, Garrett and a dozen hand-picked men rode north toward the border and the Brazos River. They rode relentlessly, traveling through the dense chaparral and craggy hills between Camargo and Austin. The trail was fresh, ever indicating that a band of riders were just ahead, but the *guerrilleros* seemed to melt away into the dense underbrush. The men caught snatches of sleep during the chase, but there was never time to set up camp any longer than was necessary for the horses to rest.

Winter was fast approaching, and the farther north they went, the more turbulent were the storms of dust that plagued the harsh terrain. A few miles north of the Nueces River, they were forced to seek shelter from a howling storm. The air was so filled with driving sand and dust that the midday sun was nearly obliterated and visibility was shortened to mere inches ahead of them. They barricaded themselves inside an abandoned shack, grateful that the slatted wooden walls kept out most of the suffocating dust. The choking dirt bombarded the rustic enclosure for days, fraying nerves and coating the men with a dry film which they couldn't wipe away before it returned to cover them again. They were bone-tired, and their enforced wait provided a needed rest but also added to their frustration.

"Torres may have reached Tierra already. He could have raided the place and gotten away while we eat dirt in this damned hellhole." Garrett pounded one fist angrily on the flimsy wall of the shack. "Simon, we have to pull out soon. I have to know if Catherine is all right. If he's hurt her, I don't know what I'll do."

"I know." Simon pulled on his thick wool poncho and wiped a grimy hand over his dirt-streaked and bearded face. He looked at the sleeping men curled up on the floor, and his expression was grim. "These are good men, Garr. We can't ask them to ride out in this grit. We stand a good chance of losing our mounts as well as our way. We have to wait. Torres is a shrewd operator; he won't raid Tierra if there's a chance you are there. The men on your place are like your own private army. If he thinks you are there to lead them, he won't risk it. He couldn't have known you would leave home and go after him."

"He'd chance it if he thought I died back there outside of Nacogdoches. I'm counting on his hearing somehow that I had returned alive." He paused for a moment and then continued. "It isn't common knowledge, but who's to say Jason didn't impart his tale of woe to anyone who would listen? He knew damned well what I meant to do. Word like that spreads." Garrett turned to Simon. "What can I say? I can't forgive Jason and Elena for what they did."

"I can't forgive them, either." Simon grimaced. "Elena had better hope Jason plans to take care of her. She's a vicious little schemer, but I hate the thought of what might happen to her if she's left on her own. She is my sister." There was a slight hint of apology in his voice, which Garrett instantly waved aside.

"It's all over now, Simon. It was none of your doing."

"If I had been there, none of it would have happened. 'Course, far as Jason goes, he would have shown his colors eventually. I never did trust him. Better now than later, I say." He read Garrett's thought. "Catherine will be waiting for you, Garr. I can feel it."

"If Torres is up that way, I hope she's gone. I hope she took my money and went back to England." Even as he said it, he knew he didn't want it to be true. He fought off a painful vision of deep violet eyes and silver-gold curls. He was forever haunted by her face, could hear her calling his name every mile along the trail. He knew it would be too much to hope that she might still want him, but his need for her grew stronger with each passing day. He ached inside, but he realized that she would be better off in England. She deserved to be happy, and he wanted to know that she was safe—that Torres had not commenced his raid. The uncertainty was steadily driving him insane. He was growing more and more short-tempered as their enforced stay in the dust-battered shack dragged on. He kept recalling Torres's hands ripping Catherine's nightgown, and her screams during that long night. He had to get to Torres before he could hurt her again, before he. . . . "I'm going," he announced in a gruff tone.

Simon made no attempt to stop Garrett as he pushed open the ramshackle door and took the full force of the howling, dirt-charged wind. It was only a few seconds later that he was fighting to reclose the door, with Simon pushing alongside. Both men were choking and wiping tears from their dust-whipped faces by the time they got the door shut. Simon threw an arm over Garrett's shoulder. "Be patient, man. It will blow itself out, and we'll ride. Torres isn't safe from this weather, either. He's probably holed up same as us. He's only a day ahead of us."

Simon's prediction came true two days later. The storm faltered and died, and once again they rode north. They set up the same grueling pace, stopping to rest their mounts as infrequently as possible, but it was still weeks later that they reached the hill country. The terrain changed gradually, with granite cliffs rising in higher and higher shafts to the sky as they neared the Torres homestead. At last, they made camp on a cliff above a narrow creek that wended its way between the sheer rock hills of Torres's land. It was late April, and it had taken them months trailing just behind Torres until they were back to a place only twenty miles away from Tierra. While they planned their attack, they kept their campfires small in case Torres kept lookouts posted in the outer reaches of his hideaway.

"According to the men at the garrison, Torres has holed up in his pa's place, all right. There is no word that Tierra has been raided." Simon had just returned from Washington on the Brazos with supplies. "They hit the Vallez place on their way in. Took enough supplies to last them months." Simon squatted down before the campfire and poured himself a cup of black brew. He looked tired, and his eyes were dulled to mud green. He avoided Garrett's face, stretching his legs out to relieve the cramps from long hours in the saddle.

"And?" Garrett hunkered down beside him, crossing his legs Indian fashion, as he gazed into the burning embers.

"And nothing. I've requested reinforcements, and they'll be here in a week. Torres will be taken before he knows what hit him."

"Give, Simon. What else did you hear?" Garrett knew his friend too well. Simon was hiding something.

Simon rubbed his neck and snapped harshly, "Leave it. We'll get the bastard and haul his carcass to Austin for hanging. If Tierra had been hit, they would have heard of it in Washington, but no one said a word. Relax, damnit."

"Ramón Vallez and his wife were killed, weren't they?" Garrett could tell by Simon's face that it was true, but there was still something else. He stabbed Simon with his eyes until he got an answer.

"The little girls. Both of them." Simon looked as though he were carved out of stone. "I'd like to hang him myself."

Garrett's jaw worked convulsively as he listened. He had known the Vallez family for years. Ramón had worked on Tierra until he had earned enough money to start his own spread and raise his family on his own land. "The pleasure of killing him will be mine." Garrett stood up and moved to his horse, removing a long-barreled gun from its holster and pulling out his stash of bullets from the saddlebag. He heard Simon moving behind him and said nothing when Simon kicked a small rock with his boot, sending the stone shooting off the edge of the cliff like a ricocheting missile.

"I knew you'd go off half-cocked. Torres is going to hang for his crimes in the state capital. We've got orders to take him in alive, and as soon as we have enough men to make it through that damned pass, we'll do it. You ride in there alone and his snipers will plug you before you make it a foot."

"Would you try to stop me, Simon?" Garrett loaded the rifle and began digging through his saddlebags, his attention seemingly on the contents of the leather bag and not on Simon's fierce face.

"You'd have to shoot me before I'd let you ride in there to get yourself killed. You'll have your revenge on Torres, but it will be nice and legal, and when I say the time is right. You are under my command for a change. These men follow my orders, and they will stop you if you get past me."

Garrett laughed at that. "Still think I can beat you, don't you?" He brought a folded piece of paper to the fire and knelt down on the hard ground, spreading the paper out on a rock as he used his knife to sharpen a stubby piece of lead. "Come here and look at this," he said as he began drawing.

Thoroughly confused, Simon walked to where Garrett was kneeling and came down beside him. He concentrated on the rough diagram Garrett had drawn, and finally comprehension glowed on his face. "Well, I'll be damned. The mine shaft!" he exclaimed, slapping his forehead. "I forgot all about it."

"I thought a good Ranger never forgot anything," Garrett teased, humor softening the deep-carved lines about his mouth.

"It just might work." Simon picked up the drawing and walked over to his men. The other Rangers were soon apprised of the existence of the tunnel, and plans were made for an assault on the Torres stronghold. Garrett knew that it wouldn't be long before he was faced with his enemy, and only one of them would walk out alive. He looked out over the bluffs, watching the sun drop behind the sheer rocks to cast long black shadows over the sienna hills.

Twenty miles north lay Tierra. Was Catherine gazing out into the vast sky and thinking of him, or was she walking through the quiet halls of Bannerfield, thousands of miles away? He tossed a few pebbles over the edge of the cliff and listened as they rebounded endlessly down to the shallow creek bed below their camp.

A shiver ran down his back when the night wind picked up. The sharp breeze bent back the mesquite bushes that dotted the crevices above and below him, and he pulled his hat farther down on his brow. After a long time, he walked away from the edge of the cliff and pushed away his dark thoughts. Then he rejoined the other men to go over his plan and commit it to memory.

Chapter 20

The frigid wind howled around the great house at Tierra Nueva, plastering ice and snow against the adobe walls. The constant fire that blazed in the huge stone fireplace of the *sala* couldn't abate the creeping cold that permeated everywhere. The three women huddled near the fire were clad in heavy woolen dresses, with colorful knitted shawls draped around their shoulders. Catherine had pulled on the uncomfortable long johns that the men wore beneath their pants, tying a string at the waist, but they were still far too large and itchy.

It had been six months since Garrett had ridden

away—six months of agonizing worry that he would never return. Burt and Robert tried to reassure her that Garrett knew how to take care of himself, but Catherine was constantly plagued with nightmares of Torres. If the two men met again, Torres wouldn't hesitate to kill Garrett. She couldn't shake the feeling that Garrett would die before finding out that she loved him desperately and that she carried his child. In her sixth month, Catherine was already quite large, and although the baby's constant movements were reassuring, every one made her think about the baby's father. Garrett was out there somewhere, thinking that she had gone back to Bannerfield.

She stared into the fireplace, holding her numb fingers in front of the flames until they felt warm and tingly. "Are Burt and Rob back yet?" she asked Hannah, who sat huddled in the next chair. The flickering firelight barely softened the lines of worry about her mouth.

"They must be holed up in the line shack, waitin' for the storm to blow itself out." Hannah looked up from her knitting to watch the flames dancing along the stack of logs.

"Rob is afraid we'll lose a lot of livestock. Can they survive this storm?"

"I don't worry about the animals. Mostly they sense a storm coming and huddle together with their tails to the wind. But the men ain't half so bright. I just hope they were close to the shack when this hit."

"Burt's got good sense, Hannah. This can't be his first bad storm. What was it you called it?"

"We call 'em blue northers. They come every year, almost. You're right; he's been through them before; but it don't keep me from fretting." She turned to Maria, who sat embroidering a small jacket for the baby. In rapid Spanish that Catherine was slowly beginning to understand, Hannah instructed the girl to go to the kitchen to brew some tea.

Catherine watched Maria leave. The Mexican girl had become her constant shadow, ever since it was announced that Catherine was carrying a child. The pretty, dark-eyed girl with the shiny single braid to her waist had taken over duties as Catherine's maid. She had introduced *la patrona* or Doña Catherine to the Mexican families, and in the few English words she knew, she tried to interpret. Slowly the two women were coming to understand each other.

Maria was very adept with her hands. She seemed to enjoy brushing Catherine's long, silken, gold hair, marveling at the color and fine texture. She was also a skilled seamstress, and had patiently helped make an extensive layette. She taught Catherine to make the tiny stitches for the seams and how to embroider the intricate designs.

Catherine poured the tea when Maria brought in the tray. She had persuaded Robert to bring back the fragrant brew on one of his trips to Austin for supplies. She had tried to like their coffee, but it couldn't replace her English tea. During the first months of her pregnancy, it seemed the only thing that would combat her nausea. She had instituted an evening teatime that Hannah and Robert seemed to enjoy, but Burt could not give up his coffee, saying, "That stuff is too weak for my tough old gizzard." Catherine sipped her tea and gazed sadly into the fire.

"You aren't feeling poorly, are you?" Hannah inquired.

"No, that has passed."

"Garrett will be so proud. I bet it's a boy." Hannah had been saying that since the day Catherine's condition had become known.

"Why? So in case he never comes back, there will

still be a Browning to carry on his name?" She regretted the words as soon as they left her mouth. "I'm sorry. It's just that I'm so worried about Garrett. He might die without knowing about the baby. Even if he found out, he'd think I was staying here because of the child."

"Honey, it will be over soon. Garrett is young and strong. Fast with a gun. Torres was always a no-good coward. Garrett beat him once; he'll do it again. You have to believe that. When he gets back, you will be waiting, holding his son in your arms. How could the fool not believe that you love him then? Besides, I still say he knew what you felt, but he couldn't stop doing what had to be done. Torres has to be stopped."

Hannah didn't let Catherine know she doubted her own words. Garrett would have trouble believing anything a beautiful woman told him. Celeste had beaten out his trust, and she had left a lasting scar. Catherine could not give up hope, not in her condition. Her pregnancy had brought color back to her cheeks, but as the months passed with no word, her eyes had become shadowed and her skin translucent.

Hannah put another log on the fire. "You realize there's no way to get word through. Garrett's probably a long way south. He'll hightail it back here come spring."

"I hope you are right. I can't stop wondering. Just like you are worrying about Burt. That's the third time you have pulled out that row of knitting."

Hannah frowned at the loose yarn in her lap, and they both returned to their own thoughts. If only there were some word, even one reassuring word.

Hours after Garrett had left Tierra, Elena and Jason had stormed back to the house and, without answering any questions, gathered their belongings and left together. By the time the men had returned the next day, Catherine was beside herself with worry. They tried to reassure her, but she was positive they weren't telling her everything. Robert seemed to have grown up overnight, sharing the responsibilities of the ranch with surprising maturity. But Burt seemed to wear a perpetual frown on his face. Each man answered her questions with vague platitudes and assurances.

During the ensuing months, Robert confessed that his interest was law. Catherine helped him delve into the thick, leather-bound books in the library, surprised to learn that Hunter's father had been a successful attorney in Louisiana. She and Robert became close friends as they spent their evenings discussing the possibility that one day Robert could take over the legal business of Tierra.

Sometimes they talked about Garrett. It was through Robert that Catherine got a glimpse of Garrett as a youth. Robert told her the stories he had been told, as if by talking about Garrett, they could pretend nothing was wrong. Most of the time, Catherine was able to smile, but sometimes she would catch a certain look on Robert's face, and the subject would switch to something else.

As the fire burned lower, Catherine's thoughts went to Bannerfield. She missed Colin very much and read and reread his letters. He was doing well in school, and she was sure it was due to Allen's influence. Colin truly liked the baroness, and he wrote about her often. He asked repeatedly when he could come for a visit, but Catherine had no idea if that would ever be possible. She might be back in England, a widow, before Colin came to Tierra.

"Would you like more tea, honey?" Hannah's voice was a welcome interruption. "I think we should turn in oon. You need your rest. Maria started a fire in your oom awhile back, and it oughta be going strong by ow."

"Stop fussing. Between you two, I can't move. I ould have laid the fire." Someone was always hover-g, seeing to her slightest whim. She was never alone, xcept during the long, lonely nights in the big brass ed.

A loud thud of the veranda was followed by insistent ounding on the carved oak door. They all jumped.

"It must be Rob and Burt." Catherine ran to the oor, but Hannah stopped her.

"Wait! Let's not take chances." She reached for the ifle that hung over the fireplace. There was an eerie ilence.

"You're right. Let me hold the gun, Hannah. You go o the door."

Hannah looked doubtful.

"Don't worry, Garrett taught me to use these hings." Reluctantly Hannah gave her the rifle, and she laced it on her shoulder.

Hannah stayed well behind the door as she pulled it pen. The snow swirled inside in an explosion of white owder. Catherine staggered back but maintained her old on the gun. There was nothing there but the cold lack night, the wind and frozen particles of ice. She lanced at Hannah, who shrugged and slowly stuck her ead around the door.

Suddenly she jumped and ran outside. Catherine ook aim, her heart pounding. "Hannah?" she whis-ered. She pointed the gun into the cold winter night.

"It is me, *patrona,* Ana," Ana Morales shouted bove the storm. With great relief, Catherine replaced he rifle as Hannah helped Ana inside and over to the ire.

"Land sakes, Ana, what brings you out in a storm like this?" Hannah exclaimed as she pushed a steaming cup of tea into Ana's shaking hands.

"It is my Raúl. I cannot get him in from the stable. His little mare is foaling, and the boy will not leave her side. There is no one to help him. The men are in the hills with the stock, and the only hand left in the bunkhouse is that *loco* Roy, who doesn't know a fine animal needs special care. *El patrón* gave the mare to my *niño,* and the little horse is very *precioso* to Raúl. It is her first, and something is wrong with the birth. I came to see if Hannah can help."

"I will come, too." Catherine began wrapping her wool cloak securely around her full figure and took a long scarf down from a hook on the wall. "My old stable master taught me something about animals. Old Binning had many tricks to help a mare in a bad lying-in. Maybe I can help. Raúl is too little to be out there all night. We will convince him to go home to his nice warm bed. He will listen to me, Ana. Do not worry."

The older women looked horrified as Catherine stepped to the door. "Catherine, you will do no such thing. You are carrying your own child, and I won't have you out in this weather. I will go with Ana and see to both the boy and his horse," Hannah scolded, taking Catherine's arm to pull her away from the door.

Ana Morales murmured softly, *"Dulce señora,* think of your own *bebé.* The *vaqueros* will return soon, and Raúl must understand the harsh ways of life. If his little *yequa* does not live, he will be made stronger in the heart."

Catherine remained adamant. "The mare is Raúl's friend, Ana, and a special gift from my husband. Besides, I am not as fragile as all of you seem to think I am. I will stay warm in these heavy outer clothes, and ou both will be there to do what needs to be done as I ell you."

She finally got their reluctant agreement, and togeth-r they began forcing their way through the strong wind nd swirling snow to the stables. Hannah tied a piece of ope to the door of the hacienda, and they held onto he thick hemp as they walked slowly toward the lighted vindows where little Raúl Morales sat in vigil with his nare. Once they got inside, they stamped the snow rom their feet and removed their heavy cloaks.

Catherine walked quickly to the small room behind he tack room, where the herbs from the kitchen arden had been hung to dry. She quickly mixed a few ecessary ingredients together into a coarse, mealy aste as Binning had taught her. When she was done, he walked to the stall that held the Appaloosa mare, vho was lying on her side in the straw.

"*La patrona!*" Raúl's soft gasp revealed his awe at Catherine's presence in the stable.

She placed her hand on his soft brown cheek and aid, "Raúl, it will be all right. I will help your Nita. You must go with your *madre* and get some rest. Nita vill need you in the morning to help with her *potro.*"

The little boy got slowly to his feet and looked at his nother, who nodded her head. He wiped a tear from is dirty face and took Catherine's hand and kissed it everently.

He looked up at her with his tear-filled brown eyes, s soft and limpid as those of a doe. "*El patrón,* he will e angry with me if I do not take good care of Nita. He ay she is my re . . . respon. . . ."

Catherine bent down until her face was at the same evel as the eight-year-old boy's. Taking his face in her ands, she said, "Your responsibility?" When he odded, she continued, "*El patrón* will be very proud f you, Raúl. He will know as soon as he sees Nita that

he gave her to the right person. You have done wel
with her. See how her coat shines? Right now Nit
needs your mama, Hannah and myself. We will kno
what to do for her." She gave him a small hug an
gently urged him away. "Go now. I will see you in th
morning, *muchacho*."

Hannah watched the little boy and his mother unt
they gained the safety of their small adobe home. He
eyes were wide and her mouth open in amazemen
when she turned to see Catherine kneeling in the stal
crooning to the laboring mare and gently coaxing th
animal to take the herbal paste she had prepared
"What is that you're feeding her?"

"It's something to calm her a little, so she will accep
our help." She ran her fingers down the swollen belly c
the small animal and gently prodded. "I think the foa
is turned wrong. When Ana comes back, the two of yo
should be able to get the foal placed properly. I will te
you exactly what you must do."

When Ana returned, the women went to work
following Catherine's quick, confident orders as bes
they could until the labor was able to proceed normally
Two hours later, they stood watching as a slick, shin
colt made its first attempt to stand on quivering, thi
legs.

"Raúl will be so happy when he sees this fine youn
colt," Hannah said. Then she turned her attention t
Catherine, who was leaning tiredly against the stall, he
head resting against her arms upon the top slat. "T
bed with you, my girl." She hustled Catherine into he
warm clothing, making sure that her head was covere
and her body well protected by her hooded cloak.

"*Gracias*, Doña Catherine. *Muchas gracias*," An
thanked her for her help. "You are as kind as *el patrón*
and we are proud that you are with us on Tierra. I wis
not to speak ill of the dead, but Doña Celeste woul

have let Nita die, and my Raúl would be weeping *mañana*. Instead, he will be puffed with pride and crowing to the *vaqueros* upon their return."

Catherine clasped Ana's hands warmly in her own, and there were tears in both women's eyes. "Ana, thank you. I want to know the people on Tierra, and I want them to like me. Your little Raúl is a fine boy, and I am glad I was able to help. It would make me very happy if you would be my friend."

There was only a flicker of hesitation in Ana's soft brown eyes before she smiled warmly. "Doña, everyone on Tierra will be your friend. *El patrón* chose well when he made you his wife." As if she were suddenly embarrassed by talking so intimately to Catherine, the woman hurriedly bid them both good night and left the stable.

"Honey, that was a fine thing to say to Miz Morales. The Mexican people have been a little afraid of you after all the years that Garrett's ma was *la patrona*. She weren't the same kind of lady you are—fact, she weren't in the same class. After tonight, they are all going to know what I know'd the first time I clapped eyes on you."

Catherine looked surprised. "Whatever do you mean? I only helped an animal that needed it, and I really do want these good, gentle people to be my friends."

Hannah placed an arm around her shoulders as they started for the stable door. "That's just it, child. There's a goodness about you that I saw right away, and now they all know it, too. Yep, Garrett Browning got himself one fine lady."

Inside the hacienda, Hannah led Catherine upstairs to her room, helping her undress and get beneath the sheets, which had been warmed by the hot bricks Maria had placed there. Hannah made sure Catherine was comfortable as Maria offered her a cup of warm milk to help her sleep.

Her eyes closed, her energy spent, Catherine fell quickly asleep, warm with the knowledge that the Mexican people might not remain so shy and distant from her. It had been a situation that had puzzled her, and now she understood. Her exhaustion sent her into a dreamless rest, the first since Garrett had left.

Spring came slowly. The great drifts dissipated, and the beautiful hill country grew green and wild-flower fresh. Catherine was approaching her time, and her spirits were low as Hannah's concern rose higher. Hannah was like a brooding hen with a new chick, scolding and clucking if Catherine so much as lifted a finger.

She was allowed a short walk every day to the cluster of adobe houses outside the walls of the main house, but she was always accompanied by either Rob or Maria. She was beginning to feel like some sort of invalid when all around her she saw happily pregnant Mexican women going on with their work. *La patrona*, on the other hand, was always made to sit down. Her greatest exertion was cuddling a plump brown baby on her lap as its mother made her something to eat or drink.

The Mexican women had been shy around her at first, but she won them over with a warm smile and her willingness to listen. They regarded her worshipfully, but were always kind. Sometimes, when her thoughts would stray to Garrett, a warm brown hand would reach out and pat her, and she would hear a soft, *"El patrón es seguro."* Catherine murmured, *"Gracias,"* and prayed they were right.

One day, while sitting inside the door of the Morales cottage, enjoying the warm sun on her face and the pretty view of the blue-bonnet-covered ground, Catherine felt a cramping pain in her belly. She ignored it for a while, but less than an hour later, it grew more intense and began to come at regular intervals. A strong contraction gripped her as she attempted to get up and go back to the main house.

Ana Morales was with her immediately, calling for Robert. *"Está el bebé! Está el bebé!"* She held Catherine's hand tightly, excitement on her wide-grinning face. Robert came running, white as a sheet. He scooped Catherine up and ran for the house.

"For heaven's sake, Rob. I'm not going to die." She grinned at his fearful expression, but he didn't slow his pace.

Hannah was waiting for them by the time they reached the house, for Ana Morales had begun ringing a brass bell that stood in the courtyard. Catherine could hear the happy laughs of Tierra's workers as they heard the news. She felt like a long-barren queen who was suddenly blessed with a child, for all the commotion they were making.

"It's time, Hannah." Catherine offered a tremulous smile.

She saw Burt and Maria retreat into the kitchen as Hannah ordered, "Start boilin' some water, Burt. We're about to have another Browning on our hands."

A few hours later, Catherine was in the grip of unbearable pain that lasted for long minutes, then came again before she could catch her breath. Hannah tied a leather strap to the bedpost, which Catherine gripped with all her strength. Both Ana Morales and Hannah stayed in the room to help with the birthing.

"Push, honey," Hannah shouted, while Ana gently wiped Catherine's brow with a cool cloth. She bore down, and like a miracle, the pain disappeared. She opened her eyes to the sound of a lusty squall.

"A big, beautiful boy, all his parts and the spittin' image of his daddy," Hannah said with a chuckle, handing Catherine a cotton-wrapped bundle.

Tears streamed down Catherine's face as she looked into the stormy blue eyes of her son, angry with the world for his rude entrance. "Oh, Garrett," she murmured softly as she studied the tiny male body in her arms. She saw dark curly hair, still damp, and a face screwed up in a furious frown—a miniature version of a much bigger man. She ran one finger down the infant's soft cheek, and his crying stopped with a satisfied gurgle.

"Don't that beat all?" Hannah laughed at Ana, who nodded her approval.

Ana stepped to the veranda outside the room and flung upon the doors. A great cheer welled up from outside.

Catherine listened, her heart swelling with fierce pride as the baby was held up for the workers to see. She listened to the joyous shouts, blushing at the flowery compliments about her part in the birth of the Browning heir and the next *patrón.*

Burt came in and took her hand. He was followed by Rob, who looked awestruck. "Garrett picked a real good woman," Burt announced gruffly, and he strode out of the room before anyone made a comment on the wetness of his cheeks.

"Can't say my big brother deserves all this, but you do. He's a fine-looking boy." Robert dropped a kiss on her forehead. "Have you thought about a name?"

"I'd like to call him Andrew, after his great-grandfather. I'm told that Garrett resembles him, and I think Drew will, too. Andrew Parkinson Browning. What do you think?"

"You've made the Browning family very happy, Catherine. We've all heard tales of our great-grandfather in the baroness's letters. She'll be so proud."

Hannah dragged in a large, handmade cradle that was beautifully carved. She shooed Robert from the room. "We'll put him in his daddy's old bed." She took the child and placed him on his stomach in the cradle, watching as he snuggled to sleep. The strains of music and singing drifted through the open window. Everyone was celebrating little Drew's birth.

Catherine fell asleep with her hand resting on the edge of the cradle and dreamed of a man with dark blue eyes and wavy black hair. The green emerald she wore on her hand glinted in a ray of sun and cast a soft, flickering light over the sleeping little boy in the cradle.

Chapter 21

The stale smell of tequila permeated the small cabin. An empty bottle was balanced precariously on the bedpost; another was on the table and several more were scattered on the floor. The old man who tended the sputtering small fire seemed almost dead. His eyes were sunken and dazed, and a drop of spittle fell from his chin unheeded. The marks of several beatings stood out on his weather-beaten face. One cheek still oozed a bright red flow of blood.

"Old man! Get your carcass outside. I need some water." Alejandro Torres laughed at his father. To think that a few years ago, it had been Alejandro who had cringed in a corner at the old man's feet. It was all different now. A week ago, he had ridden into his old home, leading twelve menacing men. His father found that with one word from his son, they ran to do his

bidding. In a few more days, they would follow Alejandro as he invaded the Tierra Nueva ranch. Alejandro
would let one of them kill the old man before he left.
After all, the man was his father; he couldn't kill his
own father, could he?

"Eh, Miguel. Your cooking is worse than *mi padre's*.
What poison is this?" He threw a tin plate on the
already filthy floor.

Miguel Tahal eyed Torres with a mixture of disgust
and fear. Torres had grown mean over the long winter,
obsessed with the idea of destroying the Tierra Nueva
ranch. What had once seemed like cunning now
seemed like madness. Miguel couldn't wait to part
company with the deadly group of men who followed
Torres and encouraged him with their own crazed
thinking. Each day they spent together brought them
closer to turning on one another. Already one man had
been murdered by his bunkmate in an argument over
cards. Their supplies were low, and Torres was willing
to leave the safety of their stronghold to start raiding
again.

"*Pardón, Capitán.* Cooking is not my specialty,"
Miguel apologized woodenly. "Soon we will go to
Mexico and eat our fill of good Mexican food."

Torres spat on the floor and looked slyly at Miguel.
"You think I will ride south, when all I require is less
than twenty miles away? I will raid Tierra, using the
new gringo guns. They will not have a chance. Tomorrow we start practicing with them. First I will make sure
mi amigo Browning did indeed die, and then I will have
his golden-haired woman squirming beneath me." The
crafty look, so often on his face these days, was
directed at Miguel. "Perhaps you don't agree, Miguel?
You don't have to ride with me, do you?" The words
were meant as a threat.

"I ride with you always, *Capitán*. How could you doubt it?" Miguel lied desperately.

Torres laughed spitefully. "I am not blind, Miguel. You could not hide your disgust when we invaded the Rancho Vallez. Some of us think you may prefer boys, eh?"

"I prefer women, with women's charms. The Vallez daughters were mere children," Miguel insisted, seeing, too late, that his words made matters worse.

"I had them both, Miguel. Are you telling me that I do not like real women?" Torres reached for his knife.

Miguel blanched. "You are more man than I, *Capitán*. If I took what was offered, all of you would know my shame. I . . . I cannot perform . . . before others," Miguel stammered, watching the knife with downcast eyes, seemingly ashamed. Miraculously, it was enough. Torres laughed gutturally.

"See what your fine manners have brought you. You spent too much time with the Franciscan Brothers. I can fill a woman until she screams—and in front of a whole regiment. At Tierra Nueva, you shall have the pleasure of learning at a master's side. You shall watch me take the Browning woman, and I shall watch you do the same. You will not fail again. Would you like that, Miguel?" His snakelike eyes were ready to strike.

Miguel hid his distaste, fighting the nausea. *"Sí, mi Capitán."*

For the remainder of the day, Miguel avoided Torres. He constantly scanned the uphill trail, hoping he would discover a guard who had left his station. He had to escape before he was murdered for his inability to rape and kill helpless women and innocent children. He had been in this always for the money, and now money was scarce.

Darkness fell, but Miguel was not anxious to return

to the cabin. He would have to soon. Already he heard the drunken laughter coming from the shabby bunk house. The men, who snored in drunken stupor all day were beginning to repeat the process once more.

Miguel walked to the house. He was hit from behind and before he could yell, darkness overcame him. He didn't feel the ropes at his feet and arms, or being dragged into a dark shaft.

"Gag him," Simon ordered in a whisper. They dragged Miguel as far into the shaft as possible. Garrett stripped off the Mexican's clothes and put them on. He pulled the wide-brimmed hat down low over his face. "That's one. Let's take the house first."

Simon said, "I'll signal when to take the bunk house."

Together, Garrett and Simon crept stealthily through the shadows until they could gaze through the cabin windows.

"Wish me luck." Garrett grinned at Simon, who crouched at the door, his weapon to the jamb. Garrett opened the door and walked in.

"Madre de Dios!" Santos Torres screamed in relief knowing immediately it was not Miguel.

Garrett turned instinctively, and in that second, the younger Torres drew his knife and leaped at Garrett's throat. Garrett caught the weight of the flying body and both men crashed to the floor. Desperately Garrett tried to ward off Torres's upraised arm. Simon was unable to help, as the old man's scream had alerted the men in the bunkhouse. After raising the signal to his men, Simon came back to the struggling figures on the floor of the cabin.

Garrett clutched the front of Torres's shirt, twisting away from the descending blade. The gleaming steel was inches from his chest when he felt Torres arch his back. The hate he saw in the obsidian eyes faded to blank pitch. Garrett barely managed to push aside the knife as Torres fell on top of him.

Simon pulled his knife from Torres's back. "Guess I forgot I owned one."

Dazed, Garrett threw the body off of his chest and stood up, wiping an arm across his sweat-drenched face.

"Took your sweet time, my friend." Garrett grimaced at the malevolent, unseeing eyes of the body on the floor. "Sorry, Santos." He looked at the dead man's father.

"A crazed animal must be killed, *señor*. I am grateful you came." Santos Torres's voice was thick with emotion. "I will carry the scars of my son's hatred to my grave. He bragged about torturing you and thought he had killed you. I am glad you survived." Turning to Simon, he held out his hand, and it was taken in a sure grip. "What a fine man you turned out to be. It is good to see you, also."

"I'll have one of my men bury Alejandro for you."

"For all his hate, he was my son. I wish to do it."

Simon called for two of his men to take the body outside. As predicted, the men in the bunkhouse had been too drunk to put up much of a battle. They were all in custody.

Garrett propped his rifle against the wall and walked over to the table. He picked up a bottle of tequila and took a long swig of the burning liquor. "You got any smokes on you, Simon?"

Simon threw him the makings. He watched Garrett roll the tobacco into a paper and seal the edges with his tongue. "That's the end of it, Garr. I'll take these bandits to Austin for trial."

Garrett watched a thin column of blue smoke from his cigarette rise to the ceiling. He took another swig of tequila and shrugged his shoulders out of the poncho he

had taken from Miguel Tahal. "I won't be there to see
it. I'm going home."

"You really miss her, don't you?" Simon sat down
and brought his legs up on the table, drinking the
remaining contents of the bottle.

"Yes, I miss her, and I hope she's still there. I can
still hear her shouting that she loved me that day I rode
away from Tierra. I wouldn't allow myself to believe it.
I was feeling too damned sorry for myself that Catherine had believed the lies that Elena and Jason had told
her. I didn't leave her with much reason to believe that
I would be back."

Simon smiled reassuringly. "She'll be there."

"I don't know if any woman would stick around
waiting with so little to hang on to. She admitted that
she had been wrong, and she wanted to be forgiven for
believing their lies, but I couldn't do it." He flicked a
burning ember onto the floor of the cabin, crushing it
beneath his boot. "All I could think of was getting
away. I thought I was leaving because I had to get
Torres, but that was only part of it. I had to get away
from Catherine and find out how I really felt about
her." He took a final draw from his cigarette and
flipped the remains into the fireplace, staring sightlessly
into the low-glowing embers. "I was so scared of loving
a woman that every time I came close to admitting it, I
made some excuse to back away."

"Where Catherine is concerned, your thoughts have
been easy to read for some time. I've always known
you've loved her."

Garrett lifted his shoulders in a gesture of silent
acknowledgment. "I didn't give her much of a chance. I
was sure she was like my ma. I couldn't bear to hear her
say she loved me and then find out she didn't mean it.
Ma did that to Pa too many times." Bitterness twisted

is lips, but he forced away the past. "Since I've been away, I've realized just how much I love Catherine and need her. I only hope I have the chance to tell her."

Simon was pleased that Garrett was openly expressing his feelings. "Catherine has stuck like glue to you since you left England," he said encouragingly. "I'd say she's stickin' this out, too."

Garrett nodded, but he didn't look as if he really believed it. "I could use a bath." He searched the cabin for a bar of soap and a towel. "Remember the old days? That creek is low, but it still has enough water to do the job." He finally had to settle for a decently clean tablecloth that had been stored on the top shelf of the small kitchen cabinet. "You coming?"

"You're crazy! It will feel like ice. You might need a cold bath, but I can survive another day or two!"

"Not if you're sleeping in here," Garrett declared. "You smell as bad as a mangy polecat!" He took a threatening step in Simon's direction. In seconds, they were rolling over the floor like two battling youngsters. It was Garrett who came out the victor, unrelenting until he had Simon down and agreeing to a quick dip in the icy water of the creek.

The next morning they got up and loaded the prisoners into the wagon. Simon and Garrett ate a last meal together before they had to go their separate ways. It would probably be months before they saw one another again, since Simon planned to rejoin Colonel McCulloch after he delivered Torres's gang to the authorities in Austin.

"Blast it, Garrett. My throat's burning so bad I can hardly swallow." He emitted a loud sneeze and began to cough, and his eyes were streaming. "I needed this as much as the plague."

Garrett tried not to laugh, pouring a peace offering of steaming coffee for his hoarse friend. "When you get to Austin, I'm sure you'll find a pretty girl to tend your poor aching head."

"Hmmmph." Simon gave a surly growl. "How is it you never suffer the aftereffects of the things you drag me into?"

"Who knows? I might be suffering tonight. If Catherine has gone back to England, I'll feel a whole lot worse than you feel now." He kept his voice deliberately light, wanting to part company with Simon on a casual note. It was hard enough to know he wouldn't have Simon around to share his fears. After this morning, Garrett was on his own. He didn't want to think about his future if Catherine wasn't going to be in it.

"It's time I pulled out." Simon dragged a poncho over his head and thanked Santos Torres for the fine breakfast. Garrett walked with him outside, and they shook hands. Simon climbed up on the wagon seat and took hold of the reins. "Kiss your lady for me, Garr. I'll be stopping in one of these days, and I'll expect to find you two acting like a couple of lovebirds." He sneezed again, swearing as he reached for the bullwhip to start up the team. "Hope all is going well when I get there, because after I arrive, I plan to dunk you in a horse trough until you catch the biggest damn chill you've ever had."

"I'll miss you, too, Simon." Garrett flashed a broad grin and received one in return as the wagon pulled away.

Garrett walked to the cabin and made his farewells to Santos. He mounted Trojan and started up the trail that would take him home. Fear of what he might find when he got there made him dig his heels into Trojan's flanks, speeding the roan stallion on his way to Tierra and, hopefully, the woman he loved.

Chapter 22

The flaming glow from dozens of torches lit up the night sky above the courtyard of the hacienda. The gaily dressed dancers spun and twirled like multicolored flashes of light around the cobbled floor, spiraling particles of dust into the air with their stamping stiletto heels. The clicking cadence of castanets echoed away into the vast, starlit sky until it reached the ears of the solitary horseman who watched the festivities from the high ridge overlooking Tierra. The impassioned strains of Spanish guitars began a flamenco tune, and Garrett had to restrain the restless movements of his blooded stallion as the music called out to him.

"Easy, son," he ordered in a low voice that was husky with emotion. At long last, he was home, and below him lay his valley, where his people were gathered together for a fiesta. What were they celebrating? Perhaps one of them had married or had been delivered a healthy firstborn son. A lump closed his throat as the fervent music of the dance swelled around him and claimed him as one of its own. Even if Catherine had left Tierra, he still had a place here in the hearts of his people. There was no longer any reason to linger on the ridge. His family was saluting some small personal triumph, and he wanted to add his blessing and take his rightful place among them. He spurred Trojan into a gallop, and they descended into the valley.

Catherine clapped her hands in time with the music. Robert, dressed in the traditional garb of the flamenco dancer, faced Maria with his arms raised over his head.

293

Slowly the two young people began to sway to the music, moving apart and coming together in an ever-increasing energy of motion. Maria portrayed the seductive soul of women everywhere as she enticed Robert with her swaying hips, smiling with pleasure as he captured her within the tempestuous tempo of the dance. Catherine was delighted to see that the attraction Maria felt for Robert was reciprocated. She watched as the floor filled with couples who danced energetically as the guitars played louder and the castanets punctuated the excited rhythm of the song.

"This is not like a ball in England," Catherine said, laughing to Hannah, who stood beside her holding Andrew and swaying to the music.

"No," Hannah agreed, smiling back as she rocked the baby in her arms. "Your boy will have this music in his blood. Look at him, Catherine. He is smiling because he knows this celebration is for him. Someday he will dance at his son's christening. I hope I live to see that day."

Catherine looked down at her wide-eyed son. It was almost as if he waved his small fists in time with the music. She reached out, and Hannah placed the baby in her arms. Her fingers touched the smooth material of his christening blanket, only one of the beautiful gifts she had received for him today. She tucked a corner of the white satin under her arm, making sure the intricately embroidered initials of his name showed as she began walking toward the white latticework portal for the traditional ceremony.

"Do I look all right, Hannah?" she whispered as she took her seat. She was dressed in a hyacinth lace dress that matched the soft iridescence of her eyes. It left her shoulders bare, to gleam like pearl beneath the matching lace mantilla, which covered her hair and swept delicately past her waist. The mantilla was held in place by a white gardenia pinned over one ear. The full skirt of her gown was layered with wide ruffles that cascaded from her tiny waist to a few inches above her ankles. Her only jewelry was a thin black satin ribbon that encircled her slender neck and the small cameo at the base of her throat. She didn't realize it, but if not for the silver-gold color of her hair and the white, creamy skin of her breasts that swelled above the intricate lace bodice of her gown, she could have been taken for a Spanish aristocrat.

"I have never seen you looking more beautiful, *Patrona*," Hannah murmured reverently.

Catherine felt a quick spurt of tears moisten her lashes. Hannah had never addressed her as *Patrona* before. She was still not accustomed to her new title, but tonight she truly felt as if she belonged with these people. They were honoring her son, but she knew that their happiness was also for her. She smiled brilliantly at the crowd of people who stood before her and held Andrew so that they could see his small face. If only Drew's father were here to witness this wonderful moment. Pride darkened her eyes to the shimmering purple of a late summer sunset in an endless Texan sky as she beckoned to the children.

Their shy, laughing faces were like precious gifts as each ascended the steps and placed a blossom in her lap or on the floor by her feet. Bright red roses and white daisies, bunches of honeysuckle and cloudy pink mimosa were scattered like soft-colored jewels all around her. Their fragrant perfume filled the spring air with a sachet of scent. Raúl walked solemnly up the stairs to her side and touched Andrew's face with a chubby brown finger. "*Muy hermosa, Patrona*," he praised, as he held out a single white rose.

"*Gracias*, Raúl," she replied softly, moved beyond measure.

The crowd began a chant of jubilation, which became a joyous crescendo as Catherine stood up in the wake of their adoration and curtsied deeply, letting her humility show in the sparkling tears that shimmered in her eyes. Robert stepped forward, his back erect with pride as he held out his hand to her. She gave Andrew back to Hannah and stepped down from the portal of flowers. As Robert drew her into his arms, the crowd made a circle around them. The musicians began a slow moving song, a beautiful, lilting melody that sounded as fresh as the new life it was meant to honor. Catherine closed her eyes and moved gently to the soft music, wishing with all of her soul that the arms that held her belonged to another.

Suddenly the musicians faltered in their playing. Then the melody faded altogether. A hush fell over the crowd, a silence that brought Robert's footsteps to a sudden halt. Catherine's eyes flew open with alarm as she stumbled and turned around, her anxious glance darting to the widening gap in the crowd. People were moving aside to form an aisle, but she couldn't see beyond the shadows behind them. She looked up at Robert, but his face was unreadable as they waited for whatever had brought an end to their dance. Her heart began to pound erratically as a soft murmuring passed through the throng and she felt their mounting excitement.

He walked slowly through the crowd, coming toward her. The nighttime shadows hid the aristocratic planes of his face as he approached. He wore the white ruffled shirt and short, embroidered black jacket of a Spanish don. A wide red silk sash was tied around his slim waist, and his long, muscular legs were encased in tight black trousers that flared below the knee. He stopped in front of her, a slow smile spreading across his face as he removed his hat and flung it away from him to the ground.

The people watched as he faced the golden-haired woman who stood alone in the circle of flambeaux. His indigo eyes never left her face as he moved closer. She stood motionless, a regal match for the man who claimed her. When he took her hand and placed it on his shoulder, the crowd cheered wildly, shouting their approval. The musicians clamored for their instruments as the man began the first enticing movements of the classic Mexican dance.

Catherine moved in a hypnotic trance, caught in the sensuous web of his compelling blue gaze. Her eyes scanned the beloved features she had been allowed to see only in dreams. Her gaze lingered on the molded lips quirking up at the corners in a remembered smile, moved to the straight patrician nose and along the firm line of his jaw, finally returning to his dark eyes. The intimate communication of his gaze was writing a message on her soul that she would remember forever. She barely heard the triumphant cries of the people chanting, *"El patrón! El patrón! El patrón!"* over and over as the flamenco music stirred their blood.

There were no words to describe the feeling of enchantment that surrounded them. They moved as one to the music. The stars in the heavens seemed to shine brighter, and the flames from the torches cast gold on their rhythmic embrace. Catherine gave herself up to the music and the man, going with him and the pulsating sounds that vibrated inside her and echoed around her. Garrett and the music existed everywhere. She relived her fervent dreams, enticing him with her smile and reveling in the flash of sensation each time their eyes met. They moved apart and together like lovers, their bodies speaking the language of seduction

as they circled one another. When the music built to
climax, they whirled in a vortex of feeling as old a
Creation, which didn't end even after the last guita
had played the final dying note of the impassione
song.

Locked in a paralyzing gaze, they stared wordless
at each other. Catherine tried to calm her ragin
senses, but new life was racing through her veins. Afte
long, agonizing months of loneliness, she was aliv
again and in Garrett's arms. Compelled by a force sh
could not control, she brought her hand to his face. Sh
had to make sure that he wouldn't disappear if sh
touched him.

He lowered his head, but was pulled away. Robert'
voice broke the spell that had held them. "You are
sight for sore eyes, brother."

Garrett was locked in a bear hug that brought a wid
grin to his face. The grin turned to laughter when Bu
clasped his shoulder and swung him around. "I kne
you'd be back, son. Did you get that snake Torres?"

Catherine watched silently, her brain just beginnin
to function once again. She listened to Garrett's expla
nation of his final encounter with Alejandro Torres
Garrett and Simon had recaptured the stolen guns an
destroyed Torres's band of irregulars. It was what ha
prompted Garrett's unheralded return to Tierra. H
had finished with his enemy and had no reason to sta
away any longer. He wouldn't have come back only t
see her again, would he? No. She had had nothing to d
with his return.

Still, the expression on his face when he had claime
his dance was soft with emotion. Was it desire? Did h
still want her? Love her? Or did he dance with her onl
out of duty, since legally she was still his wife an
mistress of Tierra? She knew that his family ties we

trong, and pride would prompt him to put on a onvincing show for the people at the fiesta. She wished he knew what his real feelings were, if he still wanted er for his wife after all this time.

As Garrett was surrounded by additional welcomers, Catherine found herself moving away. None of her uestions could be answered until the evening was ver. She was vastly relieved that there was no appar-nt injury showing from his encounter with Torres. She ad worried for months that he would die by Torres's and and she would never see him again. Now that he vas here, her fears were springing from an entirely lifferent source. Would he want her for herself or ecause she had produced the Browning heir?

Hannah came to her with Drew, pushing her way hrough the crowd. She placed the baby in Catherine's rms. "You must be the one to introduce this little eller to his daddy. I'll clear the way, honey."

Catherine's trepidation increased. She forced herself o follow Hannah, holding the baby tightly to her reast, wishing she could take comfort from the small ody nestled against her. What if Garrett felt trapped n their marriage because of Drew? What if he no onger loved her? He had left her alone for months. Could he possibly feel the same as before he had left? By leaving, he had denied his feelings. Would he do so gain?

Catherine hung back as Garrett spied Hannah and wung her off her feet. "Let me down, you big lug!" Hannah laughed at his boisterous greeting.

As he lowered Hannah's feet to the ground, he ooked past her to Catherine, and his eyes locked on the mall bundle in her arms. His wide grin disappeared. He firmly set Hannah away from him, but his eyes ever left the baby.

"This is your son, Garrett." Catherine kept her eye downcast, afraid to look at him. "Andrew Parkinso Browning."

Garrett found himself staring into a tiny replica of h own face. The baby seemed to size him up as his intens blue eyes stared back at him. Garrett swallowed con vulsively, completely awed when Catherine placed th small, warm body into his arms. One tiny fist graspe hold of a ruffle on his shirt, and a delighted gurgl spilled from an incredibly small mouth. Garrett didn think he could stand it; the feeling of exultation was s strong he wanted to shout.

"My son?" He didn't know the words were audibl until he heard the laughter of the crowd. A voice insid his head kept repeating, *my son, my son,* as if it woul never stop.

Catherine's troubled violet eyes scanned his face "Do you like him, Garrett?"

"He's little, isn't he?" Overwhelming emotion thick ened his voice. He could think of nothing else to say

Hannah burst out laughing. "Well, sure he is. He' only two months old."

Garrett's smile was rueful as he adjusted the infant i his arms. He was afraid the fragile baby might be hur by his clumsy grasp. He looked at Catherine for help

Catherine felt close to tears as she looked straigh into the dark fathoms of smoke in Garrett's eyes. Sh could easily read the fierce pride reflected there. Ther was nothing she could say as she took Drew back fror him; his expression said it all.

"*Patrón,* may I be the first to toast you and you son?" Juán Morales's gentle voice came through th hushed crowd. Garrett was drawn away by the me who wished to share this proud moment with him Catherine smiled with understanding as the men move to the center of the court and began lifting their glasses to salute Garrett and his son.

"They will be drinking to Garrett's and Drew's health for hours," Hannah said. "No sense us women-folk hanging around. After all, all we do is have the babies those blamed men are so proud of. Drew has had enough excitement, and I think that his mama has had enough, too."

Catherine allowed herself to be ushered into the house. She needed some time alone before the inevitable confrontation with her husband. Her future happiness would be determined before morning. Hannah understood when Catherine told her that she would take care of Drew's needs by herself. She gave Catherine a quick, hard hug before Catherine mounted the stairs.

Catherine took Drew into the nursery which adjoined the master bedroom, and sat down on the hand-carved rocker. As she nursed her son, the uproarious voices of the men drifted in from the open doors of the balcony. She could smell the fragrant essence of flowers and feel the cool breeze of the evening as she slowly rocked in the chair. After a time, the voices outside became fewer, drifting away. The celebration was over, and the people gathered for the christening were returning to their homes. She saw that Drew had fallen asleep, and she lifted him away from her breast and into his cradle.

A tight tension mounted inside her, stiffening every muscle, as she waited for the sound of Garrett's step in the hall. She was terrified that he would come to speak with her and even more afraid that he would not. Some inner warning system brought up the fine hairs on the nape of her neck. She lifted her eyes.

He stood inside the door. She couldn't speak. Her

throat closed with unease as he reached behind him to slip the latch into place. He came toward her, but his gaze shifted to the cradle. He looked down at his sleeping son. "I want to thank you, Catherine. Thank you for my son."

The air was charged with feeling, the taut awareness that stretched between them as pronounced as ever. Their gazes locked, but a shutter came down over his face, and she could not tell what he was thinking.

Garrett fought for control. He didn't want her to see how badly he needed to pull her into his arms and tell her how much he loved her. He had thought he would get the opportunity after the dance, but Robert and Burt had prevented it. Then she had brought his son to him, and he had realized that she had stayed on at Tierra because of the baby. There would have been no way for her to get to England safely when she was pregnant, and she was probably waiting until the baby was old enough to travel. The day he had left, he had negated the promise he had extracted from her to keep Tierra safe for his son by throwing a bag of coins at her feet. Because of the kind of woman she was, she had stayed in order to honor her promise and ensure Drew his rightful share if her husband didn't come back. He had returned safely, so she was now free to go. He had to let her leave, if that was what she wanted. He owed her that, and much more.

"I won't hold you to the promise you made me, Catherine. If you want to leave, I will let you go, both you and the boy." He saw her bow her head and assumed she was feeling relieved that he was making it so easy for her. What had he expected? A muscle jerked convulsively in his cheek. He didn't stand very high in her estimation. "I would not part a mother from her son." It sounded like an accusation.

Catherine turned away, tears gathering behind her

eyes that she refused to shed. He barely heard her tight whisper. "No. Only a wife from her husband." Then she was gone, running through the adjoining door to escape from him.

It took several seconds for her words to get through to him. Finally he grasped the meaning of her soft statement. He crossed into the bedroom, locating her outside on the balcony, standing rigidly with her back to him. He drew a deep breath and went out to her. When he placed his hands on the curve of her shoulders, he felt her stiffen. He took a gamble and gently ran his palm along the exposed skin above her low-necked gown. "Catherine? We have to talk."

She stepped away from his touch but turned back to face him. She lifted her chin. "When do you want us to go?" She was dying inside. How could she leave, when all he had to do was touch her and she wanted to beg him to love her? What could he do if she refused to go? Wouldn't life with him on any terms be better than never seeing him again? She stared sightlessly into the dark night, not daring to guess why he was not answering her question. She took a ragged breath and uttered the words that would determine her destiny. "What would you do if I told you I didn't wish to leave?"

His answer came swiftly, so swiftly that Catherine was thunderstruck. "If I had my way, you would never leave me." Her eyes shot to his face and read the love and compassion written there. A spark of hope ignited inside her and burned ever higher as he went on. "I want you to stay, Catherine. I don't care what reason you come up with. Having you with me is all I could ever want."

It was like being released from darkness into light. "Oh, Garrett! I love you so," she cried, and threw herself into his arms. She melted with undisguised abandon against him, and he quickly returned her joyful embrace. He lifted her chin and captured her mouth, devouring her softly parted lips with a fierce hunger that consumed them both. Months of not being able to touch were forgotten as their desire soared. The kiss was endless, a renewal of their love that was necessary to them both and also a promise of the ecstasy to follow.

When they were at last able to let each other go, they were both breathless with reaction. His voice was a low throb in her ear. "I have loved you from the beginning, *mi esposa,* and I'll love you forever." His lips moved along the sensitive cord of her neck. "If you had left me, my heart would have gone with you." He kissed every feature of her face, her eyes, her nose, her lips, telling her without further words that she belonged to him and he to her.

He took her hand, and together they moved to the bed. Tenderly he drew the lace gown away from her shoulders and removed her petticoats and chemise until she stood naked in the circle of his arms. His eyes never left her face as he stepped back and she helped him remove his clothes. Together they sank to the softness of the satin-covered mattress, and she welcomed him with the flame of passion that burned only for him. Their mutual desire soared higher than ever before. All the pain and loneliness was erased in the ecstasy of remembered passion that enveloped their flesh. Their culmination brought a new freedom to their lovemaking, the freedom of reciprocated love that was forever new and renewing.

It seemed hours later that they lay nestled together, Catherine's head resting contentedly beneath Garrett's chin. He took a long breath, the fresh, sweet scent of her hair filling his nostrils and the lush softness of her breasts rubbing against his chest.

She lifted a hand to stroke the damp hair away from his temple. "Garrett?"

"Mmmm?" he answered in a lazy, satisfied drawl.

"How long were you home before you made your grand entrance, *mi patrón?*" The playful query placed emphasis on his title.

His grin flashed in the moonlight. "When I rode in, I knew there was a fiesta going on. I slipped unseen into the house to clean up and dress appropriately for the occasion."

"I felt as if a king had arrived to pay me homage," Catherine admitted, recalling how her breath had been taken away when he first appeared. He was splendid to look at, and every time she did, she wanted him to make love to her.

"You will get a lot more than homage from me, *mi patrona.*" His lips moved down her throat and across one breast until she gasped and moved away.

"You were gone too long," she said when she regained her breath.

"I know." He brought her close to his side, placing one arm beneath her shoulders so she could rest her head on his chest. "It took a long time to catch up with Torres, and it took me every bit of the time to sort out my feelings about you. It looks like I've been slow-witted where you are concerned, doesn't it?"

"Were you so unsure of me?"

"More of myself than of you," he admitted. "When I left Tierra, I was too angry to think straight. I knew I loved you, but I couldn't accept the fact that you loved me. After Jason and Elena convinced you that I was as immoral as they were, I was sure you couldn't really love me, not if you could believe something like that about me."

"I should have trusted you more, Garrett. I hope you

can understand that I was unsure of your feelings, just as you were unsure of mine. I thought you would forget me when you stayed away from me all those months."

His hand began a gentle stroking of her hair. "I do understand, *querida,* more than you know." He hesitated, as if uncertain of how to continue. Finally he said, "I didn't know there was any such thing as love. When I met you, I couldn't control my feelings, but I kept trying to prove it wasn't the real thing. No matter what I did, the feelings got stronger and stronger every day. I didn't want it to happen, but you got to me, witch. My mother . . . Catherine . . . she was . . . not. . . ."

"Don't." She placed soft fingers over his lips. "You told me all about her long ago, my darling. You were delirious for days in Nacogdoches. None of that matters to us anymore. We can't let the memory of a sick, unhappy woman separate us to destroy the happiness we have together. Drew and I are your family now, and we will always love you."

At the mention of their son, Garrett's brow creased in a slight frown. "I hope I'm up to this. I have no experience with babies."

There had been enough emotional upheaval for one night. Catherine's eyes lit up with mischievous appeal, and she lifted her chin at an impish angle. "You'll do." She grinned cheekily, mimicking the words he had once said to her long ago in an English rose garden.

One brow rose incredulously. "Wretch!" he accused as he rolled over on top of her. "I may have conquered the memories of my past, but I have yet to succeed in subduing you, my love."

"Would you really want to subdue me?" She pulled his face down to her mouth. "Isn't this better?" She breathed against his lips and proceeded to show him how completely victorious he could be.

About the Author

Janet Joyce is two Ohio housewives who have combined their first names and talents to form a writing partnership. They were introduced by a mutual friend who knew that Joyce wrote fast-moving stories about naked people in vague places, while Janet wrote of exquisitely dressed people locked in detailed times and places. The friend thought they would do better together.

Janet, a born Buckeye, lives with her optometrist husband and three children. She holds a degree in education from Ohio State University, loves history and is active in Girl Scouting. Joyce, a Minnesota native, recently moved to Ohio from New York. She majored in English at the University of Minnesota and lives with her architect husband and two children. Both women married dedicated professionals and, since the start of their writing partnership, have discovered that workaholism is a family trait they all share.

Their combined children, two boys and three girls ranging in ages from seven to twelve, have taken over as cooks, housekeepers, baby-sitters and advisors during the times when Janet and Joyce work on their manuscripts. Their two husbands share such similar attitudes and habits that Janet and Joyce have often speculated that they are married to one man who has devised an ingenious disguise.

Although many partnerships might falter because of personality conflicts, Janet and Joyce realized early that they were both too cowardly for confrontation. They appreciate each other's abilities and have formed a mutual support society, recognizing that each complements the other. *Conquer the Memories* is their first novel, and they are currently completing another.